THE EPIC UNDOING
OF HALEY ANN EWING

A Novel

Willow Feller

Do not judge others, and you will not be judged.
For you will be treated as you treat others.
The standard you use in judging is the
standard by which you will be judged
(Matt 7:1-2 NLT).

E ergreen PRESS

Mobile, Alabama

Evergreen Press
P.O. Box 191540 • Mobile, AL 36619
800-367-8203

To my husband, Mike,
a handyman/woodworker/
deep thinker extraordinaire,
whose invisible fingerprints
are on every chapter of this book.

And to my six quirky kids:
Nick, Alison, Annika, Irina, Zach, and Gabe.
Thanks, guys for driving me over the edge—
the view is so much funnier
from down here.

PROLOGUE

His surveillance subjects sat on a circle of chairs in the middle of the expansive room. They were on the light side of the heating vent, while he sat coiled, patiently lurking in the shadowed night side. Equipped with a shrewdness borne from millenniums of practice, he knew exactly what to look for in the human females' movements, sounds, and scents.

He flicked his tongue in and out of the metal slats, collecting light and vibration wave particles. His eyesight was poor, but his supernatural extrasensory capabilities were unmatched by any other earthly creature. Like an ultra-fast computer, he gathered information and processed it in fractions of seconds.

It only took moments for him to sift through the feel of each woman's words and the tone behind each individual's mood to zero in on the most viable candidate. He purposely waited, though, before going any further. His dark mission was far too important for him to act in undue haste. He knew better than to waste even a drop of his precious venom on anything less than the perfect prey.

His senses had alerted him to the energies of one young woman in particular. She was responsive, yet guarded, and more than anyone else in the group, showed signs of possessing the one vital trait that would ensure her loyalty to his cause once he infected her.

The fact that his special toxin always blinded his victims to their need for healing made his mission especially satisfying. The longer the poison circulated through their veins, the farther they walked away from the door that opened to the only place where the cure existed. He tightened his coils in anticipation. The sooner he could get a dose into her the better.

Still, he waited. Playing this game for centuries had made him as cunning and astute as the original infecting agent—astute enough to keep his fangs folded neatly up inside his mouth, even though the glands in his head were bursting with venom. He was waiting for one last sign, one final look or gesture to indicate that she really was exactly what he craved.

He only had to wait a minute longer. He pushed his triangular head against the vent and strained to watch his subject through the slits. Squinting through his nearsightedness, he watched her force a smile to cover the disgust in her eyes when she looked at one old woman in particular. A delighted shiver traveled his entire length. Ah! She was a splendid actress, a veritable deceiver of the most pious sort. He was certain no one else suspected that she really despised the old lady.

Satisfied, he flattened his body into a narrow black belt and slithered silently through the vent. He sliced through the light of the room like a killing knife, leaving a trail of darkness like blood behind him. Following his razor-sharp senses, he headed straight for his prey. Even though he was invisible to the humans, he sidled against a wall, darting quickly between objects like an invader in enemy territory.

He wasn't in enemy territory, though.

This was his home.

This was his church.

1

"Lederhosen?"

"Lederhosen!"

"Oh." I held up the dark brown shorts with attached suspenders. I didn't know what to say. Neither did anyone else around me. The odd gift muted the cheery chatter of the baby shower attendees like the eerie silencing of birds right before an earthquake.

"I'm happy to hear that you know what they are and that you know the correct German pronunciation—how fun!" Great-aunt Winifred exclaimed, clapping her hands.

The way she bobbed her salt-and-pepper cap of hair around reminded me of a budgie bird named Bruce that my brother kept in his room when we were kids. I could almost picture Aunt Win taking flight and flittering erratically around the church basement like Bruce did in Josh's room when the cage was opened.

"Heh, heh..." I forced a chuckle that was somewhere between a laugh and an exhale, unsure if this gift was serious or a deliberate joke.

Like me, the group remained silently puzzled. Unlike me, though, the rest of the ladies were probably not envisioning binding, gagging, and throwing elderly Aunt Winifred into the trunk of a car and depositing her at the door of der local Hasenpfeffer Haus where she might find a more appreciative recipient for her lederhosen. She was small, and didn't look like she'd put up much of a fight. *Who invited her, anyway?*

"I think we spent way too many hours working on the set of *The Sound of Music* to not know what lederhosen are," my fellow English teacher, Stacie, commented after a few uncomfortable seconds.

"Mm-hmm," I replied, purposely omitting polite pretend talk. This baby gift was weird—the shorts were obviously big enough to fit me—and I wasn't about to gush over it like I had when I opened the other tasteful gifts given by normal women with a normal sense of normalcy.

Stacie fidgeted a bit when I didn't say anything else. She chatted on in a phony voice, filling my politeness vacuum. "Um, we made suspenders out of wide ribbons and pinned them to the boys' shorts to look like lederhosen. Er, these are, um, the real thing, though, aren't they, Winifred?"

"Ouch!" Something poked the side of my hand when I set the wrapping paper down on the carpet beside my chair.

Seated next to me, my sister, Danielle, leaned over and looked at my hand as I held it up to my face. "What'd you do?" she asked.

"I don't know," I answered, watching two pinpoints of blood appear on the side of my right palm, "all I did was put the shorts down. Do you see a tack or staple or something down there?" It was as puzzling as it was painful.

Danielle carefully brushed the carpet around the lederhosen. "Nothing. I wonder what poked you. Does it hurt?"

"A little." I dabbed the spot with a tissue.

Win prattled on in response to Stacie's question. "Yes, they're traditional Bavarian boys' lederhosen—soft goat suede, as a matter of fact."

My hand injury took a back seat to my aggravation with Aunt Win. Why would she give me this anomaly of a baby gift? And how could she have missed knowing that we were having a girl? I knew my church friends wouldn't have omitted that important piece of information from their shower invitations.

I glanced over at the table where the rest of the opened gifts were placed after each was passed around the circle of women. A blessed abundance of offerings fanned out, ranging from the usual and necessary baby items to the indulgent and expensive. The only other slightly atypical gift was the mini food processor that our pastor's wife, Lorna, had given me. But even this resulted from the time she overheard me talking about wanting to make my own organic baby food. She had thoughtfully included gift certificates to a local organic produce market as well.

The fact that my friends had invested a huge amount of time and resources to make this shower a luxe event further highlighted the incongruity of Win's gift. Everyone else had figured out a way to integrate the shower's ethnic Indian theme into their present for me, whether in the wrappings, the color choice, or within the gift itself. I was awestruck by the vivid colors and silky fabrics that showed up in the blankets, bedding, bibs, and towels that I unwrapped. Even some of the accessories reflected the distinctive bright designs of art from India.

Win's gift stuck out among the others like Swiss Heidi would on the streets of Calcutta. Actually it was worse than that. It was like seeing Mother Teresa ministering to the Indian impoverished while wearing a short, aproned dirndl dress and sporting perky braids coiled around her ears. Or maybe like seeing the panic on Heidi's face as she's tumbling over the edge of a steep alpine cliff because she tripped on the hem of a long, nun-type sari while chasing her goat herd. Culture shouldn't be messed with that way. Curry doesn't go with sauerkraut, and cooking wiener schnitzel in a tandoor oven would be a sacrilege. Win's choice was out of place and distasteful. Period.

Her contribution really shouldn't have surprised me, though. She had pulled the same stunt at our wedding reception, five years previous. That was the first time I met this elderly aunt from my husband Rick's side of the family. She had attended our wedding with her sisters, Gracie and Penelope. They were both polite and quite ordinary—completely unlike tacky Winifred.

Back then, Aunt Win had presented us each with seven pairs of colorful, holiday-themed socks and a gift certificate for a website called, "Gerta's Gizmos." That site turned out to offer nothing but junky gadgets. We had a terrible time finding anything even remotely useful to order. After narrowing our choices down to an electric slipper warmer, a battery-powered Rolodex file that looked like a 19th century Ferris wheel, and a musical indoor/outdoor weather station that played certain songs at certain temperatures, barometric pressures, and humidity levels, we opted for the weather station. Rick loved the Meteorologic Melodies Weather Watcher, but I would live to regret the choice. Particularly so, because the stupid thing refused to die out, even after five years.

But what really bugged me was that Rick didn't share any of my annoyance with his loony aunt. He liked her. He called her quirky. I didn't like her. I called her a freak. It was easy to see why she had never married—as far as I knew, anyway. The only person I could picture her with would have to be a lot like ethereal-haired Richard Simmons. In a brief and horrific brain lapse, I imagined the two of them standing at the altar in matching short shorts. *Eeeww!* I quickly forced a picture of a basket of kittens into my mind to cleanse my thought palate.

"Are these a family heirloom?" my diplomatic mom asked as she leaned across Danielle's lap to stroke the lederhosen's soft suede.

"No," Aunt Win stopped and smiled as she cocked her head to one side, "but, in a way, I guess they do contain a bit of family history. I replaced the buttons on the front with some that I carved from deer antlers. That deer was a nice five-point buck I shot when I was hunting in Wyoming many years ago. I also made decorative spoon handles from the same set of antlers."

Win's remarks elicited a gasp from Dolores, an ardent animal lover. Dolores sang in our Sunday worship team and wrote original songs based on scriptures that used animal metaphors. On the previous Sunday, she had performed an interpretive dance in which she leapt and panted like a thirsty deer to a modernization of the chorus, "As the Deer Panteth for the Water."

Sharp irritation rose up in me at the same time that the baby bumped against the inside of my rib cage. Leave it to someone on Rick's side of the family to dampen such a nice gathering.

Knowing that I was apprehensive about leaving my career in education to become a stay-at-home mom, my friends were obviously trying to affirm and encourage me through the lavish shower. Under the direction of beautiful Nilima, a college exchange student from Delhi, they had converted our modest fellowship hall into a luxurious Indian banquet room, fit for a rajah and rani. Rich fabrics in shades of gold, red, and orange cascaded across the walls and over the tables. The arresting accent of a sitar singing through the wall speakers accompanied the dance of flickering candlelight around the room. Sandalwood incense mingling with heady food aromas furthered the exotic ambience.

My friends' efforts were all the more special in light of the fact that our church, Artos & Ichthus Fellowship, was committed to social justice as well as eco-minimalism. We purposely steered clear of megachurch showiness by exercising tasteful austerity throughout our facility and making sure a large portion of our resources were directed toward community projects. But on this morning, I knew the uncharacteristic display of opulence was an out-pouring of love toward me.

In contrast, Aunt Win's behavior did nothing but detract from the special-ness. She had a way of ruining the moment the way a huge fly would if it landed in one's bowl of decadent lobster bisque.

I pursed my lips to hold in caustic comments regarding the use of animal body parts for fasteners and nervously fingered the clean edge of my brand new just-above-the-shoulder haircut instead. *At least my hair is great.*

My early morning hair appointment in a pricey downtown Philly salon had been the perfect precursor to the baby shower. Not only did I get the cut of my life, I was now the proud bearer of a Solar Soak Shine Treatment, guar-anteed to last through thirty shampoos. My sandy brown, usually feeble strands had never felt so beefy before. I shook my head just to feel it swing lustily, exactly as the poster above the hair dryer said it would.

"Why are you giving large lederhosen to the baby?" Rick's grandma, Penelope, asked. As Winifred's sister, she easily raised the question that the rest of us were too polite to ask.

"Oh, these aren't for the baby—these are for Haley."

I recoiled involuntarily. *What does she think I am? A circus freak, like her? I wouldn't be caught dead in those shorts!* I purposely ran my fingers through my hair again, like a baby grabbing for her security blanket. The sleek texture was unlike anything I had ever thought I could attain in my twenty-eight years on this planet. It comforted me, calmed me, reminded that not even a deranged, elderly in-law could ruin such a special day. My hair would get me through.

"Well then, Winifred, what possessed you to get those for Haley?" Grandma Penelope didn't mince words.

"Oh, I know it seems a little odd, but I researched these extensively before I ordered them off the internet. These are maternity lederhosen."

Penelope clucked her tongue. "Win, learning how to use the computer at the senior center has made you a menace to society."

Ignoring her sister's comments, Win flew up from her chair perch and snatched the lederhosen from me. She raised them above her head with both hands as she strode the radius of the chair circle and cleared her throat in preparation for some sort of uninvited demonstration. A disgusting wash of white pet hair coated the back of her dark skirt.

I knew immediately who had brought her here. Beverly. My thorn-in-my-side mother-in-law. The loud, chaotic, too-happy woman who had barged into my ordered world on my wedding day and showed no signs of retreating into the background. The worst part was that Rick had a great relationship with his mom. He adored her. I admitted that Beverly was a good person, but most of her habits were intolerable. Even though she made a decent living as a real estate agent in suburban Philadelphia, she was anything but professional. As a specialist in lower-end homes, she toted clients around in an old SUV filled with dozens of discarded paper coffee cups and white dog hair coated upholstery. She talked nonstop and constantly texted, ate snacks, and drank coffee while driving with her Pomeranian, Bootsie, on her lap. I never saw her without at least one food stain on her front.

Beverly relentlessly pursued a friendship with me, but I dodged her as much as possible. I simply refused to be seen with her. However, after a year of arguing with Rick over my rejection of his mother, I had finally compromised by visiting with her periodically but only in her home or mine. When I went to her house, I wore old clothes and brought my lint brush with me. Today, of course, we were thrust together into the public eye. It made me uncomfortable. Her huge greeting hug had left me wishing my lint brush was in my purse.

With all the flair of a TV announcer, Win, in her dog hair covered skirt, went on to launch a spiel that described the function of maternity lederhosen.

"Now, if you will observe, the front of these lederhosen is hiding elastic panels that allow the waistband to expand significantly. This expansion not only provides comfort, but also support for the mother's mushrooming torso."

Win pulled on the front flap and revealed huge, scary-looking elastic straps. "Look," she said as she pulled down, "these panel straps form a type of shelf that mother's belly can sit right up on."

Horrified, I instinctively cupped my stomach with my hand. I had shelled out far too much money on specialized pregnancy workouts with my personal trainer, Charmaine, to allow my body to degenerate into mushroominess. And even though in my third trimester my midsection was taking on the look and feel of a beach ball, I could not imagine needing a shelf in my pants to set my stomach on. Win's gift was getting more ridiculous by the minute.

Penelope was not impressed. "But why lederhosen, of all things? Why not put that system in some regular shorts or pants?"

Win straightened her tiny, wiry frame and lifted her chin with authority. "Penny, I am getting to that. Please don't interrupt."

Interrupt? You are the interruption, silly woman!

Penelope sniffed and, unfortunately, Win continued. "The suspender system on the lederhosen provides the key to their effectiveness. As many of you know, regular maternity pants or support belts are in the habit of sliding down constantly. These straps make sure that never happens." Win held out the shorts with one hand and executed presentation-type gestures with the other hand. With longer hair, longer legs, and an industrial-strength facelift, she could have been one of Barker's beauties for the Price is Right game show.

"Lyla Wittenbow, a seamstress from Cincinnati, got the idea for maternity lederhosen when, while participating in a cultural job exchange program, she worked as a beer-slinger at the Oktoberfest in Munich, Germany, back in 1990. Her website tells the story of the inspiration she gained from watching how some older German men would unhitch the front flaps of their lederhosen in order to accommodate their growing beer bellies as the week progressed." Win paused and pivoted so that everyone in the circle could see the elastic straps.

My face flushed. Everything that Win said or did was absurdly out of sync with the rest of us. Her talk of deer shooting and beer slinging and beer bellies felt downright wrong in our beautifully decorated church basement. Even more so, in light of the fact that almost all of our church people were either nondrinkers or in some sort of substance abuse recovery. We did not joke about such things.

We didn't take propriety lightly, either. Like me, my closest Christian friends were all careful to preserve a clean and appealing witness to the world. I loved being part of a group of attractive, intelligent, and energetic women. We had standards. High standards. Standards that I was proud to uphold.

Obviously devoid of any standards, Win mercilessly continued. "When Lyla returned to the States, she went right to work, securing a leather lederhosen supplier and adapting the garments to meet the needs of pregnant women everywhere. Her design proved so popular that she patented her design, and voila! Lyla's Lifting Lederhosen has become a household word throughout the globe."

"Well, how clever!" Beverly leaned forward as she exclaimed, sloshing some of her coffee onto the front of her lemon yellow blouse. She started dabbing at it with a soggy tissue. It was a futile gesture considering that the coffee splotch had plopped itself neatly beside a reddish food stain that she had already been sporting all morning.

The dreaded silence returned as no one supported Beverly's observation. The lederhosen were not clever, they were lame, and however custom-made and expensive they might be, everyone else knew they were lame. I was now beyond embarrassed. I was mad. And if someone had tried at that moment to convince me that my rage was simply due to pregnancy hormones, I would have put an armlock around their neck and body-slammed them to the ground.

An awful moment ensued. I knew I was being watched, maybe even tested, to see if I would dutifully pull my Proverbs Thirty-one Woman costume out of the prop closet and don her robes the way a proper church girl should. I balked, though, as a twisted and unforeseen moral dilemma presented itself. Which was worse—to be dishonest and say fakey nice things about the lederhosen in order to "love" Aunt Win, or to be honestly and openly irritated to receive the stupid gift? Could true Christian love ever involve dishonesty? Or could true honesty ever involve brutal unlovingness?

In a split second, I made up my mind. I would be honest, because it would ultimately benefit Aunt Win to know her place. She needed to be reminded about where she fit in and where she didn't. Over ten years earlier, I had done the same thing to my nerdy cousin Polly in high school. When she tried to sit with me and my friends at lunch on the first day of our junior year, I swiftly and honestly sent her away. It was better to let her know right away that she wasn't one of us. It would have been mean to string geeky Polly along and then have to crush her with the truth later.

I looked down at my lap and stated, "Hmm—I don't think that I'll ever have a place to wear these—"

My mother, always needing to fix things, broke in with a practiced cordiality that was as automatic as her heartbeat. She spoke into the uncomfortable moment with conciliation, feeling the urge to bridge the chasm between Win's world and the familiar world as the rest of us knew it. I would have been quite content, even thrilled, to leave Win on the far side of a canyon, but Mom was habitually nice.

"Aunt Winifred, you certainly get an award for the most unique and entertaining gift. I'm sure these durable lederhosen will become a treasured heirloom in Rick and Haley Ann's emerging family line."

Even though Mom's persistent inclusion of my middle name riled me, I was actually glad she spoke up. Borne from almost thirty years of living with my critical, touchy father, her calculated tact was unsurpassed. She was a pro when it came to keeping up appearances while satisfying Christian rules of faith and obedience. I knew she was as horrified with the lederhosen as I was, yet she had managed to say something nice without lying and had not committed me to ever having to wear them. Which, of course, I wouldn't. *Ever.*

Win smiled and placed the offensive garment back on my lap. I leaned away from it as if it were coated with the bird flu virus.

"Oh, yes," Win said, "these shorts are definitely durable enough to be used through multiple pregnancies. My darling friend Betty bought a pair for her daughter, Missie. She said that Missie ended up wearing them every day for the last month of her pregnancy. She was a husky woman, even before she got pregnant, and she said the lederhosen provided extra back support for her long hours on the road."

"On the road?" Danielle asked.

Shut up, Dani! Don't encourage her. I had to restrain myself from slapping my one and only biological sister.

"Yes, Missie was a long-haul truck driver. She drove her eighteen-wheeler across the country right up until the day she went into labor at a truck stop plaza in Reno, Nevada."

"My goodness!"

"Really?"

Exclamations erupted from all the other women. The last thing Win needed was a responsive audience. The last thing I needed was a mental picture of a large, pregnant truck driver's belly spilling out from the suspenders of lederhosen that had been worn for thirty consecutive days and probably weren't water washable.

Win balanced on the edge of her chair as she prattled on. "Betty told me all about it. There was no time for Missie to get to a hospital. She birthed little

Walter Junior on a couch in the truck stop casino. It's an amazing story. It seems that a casino patron hit the jackpot on a poker machine the moment little Walter entered the world. Bells and whistles started blaring, lights started flashing, and Walter screamed his first scream. Healthy little bugger, apparently."

Oh, great—now we can add gambling to the list of lurid subjects that Win has decided to titillate us with at church today.

"What about the father?" Mom asked. Even my cautious mother was sucked into Win's stupid story.

"Oh, that part is sad. Missie's husband, Walter Senior, died unexpectedly right after they found out they were having a baby. He was a truck driver, so Missie decided to take to the road in his honor. When the birth happened at the moment of the jackpot, Missie took it as a sign of comfort from God. She figured that it was her husband's way of letting her know that everything was going to be all right. To this day, little Walter goes by the nickname of 'Ace.'"

Beverly actually started dabbing at her eyes. I rolled mine. Win's hammy pathos, even if it was true, sickened me.

"Well, it sounds like poor planning and irresponsibility on Missie's part to me." I raised my teacher voice in an attempt to regain control of the crowd. "I'll certainly not take any chances near my due date—my daughter will be born in a medically safe environment."

No one heard me. Win's coarse drama was inexplicably more compelling. One of the older women spoke up. "How did Walter Sr. die?"

"Oh, it was quite a freakish incident—"

Nilima, exquisitely enfolded in a gold-bordered, violet silk sari rose from her chair and thankfully cut Win off. "I think we should have our lunch now. I'm afraid the food is getting cold."

One of the older women piped up. "Wait—there's one more gift left to open." She pointed toward a bundle wrapped in fuchsia tissue paper and tied with a wide, shiny gold ribbon.

"Um," Nilima glanced over at the lederhosen in my lap and hesitated. "We'll save that one for later."

I stood, grateful that Nilima pulled the plug on Win's rude exposition. Besides, I wanted to find a bandaid and some hydrogen peroxide for my hand. Not knowing what pierced my skin, I figured I should disinfect the area, even though it seemed minor.

I pulled the tissue away and looked at the spot again. It was swelling up, like a reaction or something.

Hmm. Weird…really weird.

2

The fact that Win was wearing a bright blue blouse only reinforced her resemblance to Bruce the Budgie in my mind. Her black and white head, her beady eyes, her screechy voice, and flittery mannerisms—it was uncanny. I wondered if Danielle or Mom noticed it too.

Josh was eight, and Danielle and I were ten and twelve, respectively, when Bruce entered our home. Without my parents' permission, Josh had volunteered to keep the second grade classroom pet over the summer for his teacher, Miss Riley. Dad hated that bird, which was undoubtedly the single greatest motivator for Josh to keep Bruce for as long as he could.

Dad was angry with both Josh and Miss Riley. Every time Bruce would chime, "Go away, go away" as Dad walked into the room, Dad would throw something at the birdcage and mutter about irresponsible young women who had no business saddling their students with their burdens just so they could run off with their shiftless boyfriends to Greece for the summer.

We learned to throw a blanket over Bruce's cage when Dad came home from work each day. For some reason, Bruce would only speak when Dad was around. When he learned the phrase, "Pretty, boy, Pretty boy," Bruce's cage was swiftly transferred to Josh's bedroom. On more than one occasion, Josh had to plead with Dad not to kill the bird.

Josh's vigilant protection of Bruce became even more essential when the start of the school year rolled around, and it was announced that Miss Riley would not be returning. Miss Riley's replacement, Mrs. Percy, refused to allow Bruce back into the classroom because she suffered from a virulent bird allergy that she called, "bird fancier's lung"—something that could kill her on a moment's notice if an attack was triggered. Josh's third grade teacher, Mrs. Levy, also refused the bird entry into her classroom, saying that she preferred the muteness of fish and reptiles. So Josh brought the birdcage back home and Bruce lived in exile for the rest of his life in Josh's bedroom, much to our dad's vexation.

Dad's harshness was not limited to budgie birds. He was a strict authoritarian in the home and sincerely believed that the divine mandate for his life was to raise an ordered, disciplined, and industrious family. He was also a junior high algebra teacher, which probably better explained his approach to parenting than any directive from God might.

He was passionate about constants, variables, functions, and especially order of operations. In Dad's black-and-white way of thinking, everyday life and relationships were just sets of equations. All one needed to do was properly arrange and methodically solve every situation until each unknown equaled something. Dad took pains to reduce everything in his life, even his faith in God, down to something concrete and logical.

As a church board member, Dad enjoyed a reputation as the sober-minded elder—the calm, rational man who wouldn't change church policy merely because someone, even the pastor, felt led by the Holy Spirit to do so. His biggest fear for the church was that it could be infiltrated by crass emotionalism or "flaky woo-woo" ideas. He held his church office through three pastors, each voicing both admiration for, and aggravation with, my doggedly incontestable father.

Dad was also a stickler for appearances. His math students knew all too well that if each equation wasn't properly written out on the page it could be counted as incorrect even if the answer was right. The problems had to look right to be right. This highly visual approach sometimes followed Dad out of the classroom and into different areas of family, home, and church life. He even applied it to our clothing choices.

Dressing for church often disintegrated into a ritual of heartbreak due to what Dad called the "binary nature" of church clothes. He insisted that reverence displayed on a person's outside would translate into reverence on the inside. As teenagers, Danielle and I resented having to wear skirts every single Sunday when the other girls were all allowed to wear pants. Some of the coolest dads even let their daughters wear jeans to church.

Hairstyles were not exempt from scrutiny either. On one unforgettable Sunday morning, when Josh got into the car with an irreverently gelled-up, punkish hairdo, our horrified father bellowed, "You can't go to church looking like a threatened pufferfish! You're a board member's son—*what will people think?*"

————◆◆◆◆———

It would have been easier on me if Aunt Win's weirdness was limited to something like a gelled-up hairdo. I knew I let her bother me too much, but I couldn't shake the feeling that she reveled in purposely bucking all societal norms as if she were flaunting her freedom from something that one should not be free from. I resented her presence. The binding, gagging, and depositing option was looking more attractive with every minute that passed.

I stood, took a deep breath, and made my way to the food table with the other ladies, oohing and aahing with them over the sumptuous foreign feast that awaited us. Two large tables were pulled together to accommodate aromatic platters of meat, vegetable, and rice dishes, as well as baskets of flatbread. Colorful glass bowls filled with various fruit chutneys and a three-tiered crystal dessert stand graced the far end of the buffet.

"Nilima, this is amazing! You went to so much trouble—" Overcome with awe at the sheer beauty of the event, I choked and my eyes filled with tears. The last trimester had brought with it some sort of hormone deluge that threatened to completely drown my customary composure. I felt thrust onto a wild emotional roller coaster—one minute I was happy and excited; and then, without warning, I would slide wildly down into weepiness, despair, or even rage. It was scary and embarrassing and necessitated a switch to waterproof mascara.

It was also totally out of character for me. I found myself thinking and saying things—mean, even cruel things—that I wouldn't have dreamed of voicing only months earlier. I wondered if a pregnancy hormonal shift was similar to a menopausal hormonal shift. Maybe something like "the change" my grandma used to refer to when she recounted stories of the temporary personality distortion she experienced around age fifty. Grandma remembered impulsively throwing a hymnal at the pastor during a Sunday morning church service when he preached on Peter's reference to women adorning themselves with a meek and quiet spirit. Grandma said it felt good at the time, but she was really embarrassed about it later.

Nilima simply smiled at my emotional overflow and placed a perfumed arm around my shoulder. "Haley, this is no trouble—it is our pleasure to do this for you. Please, just enjoy it like we are."

Frowning as she surveyed the platters, Beverly asked, "So these are all foods from India? What are they, anyway?"

"These all represent various Indian entrees and side dishes." Nilima pointed at each plate as she spoke, "This is Chicken Vindaloo—spicy chicken pieces, potatoes, and onions simmered in a tomato-based gravy. And these lamb kebabs were marinated in a pungent yogurt sauce, skewered, and grilled. But because India is a predominantly vegetarian culture, I decided to fill today's meal with more vegetable and rice dishes than with meat."

Nilima proceeded down the length of the tables, naming each dish and listing the ingredients. As an amateur nutritionist, I was delighted with the variety of healthy choices. There was lentil curry, spinach with grated coconut, and a nut, fruit, and basmati rice dish that smelled heavenly. Several intriguing salads rounded out the entrees. The dessert portion included diamond-shaped, sweet groundnut bars, minted fruit chutney, and small cups of mango mousse.

Nilima reached the end of the line and pointed at one of the tiers of the crystal dessert stand. "These round cakes are called Gulab Jamun. They are similar to a small doughnut; and because they are deep-fat fried, they are admittedly quite unhealthy." She laughed, then continued, "But I didn't think that it would hurt to include one indulgent food. You must try one—after they are fried, they are soaked in a sugar syrup, flavored with essence of rose."

Beverly leaned down and sniffed the plate. The stained ruffle of her blouse brushed against the cakes. "Well, goodness sakes—they do smell just like roses!"

I winced, noting in horror how the window behind her silhouetted the brushy hairs that poked through her pantyhose. She often joked about giving up the battle with her head of dark, dense, and defiant hair. Like her Mediterranean grandmother's hair, Beverly would say, her own wiry curls had a wacky mind of their own. Apparently, she had surrendered to her leg hair as well. It looked like she was wearing a skirt over the bottom half of an ape costume. *She could at least have the decency to wear pants if she's too lazy to shave her legs.*

Nilima smiled and asked Lorna to pray before we started dishing up. Lorna cleared her throat and in her clear, sweet voice led us in singing a familiar prayer song. The ladies sounded like a chorus of angels. My fabulous friends had truly outdone themselves.

I was happy that Rick and I had chosen this church several years previous. Artos & Ichthus Fellowship was exactly the kind of modern, yet grounded church that met both my spiritual and social needs. Its name alone, based on the Greek words for bread and fish, reflected perfectly my acknowledgment of Christ's provision for hungry people. I had arrived at this church with a hunger for something that neither my dad's legalistic type of Christianity, nor my stuffy childhood church could ever fill.

After spooning carefully chosen selections onto my plate, I sat down between Danielle and Stacie at a round table. Two of our church's orchestra members, Tara and Natalie, were also at the table.

"Haley, your hair is gorgeous!" Natalie raved. As an older woman, cultured and refined Natalie was living proof that age wasn't an excuse for boorishness. She was the antithesis of Win in every way. Her fashion sense and social graces were impeccable.

"Thank you," I said as I tossed my head. My tresses swung lustily, then settled sweetly back into place. I could almost feel the shine emanating from my scalp. To receive a compliment from Natalie was a highlight, or maybe even more of an achievement.

I handed Tara my phone. "Tara, would you please take a picture of me and Stacie?"

"Sure," Tara said as she snapped a great pose of Stacie and me leaning into each other. Stacie was almost as gorgeous and fun as my church friends. Tara passed the phone back and I quickly clicked through all the shots that Danielle had taken on it for me while I opened the presents. I couldn't wait to post all the shower photos on my Facebook page—all the photos except the ones of the Win and the lederhosen. Those would be deleted later.

"So, Haley, will you be taking on some part-time hours at school after your maternity leave is up?" Stacie asked.

I opened my mouth to reply but was interrupted by Win's shrill voice as she sat down across from me. I bristled. *Why can't she leave me alone?* Even Beverly knew enough to sit on the other side of the room, at a table with the rest of Rick's rowdy relatives.

"What a delight—pumpkin pieces and radishes in the same salad! As un- likely a combination as Aunt Letha and Uncle Juji." I stifled a groan. Win bent her head down to within a few inches of her food and started separating the ingredients into small groups on her plate. "Hmm, but you know, even though Letha was over six feet tall and Juji, from Japan, was barely five- three, they had a long and happy marriage." She popped a forkful of vegeta- bles into her mouth. "Ooh, very nice! Tangy, yet sweet—just like Letha and Juji. A match made in heaven." She closed her eyes and nibbled her vegeta- bles noisily, again reminding me of unruly Bruce.

I turned back toward Stacie, openly and deliberately ignoring Win. "I've pretty much decided to forego even part-time work. I'm mostly concerned about finding quality child care. Since Rick's job has really picked up this year, we should be okay with just one income, for several years anyway."

"So you think you'll stay home fulltime—"

"Ooh, look—this chickpea salad is hiding lime chunks!" Win interrupted. "They're treasures, like little emeralds in the sands of the seashore!" She picked through her salad like she had lost something in it.

Forgetting to finish her sentence, Stacie stared at Win. I really wanted her to ignore the batty old lady like I was, but with a curious expression on her face, Stacie stared at Win instead. That exasperated me even more. I had hoped that my table mates would join me in an all-out team snubbing event. I experienced a moment of fondness for dear cousin Polly—at least she was smart enough to know how to respond properly to dismissal. When I let her know that she had accidentally climbed the wrong ladder, Polly backed right down. Win, though, had not only inappropriately scrambled up the rungs occupied by me and my friends, she was managing to dodge my ejection kicks by swinging around us like a silly monkey.

Win turned her inspection to the appetizer-sized kebab on her plate and commented in a quieter tone, "I would never have expected to eat lamb meat at a baby shower." She raised her head and slowly rotated the bamboo skewer as she studied it intently. "Hmm." Her eyes drifted beyond her kebab and locked onto something on the gift table next to us. In unison, all heads at our table turned to follow her gaze. Win was looking at a large gift bag that bore a picture of a smiling lamb. It frolicked underneath the printed words, "Welcome Little Lamb." Win's eyes fell back to her kebab and then back again to the picture. Silently everyone at the table did the same.

The baby started fidgeting around inside me as I looked down, uncomfortably, at the kebab on my own plate. No longer the picture of a harmless domesticated birdie, socially-impaired Win reminded me more of a mangy turkey vulture, trespassing in an exotic parrot aviary.

I raised my head just in time to watch Win brandish her meat above her as if she was raising a glass to propose a toast. "Ha!" she exclaimed. "Jesus told Peter to feed his sheep, but today the sheep are feeding us!" She lowered her skewer, tore off a chunk of meat like it was a piece of carrion, and chewed with gusto. "Mmm, tasty—positively tasty," she squawked.

I wished I could throw a blanket over her.

Looking back down, I winced at a twinge of pain in my hand; and suddenly, for the very first time in my life, I felt a twinge of empathy for my father.

3

After the shower ended, I uploaded the pics from my phone onto Facebook while I was still in my snappy hybrid car in the church parking lot. Knowing how much I adore being connected, Rick had surprised me at Christmas with one of the smartest cell phones available on the market. I loved having the internet, and thus my social circle, at my fingertips at all times. And as I acquired more and more apps, I began using it for more than just communication. With instant weather info, nutrition calculation, radio stations, the complete Bible, and shopping comparison capability, my phone was becoming as indispensable to me as one of my vital organs.

I started to delete pictures of Win and the lederhosen but hesitated as a novel idea nudged the creative side of my brain. *Hmm...that would be fun.* I began to envision yet another Facebook album. An entertaining album. An album that my friends would get a kick out of and could even contribute to if they wanted. My own FASHION FAIL spot, with Win holding the lederhosen as picture number one. Clever captions for that one immediately started buzzing about in my mind. Chuckling over others' clothing mishaps could provide a much needed diversion for me and my hard-working friends. We were all a little too driven at times.

I reasoned that Win, being about as tech-savvy as a feeder rat, would most likely never see her gift made fun of on Facebook. All she ever used the internet for was to order useless junk from a computer at a senior center. And even that was only a weekly event for her. She had announced at the shower that looking for things on the Worldwide Web was like walking into a shopping center of "universal proportions and endless possibilities." She could only digest it in limited bits.

I started clicking back through the pictures a second time, searching for a photo of Beverly. *Oh, man—a picture of her with the sun behind her legs would be perfect.* I was disappointed that I didn't have any such images of Beverly but knew another opportunity to catch her in a Fashion Fail would certainly arise again. I was pretty sure she wasn't on Facebook, either.

Smiling to myself over my own ingenuity, I finished the task, set the phone in my cup holder, and headed for home. The noonday sun warmed me through the car window as I zipped around on the quiet side streets. Once on the interstate, however, the traffic in front of me started thickening and slowing like cooling wax. I inhaled deeply and exhaled slowly as I pressed down on the brake pedal, making a conscious decision to stay in a good mood. I didn't want to let anything ruin my nice day. In spite of Aunt Win's antics, my morning had delivered some delicious surprises, and I wanted to savor the memory of those for as long as I could.

One of the best shower moments occurred right before I left. Displaying the characteristic politeness of her culture, gracious Nilima had waited until most of the ladies were gone before giving me the fuchsia wrapped present to open. Nilima was worried that her gift of a maternity outfit could somehow upstage Win's gift. I really wished she wouldn't have been so careful. Her good manners had denied me the opportunity to publicly rhapsodize over and even model two gorgeous Indian kurta blouses.

These were embroidered and beaded tunic tops, one navy blue and one cream-colored. They were roomy and long—perfect for the last two months of my pregnancy and beyond, if necessary. Their bohemian, yet classy, look was definitely me. I would have welcomed the chance to show off my toned physique. It might have opened up a discussion on the benefits of pregnancy nutrition and fitness. As a health minor in college, I loved teaching others about how to eat well and stick to a regular exercise routine.

A warm feeling flowed through me when I reflected on my blessings. It was a sensation of gratitude that overshadowed the strange hostile feelings that had been dominating my psyche all morning. I knew I needed to rein in some of that uncharacteristic negativity. It was like something dark had come over me and it suddenly seemed a bit frightening. The real me wasn't usually that edgy.

I started thinking about crafting some really special handmade thank-you notes for my friends instead. Maybe I could look on Martha Stewart's website and get some stamping and gluing ideas. That actually sounded more fun than posting Fashion Fails. A spontaneous praise song erupted from my lips as I drove, making me feel a bit more like my regular, nice self.

The traffic continued to slow, but I deliberately kept my thoughts positive. A sign pointing the way to a downtown arterial reminded me of my pre-shower appointment in the posh salon. It was an artsy establishment with highly trained, up-to-the-minute stylists. Disappointed that the salon's liability regulations prevented pregnant clientele from using their eco-friendly, pedal-powered hair dryer, I had consoled myself with the chai tea and buckwheat biscotti that my stylist, Josie, brought me while I sat under a regular hair dryer.

As the Philadelphia skyline slowly passed by my passenger window, I thought about how much I enjoyed the energy and bustle of the city itself. The way the clean lines of the Philly skyscrapers defined the high spaces around them always made me feel like I was in the middle of something important. Even on a weekend, the atmosphere in the shadow of the tall buildings was more formal than in the suburbs. It was refreshing to take a break from my suburban mediocrities once in a while.

I glanced at myself in the rearview mirror. Bolstered and polished to a gleam by the Solar Soak Treatment, my new hairstyle was definitely worth its exorbitant Center City cost—something that I would avoid revealing to Rick, of course. The even more horrific price that I paid for an assortment of special hair care products warranted that I seatbelt the bag in the passenger seat next to me. I wouldn't risk spilling even a drop of the miracle fluids that would carry my style through the last ungainly months of pregnancy. The raffia-tied salon bag sat regally upright, like it was Queen Elizabeth being transported to her next important engagement.

I refused to feel guilty about spending so much on my hair. I figured it was better to spend the extra while I was still teaching fulltime. After my maternity leave was over in the fall, I planned to stay home for at least a year. I would adjust to a tighter budget then, but I didn't have to yet. And, to my credit, I had refused the stylist's offer of a highlighting job because of the price. So, essentially, I was frugal.

The traffic slowed even more. How bad could a traffic jam get on a Saturday? I strained to see what was holding up the flow of vehicles, but the semi-truck directly in front of me blocked my view. While inching forward in the middle lane, I continued to breathe deliberately, telling myself that it was actually beneficial to have this childbirth breathing practice time.

The cars in front were merging to the left. I signaled to the left, but no one in the endless line of cars would let me jump in. I was usually an assertive driver, but as I approached the mysterious roadblock, I realized that I should have merged much sooner. If I couldn't get into the open lane within a few moments, I would be forced to stop on the crowded interstate—a situation that I usually would never allow to happen. Through clenched teeth I reprimanded myself for daydreaming too much. My hair wonderment was dangerously distracting.

Flaunting his mass, the semi-truck barreled to the left and impudently sliced a space for his rig in front of a honking and gesturing motorist. The cutoff vehicle in the left lane slammed on his brakes, causing everyone behind him to experience a moment of near rear-ending terror. Brakes screeched, horns blared, and one man even stuck his head out his window and yelled profanities at the trucker. I growled, knowing that the flare up of drivers' tempers had likely killed my chances to receive a break from anyone in the line of cars approaching from behind me. I started worrying that I would be stuck in one spot for a long time, considering that my vulnerable little hybrid car was too tiny to allow me to risk any such aggressive reentry tactic.

With the huge truck out of the way, I finally saw the traffic obstruction. It was a stalled car, now immediately in front of me. Not just any car—it was the type of bloated, gas-guzzling sedan that I considered to be an offensive and unnecessary environmental menace. It was an ancient, unhealthy behemoth whose years of indiscriminate fuel consumption had probably contributed to its own clogged systems. No wonder it had broken down. Its hood was propped up and its unfortunate driver stood, plastered to the outside of the driver door, frantically punching the buttons of her cell phone. Something must have been wrong with her phone because she kept shaking it and holding it up in between button pushing sessions. She was talking wildly to herself.

The woman, probably not much older than me, was dressed in filthy jeans and a raggedy plaid shirt. Her dark and stringy long hair loitered around her shoulders beneath a dingy, winterish hat with dangling ear flaps. She looked terrible. I wondered if she intended to look the way she did, or if she was merely a victim of hard circumstances, someone whose rough times had robbed her of self-respect and good taste.

I continued to signal, but had no choice except to come to a complete stop. The woman looked up and we locked eyes. I shuddered as my nice self suddenly ran out of my head and my hormonal mean self stomped back inside me. I didn't even try to stop it. This woman's stupid situation was not my problem. I just needed to get home and get on with my day.

I started desperately praying for a miraculous opening in the traffic. The last thing I wanted was to be accosted by the stranded driver. For all I knew, she could be dangerous—a criminal, a druggie, or an insane escapee from something. I pushed the lock button on my door panel. It would be reckless for me to risk contact with the stranger. Even if her intent was not to rob me or hijack my car, she looked dirty and smelly, and I certainly didn't need the added inconvenience of vermin infesting my upholstery.

She looked at me again and walked toward my car. My heart lurched. I continued to signal and glanced frantically from side mirror to rearview mirror. *Please, please, God—make an opening in the traffic!* She touched the hood of my car and started to walk around to my window but suddenly changed her mind and went around to the passenger side. A strange, niggling feeling in my gut started mingling with my fear. *No, no Lord. It can't be.* The woman peered into my passenger window. The faint pang of feeling tickled *my gut again. No, I'm sure it's just the lamb. I hardly ever eat meat any-more—it's just not settling well.* The woman knocked on the window, then pointed at her phone and shook her head. I refused to look her in the eye and frantically searched my side mirror for even a hint of an opening between cars.

On a momentary whim, I grabbed my phone and snapped a picture of the creepy lady. Another perfect FASHION FAIL entry had presented itself to me just like that—right in the middle of a tense moment, no less.

Seeing me hold up my phone, the woman pounded on the window again. I put the phone down and felt the baby kick at the feeling inside me. *Lord, You're not asking me to help her—it's just indigestion, right?* The woman yelled something just as a car slowed and flashed its lights at me. *Thank you.* I had my answer. It was just the lamb meat, not spiritual prompting after all.

I pushed on the accelerator and steered hard into the left lane, not even bothering to look back at the scraggly motorist. Someone else would surely come along. Besides, there was no reason for anyone in this day and age to drive such a monstrosity, and she was probably just too careless to keep her phone battery charged. In fact, I rationalized, if I helped her, I might actually be enabling her to get away with irresponsibility. I wouldn't be a good Christian witness in anybody's eyes. Her car problems and her phone prob-lems were her own fault, just like my stomach discomfort was my own fault. I was glad, though, that eating carelessly was my only mistake. It was a small one compared to a lifetime lived carelessly. *Thank you, God, that I'm not that woman.*

Relieved, I resumed a normal speed and made a mental note to stay away from meat altogether. I patted my snappy little hybrid's steering wheel lov-ingly, suddenly grateful that my dad had drilled into me the importance of self-respect. It was the second time that day that I felt a surprising apprecia-tion for my father. Maybe his insistence on proper bearing and convention, however excessive at times, had not been so wrong after all. I thought about Win's complete ignorance of social mores and shuddered. I bet the stringy-haired lady would enjoy Win's stories. *Hmm, birds of a feather, perhaps?*

After a few miles, I exited off the interstate onto the streets of our older subdivision. The March sun was coaxing leaves out of their bud casings on the various bushes and trees that lined the streets. Even though I was be-coming dissatisfied with our boxy little house, I had to admit that the neigh-borhood was quite pretty in springtime. Blooming trees and flowering perennials tended to divert attention away from the crumbling sidewalks and curbing that was characteristic of an aging district.

Beverly had found the fifty-year-old bungalow for us when we first married. It was all we could afford at the time. By moonlighting as a costume and mask designer for the high school's drama department, however, I was able to save up enough money for a smart renovation. Rick was less fussy about home decor than I was, but because I was bringing in bigger paychecks at the time, he begrudgingly agreed to hire a professional to redesign the kitchen and living room. I was proud of the elegantly understated result. In my mind the cost of the makeover was an investment, something that would pay off when we sold the house in order to upgrade to a classier subdivision—one that would be well above Beverly's market niche.

Turning into the driveway of our home, I saw Rick on the front lawn, oddly stomping his feet in a high-kneed gait across the awakening grass. *What's he doing now?* It seemed that my energetic husband was endlessly fiddling with our yard. It wasn't that he was into perfect landscaping—I would have liked that—he was just obsessed with the grass itself. He viewed hedges and flowerbeds with the same disdain that I reserved for appliquéd Christmas sweatshirts. Rick felt that anything but lawn on a lawn was unnecessary and distracting. He had an odd affinity for large expanses of grass and talked about sod the way a farmer talked of crop production. Mulching, fertilizing, watering, raking—his preoccupation made for some fairly boring conversation at the dinner table.

I pulled in behind Rick's mini-pickup. Several large bags of lawn food rested on the open tailgate. Rick dreamed of owning a bigger truck someday, but as suburbanites, I couldn't see why in the world we would need one. Rick was able to haul everything he required for his lawn hobby in the small truck, and besides, a big pickup didn't seem environmentally responsible.

"What are you doing?" I called as I got out of my car.

"Hi, hon—I'm just aerating," Rick yelled back as he did an about-face turn at our yard's border and proceeded on his exaggerated high-stepping march back toward me. I stood and waited, not wanting to have to conduct a shouted conversation for our neighbors to hear. They were probably watching Rick from their windows, anyway. His lawn projects had already become enough of a curiosity on our block without any attention-getting shouting on our part.

"Hey Babe!" he greeted me when he finished his lap. Lorna told me that Rick had known about the shower all along and had been instructed to make sure that I went to Bible study that day. "How was the shower?"

"It was spectacular! You sneak—you did a good job of keeping it secret. I can't wait to show you all the presents." I looked down at his feet and grimaced. "What in the world are those?" I pointed at the weird shoes that I had never seen before.

"These are homemade aerating shoes. Got the idea off the internet." He grinned. "It's a little labor intensive, but it saves us the sixty bucks it would cost to rent a power aerator for the afternoon. Actually, about fifty-five when you deduct the cost of the nails and the shoes."

He pulled his foot up and showed me how he had taken his staple gun and fastened each sole of a pair of moribund hiking boots to a square of plywood that was only slightly larger than the perimeter of the boots. Several neat rows of huge nails jutted from the bottom of each shoe-board.

"Where'd you get those icky shoes?" Their brown leather was grimy, stained and had the word, "Bob" written in permanent marker on the back of each.

"Thrift store," Rick beamed. "Dollar-fifty!"

I grimaced again. "Ooh, you don't know where those have been! Aren't you afraid of diseases or at least a stranger's sweat?" I immediately envisioned those shoes carrying the feet of a leprous, drug-crazed indigent on a frantic run from police officers. *How stupid of Bob to write his name on his shoes if he was going to commit crimes.* My mind went on to form a picture of the stringy-haired, interstate blocking lady as the driver of Bob's get-away car. *Good thing the monstrosity is prone to breaking down.*

"Aw, Haley, come on—you're always so uptight about this stuff. Look—when I ram my foot down, it puts aeration holes into the thatch."

I pushed aside my disturbing thoughts of criminals with stringy hair. "Does our lawn really need this?"

"Definitely. It helps the grass breathe."

"Oh." I didn't know that grass needed to breathe but didn't want to ask questions that would invite any more discussion on the topic of grass. Besides, I had much more interesting news to relate concerning the baby shower and my hair appointment. Information that he would be dying to hear all the details about, except the expense part, of course. I didn't need to bother him with that much detail.

"Are you almost finished? I need help getting all the baby presents into the house." I opened the hatchback of my car. "Oh, and do you notice anything different about me?" It seemed impossible for him to miss the sophistication of the new haircut.

"Um," he dropped his smile and shifted uncomfortably while he eyed me up and down. His look reflected the anguish of a spelling bee contestant who had just been given the word "dirigible" to spell. "Um, new shoes for you too...maybe? Or, uh, you got your eyebrow-thing, um, waxed...perhaps?"

"What eyebrow-thing? Is there something wrong with my eyebrows? What are you talking about?" I growled. "Rick, I can't believe you don't see it. It's my hair—it's a totally different cut!"

"Oh, oh, yeah. I see it now, I-I really do. It's beautiful, no—stunning!"

I started grabbing gift bags from the back of the car. "Keep your platitudes to yourself."

My hand fell on the food processor box and instant conviction washed over me. I needed to go easy on Rick. He really was a wonderful husband and we had so much going for us. Besides, I still didn't want anything to upset such a great day. "It's okay, Rick," I conceded, "and thanks for taking such good care of our place."

His smile returned as he loosened the unlikely boots. "No, problem, my brown-eyed beauty—here let me take that one, it looks heavy." He pulled a box from my grasp and noticed my bandaid. "Hey, what happened to your hand?"

"Not sure," I answered, "think I was poked by a staple on some wrapping paper or packaging at the shower. It's small, it'll be all right."

"Does it hurt?"

"Not really, I'm fine," I said, placing several gift bags on top of the box he had taken from me. He turned and padded toward the house on bare feet.

I reached for my phone from inside the car and followed him. "Rick, you should take a minute to look at all my pictures—you'll love the ones of the amazing buffet."

"So Hal was on surveillance the whole time." His tone became serious as he set the presents on the kitchen table.

Rick started calling my phone Hal when I added a voice recognition app that not only recognized spoken commands but also read email and texts back to me while I drove. Hal was the talking, all-seeing, all-knowing computer in the old movie, *2001: A Space Odyssey* that eventually gained total control of a spaceship.

Normally a laid-back, fun-loving guy, Rick was serious when he recently said he regretted getting the phone for me. He said the phone creeped him out, and he made me turn it off each night before we went to bed. Apparently, in the Space Odyssey movie, Hal purposely disabled the life support systems of three crew members while they slept in hibernation mode during the ship's mission to Jupiter. Hal was a murderer.

I frowned at his comment. "It wasn't on surveillance—it's just a cell phone. And I'm glad I had it. The shower pictures will make a great first page for the baby's memory book."

"Hmph." Rick replied. "I'm gonna finish aerating."

He went out the door, and I immediately plugged the phone into its charger, next to Rick's simpler, older phone. I reminded myself to talk to a service rep sometime about replacing the phone battery. Lately, it hadn't been holding a charge as long as it should. I tried to talk to Rick about that, but he dismissed me, saying that the battery was just tired from overuse.

I went into the dining room where I logged onto Facebook on the desktop computer, glad that Rick wasn't in the house at the moment. I hated it when he looked over my shoulder when I was online. He always made snide comments about Facebook and the stuff my friends and I all wrote to each other. He called everything petty, saying we were narcissistic.

Rick had started going on rants about instant messaging and social networking sites, saying that Americans were tying up the airwaves and cyberspace with so much meaningless conversation that there was probably no room left for the really important national security transmissions. He would say that telling someone we just ate a peach could disrupt messages from overseas intelligence relaying that a group of terrorist-launched nuclear missiles was heading for all the major dams in America in order to take out the country's power grid. Then he'd announce that we'd regress into the dark ages of handwritten correspondence and slide rules and abacuses. I asked him what those were, and he said I didn't know because Facebook was turning my brain into a mushy drivel sponge. At that point I'd yell at him to shut up. Of course, he wouldn't.

"Why would Danielle think we want to know that she's drinking juice right now? Who really cares that so-and-so's kid just squirt dish soap into the toilet? Is it life-changing for you to know that Tiffany's boy went to school in his Boy Scout uniform? It's just Tiffany's way of bragging that her darling is more special than anyone else's kid, right?"

I always got mad and told Rick that women like to know these things. Men just didn't understand. Besides that, he was being judgmental. When I would pause to think about what I wanted to tell my friends, his asinine suggestions made me want to slug him in the stomach.

"Hey, Haley, here's a good one—write, 'I just burped.'"

"Rick, stop it."

"No, no—this one's better! Write, 'my dog just burped, and it sounded human.'"

"Rick, we don't have a dog."

"Okay, okay—write, 'I just burped and it sounded like a dog.'"

"Rick, that's enough!"

My tolerance of his taunting reached its end on the day, though, when he leaned over my shoulder and read my status update for that day. I had just written, "Today I am seeing my growing body as a metaphor for God's holy growth within my soul."

"C'mon, Haley—cut the super-spiritual stuff. You are not seeing God's holy growth within you—you complain every day about feeling fat!"

That was the day I ordered him out of the room and didn't speak to him until late that night.

━━━◆◆◆◆━━━

I was surprised that manual lawn aeration could take so long. Rick returned to execute his baton-twirler's march, back and forth across our modest lot for over an hour. I marveled at his stamina. Rick had never been particularly athletic, but his constant motion seemed to build the kind of sinewy muscle that other men paid gym dues to achieve.

I finished my online communiqué, satisfied with my latest entries, and sat down on the couch with a cup of tea. As excited as I was to put away and arrange the shower gifts in the baby's room, I needed a moment to unwind. It felt good to put my feet up and pore over the Montana maps and print-outs I had taken from some travel websites.

The blasting of a tinny tune made me jump. *Ergh.* Luckily, the resulting splash of hot tea hit my brochures and not my stomach. It would have burned me, for sure. Win's other stupid gift from five years ago, the Meteorologic Melodies weather station, must have picked up on a sudden change in temperature and was bleating the song, "You Are My Sunshine." For the last five years, at Rick's insistence, it squatted on the kitchen windowsill like a mischievous howler monkey, waiting to scare me specifically when I was doing things like transferring pots of boiling pasta to the sink or chopping vegetables with a razor-sharp cleaver. I was always nervous in my own kitchen.

I took a deep breath and wiped the Montana brochure with a tissue. Because of the baby, Rick and I wouldn't be vacationing out West until next year, but I loved staring at the pictures of the serene mountain lakes and evergreen forests. It all looked so peaceful.

Rick's cell ringtone, blaring the theme song to Star Wars, interrupted my dreamy moment. I sighed, got up, and looked at the phone's incoming number. Why was Jerry calling Rick on a Saturday? I let the voice mail take the message. Rick could call back when he concluded his half-time show.

I returned to the couch and let the Montana pictures lift my spirits into the "Rocky Mountain High" that the late John Denver sang into my childhood kitchen through my mother's old cassette player. Singing pop tunes with Mom was one of the rare fun things we did together. Almost every time we sang the John Denver song, Mom would recount the one time she visited the Rocky Mountains and how much she wanted to go back someday.

Dad did not share my mom's interest in vacationing out west. At some point in my early school years, Dad conducted his own detailed survey of the costs associated with various vacation options. He divided the U.S. into six sectors and researched things such as transportation and fuel costs, lodging options, wilderness vs. commercial recreation, and relevance to overall family well-being. He developed a formula that allowed him to plug all those variables in and calculate it according to places within each sector. The results were ranked and plotted on a graph. The tourist spots of the Rocky Mountains all ended up too low on Dad's vacation viability graph for us to go there. We went to Warbling Waters Wigwam Village in Michigan instead.

That trip revealed the first of many flaws in Dad's system. For one thing, he had not factored in the different levels of truthfulness conveyed in tourist trap brochures. Our decaying wigwam bore no resemblance to the one in the pictures. Dad's formula also was too concrete to account for gray areas such as implications, rather than outright statements about the facilities each wigwam contained. Mom was horrified to find that what she had assumed would be a kitchenette was only a rusting pan of charcoal briquettes positioned below a ventilation hole in the top of our wigwam. We ended up eating acrid barbecued everything for a week. Mom almost had a nervous breakdown during that vacation and gave away our outdoor grill when we returned home.

I glanced down at a brochure of Glacier National Park. It showed a blue mountain lake framed by mountains that were so beautiful they almost didn't look real. But I knew that they were real. Rick had his own photos to prove it. He worked at a backcountry chalet in Glacier Park for two summers during his college years. His descriptions of his hikes and wildlife encounters fascinated me when we were dating, and the fact that he had relatives in other parts of Montana got my attention as well.

Dad's refusal to take us anywhere within the Rocky Mountains made Rick's association with that area all the more attractive. He had access to something that my Dad denied me and my siblings. When Rick and I honeymooned in Colorado, I felt like I had committed mild revenge against my father. It was quite satisfying.

I picked up the brochure and studied it intently. Part of me wished I could jump into that picture sooner than next year and run away from my anxieties. I hadn't yet admitted to Rick how scared I was about being a mom, or how unsure I was about quitting my job. I felt like I was in a car, barreling full speed ahead toward a huge, dark, mysterious tunnel marked, YOUR FUTURE. I wanted to slow down, size it up, maybe peek around inside it before I just blasted in, but my accelerator pedal was stuck and I had no brakes. I kept staring at the mountain picture, wishing a place like that was guaranteed to be at the end of my tunnel.

All of a sudden, Rick burst through the back door in his bare feet, bringing a loamy, new-grass odor with him.

"Haley—any calls come in for me, yet?"

"Yeah, it looks like Jerry tried a little while ago. Think he left a message."

"Oh, good." He grabbed his phone and started pushing buttons. "I'm workin' on a new job plan, honey. You're gonna love this one!" He put the phone up to his ear.

A fresh stab of disquiet poked my insides. The baby moved, as if she felt it too. The tunnel loomed closer, and the car kept going. In my mind, I frantically pushed the floppy brake pedal again. It instantly went all the way to the floor. There was to be no stopping, or even slowing, on the road to whatever lie ahead.

4

Rick snapped his phone shut and raised his arms into the air. He leapt into the middle of the living room rug like he was breaking out into song in the middle of a musical production.

"Haley, you won't believe this! This is it—the way to take our vacation in Montana this year and get paid for it!"

"*This* year?"

"Yeah, and not just that, but this could be my big break. Taking this one on could finally put me in line for the next big promotion. Isn't that what we've been praying for? You wouldn't have to worry so much about quitting your job."

Rick went on to explain that a major ranching corporation had offered his business consulting team a contract to analyze and improve its operations. It just so happened that one of the corporate ranches was located near the place where Great-aunt Gracie and Great-uncle Hank lived. Rick's supervisor had almost turned the contract down when he found out how remotely located the ranch was, dismissing it as too cost-ineffective; but Rick, predictably, had changed his boss's mind.

"Haley, this is perfect—I convinced Jerry to let me go out there and work as a one man team." Rick was jubilant. "I outlined a plan that would allow for me to draw up all the analyses myself and conference once a week with the others to make sure I stay on the right track. Jerry agreed to let me work the contract and gave me up to three months to do it."

"Three months?"

"Yeah, I'll get my two weeks of vacation and one month of expense pay. The company will let me stay up to six weeks longer without losing my job. I'm sure I could get hired on at the ranch to make whatever extra salary we need while we're there."

"While we're there? What about my job? A teacher can't just abandon her English class in the last quarter of the school year." I was incredulous. As much as I wanted to go to Montana, this was not the right time.

"Isn't that student teacher, what's-her-name, taking over anyway for the last month?"

"Well, yes, but I'm supposed to supervise Ashley. And I'm finally getting somewhere with the students' vocabularies." I didn't say it, but I also wanted to hang on to my teacher identity and paycheck until the last possible moment. Once I let those go, it could be years before I could get them back—if ever. "Rick, you'd just have to go without me."

"C'mon, Haley, I'm sure the school can work something out. Tell 'em you're taking your maternity leave a little early."

"A little early? Rick, it would still be April and school isn't out until the end of May!"

"Like I said, they could work something out."

"But what about the baby? She's due right after school's out. We had it all planned, remember?"

"Haley, this is twenty-first century America. Grassview, Montana, happens to have doctors, you know. You could deliver out there just as easily as you could here. Might even be better for you—higher altitude, cleaner air and all that."

"Rick, you can't just make assumptions all the time. How do you know that childbirth would be workable out there?" An unsolicited picture of Missie birthing Walter Jr. in the casino popped up in my mind, sending a shiver through me. "And what about the peace and quiet I need? We talked about it, remember? You promised that you would help me keep our summer as calm as possible for the baby. A road trip and away-from-home-birth does not sound peaceful!"

I continued, but my objections would never be a match for Rick's ebullient determination. I had learned after five years of marriage that trying to talk him out of one of his grand plans was like trying to circumvent an automated phone menu.

I managed to stave off Rick's scheme for exactly three days. We sincerely prayed during that time, asking God to give us some kind, any kind, of clear sign to indicate whether or not we should go through with Rick's wild idea.

I also discussed the matter exhaustively with my friends. I had several long phone conversations with Stacie and Danielle. And dozens of responses filled my Facebook wall when I updated my status with the Proverbs verse, "Plans fail for lack of counsel, but with many advisers they succeed." This opened up an entire discussion on the subject of Knowing God's Will For Your Life.

Rick didn't consult anyone other than God. This bugged me. I expected him to set up a meeting with some of the men from our church and listen to their wise counsel. At the very least, I hoped he would call one of the elders and talk about it over the phone. He cheerfully avoided performing any of these prudent measures, though, and kept saying that praying with me for a clear sign was enough. He spent two full evenings at the lawn and garden store consulting the manager, Chester, on the intricacies of nitrogen/calcium/phosphorus ratios in lawn fertilizer. He even emailed several other gardening experts, asking them for their opinions concerning fertilizer brands.

A phone call from Aunt Win proved to be the coup de grâce that Rick unquestioningly accepted as God's answer. I wasn't so sure. It didn't seem prudent of God to use a mentally unstable elderly woman to deliver His sign.

"Hey, there, Aunt Winnie, how're you doing?" Rick answered the kitchen phone with his characteristic cheer. "Really?....You're kidding!....Uh huh....uh huh—wow, what a coincidence. This would solve the housing issue."

I turned to empty the dishwasher as he said "uh-huh, uh-huh" over and over for a full thirty seconds.

"I think this really could work. Wait a moment; I'm going to put on the speakerphone so Haley can hear this." He pushed the button and Win's cackly voice echoed through our kitchen.

"Hello, hello?"

"Hi, Aunt Win, it's Haley. I'm here." My voice was flat.

"Oh, sweetheart, how are you?"

"I'm fine."

"And how's that little bun-in-your-oven doing?"

"Bun in—?"

"—Win," Rick cut in, "just tell Haley what you were telling me."

"About the neighbor's ferret accidentally calling Bucharest on their cellular telephone?"

"No, not that. About Gracie needing a house sitter."

Aunt Win explained that she had just phoned Gracie in Montana to wish her a happy St. Patrick's Day and learned that Gracie and Hank were planning to visit their daughter in Alaska for the summer. Gracie had expressed concern that the neighbor who usually looked after their place was suffering from too many health issues to be able to help them out this year. Winifred, hearing from Rick's mom about his job proposal, called us to let us know about the possibility of free summer housing. In fact, Win stated that she had actually been planning to go visit Gracie later in the summer anyway, so why not all go together? I mouthed a silent "no" at Rick as Win chattered on and on like a speed junkie. Even though I was warming up to the whole Montana plan, the thought of traveling and living, even temporarily, with Aunt Win was just too much. *He better get that idea out of his mind right now. I refuse to spend my vacation with a crazy old lady. I won't let it happen. I simply won't.*

The images that resulted from Googling "Grassview, Montana" were minimal. There was one photo of a rodeo queen wearing a belt buckle as big as a hub cap and several other pictures of oversized wheat harvesting machines. Rick got excited when he saw those. He called them state-of-the-art combines and immediately emailed the photos to Chester at the garden store. Only two other pictures came up, one of the modest, sandstone county courthouse and one of the sun setting behind some low hills. I decided to use the travel brochure pictures from other places in Montana to fill in the gaps.

Surprisingly, the consensus among my friends leaned toward making the trip. A couple of women had taken skiing and hiking vacations in the Montana mountains and reported that they had great experiences. Charmaine had even skied in a race at a posh Montana alpine resort last year. She said the town she stayed in was really upscale and fun and had one of the best workout facilities she had seen in a long time. Everyone agreed that the timing was a bit difficult; but in spite of this, they also agreed that this might be too good an opportunity to pass up.

I did some investigating and located an obstetrician in the town of Range City, about a thirty-mile drive from Grassview. A phone consultation with the doctor convinced me that he was a suitable choice for our birth. That, combined with my mother's willingness to fly out to be with us when the baby was born, put my mind at ease. The way things were falling into place was the sign I was looking for. I would go.

Not content to leave it at that, though, Rick started making a case for taking Aunt Win with us. I listened but stood my ground. He first contended that Win could be an invaluable household helper at Gracie's place. I replied that because I wouldn't be working anymore, I would have plenty of time to take care of things myself. He proposed that Win could be a great nanny after the baby was born. I reminded him that my mom would be with us. His last argument, however, jolted me. He announced that Win had offered to pay for all our trip expenses if she came along. I had no good answer for that one, especially as events unfolded over the following two days.

I still hadn't come clean about how much my downtown hair extravaganza had cost. Rick figured I had merely gotten a haircut, the price of which he had never thought to question. His buoyant dark curls and fashion apathy only warranted a periodic visit to Burt the Budget Barber for a twelve-dollar snip snip and neck shave. He was clueless about the high price of womanly beauty, and I had never bothered to enlighten him.

Admittedly, I suffered a measure of guilt over keeping my most indulgent fashion expenses hidden from Rick. The longer I practiced that marriage no-no, however, the duller my conviction became. He refused to see that designer jeans really did fit better than cheap brands and that mayonnaise was not a suitable substitute for silkening hair conditioner. Just because his mom was content to go around with oily hair that smelled like an untended salad bar didn't mean that I should do the same. What Rick didn't know wouldn't hurt him, and I was determined to protect my image, even as an unemployed mother. Dowdiness would never be an option for me. Ever.

We were eating breakfast several days into our trip planning process when Rick casually asked the one crucial question that I had counted on to never arise.

"We still have a few hundred bucks left over from the tax refund in the savings account, right, hon?"

"*Herg-aack—*" My gasp sucked a chunk of eggplant off my gluten-free bagel and into the back of my throat. I choked and sputtered.

"Haley!" Rick jumped to his feet as I coughed and hacked. He awkwardly grabbed me from behind and tried to clasp my middle.

"Rick—stop—*hack*—I'm okay—*erk!*"

"Honey, let me help!" He jumped around in front of me and tried to pull me to a standing position.

"Rick, stop!" I pushed him away and took a deep breath. "I'm okay—*cough*—really, I am."

"You sure?" He looked terrified.

"Yes, it was just a piece of food, but it went down now." I coughed again.

"Oh, man, Haley—you scared me. Glad it went down. I was blanking out on the Heimlich accommodations for pregnant women."

"I'm okay now," I said quietly.

Rick sat back down and took a swig from his coffee mug. "Well, before you choked I was going to say that I've been thinking about this whole Aunt Win thing, and I don't want you to get too stressed out right before the baby's born. Going out to Montana during this time is hard enough, and I realize it's kind of selfish of me to think it has to go my way."

My heart sunk. Rick was picking the worst possible time to be kind and sacrificial. It was awful.

He reached over the table and took my hand. I flinched, not just because the mystery injury had still not healed, but also because I felt paranoid. It was a stab of paranoia probably like one which a successful shoplifter would feel every time a mall security guard crossed her path.

"Haley, you're right—we don't need Aunt Win's help, and with the tax money and the bonus I got from the last contract we can afford the trip without her. I just want you to have a nice vacation."

If I could have, I would have crawled under the table. How could I tell him that I spent a full three hundred bucks on my hair? That the tax money was gone? From the very beginning of my pregnancy, I had been mulling over the ways I could quietly skim beauty money from our looming single paycheck budget. Rick would never trust me with our finances again if he knew I blew our refund on one single hair appointment.

I reached up and tucked some hair behind my ear. It was already losing its beefiness. "Um, actually, Rick…I, um, I really do want to take Aunt Win with us," I mumbled, my eyes down. Like a freed prisoner parroting Communist propaganda to the media in order to keep her still-incarcerated friends from being shot, I lied. I loathed the words as they tumbled from my mouth, but it was either say them or watch my whole polished image die a bloody death from lack of funding. Sadly, accepting Win's money was the only thing that could preserve my vital secret.

"What?" Rick leaned forward.

"I said—I do want to take Aunt Win with us." I spoke louder but kept my gaze down.

"Really? You'd be okay with her coming along? What changed your mind?"

"Um, mostly the expense thing." It would be a full two days before I could look Rick in the eye again. "Hotels, meals, gas—it could really add up. Uh, it's probably smart to take her up on her offer since I won't be going back to work."

I noticed a smear of tomatillo jam on the front of my bathrobe belt. The belt must have brushed across my bagel when Rick kindly attempted to wrench me from my chair. The jam smear coated the robe's terrycloth fibers, but I knew it would come out in the wash. I absentmindedly fingered my hair again. It felt deflated, defeated, wimpy, traitorous.

Like the rest of me.

———◆•◆•◆———

"We're in luck—three empty spaces in a row," Rick announced as he pulled our borrowed minivan and its accompanying utility trailer alongside the curb, across the street from Gunther's Gun Repair. Win had chosen this apartment above a gunsmith shop eight years ago, reporting that she loved the cheap rent and the smell of gun oil.

"Rick, we're across the street—we can't expect her to cross all this traffic with her suitcases."

"Okay, you wait here, and I'll go up and help her bring her stuff out."

Terror seized me. "No, Rick—NO! Stay outside!" After four years, I still hadn't come to terms with the scare I experienced during my one and only visit to Win's apartment.

"Aw, Haley, don't tell me you're still carrying on about the bullet holes in her floor," Rick said with his eyes raised toward the ceiling of the car.

"Carrying on? Rick, that woman lives in daily danger of misfired bullets penetrating her floor and killing her and/or her visitors, and you call my concern carrying on?"

"C'mon—those bullet holes were already there when she moved in years ago. It's never happened even once since she's lived there. Haley, you've got to calm down."

"Calm down? Isn't that my idea? I'm the one who works every day at keeping our lives peaceful, and you're the one who keeps stirring everything up. Don't lecture me about calming down."

Rick stepped onto the street. "It's Win's business, not ours. Besides, Win credits the shrapnel in her knee with making her less afraid of bullets."

I gasped. "Shrapnel? So she was shot!"

"No, not in the apartment. She was in a hunting accident over fifty years ago. It's quite a story." Rick sighed. "I'll be right back—I'll just stay outside her apartment door, okay?"

"Okay." I sighed too.

As Rick got out of the car, he looked over and growled when he saw me pull Hal out of my purse. He had developed some sort of immature jealousy toward my relationship with my phone. He said I paid more attention to Hal than I did to him. I wasn't sure if I should address or ignore his dysfunctional attitude. For the moment, I ignored it.

At first I thought that Rick might warm up to the phone if he started using it more himself. After all, he was a nominal techy and a science fiction buff. When Hal badly mangled the email message that Rick tried to dictate using the word recognition app, though, Rick promptly vowed he would never use it again. I tried to get him to see that the app's word recognition capability became more effective as it became more familiar with his voice, but he would have none of it. And he meant it. He acted like the phone was his mortal enemy. I often wondered what a psychiatrist would say about Rick's paranoia. It wouldn't have surprised me if it stemmed from some sort of childhood trauma—most likely Beverly's fault.

I pushed the lock button down after he got out of the car, shuddering at the seediness of the neighborhood. I couldn't imagine why Win chose to live in such a scary locale. She certainly could afford better or at least safer.

I commanded Hal to bring up Facebook. Several entries were already posted in response to my request for prayer for our trip.

Mom posted her usual motherly advice. "Please be careful and safe. Make Rick pull over if he gets drowsy. Call me each day."

Lorna posted appropriate pastor's wife advice, "Will be praying daily for you. Not only for traveling mercies, but health for you and the baby. Look forward to holding your precious girl and hearing the wonderful praise report you will bring to us when you get back."

Danielle said sister stuff. "Have a great time. Wish I could be there when my little niece is born. POST LOTS OF PICTURES!"

Stacie always made me smile. "Have a great trip and keep your eye out for an eligible, hot cowboy for me. Might pay you a finder's fee for the right one. lol." Stacie could be a little rough around the edges sometimes, but I overlooked it. She wasn't a churchgoer. Yet.

After a full fifteen minutes in front of the gun shop, Win and Rick emerged from the side of the building. Rick looked like a pack animal as he crossed the street balancing two enormous suitcases on each shoulder. Win carried a smaller suitcase, a tote bag, and a huge purse. In spite of the luggage, her tiny, wiry frame darted quickly across the roadway. She wore a surprisingly tasteful brown pantsuit and white sneakers. Sadly, however, she also wore an ugly red and white baseball-type cap which bore the front logo, "Brawny's Gas and Groceries." It thoroughly sapped the pantsuit's style vibe.

I quickly snapped a picture of her. It was a perfect Fashion Fail shot—her head was down so her face wasn't recognizable, but it showed the hat's logo clearly. I got out and raised the back door of the minivan.

"Hello, Haley, dear!" Win set her suitcase in the back and turned to hug me. "I'm glad your mother is letting us use her minivan—how nice to have so much room."

"Ooof," Rick grunted as he plunked the freight car-sized suitcases down behind the trailer. "Is it okay for these to ride back here?"

"Oh, yes, dear. Those contain my extra clothing and appliances that I'll need once we get there. I have everything I need for the trip in my small suitcase and purse."

"Appliances?" I raised my eyebrows.

"Oh, just the handy things that I use once in awhile to make life a little easier."

I started to ask what that meant but decided maybe I didn't want to know, after all. I had to deliberately disengage my thoughts from pondering the possible contents of Win's suitcases. The potentialities were unnerving.

Win placed her purse on the middle seat. "Hmm, think I'll leave my hat on. Those sly little sun rays always try to sneak up to the unshaded parts of my face and dig unsightly crevices. Never hurts to keep the shade intact."

She pulled the tacky hat down tighter onto her head. I looked at the relief map of etchings in her face and decided that a comment about "too late" would probably be too mean. I wondered why Win was so much more weathered than her sisters. There was probably a story behind that too.

Rick busied himself with cramming the luggage into the trailer. Again, I stopped myself from asking a question. I knew that snidely asking if he was glad we rented the trailer after all would just be more salt in a wound. He had insisted that we didn't need it, but I had arranged the rental anyway, knowing that I couldn't fit a summer's worth of my things and basic baby necessities into one vehicle.

Win started to get into the car but paused to look up at the sky.

"Hmm, still hazy. I can't wait to gaze upon the azure skies of Montana. The heavens are just never as blue out here. I'm so excited!" She clapped her hands and practically leapt into the seat.

I had to admire Win's agility. At age eighty, she seemed to have a lot more energy than my pregnant late twenties were affording me. My thickening torso wouldn't allow me to just jump into the car the way I normally would. Still, I knew from some of my friends' pregnancy experiences that physically, I could have had it much worse. My workouts were paying off. Charmaine continued to compliment me on my self-discipline and perseverance. I just wished that my mental state would stay as healthy. My emotions were starting to feel more and more out of control.

"What's that?" I noticed Win taking something from her purse and strapping it around her wrist. It looked like some sort of giant watch.

"Ha!" Win beamed and held her wrist out for me to see. It was a cell phone.

"Penny bought a little cellular phone for me to take on this trip. Finding this little wrist harness on the internet was a serendipitous moment, for sure."

Serendipitous. I had to hand it to her—her vocabulary was commendable.

She tightened the Velcro strap. "This device takes me back to my childhood. After seventy years, I finally have a Dick Tracy wrist radio!"

"Hey, that's cool," Rick exclaimed, settling into the driver's seat.

The phone wasn't cool, it was stupid. The small green cell phone looked like a big bug with stubby antennae.

"Penny got me a child's phone because of the arthritis in my fingers. It only has four buttons—each is attached to a single phone number. Button number one is you, Haley, in case we get separated—"

Oh, wouldn't that be a tragedy?

"—and number two is Beverly. Number three is Gracie in Montana. And number four is Chief Penny." She held the phone up to her mouth and deepened her voice. "Chief Penny, come in, Chief Penny."

She and Rick both laughed heartily. I didn't see any humor in it. In fact, the way that I found myself picturing little lightning bolt callout marks emanating from Win's phone was highly disturbing. I must have been influenced more than I realized by a communications class I once took that examined pop culture as depicted in comic strips. It was obviously a worthless course.

"I loved Dick Tracy comics—haven't thought about him in years," Rick said as he glanced in his side mirror and steered onto the road.

"He was my hero," Win replied. "Remember those despicable villains? Mumbles, Flattop, The Mole, oh, and who could forget Pruneface!"

I glanced back at Win from my visor mirror. *Pruneface, indeed.*

Rick chuckled. "Quite a trip down Memory Lane, I'd say."

"Oh, yes. Speaking of memories, is the Melodies weather station still humming away?" Win asked.

"Hellishly, yes," I muttered.

Rick frowned at me and accelerated. Something around the trailer hitch rattled.

Win, mildly hard of hearing and oblivious to my bad attitude, squealed, "Wonderful! So, what's the humidity level for today?"

"So glad you asked." Rick cleared his throat and started singing, "Look at me, I'm as helpless as a kitten up a tree—"

I cringed. Although Rick loved to sing, he was always a little off key.

"Ahhhh," Win practically swooned, "Misty—the perfect song." She closed her eyes and clutched her chest.

Rick continued, "—and I feel like I'm clinging to a cloud I can't understand—"

"Ohhh...Johnny Mathis..." Win's voice trailed off, high and breathy.

"—I get misty just holding your hand—"

"Rick!" My scream interrupted their cabaret. "The on-ramp—you just missed our turnoff!"

My peaceful vacation had begun.

5

If Rick was weirded out by my phone, I was even more weirded out by his relationship with Aunt Win. The two of them laughed and joked about things that I didn't think were funny at all. From the onset of the journey, I felt like I was the one trapped in a spaceship. It wasn't Hal that I was afraid of—he was my lifeline to the outside world—it was the two laughing and singing crew members that threatened to disable my sanity support systems.

It was horribly disconcerting to watch my crewmates simply laugh at other drivers' displays of vulgarity when said drivers were cut off by our space vessel as it careened recklessly through traffic to make a last minute turnpike entrance. I countered their unsuitable cheeriness with a stern reminder that both rear side windows on Mom's minivan bore vinyl graphics that advertised a Christian stationery company.

Mom worked from home as a sales rep for a business called ChristianPaperWorks.com and decided that letting us use her car was a fair trade-off for free advertising on roads across the eight states that we would be driving through. The lettering on the windows read, "WRITING WITH THE RIGHTEOUS TOUCH – CHRISTIANPAPERWORKS.COM." I delivered a sobering lecture about the importance of staying constantly aware of the kind of witness we would bear throughout our journey. Mom was counting on us to represent her company in a godly manner.

As the miles flew by, though, it quickly became apparent that our priorities and expectations for the trip were miles apart. I expected to enjoy a quiet, albeit long, drive. I looked forward to a break from work and home duties, maybe even an extra nap or two during the day. And reading, lots of reading. There were several novels I had wanted to read all winter, but had not had the time. Now was my chance.

Rick, in turn, expected adventure. He designated himself as sole pilot of our vessel, happily taking on most of the driving. That part was a relief for me, and as long as his adventure didn't collide with my vacation, I figured we'd be fine.

Win expected…well, I wasn't sure what in the world she expected. I decided she entertained delusions, not expectations. She seemed to be content to enter any environment and enjoy it. If she ever found herself homeless, she would be the one to organize a white elephant Christmas gift exchange among her fellow vagrants. She'd host a party at her cart and regale her huddled guests with tales told around a barrel fire.

I certainly would have welcomed a different audience that morning for her stories and trivia about the history of the Pennsylvania turnpike construction. She clapped her hands and cheered each time we went through a tunnel, exclaiming over what an accomplishment each one represented for the era in which it was completed. I couldn't care less. I just wanted to be left alone to read the ebooks that Hal had efficiently downloaded for me. After all, I had chosen to teach English, not history.

Unfortunately, Rick also remained bright and chatty throughout the morning. Even my need for frequent stops at service plazas along the turnpike had not seemed to bother him. His and Win's exclamations over the wooded rural Pennsylvania landscape kept distracting me, forcing me to disengage from my ebook. I agreed that the drive was a refreshing change from the city but couldn't figure out why they had to go on about it the way they did. Win kept tapping my shoulder, pointing out some mountain, or wooded ridgeline, or river crossing. I had to resist the temptation to slap her hand.

We motored through Pennsylvania and traversed the narrow northern panhandle of West Virginia. Rick made the decision to exit the turnpike before Pittsburgh and to continue on I-70 to Indianapolis in order to avoid paying more tolls. Sometime before we crossed into West Virginia, Win switched her history narrative from recounting turnpike construction to facts about the much older National Road building project.

"Oh, look—there's another sign for Highway 40!" she exclaimed, nodding her head up and down repeatedly as she leaned forward to peer at the sign through the front window.

Her mysterious head-bobbing was as distracting as her shoulder-tapping. Even when I didn't look at her directly, I could see her nonstop nodding in my peripheral vision. We were not more than a couple hours into the trip when my irritation reached a critical level. Casting aside any sensitivity to what might be a medical issue, I bluntly confronted her.

"Aunt Win, why do you nod your head so much?"

Rick frowned at me, like I was the one committing some kind of social blunder. I frowned back.

Win just smiled and brightly answered, "Oh, is it that noticeable? It's my glasses—I'm still trying to figure out how to use these baffling trifocal lenses. I can't ever figure out if I should look at things through the far, middle, or close distance prescription part of these things."

"Oh." It wasn't often that Win offered a legitimate reason for something she did.

"You, know—I wouldn't mind any creative suggestions you might have to help me solve this problem. My optometrist says it's either wear trifocals or carry different pairs of glasses around. I tried that, but all I ever did was misplace them. I bought cheap reading glasses by the case, but still lost most of them in the first week. If only I could find a way to permanently attach reading glasses to a part of my body, I could go back to just wearing bifocals. For years, I handled bifocals just fine without having to move my head too much."

"What about wearing them on a chain around your neck?" Rick asked.

"Oh, dear, I tried that for awhile but had a terrifying incident with a paper shredder. The glasses got sucked in when I leaned down too far. Came within a millimeter of making noodles out of my chin."

"Ooh, ick." I really wished I wouldn't have heard that. The subject of the Old National Road suddenly interested me. "So, how do you know so much about road-building history, Aunt Win?"

"From reading! Lots and lots of reading," she replied. "Something Americans need to do more of."

"If only they could..." My voice trailed off as I put Hal down to crack my window for a moment of fresh air. The instant I did this, I felt my expectations slip right on out, laughing at me as they went to frolic in the roadside ditch. I didn't blame them for not wanting to hang around in our stuffy space, though—it wasn't a healthy environment for expectations such as mine to live and thrive and have children. Certainly not with Aunt Win in the car.

———◆◆◆———

It had taken us well into the afternoon to cross Pennsylvania, and I was ready to call it a day when we hit Ohio. Rick, though outwardly agreeable, didn't give any indication that he was going to stop short of his intended first-day goal of Indianapolis.

I needed to recharge Hal. The wilds of western Pennsylvania had presented me with a few highly disturbing gaps in cell phone service. I wasn't sure if there really were places in the country that still didn't have reception, or if Hal's battery was just getting too low to pick up on the weaker signals in certain valley bottoms. I couldn't imagine that in this day and age there could be anywhere in the U.S. that didn't have cell phone reception.

"Rick, there's a rest stop sign—please pull in there." We were approximately fifteen miles inside the eastern border of Ohio.

"Again? Haley we just stopped a half hour ago."

"Well, it's not like I can help this." Certain parts of my pregnancy were starting to annoy me. All the muscle tone in the world couldn't stop the growing baby from planting herself squarely on top of my bladder. Not even Charmaine could do anything about that one.

"It's fine, Haley. I wouldn't mind stretching my legs, anyway." Rick's voice remained pleasant.

He exited and parked among an array of diverse vehicles. I unfolded my stiff legs and shuffled toward the blocky restroom house. I sincerely hoped that there wasn't a waiting line. Win flitted along beside me, chattering about how the section of I-70 we had taken through West Virginia was the shortest stretch of interstate in any of America's highway system. She went on about the evolution of the interstates and their accompanying rest areas. I wanted to tell her to save the fascinating details for when I needed to take a nap in the car but nobly kept my mouth shut.

The late afternoon sun glinted off parked car windows with all the promise of an early summer. A brisk, warm breeze pushed litter pieces into the leaves of a budding bush on one side of the parking area and sent fast food bags into hiding underneath the back of an eighteen-wheeler. The rest stop was a busy place for a Tuesday afternoon, and I questioned why so many people would be traveling in late April.

"You know, we Americans truly are creatures of culture," Win commented as we approached the lineup of women that spilled out the door of the restroom. There was no line at the men's, of course.

"Why do you say that?" I would soon learn to not encourage responses from Win when she broached philosophical subjects in public.

"Well, it seems that Americans in general combat their boredom by consuming tasty treats and drinks." Her declaration was noticeably loud as we joined the bathroom line.

"What?" I lowered my voice, hoping she would follow suit. In all my fretting over having to travel in a confined space with her, I had forgotten to worry about how embarrassing it would be to appear with her in public. With her irritating voice, her ugly hat and her lime green cell phone bobbing around on her wrist, she was almost as bad as Beverly.

She spoke up louder. "I mean that all these travelers have probably over-filled their insides while driving long distances. We are living in unhealthy times—"

"Win, please!" I glared at her, thinking of our van's advertising and our obligation to act properly.

I resisted the urge to dance a bladder-control dance. The baby moved around and nearly sent my herbal health tea to a premature exit. I began shifting my weight from leg to leg every few seconds, fearful of the unexpected length of the waiting line. At least I was wearing my expensive, super-comfy shoes. The pillowy, yet supportive sandals were proving to be just the ticket for my expanding, hurting feet. I had purchased the shoes upon Lorna's recommendation. She said that these were the only ones that her feet could tolerate during her pregnancy. I was glad I had taken her advice. They were proving to be well worth every penny.

Win, observing my leg-shifting, piped up, "Haley—you definitely need the Trav-A-Lav now. It's in a suitcase in the trailer. It shouldn't be hard to get to—let me go get Rick—"

"Win, no!" I hissed. I had already rejected her three previous Trav-A-Lav offers in Pennsylvania.

"The Trav-A-Lav?" A large, middle-aged woman yelled from the center of the line, proving that people were listening to us. "You have a Trav-A-Lav?" The woman wore a sparkly blouse: grape cluster-sized, beaded earrings, and chintzy, flowered flip-flops. I shivered at the thought of having such thin soles as the only barrier between my feet and a nasty public restroom floor. I wouldn't ever wear cheap flip-flops outside the safety of my own home.

"I certainly do," Win replied with obvious pride.

"Wow, I saw it advertised on channel sixty-two and almost ordered it the other day. Does it work?" The woman's earrings bounced around with her excitement.

All the ladies' eyes were on us. I would have fled the scene if I hadn't needed the bathroom so desperately.

"I haven't had a chance to try it out yet—it's still in the box. But it came with a satisfaction guarantee, so I'm sure it will work as promised."

"Well, if this line doesn't start moving faster, I'd be tempted to pay you to set it up and let me use it," the earring lady bellowed.

"What's a Lav-A-Trav?" a little girl asked. Her mother shushed her.

To my complete chagrin, Win stepped out of line and faced a wide-eyed audience.

"So glad you asked." Her voice deepened slightly and she took on the tone of a radio announcer. "The Trav-A-Lav is a personal, portable toilet that can easily be set up and used inconspicuously in almost any situation. It's fully—"

A startling ruckus from the pet area interrupted Win. I had never imagined that in my lifetime a dogfight would rescue me from an uncomfortable moment. A pony-sized Great Dane was cowering in the face of a tiny Boston terrier's fierce barking. The terrier lunged repeatedly at the quivering Great Dane, backing the larger dog onto the sidewalk. As the ladies all turned to watch the Great Dane's owner rush to save it, I darted to the head of the bathroom line and slipped into a stall before the next girl even knew what happened.

I returned to our car to see Rick absorbed in a conversation with a trucker on the other side of the lot. They stood in front of the driver's enormous tanker, deeply absorbed in whatever they were talking about. I fished around in the glove box of the van, found my noise-canceling earbuds, and hefted myself into the back seat. I decided that restfulness would not happen without some work on my part. I determined to force some relaxation out of the remainder of our first day's journey.

We reentered the flow of traffic in the westbound lanes of the interstate. Win had taken my place in the front passenger seat and settled in as a rapt participant in Rick's intriguing discussion of crop fertilizer transportation. His newly-acquired knowledge of the debate over railroad vs. tanker truck shipments of anhydrous ammonia apparently provided much fodder for engrossing discourse.

Their rousing topic had prompted Win to use her phone for the first time that day. She called Penny to ask her if she could remember what their father used to fertilize their garden with in the old days. It was unnerving to watch her awkwardly hold her elbow in the air while she keeping her wrist up to her ear to use the phone. She shouted through the whole conversation.

Thankful for more space between us, I put in my earbuds and snuggled into a pillow against the rear passenger window.

"Email," I directed Hal. He obeyed and presented my inbox. Nothing new in the last hour.

"Facebook." Not much new there, either.

I felt restless in a tired sort of way. I needed to talk to someone—to process the events of the last few days. It had been hard to pack up my things in the classroom and say good-bye to my students. But, true to Rick's assumption, things had fallen into place and the English department had graciously facilitated my early departure. I appreciated their flexibility, but it was slightly disturbing to see how easily I could be replaced. It was equally disturbing to think that I might have wasted a ton of money on an education that I would never use again, or at least not use for a long time.

With serendipitous timing, as Win would say, Hal started singing "Shout to the Lord." It was Lorna's ringtone. *Oh good.*

"Hi, Lorna."

"Hi, Haley, is this a bad time to talk?"

"Not at all, it's actually perfect."

"I only have a few moments, but you were on my mind. Thought I'd check and see how your trip is going."

"It's going pretty good. I have to go to the bathroom a lot, though."

Lorna chuckled. "I remember those days. Have things been okay with you and Rick's great-aunt?"

"Well—" I hesitated, quickly scanning my brain for the proper answer, "—she's a bit of a handful, but I think that God is using her to teach me more patience. I think I'm being tested through this and that keeping my cool during this trip is the best way to glorify God in my life."

"You have a great attitude, Haley—keep it up."

"Well, having a sister in the faith like you has certainly helped me grow."

"Thank you, Haley, but I'm afraid I can't stay on the phone very long. The church's poverty relief committee is meeting at our place tonight, and I need to come up with a finger food to serve. I'm putting together a veggie and hummus tray but wish I could come up with something else kind of special. Any suggestions?"

It was gratifying to have my faith mentor ask me for advice. "Hmm, what about Asian? You could make those Nigiri bundles—you know the sushi and rice ones that you tie with seaweed strips?"

"Mmm, yeah. Except I think Natalie has issues with sushi. Seafood's a good idea, though."

I thought harder. "I've got it—what about wonton cups with seared scallop and wasabi filling? I just saw that recipe on a blog earlier. It looked easy."

"Oh, now you're talking. That sounds impressive."

"Yes, and with fresh scallops it would be healthy. I'll email you the link to the blog right away." I paused to let the next great idea form. "You know, you're not real far from Harmony's Fish Market, are you?"

"No, it's pretty close to the produce market—I was going to run over there in a minute to grab more veggies."

"Perfect. Harmony's always has the freshest scallops. Better yet, my brother Josh works there. Mention my name and he'll throw in a little extra."

"Have I met him? What does he look like?"

"I think you met him at Christmas when he came to church with us. He's tall and thin and has long, dirty-blond dreads."

"Oh, yeah—I remember him! He had on that, um, unusual coat and he was wearing sandals even though there was snow on the ground, right?"

I laughed. "Yep. That's my brother, all right. Say hi to him for me."

"I'll do that. I better go now, Haley, if I'm going to get this all put together in time. Thank you so much for your help."

"No problem. Almost wish I could be there tonight."

"Well, you're on a whole different journey for now. We'll all be here when you get back. In the meantime, rest assured that Mitch and I will be praying for you every day. Have a wonderful time—bye!"

"Good-bye." I hated to hang up. Even though it felt good to help Lorna out, I really needed to talk more about my problems.

I emailed the recipe link to Lorna then looked out the window and watched the wooded hills and valleys of eastern Ohio skim past. It was a little bit mesmerizing. I realized that I should have retreated to the backseat much earlier in the trip. But the extra few feet from Win and the view outside still couldn't quiet my soul.

I needed to talk. I scrolled through my contact list and settled on Danielle. She was a good listener. I clicked off a quick text message.

Hey Sis, still on the road. Need to talk. Call me when you can:)

I had barely set the phone down beside me when Danielle's ringtone, the song "Hey Soul Sister," sliced into the space around me.

"Hi, Dani, that was quick."

"Yeah, I was already here at home—I got off work early. I'm kinda surprised to hear from you today. Where are you right now?"

"Ohio."

"Wow, you've made good time. What's up?"

"Well, I think I just need to debrief for a minute with someone who understands me. I'm still stressing about quitting my job and, well, other stuff."

"Okay, I'm listening—what other stuff?"

"Um, I'm actually scared about becoming a mom. It's like, I guess, well, I don't want to be like our mom. Know what I mean?"

"Of course I know what you mean, Haley. But come on, Sis—you're way different than Mom, and Rick is way, way different than Dad. I don't think you have to worry at all about taking on a life like Mom's. You know you wouldn't let that happen."

"Well, I wouldn't think so, but lately I see little things about Rick that scare me."

"Like what?"

"Like you know how Dad controlled everything—especially the money—and Mom was always trying to appease him?"

"Yeah, but you definitely don't act like that around Rick."

I glanced up at Rick in the driver's seat, still talking animatedly with Win and quieted my voice. "It's not that, it's just that Rick doesn't understand how much stuff costs. You know, like nice clothes and good accessories. I'm afraid we'll fight constantly about what I spend when I'm not making my own money anymore. Just yesterday, I tried to talk to him about it, and he just said we could sell my car if making the payments became too hard once I was home."

Danielle gasped, as I knew she would. We thought a lot alike.

"That little car is a prize, Haley. You need to hang on to it. Isn't there any other way you could pinch pennies?"

"Not really. I've boiled our budget down to just the basics."

Ouch. The baby kicked up high in my torso. I sat up straighter in the seat and kept talking. "I'm pretty sure we won't have to resort to selling the car, though. Rick's job prospects, even beyond this Montana thing are looking good." I paused to let the mist clear away from my venting process. "Hmm, now that I'm talking this out, I do think it's the staying-home part that scares me the most. I mean, fulltime homemaking seems kind of insignificant."

"Insignificant? Haley, you'll be raising a child! That's pretty significant."

"I know, I know. But child-raising has been going on forever. I know it's important, but honestly—it's also really ordinary."

"Common, maybe, but not necessarily ordinary. I mean, you'll be home shaping a little baby girl into a smart, decent woman. That's a pretty important job, if you ask me."

"I know that. But am I going to still be respected?"

"Haley! Look at you—what's not to respect? Quitting your job can't change you that much. You'll still be your smart and feisty self, even when you're not expanding the horizons of other peoples' kids."

"But Dani, teaching has given me so much purpose. I know I'm gifted for it, and it's hard to give it up, but I really want to be home with the baby…it's all so hard."

"I hear you."

We were both quiet for a few seconds. I appreciated that Danielle was at least listening to me.

"Hmm, Sis, an interesting thought just hit me. You know I'm not usually real spiritual about stuff, but think about it this way—maybe God has a whole plan for you that you're not seeing at the moment. I mean, what if this trip to Montana is meant to launch you into something even better?"

"What are you talking about?"

"I don't know, um, like maybe you'll still be teaching but just have different students in a different setting."

My sister's inspiring words gave a little push to my emotional roller coaster car. It very slowly started to creep upward.

"Whoa, you're sounding like a preacher now. But keep going."

"I don't know, um," Danielle paused and continued, "maybe you're on a missions' trip…or something."

My heart started to beat a little faster as my coaster car crept higher.

"Whoa, Dani—" I caught my breath, "—a mission? Like there'll be more to this than just an extended vacation?"

"Yes."

I paused to ponder my future from my elevating vantage point. Danielle's encouragement was pushing me above my fears and my view was becoming clearer, brighter, unveiling all kinds of possibilities I hadn't thought of before.

"Wow, maybe there is a higher purpose in it."

Danielle was also buoyed by her own words. "Yes! And you know, maybe Aunt Gracie's home could become some kind of a base of operations…or something."

We both fell silent again as the full impact of our shared prophecy hit us. After a few seconds, Danielle replied with quiet reverence. "Uh, Haley, it's quite possible that someone's life will be changed in Montana because you've had the guts to quit your job and follow your husband out there."

Hmm. Quite possible, indeed.

We chatted for a few more minutes and said goodbye. I sat there feeling lighter as I imagined something completely new filling the rest of the car interior around me.

It suddenly seemed okay that my smaller expectations had left earlier to cavort in a Pennsylvania ditch. There was now room for bigger, more important ones in the seats. These were the type of expectations that promised to deliver weighty, important results. They had a presence all their own, an awesome presence—a presence too big for even Win to chase away. And they were going with me.

All the way to Montana.

6

At some point in my adolescent years, I remembered vowing that I would never be like my mom. As a fulltime mother, she acted powerless, voiceless. Everything always went the way my stubborn dad insisted it should. There were times when I longed to see Mom stand up to Dad. On all but a few rare occasions, she deferred decisions to his final approval, even when the rest of us knew she wanted to do something else. She simply had no backbone and all three of us kids didn't like it.

One of her few courageous episodes, however, stuck in my mind forever. It happened on Halloween, in the same year that Bruce came to live with us. We were not allowed to celebrate that day the way other kids did. Dad said Halloween was a holiday with occultic roots and was set aside for devil worshipers to extol their evil practices. As such, we were only permitted to attend a church "harvest party" every year in which our costume choices were limited to the sanctity of Bible characters.

Josh, always on the lookout for loopholes in Dad's systems, came up with a novel harvest party costume idea. He announced at the dinner table one night that he wanted to dress up as a budgie bird. Dad, of course, scoffed and flatly refused the request, crushing eight-year-old Josh's feelings.

My mother's reaction surprised us all. We watched with a mixture of apprehension and awe as she flushed, looked Dad in the eye, and asked, "Why not?"

Dad, raising his eyebrows but not his voice, replied, "What do you mean, 'why not?'"

"Why can't he dress as a bird?"

"It's not a Bible character. My rule has always been that our children should emulate the great heroes of our faith."

"I know, but a bird is part of God's creation."

Dad leaned forward. "So is Charles Manson."

Mom didn't flinch. "Budgie birds were probably in the Garden of Eden."

"And so was the serpent. I would classify both the serpent and budgie birds as evil beings which would best belong in secular Halloween parties, not Christian ones. My answer is no."

Mom didn't reply, but the way her jaw tensed and her eyes glinted told us that the matter wasn't settled yet. She didn't slump down in defeat like she ordinarily did. She just stayed straight in her chair and looked at Dad like she was thinking about what she wanted to say, but didn't dare. Josh's eyes watered, but he didn't protest. There was something unusual in the air, and all but Dad could feel it. He simply adjusted his glasses and finished devouring his casserole without a word.

We came home from school the next day to find Mom sitting in a huge mess in the dining room. A dripping bowl of white soupy goo sat in the middle of paint-splotched newspapers that covered the entire table. Strips and shreds of more newspaper littered the table, the chairs, and even the carpet. Paint brushes, spoons, rulers, and a pair of scissors lay haphazardly strewn around the bowl of goo.

Mom was a mess too. Her hair flew in all directions and she had crusty white stuff smeared on her face and shirt. We had never seen her like this.

"Kids—just in time!" She carefully lifted something from the table and held it up. "It's not quite dry yet, but we can try it on you, Joshua, if we're careful."

We all gasped. It was a gorgeous, painted paper-mache mask—a budgie bird mask.

"Mommy, it's so cool!" Josh was delighted.

I was amazed. It was a white and gray half mask—a detailed, elaborately painted sculpture, with holes for eyes and a curved yellow beak. I couldn't believe my mom had made it.

"So, Joshua, I think we can make a headdress from one of Gramma's old wigs, and we can dye your white dress shirt blue. Wings will be easy to make from freezer paper, and you could wear a pair of Danielle's pink knee socks."

"Yay! I'm going to be Bruce!" Josh started jumping around and flapping his arms. "Pretty boy, pretty boy!" he squawked.

"What's going on here?" Dad bellowed, standing in the doorway.

We all fell silent. Mom swallowed hard and looked down. I could see her hands were shaking. "I made a bird mask for Josh to wear at the harvest party." Her voice was almost a whisper.

"Let me see," Dad took it from Mom and scrutinized it for a full twenty seconds. His expression softened as he said, "It's really something, Ellen. I didn't know you had it in you." He continued to study it, enthralled.

Mom exhaled and looked up. "You like it?"

"I do. You know masks have always interested me." He looked over at Josh and the spell broke. His face went back to its usual stony frown. "You can wear the bird costume—but only, and I mean *only*—if you do not make those disrespectful bird noises. You hear me?"

Josh nodded meekly. He ended up being the most beautiful character to ever attend the harvest party.

———•◦•◦•———

The baby kicked my ribs and woke me from a clammy sleep. I painfully pulled myself away from the pillow that was stuck against the window and winced with lower back pain as I eased into an upright position. The sun, shining straight through the middle of the windshield, sent a headache-inducing odor of plastic and warm upholstery wafting throughout the car's interior.

"Where are we?" I called from the back seat.

"Hey, sleepyhead, you're awake. We're just hitting Columbus." Rick looked back at me from the rearview mirror as he spoke. "Are you hungry? I'm thinking about stopping for a real meal."

"That'd be great, hon." I really wasn't all that hungry, but a restaurant stop would give me another excuse for a bathroom break. We had managed to avoid restaurants all day by eating the veggie wraps and fruit that I brought along.

Win had refused my food and pulled her own edibles out of her bottom-less purse. When she wasn't chewing on a creepy assortment of leftovers from her fridge that she toted along in plastic bags, she was nibbling like a messy rodent on little packages of crumbly crackers, sesame sticks, and fortune cookies—a perturbing activity, given the spotless interior of my mother's van. She said that collecting cracker and condiment packages from restaurants, airports, and convenience stores was one of her hobbies. To me, that kind of collecting constituted a disorder, not a hobby.

"Fast food or sit down?" Rick asked as I maneuvered my achy, baby burdened self into the middle seat.

"Ooh, if we go to fast food, I vote for Taco Tango," Win stated. "That chain has a lovely selection of mild to hot salsa packets. I think I still have some in here somewhere." She started rummaging through her bag.

"Let me see..." I started scrolling through the restaurant nutrition guide app on my phone. "Columbus, Ohio," I spoke clearly and distinctly to Hal.

"Aw, c'mon Haley," Rick whined, "do we always have to go where Hal tells us to?"

I ignored him and kept scrolling. "Oh, good—there's a MaryBerries Restaurant in Columbus." I addressed Hal again. "Find MaaarrryBeeerries." I purposely drew out the short "e" sounds to prevent Hal from confusing his vowels.

Rick was not pleased. "MaryBerries? I don't want to eat in that hippie franchise. Everything in those places is too healthy and crunchy." His cheeriness was finally showing signs of diminishing.

"Their food is crunchy because it's not soaked in fat," I stated, waiting for the GPS map to display the directions. "You might like their forest mushroom quiche. That wouldn't be crunchy."

"Forest mushrooms? Eeesh, sounds like the stuff of psychedelic dreams to me. I wouldn't touch that with a ten-foot pole. I don't want to spend a ton of time searching for something. We need to stay on schedule."

"Does that restaurant have liver and onions?" Win asked. "That's one of my favorite things to get when I'm on the road."

Win's words finally answered something I had wondered about all my life. I now knew not only that there was someone on earth who really did order liver in a restaurant, but I also now knew what type of person it would take to do such a thing.

I needed to set her straight. I wasn't about to sit across a table from someone consuming a mushy bovine blood filter. "Actually, cow's liver contains high concentrations of trace metals—" A beep from Hal brought me back to a more pressing issue. "Oh good! Hal's GPS says MaryBerries is just off the next exit—"

Rick growled.

"—and I really have to go to the bathroom again."

Rick pursed his lips and hit his turn indicator. After signaling to the right and checking his mirrors, he guided the car and trailer up the off ramp.

"Now where?" There was a distinct edge building in his tone.

I peered into Hal's screen. "Okay, it looks like you need to take a left."

"Here?"

"Yes, now."

Rick growled again, but the traffic light turned green, allowing him to smoothly turn left in submission to Hal's capable leadership.

I dictated Hal's directions from the phone. "Now, go one block ahead and make a right turn."

"Up there?" Rick pointed at a busy intersection. "Is there a turn lane?"

"Um, doesn't look like it—start signaling, anyway."

"Haley, there's no room; no one's gonna let me in."

"Oh keep signaling—we have to turn there!"

Rick slowed down in the midst of the surging traffic flow. Horns started blaring at us. Rick stayed steady in the middle lane, having no choice but to continue going straight through the intersection.

"Now, what?" Rick's cheeriness was now completely gone, and something much more unpleasant was threatening to fill its vacated place.

"Oh, great," I winced as the baby rolled around on my bladder, "we'll have to find somewhere to turn around. Doesn't look like any of these other roads connect to the one that goes to MaryBerries."

"Turn around? Haley, I'm towing a trailer!"

"Okay, okay, let me see if there are any alternatives."

"Better come up with something quick. Looks like we're getting into some industrial stuff—no restaurants around here." Rick's face was red and his knuckles were white.

Win, after having been uncharacteristically quiet for a few minutes commented, "My, this is an interesting neighborhood."

I stayed focused on my phone. "Um, okay, let's see. Wait a minute— there's another street just ahead that might… Uh-oh." I tapped Hal's screen.

"Might what?" Rick asked.

"Oh, shoot, Hal's glitching.'

"What?"

"Hang on, hang on…he's coming back," I frantically skimmed the screen with my finger. "Phew…okay, a right turn at the next intersection should connect us to a street that looks like it comes in behind the restaurant. But hurry—I've really got to go!"

Win spoke to me over her shoulder. "Haley, this is definitely the time for the Trav-a-Lav."

"No, Aunt Win."

"But look—we could pull right into that lot beside that large hedge-growth thing. Goodness, that hedge is quite overgrown." Win pointed as she peered out the window. "It appears to be harboring a small car."

"No Trav-A-Lav—don't mention it again, Aunt Winnie!" I didn't like getting loud and cantankerous, but she had left me no choice.

Rick signaled and found just enough of an opening to slide into the right lane. He pulled to a stop and waited to make the turn. We sat in tense silence, listening to the ticking of the blinker.

I compared the corner street signs with the street names that Hal indicated. Something didn't seem right at all, yet the names all matched. I was sure we would get back to the right neighborhood in a few blocks.

Rick steered onto the side street. It was narrow and dingy, lined with older residences and a few boarded-up warehouses. "Interesting" was not the right adjective. I would have used words like "bleak" or "unfavorable" or even "frightening."

"Where now?" Rick was getting really angry.

I pulled Hal up closer to my eyes. "Um, it looks like you'll need to go straight for three blocks and then turn right."

Win kept staring intently out her window. "Look at all those cats on that porch! Must be some sort of feline farm."

I ignored her. I was completely occupied with executing my navigation duties at the same time that I desperately, painfully worked to keep my bladder from spilling over.

"Here?" Rick asked after almost three blocks.

"Yes! It looks like MaryBerries should be just down on our left."

Rick slowed as we approached the only business we had seen for blocks. It was a three-story, decaying brick corner building with bars over windows that were painted opaquely dark. A huge, black-lettered sign hung above the door.

"Scary…Larry's…Pawn…and…Piercing…Parlor." Rick spoke in an ominously slow monotone. "Hmm. Should be really good food."

"Oh, no!" I lamented. "Hal got his consonants mixed up this time!" I started shaking my legs and hitting my thighs with my palms.

Win, respectfully staying quiet about her blasted Trav-A-Lav, quietly asked, "Is that a hat or is that a hairdo?" as she watched several patrons going in the main door.

I thrust naughty Hal into my purse. He had let me down. "Do you see a gas station or anything down the street?"

"Nope, just more houses," Rick replied, "you're gonna have to go visit Larry's bathroom."

I gasped. "No! That place looks dirty and dangerous!"

Rick pulled the car and trailer over to the curb. His voice softened. "I'll go in with you."

Three thug-like teen boys were approaching Larry's parlor on the other side of the street. In their varying degrees of black clothing and boots, they looked tough and threatening.

"Those young men are pointing at our van, " Win said. "I think they're trying to read your mother's advertising."

"I see that," Rick replied. "Haley, I think I better stay out here. Win— please go in with her and help her find the restroom."

"Certainly." Win adjusted her wrist radio and grabbed for her purse.

I was dumbstruck with horror. "Rick you can't let me go in there without you! Even the sign says Larry is scary!" I shook my legs harder. "And, what about our witness? People riding around with a Christian sign on their car shouldn't be seen going into, into—there! Mom would not appreciate it."

Rick turned around, leaned toward me and looked directly into my face. "Well, Haley, I don't think your mother would appreciate peed-on upholstery either. We can't leave our stuff untended here, so the way I see it, you have three options—go in there with Aunt Win, use the travel toilet out here some-where, or wet your pants. It's your choice." He turned back to face the front, his jaw set. I hadn't seen such a hard-hearted side of my husband before.

Win spoke with inappropriate cheer. "Oh, dear—are you afraid? Don't worry, I'm with you. Besides that, I'm sure Larry just says he's scary as an advertising stunt. He could actually be a very nice man."

Being constrained to choice number one felt like a death sentence. I reached for my purse, then put it back. I didn't want to provide temptation to a paroled robber.

Unmindful of the peril we faced, Win jabbered on as we got out of the car. "This isn't near as scary as the time I was visiting a North American wildlife exhibit in Canada and the wolverine escaped. He leapt, snarling into the crowd—"

"Win, please!"

As we crossed the street, I thought about what Danielle had said. Maybe the mission part of the trip had already started. I decided to be brave.

We entered through the heavy barred and marred door and stepped into a musty junk galaxy. An entire Milky Way of random objects filled every single millimeter of area in the small store. It was the Black Hole of all pawn shops—a region of space that had sucked in all other pawn items in the uni-verse and compacted them into a dense mass. Every sort of rusty tool imagin-able, from chainsaws to buckets of greasy wrenches lined one wall, and defunct kitchen appliances—a lidless blender, a one-armed hand mixer, and carafeless coffeemakers and coffeemakerless carafes lined the other. Dented musical instruments hung from the ceiling beside fringed leather vests and fantastical motorcycle helmets with attached wings, horns and tusks. I looked over at the blackened windows, knowing that even light could not enter or es-cape. I felt a sense of claustrophobic doom.

Win's expression, however, conveyed pure awe, like she had just stepped through the senior center's computer monitor and into her "Worldwide Web Shopping Center of Universal Proportions and Endless Possibilities." My death and doom was her light and life.

As we stepped around a stained, gold crushed-velvet easy chair, a loud hooing noise startled me. I jumped, stumbled, and ended up grabbing onto the head of a four-foot high concrete statue to keep myself from falling into the fetid chair.

"Hoo-hoo. Hoo-hoo."

A large owl figurine, perched on a shelf above us, spun its head and hooted as it sensed our motion near it. I righted myself quickly, ashamed to find that I was hanging onto a brazenly topless mermaid statue.

"Oh, a garden owl! Those repel pesky birds and rodents. How de-lightful!" Win exclaimed.

She walked right up to the front counter and confidently addressed a man that I presumed was Larry. Planted squarely like a gravestone behind his glass case, he looked like a monument with a hairless head, a Fu Manchu mustache growing lustrously down both sides of his chin, and a face riveted with metal piercings. Magnets were probably the only thing he avoided having anywhere in his shop.

Win cocked her head to one side and peered at his two symmetrically placed eyebrow piercings while she asked, "Sir, do you have a bathroom that my niece here could use?"

He eyed me up and down for several agonizing seconds before grunting, "Not for public use but go ahead. To your right."

"Thank you," Win addressed him with undue respect.

I looked over and saw a narrow wooden door with a greasy knob at the end of the counter. Just beyond that was another open doorway that exposed what looked like a clutter-laden living room. A TV blared from somewhere inside it. *Does Larry actually live in this place?*

"Aunt Win, come with me. Guard the door," I whispered.

We walked past bins of old videos and I squeezed into the tiniest bath-room I had ever been in outside of an airplane. I didn't see how Larry could fit his mass in the space. The facilities were surprisingly clean, but the walls were hideously covered from top to bottom with magazine photos of tattoo and piercing art. I felt exposed, watched by hundreds of gothic, black-lined eyes. It was horrible.

I got out as fast as I could only to find that Win had left her post and was engaged in a discussion with Larry. A young woman with a green, spiked, Statue-of-Liberty-Crown hairdo leaned on her elbow on the counter, looking up at Win with inquisitive eyes. A Fashion Fail snapshot for sure, but even if I had brought Hal in with me, I wouldn't have dared to risk offending anyone in there.

"So, how much would you charge for two smaller eyebrow rings, right up here?" Win asked, pointing with both index fingers at the top of her glasses.

"Aunt Winnie!" I caught my breath and grabbed her arm. "We're leaving now!"

"Just a minute, dear—I'm negotiating—oof." I pulled on her like she was about to go over a cliff. "Haley, please, I'm not done, and I have a purchase to pay for as well."

The stupid hooting owl stood on the counter. Win handed grim-faced Larry a wad of bills.

"Hoo-hoo. Hoo-hoo." The statue turned its head and hooted at me as if I were a garden pest that must be repelled.

"Enjoy Herman Hoot Owl, Ma'am," Larry spoke in a serious monotone, like he had just sold Win a handgun.

"We don't have room for that…," I trailed off, realizing that arguing with Win would only slow our exit from the premises. "Just hurry up," I hissed through tight lips.

I didn't even offer to help Win as she threw her purse strap over her shoulder and pulled the bulky owl off the counter with both arms. I marched out the door behind her, not saying a word until we were safely back outside.

"Aunt Winnie, what were you thinking? Have you lost your mind? You're too old for eyebrow piercings!" I breathed hard from a mixture of incredulity and exertion. "And why would you buy that ridiculous bird thing?"

"Oh, goodness, I should have made myself clearer. I was only looking into getting two very tiny rings implanted above my eyes. Not for decoration, but for utility. And the owl is a gift for Gracie."

"What? Let's talk about this in the car. Put the owl in the back seat for now—we need to get out of here." I didn't want to discuss anything else until we had put miles between us and Larry's suffocating little lair.

It was unimaginable that anyone could stay in such a confining atmosphere filled with germy, dusty junk for five minutes, let alone a whole day. I thought of my own little house, thankful that I knew how to decorate with tasteful austerity. *I will never stoop to living in unnecessary clutter. Thank you, Lord for giving me an appreciation for quality, not quantity, of things.*

Once we were safely back on the road, Win explained that seeing Larry's piercings had sparked a wonderful epiphany. She said she began envisioning a way to slide a lightweight bar between two eyebrow rings and attaching flip-up eyeglass lenses to it.

"Finally—my dreams of permanently affixing my reading glasses to my head seem attainable. I could get rid of these bothersome trifocals once and for all. Larry said nobody has ever approached him with that idea before, but it might be possible. If I could find a really lightweight metal for the cross-piece, that is. Hmm, you know I just might have something like that in my handbag..." Win's stream-of-consciousness talking flowed unchecked while she started digging around in her purse. "...Mr. Gunther, my landlord, sometimes has metal scraps that he lets me take for different uses. I know he gave me a small rod of titanium once. That's an extremely lightweight metal, you know—hmm, well what have we here?" She pulled out a slim black vinyl case. "Hooray! I did bring it after all!"

"What's that?" Rick asked. He had resigned himself to retracing our driving path back to the interstate.

"It's my Eezy-Tweezy twenty-times magnification mirror. I ordered it quite awhile ago, but haven't had the time to sit and use it. This trip is the perfect occasion!"

"Wow, twenty times—that's powerful. What do you use it for?" Rick asked. His curiosity must have eclipsed his crossness.

Win snapped the case open and pulled out a rectangular mirror, edged in a metal frame. "Well, having inherited Granny Nicolina's hirsute genes, I must tweeze often and regularly. Sneaky little hairs grow everywhere but where they should," she giggled, "even at my age."

Only half-listening to Win's gibberish, I went back to my restaurant search. This time, though, I typed my commands to Hal rather than speaking them.

Win seemed to have already forgotten about her piercing epiphany. As her chatter switched without pause into a whole new topic, I made a mental note to research information on adult ADHD later. Maybe the right medication could help her.

"Poor Granny Nicolina, she fell prey to a turn-of-the-century snake oil salesman. He sold her a supposed hair removal ointment that ended up burning off the tops of her ears."

"Her ears?" I could see Rick's frown in the rearview mirror. *Errr.* I felt like I was back at the baby shower, wanting to slap someone for encouraging Win to keep telling her tale.

"Yes—she had unwanted hair growing everywhere. After that, she always kept her hairdo artfully arranged over her ears. Her husband didn't even see the burn area until their tenth anniversary. I saw them once when I was nine years old and had ear nightmares for years. As a result, I still won't trust those electric needles or killer waxes—I just tweeze my stray hairs. It's safest."

"Hoo-hoo." Something had triggered Herman Hoot Owl which triggered something in me.

"Aunt Win, what makes you think Gracie would want that hooting owl in her house?" I was embarrassed to even admit that the thing was in our car, let alone give it to someone as a gift.

Win looked back at her prize and smiled. "Oh, Gracie likes these sort of things. I know she'll be thrilled."

As thrilled as I was to get the lederhosen, I'm sure.

"It's not for in her house, anyway," Win continued, "it's to keep the snakes out of her yard."

"Snakes? What kind of snakes? Nobody said anything about snakes in Montana." This was not something I wanted to hear.

"Oh my, yes—"

Rick broke in. "Hey, those signs are promising. I'm taking the next exit."

I tapped Hal's glitching screen. "Give me a minute, Rick—Hal is coming up with something within a two-mile radius. Wait, I think there's a Lettuce Patch Deli at exit number—"

Pointedly deaf to me, Rick silently steered off the freeway and turned smoothly into the driveway of a gaudy fast food hut.

"Hooray! Taco Tango!" Win clapped her hands.

"Hoo-hoo. Hoo-hoo," With the motion-sensing capability of a California seismograph, Herman Hoot Owl affirmed the restaurant choice from his perch in the back seat. He followed his hooting with a chilling head spin, making me wonder if we should stop at the nearest Catholic church and request an exorcism.

"Win, you're pulling the batteries out of that monstrosity when we get back from eating," I commanded as I slammed the car door shut.

"Can't do that," Win said with an innocent smile. "Herman is solar powered. No batteries needed."

"Hey, Haley, that should make you happy—the owl's environmentally friendly!" Rick's two cents' worth wasn't even worth two cents.

"Yeah, well so was Ted Kaczynski," I muttered, no longer caring that I sounded just like my father.

I marched toward the restaurant door in a fit of resigned disgust. Charmaine would have had a cow if she knew where I was. She probably would have thrown her own buff body in front of the door and physically prevented me from entering the faux food franchise if she was there.

But she wasn't there. She, along with the rest of my sane life, was already a very far four hundred fifty miles behind me—and getting farther with every minute that passed.

I ended up eating the only non-meat item on the menu board. It was a chubby bean burrito that was surprisingly savory. So much so that I ate the whole thing. Rick, with chimichanga-lifted spirits, discussed our trips plans while we ate, and because of my physical complaints, sacrificially agreed to call it a night before reaching Indianapolis. I, in turn, compromised by agreeing to travel an hour or two further west before stopping. Win stated that now that she had found her Eezy-Tweezy mirror, she was content to go along with anything we wanted.

Herman was not consulted. His menacing glow-in-the-dark eyes were the last straw for me. I banished him to a spot deep in the trailer where I hoped his solar cells would die a dark and painful death.

And so, after enduring twelve hours on the road and viewing the skanky insides of exactly eight public restrooms and one semi-public restroom, Day One of my peaceful vacation concluded in a noisy motel, just inside the eastern border of Indiana.

7

Rick coaxed me awake at five-thirty the next morning. Even though I had slept surprisingly well, I couldn't seem to heft myself out of bed. My body felt twice as big as the day before, as if my entire torso had expanded substantially overnight.

Rick saw me struggling to get my legs over the edge of the bed and bounded to my side. "Here, Haley, let me help."

"Ooh, something's wrong. I feel ginormous today—oof," I mumbled and grunted while Rick grabbed my hands and pulled. I winced when he touched the sore area on my hand. After almost two months, the two spots where I had been poked at the baby shower still hadn't completely healed.

"I hope it's just, *erf,* fluid retention, *mmph,*" I said, letting Rick's muscular forearms do the heavy pulling.

"I bet it's last night's burrito."

"What?"

"Remember when I used that Maxagro grass growth stimulator on that dry patch in the backyard? Remember how that spot grew almost right before our eyes?"

"No." I waddled over to my suitcase.

"You don't remember that, Haley? It was amazing! The way that Maxagro stuff made the grass shoot up overnight was practically miraculous. I would have put it on the whole lawn, but it was too expensive."

I pulled out my denim stretch capris. They looked tiny. "Rick, I don't want to start talking about grass right now. It's too early."

"No, listen—I'm sayin' that you finally ate something with a healthy dose of fat and calories last night. That burrito probably hit our little girl like a big shot of Maxagro. She's probably happily growing as we speak."

"Rick, no. Please—I said I don't want to talk about this. You're not helping." I didn't want to admit it, but the thought of overnight baby growth scared the heck out of me. *Is it just from too much sitting and no working out, or am I...mushrooming?*

I unplugged Hal from his charger and put him in my purse. I would text Charmaine once we were back on the road. Getting overlarge was unacceptable. I had vowed from the very beginning of my pregnancy that I wouldn't let that happen. And Charmaine had assured me that as long as I was careful, it wouldn't. She said her unique Extreme Expectancy Exercises were responsible for how great she looked in spandex biking shorts when she competed in a triathlon only three weeks after birthing her third child.

Working around my grumpiness, Rick managed to cajole me through my morning hygiene routine and usher me into the motel coffee room by six-fifteen. Win was already there, sifting through the jam and honey packets at the toast station. She was wearing another of her ugly baseball caps. This one had the words, "Spinning Lizzies Fiber Arts Powwow, '02" written across the front.

Groggy, I sat with a cup of tea and waited while Rick opened up the road atlas and found the Indiana page.

"Um, I think we should make today a long day." He spoke quietly.

I stopped in mid-sip. "How long?"

He cleared his throat and avoided meeting my questioning gaze. "Uh, eight hundred...miles...or so—"

"Eight hundred miles?"

My shriek shoved him directly into his salesman act. "It's actually not as far as it sounds. Look," he pointed to the map, "it's a pretty straight shot from here in Indiana—" he flipped over to the full country map at the front and traced the route with his finger, "—through Illinois, Iowa, the bottom of Minnesota, and into Sioux Falls, South Dakota."

"Rick, that's two hundred more miles than we traveled yesterday! That's a huge chunk of the entire Midwest, and I'm pregnant!"

"Okay, okay, I know, I'm aware. But listen..." he knew I disdained placation, but he always resorted to it anyway when my reactions made him nervous, "...if you can stand up to fifteen hours on the road today, we could actually have two short sightseeing days in South Dakota. You could sleep in, and we could tour the Badlands and the Black Hills at our leisure."

"But what about Aunt Gracie and Uncle Hank? They're expecting us in Grassview, when?"

"Friday, and, we'll still get there on Friday. The days are just broken up a little differently."

"I don't know..."

"You could actually enjoy two much more restful days if you sacrifice today or maybe even have time for a morning workout in our next motel." He was openly manipulating me, using one of my greatest fears to his own advantage.

It worked. "Okay, fine—but you need to let me make all our food decisions."

"Consider it done!" He kissed my cheek. "Finish your tea while I check the trailer hitch and test the tail lights." Reaching down, he patted my tummy. "How's my little girl, doin'?"

"Restless, like her dad." I tried to sit up straighter, but my stomach hit the edge of the table. "And growing."

"Good! She'll need to be a brawny one if she's going to operate Daddy's tractor."

"You don't own a tractor."

"Someday, someday…" Rick smiled and strode out the door.

"Hooray!" Like Rick, Win was already wide awake and ready for action. "Haley, look—sealed peanut butter tubs!" She sat down at the table with me and displayed her bounty. "You know, if I combine these with the hot sauce packets from Taco Tango, I can make Indonesian satay sauce. Oh, boy, if I collect enough ingredients, I can cook us up a real ethnic smorgasbord at Gracie's."

"Wonderful." My tenuous morning appetite fled, leaving plenty of room for sarcasm to fill the void. I was afraid it was going to be a long day in more ways than one.

◆•◆•◆

Interstate 74, like a conveyor on the Corn Belt, pulled us smoothly through pastoral western Indiana and into the farmlands and urban centers of the Illinois heartland. The Mississippi River crossing on the Illinois-Iowa border funneled us onto I-80, depositing us directly into the "Fields of Opportunities" that the Iowa welcome sign announced at the state line.

This was true farming country. Newly-birthed green rows of delicate soybean and corn plants coated the expansive fields like strokes of watercolor on brown paper. Farmsteads, consisting of homes, barns, silos, and outbuildings were plotted in intervals along the tidy county quadrants, appearing satisfied with their work. Even the compact farming towns, though quiet, exuded an air of capability and accomplishment.

Win's discovery of her magnifying mirror was keeping her blissfully occupied. She spent a good deal of time leaning toward the window from the middle seat wordlessly poking, plucking, and tweezing whatever the Eezy-Tweezy brutally exposed, particularly around her ears.

Charmaine did not reply to my urgent text all morning. I knew she was busy whipping other pregnant clients into shape at her Extreme Expectancy classes, but my condition was worsening. The elastic waist on my cute Capri pants was stretching unforgivingly to the max. I began to fear that my nice maternity wardrobe might not work for me anymore if I didn't take swift action. Surely there were some yoga stretches and/or special foods that would properly nourish the baby while keeping undue mother expansion under control.

Rick said it was nice to have me back in the front beside him, but I didn't share his enthusiasm. He just wanted to talk about his upcoming job and the research he had done on wheat and cattle ranching in Montana. I was too troubled about my condition to focus on what he was saying. I really needed to plug back into my understanding circle of women and draw some encouragement from them. I also felt a duty to offer my perspective into their lives.

I listened to Rick and worked on Facebook at the same time. I responded to a few of my friends' posts and updated my own status. It was helpful when Rick finally stopped talking so I could concentrate on my writing. I decided to show a positive attitude. That would bolster my reputation as a woman of faith. I wrote:

Two days into the trip and I'm facing challenges. But, PRAISE GOD! I know it's the enemy's way of trying to keep us from getting to Montana. Satan wouldn't be fighting against us if we weren't a threat to his territory, right? Pray for me as I show love and grace toward Rick's difficult elderly aunt. Also pray that I press on in spite of pregnancy discomfort. Thanks to all of you for your support!!!:)

I clicked over to my Bible app and selected a verse to paste into my status text:

For we are not fighting against flesh-and-blood enemies, but against evil rulers and authorities of the unseen world, against mighty powers in this dark world, and against evil spirits in the heavenly places. Eph. 6:12 (NLT)

My friends would like that. We shared scripture verses through Facebook all the time. I was glad that Rick couldn't see my update, though. He always said he'd be mad if his work buddies or Chester ever started spouting off random Bible verses at him. He said it seemed like showing off. He preferred they all just talk about ballgame stats and leave the preaching to the pastor. I told him he needed to get closer to God. He told me he thought God was great and to let him and his friends and God talk to each other any way they wanted.

I finished my writing and scrolled through some more of my friends' posts. Lorna's status delivered a swift poke of conviction. She spoke of how she was making the sacrificial choice to spend quality time with her husband that day. She mentioned something about how much it pleased God when we put our husbands first. I resisted the temptation to mentally list all the concessions I had already made for Rick in the last few days and sighed as I placed Hal back in the console. I would be a virtuous woman with the best of them. And then report about it later.

Rick, noticing that I put Hal down, seized the moment. "So, could you picture yourself living here in Iowa, Haley?"

I looked out the window. We were searching for a grocery store in a serene, medium-sized town.

"Hmm. Not sure. What do people do here for recreation?"

"Oh, probably agricultural related contests and fairs and things. Square dances, maybe."

"Not my cup of tea. Sounds kind of hokey." I kept gazing out the window as Rick calmly followed a store's billboard directions.

"Whoa, those churches don't look hokey," Rick stated. We were driving by two older brick churches on the same block.

I didn't reply, but inwardly conceded that he had a point. The churches were both stately and well-maintained. One had a sign announcing a worship concert. I also noticed a beautiful, tree-filled city park and playground and another large building marked as a historical museum. I could imagine myself taking the baby for walks in a place like that. Maybe I could learn to enjoy rural life. Temporarily, at least. But not permanently—I wouldn't want to end up square dancing my life away at an animal fair.

My suspicions concerning hokiness were confirmed when a worn-out, dirty farm truck pulled up beside us at the store. Its dangling tailpipe belched a cloud of lingering, fetid fumes when its engine was shut off. The passenger, a smiling, greasy-haired woman had her feet propped up on the dashboard and dangled her arm out of the open side window. The driver, a bruiser of a man in his thirties, hacked and spit when he climbed out of the cab. *Apparently, mullets really aren't just the stuff of redneck legend.* I wasted no time in discreetly nabbing another glorious Fashion Fail shot.

The most upsetting part of this scenario, though, lie in the fact that a young boy was perched, unrestrained, on the wheel well in the pickup's bed. He looked happy enough, innocently unaware that his parents were imperiling him and gambling with his very life. An unnerving host of possibilities paraded through my mind as I watched the unfortunate child stand and wave exuberantly to another child across the parking lot. What if the truck wrecked or hit a bump, and he was thrown out? What if another vehicle kicked up something and he was hit with rocks or other objects? *Shouldn't he at least be wearing a helmet? Safety glasses? Sunscreen? How can parents be so neglectful? Should I turn them in? What are the seat belt laws in this state? Besides all that, his parents don't even seem to care about his dignity. I would never transport my family in such a degrading vehicle.*

We bought more fruits and veggies and sidled the van back into an open spot on the highway conveyor belt. The neglectful parents made me again question whether or not I would want to live, even temporarily, in a farming community, but it was obvious that Rick could envision himself living there.

"Oh, man, look at that cornfield! It goes on forever. Wonder what kind of herbicides they use to keep them so weed-free?" Rick, talking happily, hardly paid attention to the curveless road. He was thoroughly enjoying himself.

I dutifully looked at the things he pointed out, but didn't have any commentary to add. Instead, I fidgeted, listening for text or email alerts from Hal. At one point, Rick looked over at me and smiled. He even put his hand on mine, like we were on a date. It only served to irritate me, though. He seemed completely unaware that in spite of grave physical and mental misery, I was yielding precious phone time to his incessant farming talk.

Rick looked at some equipment that was working the huge fields beside the interstate. "Wow—now that's one nice implement. Is it a planter or a cultivator?"

I was saved from pretending like I cared by one of Hal's strident ringtone songs. I took it as a sign that my obligation was fulfilled. Rick sighed deeply and slumped in his seat. I rolled my eyes as I reached for the phone. *His petulance is silly—I've just given him a full half hour of my attention. We really need to deal with his phone jealousy as soon as possible.*

Hal yelled out the extended opening note of the old church chorus, "Set My Spirit Free." It was Mom. Good.

"Hi, Mom."

"Hello, Sweetie. How is everything going?"

"It's going." My emotional roller coaster car took a dive when I heard her voice, causing tears to well.

"Are you okay? What's wrong?"

"Oh, it was just a difficult day yesterday, and today I woke up feeling bloated and terrible."

"Haley, those are pretty normal late-stage pregnancy problems. You just need to take it easy."

"I think that's my problem! I'm sitting too much and, and—" my voice broke, "—I'm not eating right."

"Honey, you're the most cautious eater I know. You've been so careful up to this point that I'm sure you have a lot of margin for the times when you can't eat exactly like you think you should. You'll be fine."

"My back and my legs have been hurting too." My emotional swell abated as I let my feelings tumble out. Although we didn't agree on everything, Mom was still a safe person to complain to.

"Isn't the van comfortable enough?"

"No, no—it's great. I'm really glad you let us use it."

"Speaking of which, has anyone approached you about my advertising logo?"

I paused, remembering how the thug boys pointed at it in front of Scary Larry's.

"Um, no." It was good that the car couldn't tattle on where its occupants had taken it.

"So where are you today?"

I gave her a censored version of the previous day's drive and told her about our plans for the next couple days. After some motherly advice and reassurances about how normal my pregnancy symptoms were, we hung up.

Right after the call ended, Hal emitted a puzzling low-battery beep. It was disturbing, considering that he had only been unplugged for a few hours. His inability to hold a charge for long enough was getting worse. I attached him to the car charger. Rick watched me plug him in.

"Still not holding a charge?"

"No, I can't figure it out."

"Either you need a new battery or you have some defective circuitry."

"How can we get it fixed?"

"Don't know."

"Well, do you have any ideas?"

"Nope."

Win piped up from the seat behind me. "Too bad your phone computer isn't solar powered like Herman Hoot Owl. His solar cells are guaranteed to last a decade."

Fabulous. I knew it was a long shot, but I had been secretly hoping that Win would forget about the owl and I could quietly ditch it at some point. I sighed, reminding myself that reasonable expectations could never survive anywhere within a thousand yard radius of Win.

We didn't say anymore to each other until Rick exited to find a gas station. As he drove the two blocks to a truck stop, he suddenly whistled and hit the brakes.

"What's wrong? Did we miss the turnoff?" I asked.

Not answering me, Rick exclaimed, "Whoa, am I reading that sign right?"

He proceeded to pull the car over to read a "For Sale" sign on a small, rusting, decrepit tractor parked by the side of the road.

"What are you doing?" I asked.

"Haley, we should call that number. Hand Hal over."

"Rick, you can't be serious. Why would you call on that tractor?"

"I've been thinking about getting a tractor for a while but just hadn't talked to you about it yet because of the expense. A new one costs more than a car. But, look—this one's only five hundred bucks!"

I was speechless. The only thing I could think of was that my poor husband had been driving for too long. I worried that he might be suffering from a type of road hypnosis or mind fatigue or something. He needed a rest.

"Rick, let me drive. I'll take over for a while so you can take a nap."

"Well, if you don't mind—but are you comfortable with towing the trailer?"

"I'm a lot more comfortable with towing something than with wasting five hundred dollars on a rusted piece of something."

Stupefied with admiration for the oxidizing heap, Rick was deaf to my cynicism. "Great, hon! I can make the call while you drive. This deal is just too good to pass up."

"Rick, you can't be serious. It doesn't look like it runs and how would we get it home?"

"I'm sure we could come up with something, and I bet Chester would let me use his shop to rebuild it in. He knows all about this kind of equipment."

In desperation, I appealed to his frugal side. "You hate to spend money."

"Too much money, Haley—I don't like to overpay for stuff. But this—this—is one sweet bargain."

"Rick, no!"

My screech caused Win to put her Eezy-Tweezy down. She looked out the window and exclaimed, "What a wonderful tractor!"

Oh great, just what I need—backup from the peanut gallery. Win's nauseating enthusiasm was reengaged. "It's just like the one that cousin Archie let me dig his trout hatchery runs out with. I did the excavating and he did the concrete pouring. Of course, Archie ended up abandoning the project after the mishap with the cat in the electric cement mixer, but—"

"Aunt Win, please!" I couldn't do it anymore. My head was starting to throb. "No tractor, Rick. This is not the time." Biblical submission would certainly not apply to impulsive purchases of rusting detritus. It was my wifely duty to save us all from such a fate. Unlike my mom, I had a backbone and I wasn't afraid to use it.

Rick was smart enough to stay silent, but Win wasn't. "Poor kitty. But you know, Rick, you could make extra money plowing out your neighbors' driveways in the winter. You could even pull stuck vehicles out of snow banks—"

"NO!" My roller-coaster car was plunging into a dizzying, terrifying descent, and Win and Rick were coming along, whether they wanted to or not.

"That's enough from both of you! Sure, go ahead and buy your lovely tractor, Rick—just how will you get it home? Divvy it up into pieces and let me fly home with it as carry-on? Airport security would love that. I know—cram it all into flat-rate postal boxes, send it home and kill our poor mail carrier in the process! Why not? You need that tractor, right? We need an ugly heap to grace our driveway, right? And our neighbors need more fuel for their gossip, right? RIGHT?"

Silently, Rick met my tirade with a cold stare. He kept his narrowed eyes locked on me as slowly, defiantly, he picked Hal up from the console. With slow, exaggerated movements, he held Hal in front of him and aimed his index finger at the phone's power button. I was shocked. Never in our five years together had Rick acted so cruelly. Until this moment, I hadn't even thought he could be capable of such injurious hostility. Hal was his mortal enemy, yet Rick was stooping to use him just to rebel against me. How can he coldly commit such a damaging act to our marriage?

Rick pushed the button. Nothing happened.

He pushed and held the button for two seconds. Nothing. Hal's screen remained as dark and blank as Rick's eyes. Rick pulled the phone in front his face and pushed other buttons. Nothing. He started shaking the phone.

"Rick! That's enough. You're going to make things worse."

"Stupid piece of junk—I paid how much for this?" He tapped the screen.

"Hand it over, Rick—you've probably broken it for good now." I grabbed unconscious Hal from Rick's grasp.

"Oh, right, so now you can blame me for breaking your phone. It's been glitching and discharging for days and you know it. Don't even go there."

"All I know is that you resent this phone and go on about how I use it too much; and then suddenly, when you decide you need it, you're mad that it doesn't work!"

Inside, I was really panicking over Hal's breakdown. He was my vital link to everything important to me. I was sure that Charmaine was texting remedies for hugeness even as we sat there beside the road. The stupid tractor fight was secondary. We'd get over that, but would I regain my priceless communication tool anytime soon?

Rick set his jaw and pulled back onto the road without a word. His phone was packed away somewhere with our housewares in the trailer. Before we left, he had decided that because he wouldn't call his work partners until we got to Montana, he didn't need his phone. For him, it was just another thing to keep track of; and I talked to everyone for him anyway, even his mom. Occasionally.

We drove another block and pulled into the gas station. Rick started to get out, then paused. He looked sad. Glancing pointedly down at my tummy, he stated, "Sorry, Haley. I won't buy a tractor—yet. Now please try to stay calm for the baby's sake."

It took everything I had to not scream. *Me? Stay calm?* He did it again. He was always riling me up with inflammatory ideas or accusations and then chiding me for not being calm. What did he expect? My lifeline was suddenly dead; and beside that, I doubted there was a woman on this planet who wouldn't scream if her husband tried to tote an old tractor home from their vacation. The original John Deere's wife must have been a saint. Of course, she was long dead. Probably her husband's fault.

Sweaty and red-faced, I stomped to the restroom. My headache and backache were as out of control as my mood. I momentarily considered committing a crime just so I could get arrested and spend a night all by myself somewhere.

Simply too tired to shoplift or vandalize anything, though, I returned to the car. Exiling myself to the back seat, I laid my head against a pillow and tried to regroup. I longed for my music, but Hal's malady meant I had to do without. And, unfortunately, I had given my old MP3 player to one of my students after receiving Hal for Christmas.

Win once more took my place in the front seat and, except for patting my shoulder on the way into the restroom, didn't acknowledge our blowup. She acted like we were all just one big happy family. Again I questioned her mental health.

I closed my eyes and practiced my childbirth breathing. It helped me calm down enough to think about something other than my horrible husband and the hole that Hal's absence had left in my heart. My mind wandered through several topics before stopping to ponder over Win. She was such a strange and puzzling old lady that thinking about her made me frown.

She said she was a Christian, and for the most part, behaved like one, yet she insisted on attending a flaky church that gave out door prizes every Sunday. And even her attendance there was spotty. She would take each summer off to go on what she called her Family Reacquaintance Tour. She would go to a different church every Sunday for three months for the purpose of "seeing what her fellow believers were up to." When I told her that I couldn't condone such a lack of commitment to one's home church, she just smiled and said that each fellowship was a part of her home church. When I asked her if she was worried that she could inadvertently pick up dangerous teaching, she replied that getting "stuck in a tradition box" was much more dangerous in her mind.

Dangerous? I reminded her that one of the churches she had attended in the summer made the news headlines when the pastor was convicted of fraud. This particular pastor had been embezzling church funds for years in order to finance his penchant for expensive clothes and cars. It was the kind of event that made Christians everywhere cringe—leaders like that always made the rest of us look bad to non-Christians.

Ow. The baby kicked me hard in the ribs, bringing me back to the confined and uncomfortable present. I tried to stretch out without taking off my seatbelt, but coziness was obviously not attainable in my circumstances. If only I could call someone…

By early evening, the sky started darkening as we crossed into Minnesota. Lulled by the motion of the windshield wipers swiping a soft rain off the windshield, I dozed off and on in an awkward half-lounging position in the back. We were heading straight west on Interstate 90 when another of Win's ridiculous exclamations jarred me.

"Yee-HAW—South Dakota Fireworks!"

She startled me bad. With my heart pounding and the baby kicking, I sat straight up in spite of my aching bulk.

Breathing hard, I yelled, "Aunt Win—don't do that!"

Win turned around from the front, grinning broadly. "Oh, sorry, dear. Did I scare you?"

"Ergh." I pursed my lips, too upset to answer.

"Did you see that billboard? Fireworks, a hundred miles ahead, right off I-90! We can get some tomorrow."

This time, Rick was not boarding Win's excitement train. "Why do you want fireworks, Aunt Winnie?" He sounded as tired as he probably was.

Win, showing no sign of tiring, replied, "Oh my goodness, South Dakota is known for its fireworks deals. I'd love to get some for us to shoot off at Gracie's. Twenty years ago, I bought fireworks from a highway stand in South Dakota and they were spectacular. Unbelievable prices too."

"You've been in South Dakota before?" Rick asked.

"Yes, I have. It came about when I entered a sculpting contest held at an arts and crafts museum outside Philly. The contest guidelines said that the top three entries would win a trip to Mount Rushmore and that the judges were looking for the most creative piece crafted from unusual medium. I decided to think outside the box and ended up using rolls of fine-gauge wire to crochet a bust of Mikhail Gorbachev."

"Rick—bathroom, please—" I was desperate again.

"I worked on it for weeks and nearly ground my fingers to hamburger, but it paid off. I was able to capture that gleam of glasnost in Mr. Gorbachev's eye—"

"Okay, Haley, looks like a restroom at the next exit—hang on." Rick talked above Win's wordy trip down memory lane. She didn't notice that no one was listening.

"—and even found tinted wire for his birthmark—"

Rick looked back at me through the rearview mirror with a softer expression than he had shown toward me for several hours. "It's gonna be okay, Haley. Tomorrow will be much better. It'll be a short, relaxing day, I promise."

Promises should never be made about things over which one has no control.

8

A grilling, blinding ray of sunlight seared my closed eyelids. The sudden brightness hurt. I pulled the covers over my head and yelled for Rick to close the curtains. What motivated him to always rip open the drapes in motel rooms? I spent all of my time trying to maintain privacy, both at home and on trips, but he seemed bent on exposing our lives to full view. I tried to be patient with him because I knew that as a child his home life had not included many lessons on decorum, but on this particular morning I didn't want to give the truckers outside a cheap thrill.

"Good morning, Beautiful!" Rick skipped out of the bathroom and closed the drapes. "Sorry if the light bothered you. It's just so nice today— guess the rain was heading east, not west. Feels like summer here." He bent down and kissed my forehead.

"Oh, wow, my head hurts." If I weren't pregnant, I would have been downing aspirin like nobody's business.

"Still have the headache?"

"Yeah. Might be related to all the driving, or something."

"Well, guess what? Like I promised, today will be a short day. Only three hundred and fifty miles to Rapid City. That's as far as we'll go today. See, I let you sleep in."

He held up his cell phone and pointed to the time. He had retrieved it from the trailer the night before. "Eight-thirty—can stay in bed even longer if you like."

"No, I'll get up now." Anxious to get Hal fixed, I wanted to make sure we left ourselves enough time to find a cell phone store in Rapid City. Rick's old phone was too basic for me. It wasn't internet capable and he had blocked texting from his plan to save money.

I painfully pulled my rotundity from the bed and slowly stood. If only I could have known what was ahead for me that day, though, I would have taken Rick up on his offer to stay in bed longer. In fact, I should have never gotten up. I should have stayed, safely tucked under the covers "until these calamities be overpast," as old King James so eloquently stated. I really should have stayed right there, right in that motel bed in Sioux Falls, South Dakota.

———•••••———

I went straight to the back seat when we finally hit the road in late morning. Win sat up front and provided a running commentary on South Dakota geology, a lot of which Rick appeared to be ignoring. He seemed to be lost in his own thoughts, which were probably meandering somewhere down in Tractor World. He must have completely forgotten that he was, after all, a city boy, born and bred.

About two and a half hours into the drive, the corralled and cultivated Midwest started to give way to the wandering West. Somewhere between Sioux Falls and the great Missouri River, the expansive, yet orderly, corn rows of eastern South Dakota began petering out, yielding to untamed, un-ending swells of grassland. Farms were now ranches; cropland was now rangeland.

"Man, look at all that wild turf." Rick sat upright in the driver seat, his hands high on the steering wheel. He gazed at the grass, still partly brown from winter but showing shades of green in the lower-lying areas.

"Ah, just think how jealous the corn and soybean plants must be of their truant, dancing grass cousins," Win spoke like she was reading out loud to a preschooler. I decided to add her bizarre practice of personifying everything to the list of annoyances that I held against her.

I moved up to the middle seat in order to stretch my legs. In spite of my headache, I had to admit that the scenery, or perhaps the lack of it, was inter-esting. Signs of civilization were getting farther apart, making the smooth in-terstate with all its big rigs and cars seem out of place and time. The open range somehow pulled the Indians, buffalo, and covered wagons farther to the right on our history timeline, or maybe it was pulling us farther to the left. Either way, I could almost see the Old West waving at us from beyond a far hill.

"You know, I can practically see the pioneers crossing this raw land in their wagons of yesteryear," Win stated. It was spooky that she said what I had been thinking.

She went on, of course. "This is Laura Ingalls Wilder country. Did you know that one of her family's homesteads is north of Sioux Falls?"

"Uh-huh," I said, not wanting to admit that as an English teacher, I hadn't thought about that.

Rick looked at me through the rearview mirror. "Are you feeling any better, hon?"

"Not really. The headache makes my eyes light-sensitive. Can you hand me my sunglasses?"

Win clapped her hands and turned to face me. "I know! You lay back and keep your eyes closed. I shall be your eyes—like Laura Ingalls was to blind sister Mary." Before I could protest, she turned and leaned forward with her nose almost to the windshield. "First, I see the sky—huge, blue, yet clouded as Mary's own eyes—"

I broke in. "Win, don't you have more tweezing to do? Here's your Eezy-Tweezy." She had put it down on the floor between the front seats and hadn't stopped talking since. Its powerful reflecting rays had been beaming around the car's interior, further aggravating my condition.

"Oh, no, thanks. I think I have my strays conquered for the next week or so."

Darn. It was worth a try.

Win turned back to look at the road and caught her breath. "Oh, look—a series of signs." She leaned forward and squinted to read the bright orange lettering. "Start To Slow...Now Go...And Exit Here...For Pyro Joe—what? Oh, I get it—it's the fireworks emporium! Rick—exit NOW!"

Reflexively, Rick jerked the steering wheel to the right and pressed the brakes. The car shot off the freeway, and the trailer swayed outward. We started to veer off the side of the exit ramp, but Rick corrected it just in time. We rolled to a screeching stop on a cattle guard at the top of the turnoff.

My heart raced. We all sat for a moment in stunned silence. Rick spoke up first.

"I wonder how many wrecks those signs have caused."

"My goodness, Rick dear. You saved us with your expert driving skills," Win patted Rick's knee.

I was too distressed to scold, fuss, or even pray. I just closed my eyes and performed my childbirth breathing pattern.

Rick recovered his composure and turned into the fireworks store's gravel lot. This was no ordinary fireworks stand. Win was awed by the shouting flags and pennants that garrisoned the sprawling, low-roofed building. I suspected, though, that the colorful display out front provided a distracting coverup for the dangerous nature of this establishment. I could see two small, concrete block outbuildings behind the store that resembled some sort of bunkers. It wouldn't have surprised me to see men in black suits and machine guns standing guard over their hazardous booty. Like a reverse mullet haircut, this place was "party up front" and "business"—serious business—in the back. I shivered when I noticed the large "No Smoking" signs posted alongside the banners, hoping that the place wasn't carpeted and that no one was shuffling around inside in their house slippers.

"Look at all their exciting banners—Explosive Buys! Blow-out Prices! Smokin' Hot Deals!" Win yelled like an announcer for the old WWF. "Such clever signs—what fun!"

I couldn't help but wonder why Win was so drawn to advertising kitsch. Maybe her true calling was on Madison Avenue or possibly as a hawker at the Bearded Lady booth at the carnival.

I stayed in the car while Rick accompanied Win on her shopping spree. He had assured me that he wasn't going to buy anything—spending money on stuff that only lasted a few seconds didn't appeal to him, either—but he thought he should stay with Win and make sure she didn't go overboard on her own purchases.

Other customers came and went, some carrying small yellow plastic bags with punks and bottlerockets sticking out the tops. Others carried large, cello-wrapped boxes, probably the combined package deals that included a variety of incendiary whatevers. Finally, after I had spent fifteen intense minutes mulling over in my head all ways that sparks can inadvertently be generated, Rick and Win emerged, unscathed, from the store.

"Oh, Haley, you should have come in," Win said as she opened the van's side door. "Should we store these back in the trailer?" She held up a medium-sized plastic bag of goods. It was big, but not gigantic.

Wanting to make a fast getaway from the deadly place, I answered, "No, just set it down in here, and we can store it in the back later."

"Okay, dear." She placed the crinkly bag between the front seats and jumped in. "I can't wait for you to view the effects of my 'smokin' hot deals!" She began chanting off a list as if I had asked. "Let's see, there are multiple strings of firecrackers, two Whistling Bee fountains, an assortment of Shazam artillery shells with mortar, some Deadly Decibel skyrockets, two Vulcan Roman candles, and even some smoke bombs and sparklers." She clicked her seatbelt with a flourish and adjusted her powwow hat.

I felt dizzy. Rick looked at me again in the mirror. "Do you need to use the restroom, Haley?" He asked.

I inhaled, then exhaled deeply. "No, I'm fine until we stop for lunch. Just go."

"Okay," Rick said in a tour conductor's voice, "next stop, lunch, and then we're off to explore Badlands National Park. Seatbelts, everyone?"

"Rick, please—just go!"

The Badlands tourists were a sporty bunch, indeed. Too sporty to be real, in my estimation. It didn't seem like anyone really could indulge in all the sports activities that their vehicles bragged they did. There was every kind of canoe, longboard, bike, and metal-framed backpack known to man tied to the sides and tops of many of the cars.

I was suspicious, wondering if the occupants of those gear-laden cars were merely outdoor sporting wannabes, not unlike certain people at the gym Charmaine complained about. The ones who paraded around in ultra expensive warm-up suits and running shoes, looking spiffy but never actually breaking a sweat.

One camper van, parked two spots down from ours, struck me in particular. It was some sort of homemade conversion van with an elevated top. Two kayaks and a carrier were strapped to the top and bikes hung precariously from the back end. It looked overloaded and overburdened with too much recreation.

A terrible barking fracas ensued as we walked past the camper contraption on our way to the trailhead. The van was filled with large, noisy white-coated dogs. I shuddered at the sight of all that white dog hair, again thankful for Mom's impeccably clean car. I renewed my determination to keep it that way. I also made a bet with myself that I could pick out the owners on the sightseeing trail we were about to hike. The hairy condition of their outerwear would surely give them away.

While Rick and Win gushed about the dramatic rock formations and the otherworldly terrain of the area, I turned my attention back to my own pressing matters— namely, my shoes.

When I saw that the rain from the night before had muddied the trail ahead of us, I made a last minute decision to forego my premium sandals for an older pair of running shoes. Rick retrieved them from the trailer for me and I was surprised at how hard it was to get my feet into them. I realized that I was inflating like a water balloon. As if my mushrooming episode was not enough, the two days of car riding had triggered an awful bout of fluid retention. I sincerely hoped this would not continue. If only I could contact Charmaine. I couldn't just call her from Rick's phone, though. She kept rigid boundaries around her communication with clients and would only respond to texts or Facebook messages.

Thankfully, the walk did help me feel a little better. Even though my mood had not elevated much after my outburst in Iowa, I hadn't sunk any lower into despair, either. I hoped I could maintain an even emotional keel for a little while. I didn't mind my coaster car creeping along on this level spot. I wanted to regain a bit of control over myself.

We chose a scenic stroll along a boardwalk that skirted some incredible geologic sights. In spite of the cramped shoes, it felt good to work my legs and my headache started to diminish. The light, warm breeze was a nice change from the stuffy car interior and the sun shone brightly, causing us to shed our jackets. Unfortunately, though, Win kept her ridiculous hat firmly in place.

While Rick and Win gushed about the dramatic rock formations and the otherworldly terrain of the South Dakota Badlands, I worried about my shoes. The rain from the night before had muddied the sightseeing trail that we were about to embark on, so I made a last minute decision to forego my premium sandals for an older pair of running shoes. Rick retrieved them from the trailer for me and I was surprised at how hard it was to get my feet into them. I realized that I was inflating like a water balloon. As if my mushrooming episode was not enough, the two days of car riding had triggered an awful bout of fluid retention. I sincerely hoped this would not continue. If only I were able to contact Charmaine. I couldn't just call her from Rick's phone, though. She kept rigid boundaries around her communication with clients and would only respond to texts or Facebook messages.

Thankfully, the walk did help me feel a little better. Even though my mood had not elevated much after my outburst in Iowa, I hadn't sunk any lower into despair, either. I hoped I could maintain an even emotional keel for a little while. I didn't mind my coaster car creeping along on this level spot. I wanted to regain a bit of control over myself.

We chose a scenic stroll along a boardwalk that skirted some incredible geologic sights. In spite of the cramped shoes, it felt good to work my legs and my headache started to diminish. The light, warm breeze was a nice change from the stuffy car interior and the sun shone brightly, causing us to shed our jackets. Unfortunately, though, Win kept her ridiculous hat firmly in place.

"I believe I have chosen the wrong hat for this trek," Win announced part way into our hike.

I couldn't have agreed more. After lunch, Win had exchanged her powwow cap for her "floppy sun hat."

It was an aberration of a hat.

It was the mother of all bad hats.

It was the epitome of everything that could go wrong with a hat. It consisted of flattened panels of aluminum cut from old beer cans and edged with punched holes. Fiery red yarn had been looped through the holes and was used to crochet the panels together to make a cylindrical crown encircled by a wide, floppy, beer can brim. It had the potential to be an award-winning Fashion Fail, but unfortunately, Hal, safely tucked in my pocket for comfort, was too sick to take any pictures.

The hat was such a disgrace that I tried to keep my distance away from it, but Win kept stopping and waiting for me to catch up. She never seemed to take a hint. "You know, this metal-sided hat does not work well in hot sun. I should have thought of that before I put it on. It feels like it is cooking my flesh underneath. Do I smell like barbecue?"

"Um, not sure," I muttered.

She stayed beside me. "It makes me wonder how Dotty, my next door neighbor in Mesa, could stand to wear her Budweiser bikini in the sun for as long as she did. I wonder if she ever suffered any bosom burns." Sweat trickled down Win's cheeks.

I opened my mouth to pontificate on how beer can hats could destroy one's Christian witness but was cut short by a series of popping sounds. Other people on the trail heard it too and stopped to listen.

"What's that?" someone asked.

"Sounds like it's coming from the parking lot," another someone commented.

"Hmmm, I see smoke rising." A small group of fellow hikers turned toward the trailhead. The parking area was just out of sight, beneath a low, stony ridge. A small curl of yellow smoke rose just above the rocks.

What happened next would probably best be understood by the unfortunate volcano victims of the Italian town of Pompeii in A.D. 79 or perhaps the hapless passengers on the airship *Hindenburg* in 1937. The rest of us were utterly unprepared for the fiery spectacle that was about to occur in the middle of a place that, for me, would live up to its name—the Badlands.

The popping noises were followed by a loud whistle and an echoey bang. Instinctually, like a herd of friendly tabby cats running to the sound of an electric can opener, the dozen or so hikers—including Rick, Win, and me— all rushed to the parking lot. Rick, with a distressed look on his face, broke into a full run. I lumbered forward as fast as I could, praying that my apprehension would be proven unwarranted.

I crested the ridge above the lot to the tune of high-pitched whistling noises and reverberating booms, and it was obvious that every single iota of apprehension I had ever experienced in my life wouldn't be enough to warrant the horrific sight I beheld. All the images I had ever seen of war battles, urban riots, or violent protests flashed through my mind while I helplessly watched innocent bystanders run, scream, and duck for cover from the exploding projectiles that peppered the parking lot from a single source.

Regrettably that source was my mother's once faithful and immaculate minivan.

Win's smokin' hot deals were detonating and torpedoing through the car windows. The firecrackers were firing, the artillery shells were shazamming, the bee fountains were spraying fire, the deadly skyrockets' red glare was lighting up the bombs' bursts in the air, the roman candles were erupting, the sparklers were sparkling, and the smoke bombs were smoking.

It was one big show. I almost wet my pants.

9

I stared into the truck's side mirror. "I can't see anything back there. I think we should stop and check on her."

"Just give her a call with my phone. She loves it when her wrist radio rings."

"Rick, I told you, we haven't had service since South Dakota."

"I'm sure Aunt Win is fine." Rick had to speak loud in order to be heard above the truck engine's roar. "We have to keep going or we'll be stuck searching for Aunt Gracie's place in the dark."

How quickly we went from journeying in the semi-comfort of a roomy minivan to the discomfort of a geriatric truck still made my head swim. Actually, my head wasn't swimming at all. It was drowning. Drowning in a roiling sea of madness. The kind of madness that prompts young husbands to think it's perfectly fine to let old ladies ride on the backs of a flatbed trucks while traveling on a highway to Hades.

The whole thing started when Rick used his phone to take pictures of our incineration scene in the Badlands parking lot and emailed them from the park ranger's office computer to my mom's insurance agency back East. The agency informed us that it would probably take two days for a claims adjuster to arrive in South Dakota to assess the situation. They also said that Mom's coverage might allow payment for a rental vehicle and trailer with which to finish our trip, but we would have to get the final okay from the adjuster. In the meantime, the agency had us contact a local towing company to transport the smoking carcass and scorched trailer to the nearest town, where we would have to wait out the process.

But then, because there wasn't enough room for all of us in the tow truck, we were stuck trying to figure out how we could get ourselves back to Rapid City. It was over forty miles away, and a one-way cab trip would cost well over a hundred dollars. In my shocked state that amount seemed like a steal, but Rick stalled on making the call. I couldn't believe he'd worry about money at a time like that.

Unfortunately, Win provided a solution.

As I had predicted earlier, the people from the dog-filled camper van had been easy to identify on the Badlands trail. They were a thirty-something couple, both with tattooed arms and a telltale layer of white hairs on the backs of their vests and jeans. Win had befriended them in the parking lot while I was fussing with my shoes.

Considering the extreme ugliness of our day, it was only fitting, then, that these would be the people to generously offer to take us to Rapid City. Hence I was stuck riding in a stupid van that made Beverly's car interior look like a clean room in a computer chip manufacturing plant.

I had to sit up against an old camper table with Win on one side of me and a stupid Samoyed dog named Gleb cozied up on the other side, shedding his hair all over. His stupid dog friend, Nadia, sat across the table from me, drooling and staring at me while my husband perched on the floor below us. There were no stupid seat belts, but for the first time in my life I couldn't have cared less.

Stupider yet was the fact that the dog's owners chatted nonstop about their idiotic, dog-hair sweater knitting business.

Yes, dog-hair sweaters. *Who knew?*

I was nauseous and miserable the whole stupid ride. The third Samoyed, Ivan, sat halfway on Rick's lap for the entire trip, ensuring that all three of us would emerge from our ride looking like we had slathered ourselves in petroleum jelly before rolling around in open bales of cotton. Any lint brush worth its salt would have whimpered, curled up in a ball, and died at the sight of us.

Our tattooed friends, Jack and Rachel, helped us find a hotel before heading off to their next hairy adventure. They mentioned something about answering an ad for a used spinning wheel in some remote place in North Dakota that could only be reached by bike. I made the mistake of asking how they could pack a spinning wheel on their bikes, and they said that Gleb would carry it out. Apparently, besides providing copious fibers for their sweater yarn, Gleb was also an amazing working dog. Best they ever owned, Jack said.

"Funny how Gleb took such a shine to you," Jack had commented while he watched me pick futilely at the hairs in my jacket zipper. "He doesn't usually bond that quickly."

Bond? It was more like being suffocated by a happy sasquatch.

I was mad when Rick tried to offer them money for the ride. They refused all his offers of payment, but in the end, accepted Win's offer of her beer hat. The lady thought Win's atrocious hat was "retro" and said she had the perfect sweater to pair with it. I was sure she did. Leaving that hat in the fur mobile was the only nanosecond of that day I could call good.

Continuing our journey in a flatbed truck would be the next logical step for me. That part came about when Rick spotted the ancient farm truck in a lot across from our hotel. It wore another one of those ill-fated "For Sale" signs and Rick was instantly smitten. Clutching his phone, he ran to it like a man running to his lover on an airport concourse.

He reasoned that because the minivan was beyond repair, the adjuster would just total it out anyway and write a replacement check for my mom. He went on to argue that the still-running, one-ton beast of a flatbed truck was an amazing steal at seven hundred bucks and had room for all our stuff without our having to rent another trailer. Rick even let it slip that the truck was big enough to haul equipment or maybe a small tractor, *ahem*, on the off chance that such a need should ever arise, *ahem*. Looking back, I'm sure that it was post traumatic stress that eroded my resolve. I acquiesced. I was just too exhausted and too numb to even argue a little bit. Rick made the call and had the deal sealed within an hour.

———— ❦ ————

The galumphing truck lurched us along the two-lane highway as if it had octagonal tires. The ease of the U.S. Interstate system was now a distant memory. Rick, acting like he enjoyed having his spine misaligned and his jaws unhinged, joked that his new truck must have railroad ties for suspension. I didn't laugh. Instead I entertained a picture of overdue pregnant ladies lining up for a ride in Rick's labor induction truck. He could offer his services to obstetricians all over the country.

If the doggy van was the pinnacle of stupidity, then the farm truck was the apex of sheer psychotic lunacy.

"This is ridiculous, Rick!" Too late, I was coming to my senses. "Not only is it hazardous, it's probably illegal. What about seatbelt laws? What about flying objects hitting her? Shouldn't she be wearing a safety helmet? For all we know, we could get charged with elder abuse."

"Elder abuse? You watch too many talk shows. And seatbelt laws? You didn't seem to care about seatbelts in Jack's van."

"I *did* care—I was outnumbered! You and Win jumped into that camper before I even knew what was going on. And at least no one was tied to the outside of that vehicle."

"Well, who's around to pull us over, anyway? Have you seen a highway patrol anywhere at all in the last two hundred miles?"

He had a point there. I wasn't even sure if we had seen another vehicle in the last fifty. I still had to stand on principle, though.

"Come on, Rick—you know as well as I do that breaking the law is breaking the law. Whether or not an officer is around is beside the point.

What about our logos—" I stopped myself but not soon enough.

"Christian logos, you say? Hmm. I think those are cooling off in a junk-yard right about now, though they did look more meaningful on the windows of a smoking car."

Rick grinned at the memory. "Ha! Christianflameworks.com. Sort of apocalyptic, maybe."

"It isn't funny, Rick. And it's not good for Win to be riding back there."

"Well, it's not like we forced her. It was her idea to strap the lawn chair to the flatbed."

"Sure, and do you really think she's capable of making a sound decision? The woman obviously doesn't have all her marbles."

Rick gripped the steering wheel and stopped smiling. "She's a good, competent woman. She just has some quirks, that's all."

"Quirks? Blowing up our car is quirkiness?" I hit a high F on the last syllable. "My good shoes, my best shoes—the only shoes left that I could squish my blobbish feet in are melted and squashified beyond recognition! But not to worry—it's just quirky, right?" I knew that my vocabulary was going downhill fast, but I figured that someone sporting bejeweled dollar store flip-flops shouldn't care anymore. Besides that, people generally don't worry about what they say or how they look when their emotional roller-coaster takes them into the very depths of hell.

Adding insult to injury was the fact that while my indispensable shoes had been sacrificed to the fire gods, because I had banished him to the trailer, Win's dispensable Herman Hoot Owl had escaped unscathed. He was anchored firmly in the back, hooting and head-spinning at every bump in the road.

"Haley, we can't blame Aunt Win entirely for the explosion—you told her to set the fireworks down by the Eezy-Tweezy, remember?"

"Oh, so now it's my fault? You've got to be kidding! Win should have thought to put them in the trailer before we started hiking. Or maybe you should have—" I stopped to bite back tears.

"C'mon, Haley! I didn't even know the Eezy-Tweezy was between the seats. I thought Win had put it away. You saw it there."

"Rick, how was I supposed to know that a mirror can light firecrackers? You're the one who experimented with bottles and magnifying glasses and stuff! You're the one who said you did that all the time with your brother when you were little. I think you're the one with the pyromania tendencies—don't blame me!" A couple of angry tears escaped, despite my efforts to hold them back.

"Okay, okay, calm down." Rick reverted to placating mode. "This isn't good for the baby." The baby confirmed her daddy's words by kicking my ribs hard from the inside and pouncing on my bladder.

"Oooh, Rick, we have to stop. I really have to go now."

Rick dampened his tone. "Honey, I'll do my best, but, um, where?"

A brilliant question indeed. Our drive through this far northeastern corner of Wyoming proved to be as void of facilities as I imagined a camel ride through central Libya might be. I had never seen so much empty, unfenced land before. Compared to this, Iowa was like a bustling, open-air marketplace with South Dakota as its busy parking lot. This vast emptiness called Wyoming, then, was Siberia—the place where all the thieves caught stealing in the Iowa market would be sentenced to live without bathrooms.

"Oh, this is getting bad." I started bouncing my crossed legs.

"Uh, there's always, uh," Rick cowered slightly and cleared his throat before continuing, "uh, Aunt Win's Trav-a-Lav."

I screeched and Rick winced. "The Trav-a-Lav—ugh! Do I have to go over this again? I would rather die than use that portable toilet contraption. Do you understand? I will never, and I mean never, utilize that mail order gizmo-thingee!"

My spouting off left a wake of silence resonating through the diesel-smelling truck cab. Rick stared at the road. I stared out the window. The gangly stick shift clattered. The baby kicked. The blower fan rattled. The baby kicked again.

I sighed. "Sorry."

My tone did not match the word, but I knew Lorna would expect me to at least attempt to say the right thing.

He reached over and patted my knee. "It's okay. The last two days have been kinda rough on all of us."

If the word "understatement" needed a more concise definition than the one provided in the dictionary, Rick's last sentence would supply it.

I started bouncing my legs again. Rick handed the highway atlas over to me. "Look at the map, Haley. How far to the next town?"

I squinted, trying to read the tiny mileage numbers. It didn't help that earlier Win had spilled some of her nasty carrot kugel pudding on the Wyoming page. "Um, about five miles to a place called Canford."

"Hmm, sounds promising. Can you make that?"

"If you hurry."

Rick pushed on the accelerator. "Hope Aunt Win still has her bungees hooked. Watch out the back. Yell if it looks like something's gonna fly off."

His words alarmed me. As infuriated as I was with Win, I certainly did not want to kill her. I was strangely torn between true concern for her and relief that her choice to sit back there had finally released me from having to listen to her stories. Not only that, but being crammed in the front of a truck cab with someone who has done great harm and will not take full responsibility for it, is no picnic in the park.

At one point, Win said she was sorry that her Eezy-Tweezy had set off the fireworks and then went on to find silly silver linings in the clouds of our shared tragedy. She said preposterous things like, "Maybe God allowed the van to be destroyed because it had a mechanical defect, and we would have all perished in it down the road." And, "Maybe there was a war veteran in the parking lot, and the explosions triggered some destructive latent memories that the person will now seek psychiatric help for because he or she can no longer ignore them." Or, the even more maddening, "God must have a plan in this."

I was frustrated on all levels. I couldn't believe that I was living through some of the most dramatic circumstances I had ever encountered yet couldn't distribute the details of my saga beyond a couple brief calls from Rick's limited minute voice plan. Clever and amazing Facebook updates swirled around in my brain like water in a plugged toilet. But without internet access, there was no outlet for my spiritual insights and newsy reports. And boy, did I have a report. I could have spun it to no end.

Even if he wasn't broken, Hal wouldn't have worked in this cell reception vacuum anyway. That thought afforded me a strange iota of comfort, as did the thought of my comatose little smartphone safely on his way to a repair center, thanks to a helpful customer service rep in Rapid City. He would be sent back to Gracie's address as soon as he was fixed, which couldn't happen a moment too soon. I was in full-blown withdrawal.

Unable to see through our pile of covered belongings that were lashed against the rear window, I peered again into the side mirror. I only saw a nylon strap flapping between the rough sideboards of the truck. I started to pray silently for Win's safety but felt sort of sheepish about it. It didn't feel right to pray for protection for someone that I was responsible for endangering.

I prayed for Herman Hoot Owl instead. I prayed that his bungee would be severed by the friction produced from his head rotations and that he would get bounced off the truck at a railroad crossing and ground into a million pieces by a speeding freight train. *Sense that motion, Herman...*

The mirror suddenly reflected a bony finger pointing through the sideboards of the flatbed. I sat back in my seat. "Win's okay. I see her pointing out another antelope herd."

"Good," Rick replied. "She loves spotting wildlife, doesn't she? I think she's really in her element out here on the prairie. It's kind of a homecoming for her."

"So glad we could accommodate her."

Closing my eyes, I tried to take my mind off my need for a bathroom. I concentrated on conjuring up an image of the picturesque property we would soon be living on, the peaceful place that I was counting on to make every accursed mishap of this trip worthwhile.

"Haley, look, I think that's Canford right there."

"Oh, good." I opened my eyes and leaned expectantly toward the windshield.

Rick slowed down as we passed a defunct, abandoned building surrounded by rusty car bodies and scrap metal carcasses. A bent aluminum sign displayed the faded words, "Canford Auto."

"What? Is this it?"

Rick whistled. "How does a place like this get on a map?"

Tears again sprang to my eyes as we slowly passed two rotting, forsaken trailer houses rooted deeply in the wasteland. Their glassless windows stared out at nothing, like the vacuous eyes of dead fish. Beyond them, the highway forged straight ahead through miles of lumpy, naked rangeland.

"Sweetie, do you want me to help you find a spot behind the building?" Rick was cowering again. He guided the truck onto a wide spot beside the road.

I looked back at the area around the building. Tetanus lurked around every corner.

"No," I said through tears of surrender, "tell Aunt Win we need the Trav-a-Lav."

"You know, I think I'm going to call HandiTrek Products consumer hotline when we get to Gracie's and register a complaint," Aunt Win chattered as she pushed the Trav-a-Lav box back under the blue plastic tarp. "They need to know that the pop-up privacy curtain won't withstand the stiff breeze of a passing eighteen-wheeler."

I could finally say that one of my dreams had come true. Of course, it wasn't the dream about sailing in a warm ocean on a giant fleece-upholstered recliner, or the one in which I won expensive wrought iron and glass patio furniture on The Price Is Right. No, it just had to be the macabre dream about finding myself inexplicably under-clothed in public.

I was mortified. To what had this trip reduced me? Indignity, degradation, despair—I left my comfortable life in Pennsylvania for this?

Win readjusted her yellow sun visor and pulled her hood strings tighter under her chin. She looked like a wrinkled duck. "The infomercial showed people setting the Trav-a-Lav up right next to a six-lane freeway, for heaven's sake. If it can be used discreetly in a situation like that, then it certainly should be safe to use beside a country highway. Of course, the traffic on the advertisement was at a standstill, so there wouldn't be any stiff breezes. Still, you'd think..." She babbled ad infinitum.

Fake coughing sounds emitted from behind the truck. It was the same cough Rick used in church sometimes when he was trying to suppress a laugh.

"Rick, this isn't funny!"

"I'm not laughing—it's just the dust, *cough*, from the truck, *cough*, when it passed—" He giggled, coughed again, then wheezed and started choking on his saliva.

Serves him right. I hoisted my bulky body into the pickup cab. Win climbed back onto her perch on the flatbed and waited like a patient toddler in a car seat while Rick hooked the restraining network of bungee cords into place.

The whole scenario was ridiculous. At exactly what point in this trip had my husband's endearing qualities—his spontaneity, resourcefulness and loyalty—turned against me? It was like Rick had developed an even deeper insensitivity toward me. He wasn't nearly as protective and comforting toward me as he should have been after the explosion. I wanted him to fawn over me and hold me in his arms for hours, but after a prayer and a hug, it was business as usual. I worried that the shock of our debacle could have sent me into early labor, but Rick countered that concern with a Win-like retort that, "God is in control." That hurt my feelings. It seemed like everything horrific for me had become an adventure for him.

I leaned to the side and let my head bounce against the window as Rick pulled back onto the highway. Yearning for a reclining seat, I started thinking about my snappy hybrid. I missed it terribly. It was cute, cool, efficient, and the nicest vehicle I had ever owned. Riding around in it made me feel smart and sophisticated. At that moment, I was thankful that no one I knew could see me in the lumbering truck with a deranged passenger and all our cargo strapped to the back, like the Beverly Hillbillies.

After about twenty miles, I noticed a semblance of civilization with occasional homes and ranches huddling in the draws and gullies between the knobs of the prairie's skeletal frame. The houses were all so tiny and scruffy, though. I marveled at how people could live that way and thought of all the sophisticated subdivisions that had popped up in our area over the last few years. Almost all of our relatives and church friends owned newer, fashionable homes. Even the ones who lived in older homes like ours had invested in remodeling projects.

I tried to soothe myself with thoughts of Gracie's house. I was sure that her home would be as warm, welcoming, and normal as she was—so unlike her sister, Win. Gracie and Hank had attended the last two family reunions in Pennsylvania, and I enjoyed every moment that I spent with them. Hank emailed us pictures of their home a week before we left, and it looked like a small but comfortable bungalow. I had no problem picturing myself in the quaint, older home. It was only for the summer, after all. The pictures didn't show any of the property, but Rick remembered from a childhood visit there that they had an incredible view from the front yard.

I prayed that once we arrived at our destination we could put the whole trip fiasco behind us. Maybe it wasn't too late to enjoy a restful month before the baby was born. And thank goodness, I would have computer access again. Hank had referred to "my" computer several times in his emails, so I knew he was using his own computer, not one in a public library or senior center.

"Aunt Gracie's mountain view is going to be a nice change from this," I said as I pointed toward yet another ridge of hills the color of cold oatmeal. I forgot that I had resolved to stop speaking to Rick for the rest of the trip.

"Mountain view?" Rick raised his eyebrows.

"Yes, you always said that Gracie and Hank had an 'incredible view' from their place. I've wanted to see the Montana Rockies since I was a kid."

Rick sucked in his breath. "Um, Haley, I never said they had a mountain view."

"Well, what other kind of 'incredible view' is there?"

"Think about it—real estate catalogs are full of descriptions of properties with a view. City views, forest views, pond views—practically anything can provide a view."

"So there's no mountain view?"

Rick sighed deeply. We had both done our fair share of sighing in the past few days. "Haley, look at the Montana map."

I picked up the atlas. "So?"

"Find Grassview."

"Right here."

"Okay. Now, see where the Rockies cut through the western third of the state?"

"You mean the green areas?"

"Yeah. How far is Grassview from, say, Bozeman?"

I remembered pictures of Bozeman from the web sites we had visited when we were first planning our trip to Montana. It had appeared to be in a spectacular mountain valley. "Hmm, it looks like fifty miles, maybe."

Now it was Rick's turn to holler. "Haley! Give me a break—Montana is huge. Look at the scale of miles—look at the mileage chart."

"Oh." My stomach did a twist. Math had never been my forte.

"I guess Grassview is about, um, two hundred miles from the closest mountain range," I said, my tone diminishing.

"Hence the name." Rick paused to let that one sink in but couldn't resist finishing his point. "Haley, I probably shouldn't say this, but why would you think a town named Grassview would be in the mountains?"

"Well, people and places are misnamed all the time. My dad has a cousin that everyone calls 'Baldy,' but he has a full head of thick hair." My voice had become small and whiny.

Rick, too, quieted his tone. "I had no idea that you thought we would be living close to the mountains. Didn't we talk about that part?"

"I guess not," I mumbled.

Rick clenched the steering wheel again. "Who's always lecturing who about assumptions?"

I didn't know what to say. In a way, he was right—and yet he didn't have to be so mean about it. I certainly didn't need him to punch any more holes into my sinking ship of peaceful and purposeful summer dreams. It was going down fast all by itself.

We rode along in silence until Rick's phone started singing. "We must have finally gotten back into service," I quietly commented as I fished the phone out of my jacket pocket. Rick had figured out how to use the parental controls on Win's phone and replaced Hal's number with his.

"Are you okay, Aunt Win?"

Her voice sounded absurdly distant. "Oh, I'm glorious, Haley," she gushed. "I can tell we're getting close to Gracie's—just look at the spectacular scenery!"

10

Looking back, I realize it was a blessing that we didn't reach Gracie and Hank's until dark. It would have been too much for me to digest both the interior and exterior conditions of my new living quarters in the same evening.

I stepped out of the truck and directly into Gracie's hug.

"You made it!" She clasped my hand and guided me into the front door.

Nothing could have prepared me for the extravaganza that awaited us in her living room. The cramped space was engorged with a dizzying assemblage of knickknacks and bric-a-brac. An unmatched lineup of bookcases and display cases lined the walls from top to bottom, holding every sort of figurine imaginable. Open shelved stands were even placed in the middle of the room, on either side of the crowded coffee table. My heart sunk all the way to the jewels of my flip-flops. I was back in Larry's shop in Ohio, and I was going to live there.

Gracie noticed my wide-eyed stare and chuckled. "Don't mind my stuff. I've been collecting things since we bought this place in 1965."

"Your place looks lovely as always," Win said as she inspected a porcelain leprechaun. "Still garage-saling up a storm, are you?"

"I've had to restrain myself from the garage sales since Hank discovered auctions on the computer," Gracie replied. "He's been finding the niftiest trinkets for me."

Rick walked in the door and grinned. "Cool! Just like I remember it as a kid."

His enthusiasm was riling. To me, the place looked hideous, dangerous— a housecleaner's bane. I couldn't imagine living for a few days, let alone a few months, in such mawkish environs. Base of operations? Who was I kidding? Who was Danielle kidding? I couldn't imagine what kind of mission this home could be used as the base of. Unless, of course, one was called to minister to the seriously bauble-deprived.

Rick ignored the glare I fixed on him and shook Hank's hand vigorously. Win clapped her hands.

"I have an idea. Hank, could you help me explore the computer system and find a deal on shoes for Haley? I'd like to replace the ones that burned in our little fiery time of excitement."

Fiery time of excitement?

"That's really nice of you, Aunt Win," Rick said, tossing me a say-thank-you look. I knew him well enough to know that he would regard Win's offer as satisfactory penitence for the "fiery time of excitement." He would need no additional acknowledgment of responsibility. I, however, was not satisfied. She wouldn't get off the hook that easy with me. My dad always said that taking responsibility for one's actions was a direct reflection of the depth of one's relationship with God. People who took their faith seriously took their sin seriously, as well.

"Oh, Gracie dear, I have a gift for you on the back of the truck," Win said, breathless from excitement. "But it's getting late, so it should be fine until tomorrow."

"I can hardly wait, dear!" Gracie resembled Win far more than I remembered. She turned to me. "Haley, you look pale. Here, have a seat. Can I get you something to eat or drink?"

I couldn't fault Gracie's kindness, though. My body ached all over and the baby was pummeling me again. "I think I just need to go to bed."

"No problem, dear. I have the master bedroom all ready for you. Hank and I will sleep in the motor home tonight, since we're leaving tomorrow anyway." Gracie started toward a narrow hallway leading from the living room. "Come this way."

As I turned to follow her, my protruding stomach swept against a carefully placed queue of cornhusk angels, pushing some off the shelf and sending the rest flying into a herd of crystal pigs. The tinkling clatter silenced everyone in the room.

"No harm, no harm," Gracie said cheerfully as she rushed to rescue the pigs.

"Oh, I can't believe I did that. I'm sorry." I tried to sound sincere, but I was too tired to put much effort into feigning emotion.

Rick rushed in to supply contrition for me. "Oh no—here let me help pick that up. Is anything broken?"

Gracie inspected the pigs as she returned them to their previous positions. "Not really, just one cracked ear, as far as I can see."

"Actually gives the little guy some character," Win chuckled. "Now he can boast that he wrestled an angel—just like Jacob in the Bible!"

Win's comments nauseated me. Gracie, sensing my discomfort, motioned for me to follow her to the bedroom. I gratefully obeyed, worrying that I saw a ceramic toad in a tutu wink at me. I obviously needed rest. It had truly been the longest day of my life.

———•◦•◦•———

A shriek, coming from another room, yanked me from my fitful sleep. Confused, I glanced around the bedroom, trying to get my bearings. I could hear muffled conversation from the kitchen area, and Win screeched again and laughed. I laid my head back down, and thought about the scary dream I was having right before I woke up. I had been driving a gorgeous new car in downtown Philly, when a pig with wings swooped down, landed on the hood, and leered at me. The nice vehicle morphed into a huge, boat-like beater of a 70's sedan. I was going the wrong way down a one-way street and the pig was cackling like Aunt Win did when she laughed.

Rick was already up so I couldn't talk to him about it. He'd probably just laugh at me anyway like he had beside the highway the day before. A swift kick from the baby goaded me out of bed and to the bathroom.

I emerged from the bathroom and went into the sun drenched kitchen. Muffins, pastries and breads were set out on the table on pretty platters. My heart warmed slightly at another evidence of Gracie's hospitality.

"Oh, Haley, you're going to love this vista!" Win exclaimed.

Rick rose from the table and gave me a kiss on the cheek. "Good morning, Beautiful." He was acting nervous.

"Look, dear," Win said, motioning toward the huge window in the dining area. It faced the front yard.

I blinked, then gasped. There was no way for me to conceal my astonishment. Win had been right, after all. Gracie would be thrilled with Herman Hoot Owl.

Whatever vista might exist was totally upstaged by the macabre carnival of lawn ornaments that covered Hank and Gracie's property. The array went far beyond birdbaths and Dutch windmills. I saw groupings of themed scenarios—a ceramic frog village in one corner, a grotesque metal flower garden in another. A family of bearded gnomes, lined up beside the driveway, sported hand knit sweaters.

"Isn't it beautiful?" Win was ecstatic.

I was in shock. "Um, beautiful?"

Win opened her arms wide in front of the window. "This panorama—you would never see this in our Quaker state!"

"She means the sky, Haley," Rick explained, "you're in Big Sky Country now."

I tried to figure out what Win and Rick were talking about, but all I could see was that the house was on a junk-strewn acreage that faced the lonely highway, which faced a state of cold-oatmeal-hill nothingness.

Win continued her soliloquy. "Ah, horizon, grand horizon! Wondrously revealed through the absence of man's intrusive structures!"

Hank, sitting at the table with a cup of coffee in his hand, chuckled. "Quite the fancy speech, there, Winifred. You should write that down."

Cold realization of what I had gotten myself into started creeping through my insides. Clearly, I should have researched the area and accommodations more diligently before agreeing to live, even temporarily, on these circus grounds. Moreover, I definitely should have realized that dear Gracie couldn't be as normal as I had assumed—not with a sister like Win.

In spite of her generosity, Gracie's obsession with tacky objects was baffling. I was particularly bewildered by the bust of a strangely familiar man sitting atop a tall concrete pillar in the middle of the yard. It seemed completely out of place among the mushroom and fairy statues. While I continued to gaze at the tawdry objet d'art, a short-legged, big-eared dog wandered through the yard. As if reading my thoughts, it proceeded to lift its leg and relieve itself against the pillar.

"Oh, no, it's that stray again!" Gracie yelled, "Don't let him do that—not on Winston Churchill! I just put him out for the season. Quick, Hank, get the pellet gun!"

I squealed involuntarily. "No!"

Hank smiled. "It's okay, there, Miss Haley—a pellet's only a little bigger than a BB. It'll just give the rascal a reminder of why he shouldn't be nosin' round this place."

Gracie brought the gun from the back porch and handed it to Hank. "Get him good, Hank. I'm sick of that dog chewing on the Simu-Sod mats under the ferris wheel."

"What fun!" Win said and clapped her hands. "After Hank finishes that task I want you to come with me outside, Gracie, and we'll get your gift off the truck."

Gracie giggled. "Is it the singing Liberty Bell door chime that Hank wouldn't let me buy when we were with you at Independence Park last summer?"

"Oh, no, it's something better. Much better."

———◆·❈·◆———

It was well into Saturday afternoon before Hank and Gracie departed, honking and waving from their aged, bumper-sticker-riddled motor home.

"Wow, I hope that thing makes it up the Alaska Highway," Rick commented as he watched the RV's decorated backend disappear down the highway. "They're a little old to be driving so far by themselves."

"I'm more worried about them getting blown over by these big wind gusts." I said, pushing my hair out of my eyes. My haircut was not holding up well under the barrage of westerly gales that had not stopped bullying us since somewhere in South Dakota.

Herman Hoot Owl was holding up quite nicely, though. Thrilled with the gift, Gracie had promptly stationed the statue beside a low juniper bush near the back door to the house.

"Say, that critter just might work. Sounds pretty realistic to me—that hoo-hooing will send the rattlers packin', for sure," Hank had commented, as intrigued with the gift as Gracie was.

"Rattlers?" I was alarmed.

"Yeah, rattlesnakes. Owls have been known to kill 'em on occasion. A rattler's hearing ain't real good, but it's good enough to pick up on the hoot vibrations when he gets too close. And it's not so much that the owl itself will kill a snake, it's more that the rattler just seems to know somehow that if an owl's around, there won't be many mice in the vicinity for the snake's dinner." Hank took on a teacher voice of his own.

I couldn't believe what I was hearing. "You have rattlesnakes around here?"

"Yep. Most of Montana east of the Continental Divide has 'em in the outback. There's a few of 'em in the hills out there," Hank replied, pointing to an outlying area.

Seeing the horror on my face, Gracie spoke, "Oh, now, don't worry about snakes, Haley. They're really shy—just got to watch where you step. Haven't seen one in the yard here for over twenty years. Actually, I haven't even seen a rattler in the wild more than a couple times in my whole life. And I'm not a spring chicken."

Win and Hank laughed. I didn't.

Rick changed the subject at that point by asking Hank about yard care. We ended up spending almost an hour walking around the house with him, listening to his careful explanations about things like water hose timers and attic fans.

As I picked my way around the cluttered lawn, I experienced another bout of paranoia. Not a guilty type of paranoia, but a sheer fright type of paranoia. I kept my gaze low as I walked, examining each step ahead before I took it. It was frustrating, though, that my stomach had grown to the point where it blocked my view of the ground directly beneath me. For a moment, I visualized a sort of mirror system extending from my knees to reveal my feet. After only a moment of pondering, however, I threw the picture from my mind and tried to re-center my thoughts on normal things. I couldn't figure out how I had come up with such a strange idea. I was obviously very tired.

I did feel a measure of relief when Gracie handed me a set of car keys and told me to use her car anytime I wanted. She then proceeded to go over every inch of her kitchen with me, making sure that I knew where everything was kept and that it was within easy reach for me. She had even thoughtfully purchased a few nursery items and turned the third bedroom into a temporary baby's room.

As if the thought of cohabiting with rattlesnakes wasn't bad enough, though, Hank might as well have kicked me in the shins when he casually dropped the bomb that their internet service was dial-up.

Noticing my shocked expression, he rushed to reassure me. "Oh, don't worry—it works great. Usually only takes four or five minutes to connect when you need it."

Five minutes?? I was speechless. I didn't even know that dial-up internet still existed. I thought it went out with M.C. Hammer pants and Y2K toilet paper hoarding. Dial-up seemed even more inconvenient than the two full weeks into the year 2000 that my dad rationed us each only twenty squares of toilet paper a day. He wanted to make good and sure that the country's power grid stayed operational before he let us break into our stores. Mom didn't have to buy toilet paper for almost two years. Or dried mashed potato powder.

Hank kindly persisted in shoring up my spirits. "And I've decided that I get more chores done with dial-up than I would if I had that fast speed type service."

"Get more chores done because of dial-up?" Even Rick was surprised by this news.

"Yep," Hank replied, "if we had faster internet I figure I'd have to sit in one place and just keep clicking through the pages. With my slower speed I can hit the enter button and go out and weed the tulip bed while I wait for the next page to come up."

"Oh, yes, it's wonderful!" Gracie clapped her hands just like Win. "It's been good for our marriage. Sometimes there's enough time between page-loading for Hank to fold a small load of laundry. Until we got the internet piped into our home, Hank had never, in over forty years together, ever folded laundry!"

I immediately thought of something Alice said in *Alice in Wonderland*. "It would be so nice if something made sense for a change."

———◆◆◆◆———

As dismayed as I was with their home and living habits, I felt a pang of sorrow at seeing Hank and Gracie leave. They belonged here, not me. I would never in my wildest dreams purposely pick this place as a vacation spot. Disappointment threatened to crush me. My month-long anticipation of the beauty of the mountains of Montana had latched on to me like a fun new friend. Now that friend lay dying beside me, and I couldn't do a thing about it but grieve.

Rick was excited to start his new job, and for some inexplicable reason thought that Gracie's place was fabulous. It felt like this trip had widened the gap between us that had started forming before we left Philadelphia. I feared that if left unresolved, our gap could grow into a major chasm. My hand went reflexively to my stomach as I thought about how ill-timed this disconnection in our marriage was. A huge part of our daughter's security depended on the love and communication practices in our home. Propelled by a brand new motherly instinct, I decided to confront the issue right there and then.

Rick was still standing beside me, smiling at the jam-packed lawn. Another sharp gust goaded Gracie's wind chimes into a mournful, atonal cacophony, plastering my hair over my eyes again.

"Rick, we need to talk," I said.

"Sure, hon—what about?"

"Well, I feel like we've been at each other a lot, and—"

"The earthly travelers depart, and the heavenly ones return," Win's falsetto orator voice interrupted. She was beside Rick, staring at the sky again.

"Huh?" There was just no end to that woman's absurdities.

Win pointed at the sky. "The clouds—see how they're all fluffy and individualized?"

"Yeah, I see," Rick replied.

"That's a sure sign of spring. All winter, the clouds are flat and dull. But as spring gets closer, they become fluffier and brighter." She continued to point. "And see how they all appear to be leaning forward? They are marching with their suitcases to the east. It's their yearly migration. That's why spring weather can be unpredictable—the cloud flocks stir up temperature layers and precipitation pockets in their rush to their summer homes."

Rick was mesmerized. "I...see..."

"Just watch the sky, dear. We see more by looking up with our own eyes than by looking down through those satellite lenses." Still gazing upward, she paused, then commented in a softer tone, "Or into radar or computer devices that try to squish the mighty heavens into a tiny box."

"Wow," Rick replied with reverence.

I was scared. Did Rick truly speak this woman's language? I didn't understand a word of it. I was in a strange land among strangers. Where was my husband—the loyal spouse and urbane businessman? I turned to go back into the house, letting my relationship-building intentions flutter away like litter in the wind. I was an outsider, alone in a homely country, and unable to communicate with the natives, and the empty spot in my jacket pocket where Hal usually sat reminded me that even my communication to the outside world was now gone.

———

Win's flocks of migrating clouds started huddling together into a dismal gray mass as the afternoon progressed. My attitude darkened as well. At home, when I needed a mental boost, I would curl up with a cup of tea and a book or take a walk in the tree-lined park near our home. Neither was an option for me here, however. There wasn't a room in the house that wasn't claustrophobically crammed with junk, and the property outside of Gracie's crammed lawn was agoraphobically vacant.

I vowed that as soon as I could figure out how to fire up Hank's antiquated computer, I would email Danielle. I would tell her to read and study Deuteronomy eighteen, twenty-two, the Bible verse that explains how to test whether a prophet is speaking truth or lies. If what the prophet says comes true, than that person is truly speaking for God. If the prophecy proves false, than the prophet is fraudulent. *Gracie's house as the base of missions operations, my foot. You better avoid going outside in thunderstorms until you've done some serious repenting, Dani.*

Rick and I had been tense with each other all afternoon. We couldn't seem to agree on even the smallest of decisions, and I was more upset with him than I had been in years. He told me that I was the negative one, but I knew that he was being totally insensitive and critical toward me. At one point I went into the bedroom and tried to pray, but it felt like God wasn't even listening to me.

Restless and fidgety, I stalked out the back door and onto the deck where Win was finishing up the unpacking process.

"Hooray!" she exclaimed, pulling something out of the last box.

"What's up, Aunt Winnie?" Rick called from the driveway.

"You brought the Meteorologic Melodies Weather Watcher!" Win was ecstatic. I was annoyed. Beyond annoyed. Rick might as well have brought along our neighbor's incessantly yapping dog while he was at it.

"Rick, why? The last thing we need is the sound of those grating songs blasting at random times throughout the house." I didn't care if I offended Win. It was high time she realized her gifts were dumb. I was certain there were other relatives in Rick's family who would wholeheartedly support my bluntness.

He joined us on the deck. "Oh, random, irritating songs, you say? Like your phone, perhaps?"

I sniffed and looked away.

Rick turned to Win. "I figured it might sing songs in this climate that we've never heard it sing before. Is usually way hotter and drier out here in the summer, from what I remember."

"Oh, yes, what fun!" Win held up the shoebox-sized station and inspected its gauges. "Let's set it up right away."

"Sure, but first let me put these boxes away," Rick replied, folding a carton flat to store in the garage rafters. He picked up a bundle and walked back toward the driveway. "It's nice that Hank has so much storage area in his garage."

I didn't reply. What wasn't nice about the garage was that it contained one of the hugest, wood panel-sided station wagons I had ever seen. Gracie's car was almost as bad as the one I had dreamed about. Of course Rick loved it. He said it was awesome, and a classic, and in the best shape he had ever seen a car in from that time period. It looked to me like a person would have to know a bit about ship navigation, or perhaps be a member of the Brady Bunch, to steer the beast. And, worse yet, it probably consumed more gas in one trip to town than my snappy hybrid would in twenty trips. It would definitely classify as an offensive and unnecessary environmental menace. I immediately resolved to drive on my own as little as possible.

"I'm gettin' hungry," Rick said when he returned to the deck after storing the cartons. "I bet Fern is too."

"Rick, I told you—her name isn't Fern. This is not a good time to try and discuss baby names." That subject was definitely not the one to bring up when we were already at odds. "And, yes, I am getting hungry."

"Oh," Win said, "I'd love to cook tonight. I'll make something real special to celebrate our first day together in this panoramic Land of Possibilities!"

No, dear, if you cook we'll be in the 'Land of Food Poisoning Possibilities.' I swallowed hard before saying, "It's nice of you to offer, Aunt Winnie, but I don't mind cooking tonight."

"Let's just pick up something in town and save you both the trouble," Rick offered.

"Sounds good." I really was too tired to cook.

Win suddenly snapped her head to one side and pointed her nose up, like a hound catching a scent. Her face took on an otherworldly expression and she blurted out, "You know, I think I'll go ambling across the wilderness instead." She sniffed the air. "Yes, it would be the perfect time to glean the first sagebrush cuttings of spring. It's been twenty years since I whipped up a batch of pungent sagebrush conserve."

"Are you sure it's safe for you to roam out there alone?" Rick asked, pointing toward the hills where individual sagebrush plants grew like pilled fiber balls on a rumpled bathroom rug.

Win smiled. "Safe? Why, I'd feel safer hiking the Montana grasslands than navigating my way through Lenny's buffet line on senior citizen discount day. The sharp elbows always fly at the soft serve ice cream machine."

Part of me knew I should say, "But what about rattlesnakes?" That part, though, was silenced by a newly-emerging, more diabolical side of me. It spoke up and said, "Of course it's safe. What a wonderful plan for your afternoon, Aunt Win." I grabbed Rick's arm and steered him off the deck. "We shouldn't be long—see you later!"

"Oh, shall we install the Meteorologic Melodies first?" Win asked.

Rick looked at my pursed lips and answered, "We'll get that set up later—just go harvest your sage for now."

"Yes! Ah, I must go and find the right hat." Win bounded through the back door and into the house. I knew she'd be fine by herself in the hills. She was wrapped in optimism as impenetrable as a Kevlar suit.

A one-thousandth-micron-thick piece of dust must have passed a few feet in front of Herman. "Hoo-hoo," he warned.

The highway in front of Gracie's house led straight into the heart of Grassview. Highway 32 was abruptly Main Street, just like that. I looked ahead as Rick slowed down and saw nothingness again only a few blocks up from where Main Street began. There were no traffic lights and only a few other cars.

"Um, this town is smaller than I expected," I spoke cautiously, doing my best to avoid a negative tone. I decided to try again to be nice. I knew Lorna would tell me it was my duty, and it would go toward advancing God's kingdom on earth.

Rick had no problem acting like everything was fine between us. "Yeah, it's going to be a fantastic break from the city, isn't it?"

"In what way?"

"No traffic, no noise—this is great!" He slowed the truck to a crawl to inspect the businesses lined up on each side.

I couldn't even begin to think of a reply that wouldn't include festering sardonicism, so I bit my lip and remained silent.

All the buildings on Main Street looked jaded and tired. About a third were boarded up or vacant, and the rest were marked by outdated or cheaply-lettered signs. There was an air of resignation about them as if they were all in different stages of accepting their inevitable devolution. A few attempts at storefront revival in the form of colorful awnings or newer neon signs were scattered among the blocks, but they looked lonely and vulnerable to me.

"Wow, Buffle's Insurance is still in business after all these years and look—Bob's Photo Studio hasn't changed a bit!" Rick's excited comments continued as we crept down the street. "Hmm, I don't recognize that one— Dueling Badgers Gift Haus—looks like one you'd like, sweetie."

"What do you mean?"

"Look, the sign says, 'all home decor items on sale,' and there's some trendy-looking lamps in the window. Do you want to go in?"

I wanted to scream that lamps made from animal legs with the hooves still attached were not trendy but decided to contain myself and make polite conversation instead. I wasn't sure if Rick truly liked Grassview, or if, like me, he was merely making an effort towards diplomacy between us.

"No, that's okay, let's just keep driving. Um, do badgers really duel?"

"I'm not sure. Hey, 'Pamper Parlor Beauty Shop' and 'Debbie's Pie Hut' are right next to each other—looks like you'll have everything you need right here in town, Haley."

I was dubious even though there did seem to be a bit of activity in the beauty salon. Two women exited the shop as we crept by. I couldn't help but notice that both had exactly the same super short, outdated perm-doo. It was becoming dishearteningly apparent that this dowdy prairie town and its frumpy inhabitants were the antithesis to my visions of a quaint country village. Not at all like Charmaine's special Montana ski resort town. That place might as well have been on the moon. It sure wasn't anywhere near here.

Rick's detailed assessment of Main Street continued. "The Salt Lick Saloon—I think that's always been here. Was one of the originals in the homesteading days, if I remember right."

There were two more taverns near the Salt Lick. The neon beer mug on Bison Jack's sign was hanging askew, and the upper half of the door to the Miner's Roost was boarded over where it had apparently been broken. I could almost see the rancid cigarette and stale beer odors, congealing into evil, oily, yellow clouds as they lurked in front of those establishments. I involuntarily shivered.

Rick noticed. "You okay?"

"I'm fine. Why does such a small town have so many bars?"

"Well, maybe because there's not much else to do around here. Could be sort of like community gathering places, or something."

I sniffed. That didn't sound right at all. In my world, a bar of any type was generally an establishment to be avoided.

Rick turned onto a side street. "I know there's a fast food-type restaurant around here somewhere. I remember getting a great burger here once when I was a teenager."

"That was a long time ago."

"Yeah, but it doesn't look like much has changed."

The side street was lined with a few more businesses and some interspersed houses. Some of the houses looked neat and well-tended, but many appeared ragged. All were diminutive.

"There it is—the Buffalo Shake Shack." Rick's cheerfulness and my depression were deepening in synch. "Hey, they still have the orange buffalo out front—isn't it great?" The chasm widened a few more inches.

He steered the truck into the parking lot of a dingy, metal-sided, quonset hut. A five-foot-high buffalo statue was poised in front of the door. It had a piteous grimace on its face, like it was about to throw up. Or maybe the look was more one of disgust over its own coat of peeling orange paint.

"I'm not sure about this."

"Haley, come on, you'll love it." He jumped out of the truck before I could protest further.

My doubts became stabbing blades of remorse when I saw that the menu board above the counter listed over a dozen breaded, deep-fried choices in addition to burgers with hammy names. Charmaine wouldn't have just blocked me from entering this place, she would have called the cops on me to keep me from going in. And I knew I would fully deserve to be arrested—eating this food would be a crime. I could feel the grease smell burrowing into my hair and clothing. I wanted to bolt, but of course, my bolting days were temporarily over, considering my newly acquired barrel-sized girth.

Two separate angel voices began whispering into each of my ears. One little angel on my shoulder was Lorna. She was saying, "Stay and eat something for the sake of honoring your husband. Nobody will die." The other angel was Charmaine. She was saying, "Get out—get out now! You'll be sacrificing your figure forever if you even think of consuming something from this food brothel!"

Rick was already in heaven. Life was so easy for him. "Hmm. I'll take a Brick-o-Beef burger with extra onion and a side of—wow, can't decide between the deep-fried mushrooms or the breaded ham slabs—" Rick frowned. "Oh, man, this is a hard decision. You go ahead and order, Haley. I have to think for a minute."

I paused to silently pray for courage and wisdom. The answer immediately arrived in the form of a compromise. "Do you have any salads?" I asked.

The ponytailed teen girl at the till smiled brightly. "Sure do. We have a large Bunkhouse salad with battered tomato wedges and fried cheese sticks or a smaller Line Shack side salad with plain vegetables."

I tightened my grip on my shield of faith. "I'll take the Line Shack, please."

"That's not much," Rick said. "You should eat something to boost baby growth again. At least get the Bunkhouse."

"The Line Shack will be fine, Rick." I spoke through clenched teeth.

Rick settled on the ham slabs and ordered a chicken-fried liver and onion sandwich to go for Win. He didn't say another word to me until we had gotten our food.

"Haley, you've been sort of snitty all week. What's your problem?" Burger juices dripped down his chin as he talked.

"Problem? Me? You're the one who is being completely insensitive to my emotional needs. I'm seriously questioning whether or not we should have taken this trip at all and…"

I trailed off in an attempt to lower my voice for the sake of the farm-type family that was sitting two tables away. It looked like the three young children had enough to worry about without having a loud lady shouting near them. The whole family was wearing ugly, muddy, smelly boots and the mother, heaven forbid, was wearing suspenders over a polo shirt. It was such a perfect Fashion Fail that I felt physical pain at not having Hal to capture the moment for me.

Like their parents, the kids all had pieces of straw clinging to their hair and shirts. Worse yet, they were eating corn dogs and sharing a platter of ham slabs. I was appalled that the parents could be that careless with their children's nutrition. *I will never, ever serve toxic food to my child or anyone else's for that matter.* I wondered if child neglect ran rampant in farming communities.

I resumed talking in a quieter voice. "I can't help it if I have reservations about being here."

"Honestly, Haley, it doesn't seem like you have reservations about this place; it's kind of more like, um, you have—oh, what's a word you'd use—"

I glared at him. I certainly wasn't going to help supply vocabulary to be used against me.

"—denigrations. That's the one. Put-downs, criticisms, you know? I know you're pregnant and don't feel well, but you're acting sort of superior or something."

I was incensed. "What? Superior? You're being completely unfair. I'm noticing differences between here and home, that's all!"

Rick stayed subdued for the rest of our time together. Our stop at the town's only grocery store did not go any better. I shouldn't have been surprised that it was small, dim, and not well stocked. I hadn't even been in Grassview for a full day, and I was already longing to be back where stores were spacious and modern.

"Do you have any other restaurants in town besides the Buffalo Shack?" I asked yet another ponytailed female checker as she rang up our groceries.

"Yeah, there's the Chops n' Chicks Diner and Debbie's Pie Hut. Probably the best food in town, though, is at Bison Jack's."

"The bar on Main Street?" I asked.

"Yep. They have great ribs."

Back in the truck, Rick finally spoke. "Maybe we should try Bison Jack's next time." His tone was quiet and conciliatory.

"What? I wouldn't be caught dead in that dump of a bar—ever!"

11

"Haley!" *Honk. Honk.*

The sore spots on my hand flared when I slammed the curling iron down on the bathroom counter and yanked the cord from the wall. I rubbed the side of my palm, reminding myself to ask the doctor about the persistent injury at my next appointment.

Honk. "Haley!"

Rick's impatience was downright silly. Honking the horn and yelling from the driveway could never speed up my hairstyle engineering process, especially if my results were less than satisfying. I was striving extra hard to look good for church and hoped my chic hairdo would replace some of the fashion credibility that my expanding giant mushroom physique was stealing from my appearance. I was also trying to windproof my hair with the right combination of my special products.

To make things worse, Win had emerged from her bedroom wearing an outrageous dress. It was made of a loud, scarlet bandana print material and had a fitted bodice with a gigantic crinoline-supported full skirt. It was like a knee length hoop skirt, flaring out several feet on all sides of her. I was taken aback partly because, except for the hats, Win typically dressed appropriately for an elderly woman and partly because the dress itself was simply horrific. Walking into a new church with that dress beside me would pretty much kill any good impression that I hoped to make.

Win had gone on to explain that many years previous she had a dream in which she was called to be a walking word picture of her joy in the Lord. She decided that meant that she should always wear clothes that illustrated her heart when she worshiped publicly. She couldn't find the right attire, however, until one of her neighbors passed away the previous year. The woman who died happened to have been a world champion square dancer and bequeathed all her special dance dresses to Win. Win said that the minute she saw the dresses, they said, "Rejoice!" and "Glory!" and "Hallelujah!" The bandana one was the "Redeemed!" one.

I wondered how my dad would have interpreted the binary nature of Win's dresses. Her clothing choice seemed to irreverently turn his postulate inside out. Would he have sent her back in the house to change? But then, how could he argue with joy?

I could certainly argue with it, though, because I decided Win's joy was really just pure insanity. I wanted to send her back in the house to change into pajamas and wait for a little bus to come and haul her off to the funny farm.

From its perch on the kitchen windowsill, the silly weather station warbled a tinny rendition of John Denver's song, "Sunshine On My Shoulder." I brushed past it on my way out the door, fighting the temptation to take it outside with me and throw it at Rick through his open car window. I felt the need to apologize to both my mom and Mr. Denver. I was sure that song was never intended to be so grossly misused.

Feeling the warm sunshine on my shoulder, I stomped outside with one hand shielding my hair and stoically boarded Gracie's tanker. After weighing our transportation options, we had decided that the car would allow more room for Win's dress than the truck cab would. It wasn't an easy decision, though. Choosing between the two outlandish vehicles was like having to decide between a root canal or a colonoscopy. Win had offered to ride on the flatbed again, but I had nipped that asininity in the bud.

A wind gust evilly grabbed my hair, sending it straight up, just as I took my hand away to open the car door.

"Errgh," I growled, lowering my body into the king-sized bench seat. I pulled down the visor mirror to assess the damage while Rick sailed in reverse down the driveway.

For the umpteenth time, I choked back tears. Everything seemed to be working against me. Remembering Gracie's assurances about the friendliness of her small church did nothing to calm me. In fact, it almost seemed to make me feel worse. There was no where to hide in a small group. People would notice us, and I wanted to present my best face, like I always did at home.

Win leaned forward from the back seat and patted my shoulder. "You know, dear, I saw an ad on the back of the TV Digest for something that just might work for you. I think it was called something like 'The Pump-Up' and was some sort of poofer for the crown of one's head. It's a insert that goes underneath the top layer of your hairstyle and gives your hair that high look that you like on the back of your head. It might be worth a try."

"Hmph," I said and pushed the visor back into place. I was edgy and irritable and not at all in the mood for chitchat.

"Wait a minute—" she snapped her fingers, "actually I have something even better, and I happened to bring it with me. It's called a Preservadoo and it really works."

Needless to say, Win lived in a perpetual state of chitchat, regardless of the mood of those around her. It was a form of breathing for her. She artlessly continued. "Last year, when I was hiking along the Oregon coast, I was blind-sided by a huge breaker and completely soaked, but I was wearing the Preservadoo helmet and my hair stayed perfectly coiffed underneath it. It's one contrivance that really does live up to its advertising claims."

"Sure, why not?" I practically screamed my reply. Like someone glibly pulling off the radiator cap on an overheated engine, Win had pulled out one more idiocy at exactly the wrong time. Rick hunched down self-protectively as he continued driving. He was likely bracing himself for yet another one of my emotional roller coaster car plummets.

"Okay, *sure*," I spewed shrilly, "I'll wear the silly helmet and you sit on the back of the flatbed. We can decorate it like a float. We can be a freak show, parading down Main Street on our way to church. Yeah, let's do it! No—wait a minute—I could sit on the flatbed! Oh, that's perfect. The incredible helmeted fat lady! I could sit up there and throw candy at the gawkers. Maybe they'd throw money back at me—"

"Haley, please," Rick almost ran us into a ditch as he tried to span the width of the front seat to pat my tummy while he drove. His voice sounded like it was on the other side of an auditorium. The baby suddenly hit my rib hard, like she was in cahoots with her daddy. "Haley, you need to calm down. Things aren't that bad and you look great."

"I don't look great, so stop appeasing me!"

Now it was Rick's turn to get mad.

"It's not all about you, you know. There are others that are as affected by stuff as you are," he glanced back at Win through the rearview mirror, "but they, we, choose to see the good side of life. I mean, you really are acting—" he stopped himself in mid-sentence.

I bristled. "Go ahead, say it."

"Okay—Haley, you're being mean and ungrateful."

"Oh, so yesterday I'm superior and today I'm ungrateful! Who are you to judge me?"

Rick's face flushed, but he wisely didn't reply as he drove the last few blocks and guided our vessel into the church parking lot. The smooth wave-like motion of the car's suspension system only served to amplify the silence that once again flooded our space.

Predictably, Win's sanguine denial popped her to the surface like a plastic fishing bobber as she exited the car.

"Ooh, I see that the travelers have all made it to their summer homes," she announced as she scanned the sky. "The heavenly highway is empty now."

"You're right. The sky is totally clear today." Rick, too, looked up at the sky.

How can he do that? How can he just switch his attention from our glaring problems to trivial outside matters in mere seconds? Is our relationship utterly unimportant to him?

Watching Rick and Win crane their necks to gawk at the empty sky brought to mind a sermon that Mitch had preached a few weeks earlier at Artos and Ichthus. He had quoted the passage in Matthew where Jesus accused the Pharisees of knowing how to interpret the weather by reading the signs in the sky, but refused to see the signs right in front of them—the indicators that pointed to Jesus as their Messiah. It was obvious that Rick was paying too much attention to stuff that wasn't really important and neglecting what was right in front of him—me.

Rick looked beyond the parking lot. The church was on the edge of town and bordered a vast area of cropland. "Wow! look at all that new wheat."

I refused to validate his wheat comment, concentrating instead on fluffing my staticky hair while trying to dampen my exasperation. I noticed *the sign that we had parked beside. BUFFALO JUMP COMMUNITY CHURCH—hmm, I thought that buffalo were too big to jump. But then, until yesterday I hadn't been aware that badgers dueled...and until last week, I hadn't been aware that I was married to such an unfeeling and judgmental man.*

◆━◆◆◆━━

The church's interior was dim and smelled of damp wood. Fake knotty pine paneling covered the walls and rows of rickety wooden pews lined the narrow sanctuary, their scanty seat depth testifying to an era when people's backsides reflected leaner times and larger fortitude. An unsettling number of white and ecru doilies were haphazardly strewn about on almost every flat surface in the room. Dusty silk flower arrangements stood in mismatched vases on top of more doilies on the sides of the altar. I wondered if Gracie, or someone of her ilk, had been in charge of church decorating. I also wondered if a person could end up sporting a doily if they sat too long in one place.

"Let's see, before I get to the sermon, it looks like I have a couple announcements in front of me here," the freckled boy-pastor said as he took his place behind the oak pulpit.

I was surprised to see that the young, skinny redhead who had greeted us at the door was the shepherd of this hugging little flock. He was wearing black jeans and a pearly snapped, paisley western shirt with a silver medallioned bolo tie. Like most of the men in the building, he also wore cowboy boots. He didn't look much older than a teenager himself, and in spite of, or maybe because of, his cowboy garb, I could picture my students classifying him as a geek.

"Wow, we have a busy week ahead," he said while squinting to read a small square of paper in front of him. "It looks like we're having our annual spring potluck picnic in the church parking lot on Wednesday night. Bring side dishes and desserts—" he looked up and grinned, "—ooh, I put in my votes for Joanne's double-mayo potato salad and Dora's caramel fudge balls. And—"

"Amen!"

"Amen, preach it Brandon!" Unnamed voices from the pews chimed in, inciting a round of laughter.

"—and, Ken and Charla are bringing Pofu!" Pastor Brandon proclaimed. Cheers and applause broke out from all sides of the room. It didn't feel like church.

Forgetting that I should still be mad at my clapping husband, I leaned over and whispered, "Did they say, 'tofu'?" I couldn't imagine that members of this particular subculture would cheer over tofu.

"No, I think they said, 'Pofu.' I think it's a person," Rick whispered back.

"Hmm, sounds African. Maybe he's a missionary." Whoever Pofu was, he was certainly popular.

Brandon continued, looking straight at us. "For those of you who don't know, Ken and Charla Carter own the Buffalo Shake Shack in town, and Pofu is what we call their Portable Outdoor Frying Unit. It always makes our picnics complete," he grinned again, "and tasty."

I had to keep myself from grimacing like the orange buffalo. It sounded like a church picnic in that place could seriously endanger the attendees' health. Double-mayo potato salad, caramel fudge balls, and dripping deep-fat fried everything else was simply downright irresponsible. I hoped that Rick would not want to go. Unfortunately the admiration and glee on his face, and the fact that he was licking his lips indicated otherwise.

I glanced around at all the young children in the pews with their parents. Again, parents would be exposing their children to fatty, toxic foods. Did they just not care? Or…did they just not know?

I thought back to my prayer for a purpose in Grassview. Was it possible that not all my hopes had burned up with the van? *Might I still be able to garner an important job for myself here, in spite of all the setbacks and dis-*

appointing circumstances? Hmm—is this why I'm here, Lord—to teach other women about healthy, organic food choices? My roller coaster descent slowed slightly.

"One last announcement—don't forget about Thursday's Bible study luncheon, ladies. It's at noon, right, Patti?" Brandon asked.

"Right-o, Pastor," a pleasant voice from the back of the room answered.

Rick turned toward me. "That might be a nice thing for you to go to," he mentioned quietly.

I agreed, thinking that visiting with some of the church ladies would be a refreshing change from Win. I also knew that I wasn't going to be able to get through the summer in Grassview without prayer support. And more importantly, this luncheon might be the means that God would use to get me in touch with the people I was assigned to inform. *God must have a plan for me after all. Maybe I should have waited to send that email to Danielle.* I was on my way up again.

"Now let's get on with our study on the teachings of Jesus in the book of Matthew," Pastor Brandon said while opening his Bible. "We're looking at some of the characteristics of the Pharisees of Jesus' time. Remember how last week we studied the history of the scribes and the Pharisees? Well, I thought this week we could take a look at how their nit-pickin' the law to pieces made more of a problem than it ever solved."

His demeanor became more serious. "Matthew twenty-three contains Jesus' long list of bad Pharisee behavior. We'll end up studying the whole thing later on, but for today's message, I'm going to use Mark twelve, verses thirty-eight through forty. Mark's gospel sort of sums up part of what Matthew wrote about Jesus' biggest charges against the Pharisees. Turn with me there, please."

From our cinderblock-soft pew seat in the back, I watched every ponytailed or permed head and every leathery neck look down as they riffled through their Bibles. I nervously fingered the laminated bookmarks that had been presented to us as "newcomer's gifts" and felt a little embarrassed that I didn't have a Bible with me. It made me look like an unbeliever. These people might assume that I wasn't a dedicated Christian.

What they didn't know was that I actually owned a more sophisticated Bible than all of theirs put together. Buried within precious Hal's circuitry was a whole seminary of translations, exegesis, commentaries and studies. When I held Hal in my hands, I held all the authority and power of the Word of God. I was a true Bible scholar, but unfortunately, nobody in that little dumpy church would know until Hal was safely returned to me. I prayed that he was already sitting in the outgoing mail department of the repair center, ready to be sent out first thing Monday morning.

The church service itself was about as low-tech as anything I had seen since I was a kid. There had been no polished band to accompany the worship music and no computerized powerpoint system to display song lyrics and inspirational photos. There was only an elderly lady pawing at the keys of a dusty organ, and a girl of no more than eight or nine playing along on a harmonica, of all things. Indistinct overhead transparencies projected the songs onto a tablecloth tacked to the back wall. The middle-aged man who led the singing cried his way through every song, but nobody seemed to notice. Yet in spite of the anomalous worship arrangement, I was surprised at the exuberance of the congregation's singing. The few dozen sounded like multitudes as they belted out old gospel hymns.

Win was sitting near the front with an old friend who had spotted her the moment we walked in. Naomi Stanton's baritone voice echoed through the musty little sanctuary when she saw Win. The tall lady hugged tiny Win nearly to death and escorted her around the perimeter of the church, introducing her to everyone as her "best friend from prehistoric times." I also overheard Naomi explaining that Uncle Hank was her second or third cousin and that her friendship with Win was somehow responsible for bringing Gracie and Hank together all those eons ago.

Naomi looked like no other old person I had ever seen. Her cap of white hair, sharp, beakish nose, and intense eyes reminded me of an eagle. Even when she smiled, her eyes stayed serious, almost foreboding. She had to have been at least Win's age, yet she carried her broad shouldered, lean frame smoothly with a long, deliberate stride. She wore a light green western shirt and faded jeans with a tooled leather belt and a tarnished silver belt buckle that had a slice of a polished rock set in its middle.

I had never known an elderly lady to dress that way for church. With scuffed boots and dirty fingernails, she looked like she had just come in from a barn. I frowned when I watched her take her seat up front. It seemed somehow presumptuous for someone in such irreverent clothes to take one of the front pews. To me, it would have made more sense for her to slip quietly, maybe even apologetically, into a back pew.

Granted, my friends at Artos & Ichthus sometimes wore casual clothing or even jeans to church, but they were still clean-cut and stylish. They still carried an air of respectability into the church with them. Maybe we didn't have barns or livestock to attend to before church, but even those of us who went to the gym early on Sunday morning wouldn't have shown up in our sweaty workout clothes. It wouldn't have been right. Yet, for all her shabbiness, I didn't consider Naomi a Fashion Fail candidate, and I wasn't sure why.

I decided right then that I didn't like Naomi. There was something—I wasn't sure what, but something—that was not right with her. Normally, I would have found her more serious demeanor to be refreshing compared to Win, but in Naomi's case, my instincts were alerting me to something almost sinister in the older lady's piercing gaze. Win, delighted with her unexpected reunion, was gleefully oblivious to any toxic qualities that might be lurking underneath Naomi's kindly façade. An odd, momentary feeling of protection for Win hit me, but I dismissed it. Win's weirdness protected her more than I ever could.

Brandon cleared his throat and began to read. "…Jesus said, 'Watch out for the teachers of the law. They like to walk around in flowing robes and be greeted in the marketplaces, and have the most important seats in the synagogues and the places of honor at banquets. They devour widows' houses and for a show make lengthy prayers. Such men will be punished most severely.'"

"Folks," Brandon looked up, making eye contact with different people throughout the front of the sanctuary as he spoke, "this is serious business, and isn't that much of a stretch to see how we can be a lot like those ol' Pharisees—right here, right now. I'm gonna start by throwing out the three words that summarize the Pharisees' biggest problem."

At Artos & Ichthus, this is where Pastor Mitch would have clicked on his powerpoint remote and brought up visual sermon aids to complement his teaching. He would have used a creative, catchy font for his sermon title, and clicked to the first scripture reference. His three summary words would be next. Of course, Mitch, with advanced seminary and communications degrees, was obviously much more highly educated than Brandon, so I knew I needed to lower my expectations for learning anything in this little country church. I was missing my home church already.

With his voice as his only teaching tool, Brandon kept going. "Appearances…appearances…appearances. There—there's your three words. I'm kinda talkin' like a realtor now, right? Location, location, location…ha!"

The congregation chuckled. Rick laughed. I didn't. I hoped simple Brandon could at least preach something to speak to Rick's heart. Knowing what I did about the Pharisees, I guessed that Brandon would have said the three words were something like, "critical," "mean-spirited," and "judgmental." I wanted Rick to see that he was being like a Pharisee—that he was being unkind to me and that he needed to apologize for it so we could get our marriage back on track.

Unfortunately Rick's expression remained pleasant and attentive as Brandon continued.

"But it's true—the way they appeared on the outside was the Pharisees' biggest concern. Those ol' Jewish leaders had been waiting for so long for the Messiah to show up that they must have forgotten what they should be watchin' out for. They forgot about how much God loved them and had provided for them over the centuries and instead thought they were supposed to beat each other at pleasin' Him. So they decided whoever did the most perfect job of obeying the rules would be God's favorite. But then they purposely made the rules impossible for the average workin' Joe to keep. That way they could always come out on top.

"Their teaching had become poisonous, in a way. That's probably why both Jesus and John called the Pharisees vipers at different times. They were teachin' stuff that was actually leading people farther from God instead of closer to him. They were teachin' that the Messiah would return to earth as a great political leader for the nation of Israel. They just assumed that this long-awaited Messiah was going to come as a mighty king—as a great and fancy military general with a big group of roadies to set up and tear down his production stage each night. And the Pharisees saw themselves as the ones He would choose as His opening act."

The room was hushed with concentration as each person drew their own private mental picture from Brandon's words. Without a computer screen to illustrate anything for me, my imagination took off on its own too.

"These guys spent all their time grooming themselves to be the holiest, the smartest, and the best-lookin' by far to make sure that they would be chosen to be up on stage with the Messiah Act when it came to town. That wrong expectation led those guys to focus only on outside stuff and to forget completely that God wanted His people's insides—their hearts—to be ready for him. And that's where they missed the boat. While they were watchin' the ocean horizon for a huge, fancy showboat to pull into port, Jesus came, quietly drifting down the Jordan river on a rickety little wooden raft. And His opening act—John the Baptist—was just a weird guy that ate bugs, wore clothes made with camel's hair, and sang a serious song without a microphone. The Pharisees missed the true boat completely because they wouldn't have been caught dead catching a ride on Jesus' crude little raft. It was beneath them, or so they thought. "

Brandon looked back down at his Bible. "Mark twelve, thirty-eight lists several things that resulted from them missin' the boat. The real three words that I'm preaching on today are, 'ostentation, pride, and hypocrisy.'"

Brandon surprised me by pulling out such a good vocab word. *Ostentation. That's a pretty big word for such a small town preacher.*

"First, ostentation." He lifted up a piece of paper and read directly from it. "That word means, 'showiness, trying to impress others.'" He put the paper back down and fixed his gaze on the congregation.

"The flowing robes that Jesus mentions were special outfits the Pharisees wore that were different from everyone else's. BTW—that's texting language for By The Way, in case you don't know—"

He laughed at himself again. It was annoying. Rick, of course, laughed and poked me with his elbow. I frowned.

"—the name 'Pharisee' actually means 'the separate.' They were known for purposely keeping themselves separated from anyone and anything that they considered unclean or inferior to them. They thought their clothing indicated that they were special and supposedly specially blessed by God. They took pride in looking different."

My senses were alerted. I hadn't heard teaching quite like this before. I knew I needed to be careful, to use my powers of discernment and not be swayed by false or misguided doctrine. I knew my dad would certainly not just swallow this guy's words without question.

"The Pharisees also liked to use fancy language and tried to impress everyone with long, wordy prayers. They likely said those 'preachin' prayers' that I'm guilty of saying sometimes myself when I pray in public and start saying stuff for others to hear instead of just talkin' to God directly at that moment. And sometimes, it's not just when I pray, but when I'm saying things about God in order to make myself sound all spiritual to other people that I'm talkin' like a Pharisee. That's P-R-I-D-E—pride, folks. And pride is a doozy of a sin in itself. Ostentation always leads to pride. There's no way around it."

I was getting more annoyed with each sentence he spoke. He wasn't a very good speaker. His overuse of sentence fragments and colloquialisms was too distracting to keep an English teacher connected with his intent. I wanted him to finish so I could go to the bathroom.

"When Jesus says they 'devoured widows' houses,' he was referring to the Pharisees' money swindling practices. They would act so pious that they could get poor widows to entrust their houses and estates to their cause. Those crafty guys would end up getting control of all the widows' money in the end. In Matthew twenty-three, verse twenty-five, Jesus says that they 'clean the outside of the cup and dish, but inside they are full of greed and self-indulgence.' Apparently, some of them played around with people's money to fund their own ostentation."

The baby shifted inside me, forcing me to straighten my back. I hoped Brandon was almost done. He wasn't.

"Because generation after generation of religious leaders had become so used to only worryin' about how they looked, they completely forgot about the source of sin—their insides, their hearts. When the Pharisees talked about the 'tradition of the elders,'—the ages-old rules and rituals they revered—they didn't know that not everything their elders had passed down was good. Their respected elders had also passed on to them the really wrong idea that as long as they looked good, they were good. That opened the door for them to commit fraud and crime and not feel bad about it. It also led to hypocrisy. And hypocrisy's as bad as pride.

"In Matthew, Jesus outright calls the Pharisees hypocrites. I looked up the Greek word for hypocrite, and saw that it comes from roots that refer to stage actors. One dictionary even said that the same word was used for Greek and Roman actors that played parts on a stage wearing big masks that had a voice altering device in them. Actors, people—actors in masks! That's what Jesus called some of the supposedly-godliest people of His day."

Brandon paused, then quieted his tone. "Hypocrisy is basically just pretending to be something on the outside that you're really not on the inside. Like when Clint Eastwood played Dirty Harry in the old movies. I doubt Clint was ever in his life as cool and smooth as Harry Callahan the cop. But ol' Clint made his outsides look so much like his character that we all thought he was Dirty Harry on the inside. And that's all we care about when we're watchin' the movie."

Brandon paused to smile. "Okay, okay—now don't start getting on my case about watching violent old movies with bad language in them. At least I'm honest about it!"

He quieted again, then stopped smiling. "But folks, life isn't a movie, you know? We can't play around with our relationship with God."

He stayed silent for a few more seconds before he went on, saying that the Pharisees' hypocrisy resulted in a bad habit of examining everyone else's behavior, while completely ignoring their own sin. He said they crowed like grouchy old roosters about the little speck of sawdust they might see in someone's eye but paid no attention to the fact that they had huge wooden beams sticking out of their own eyes.

When Brandon described them as, "Big ol' beams like the ones that hold up a barn roof or maybe like the ones used to build the cross they killed Jesus on," I thought that he was finally getting somewhere. I glanced discreetly over at Rick, hoping for a glimmer of conviction to show on his face. I wanted Rick to see how wrong he was for judging me as superior and critical. He looked quite comfortable.

"So now, people," Brandon raised his voice, "what do you think is the cure for pride, hypocrisy, or judgmentalism? Hmm? Well, Jesus tells us in Matthew, chapter seven."

Bible pages riffled again. Rick turned to the passage in his Bible and scooted it over for me to look on. I didn't want to look at his Bible—he preferred a translation that I didn't approve of.

Brandon read, "'Do not judge, or you too will be judged. For in the same way you judge others, you will be judged, and with the measure you use, it will be measured to you.' This is a pretty direct—it's a natural law, just like the law of gravity. Like sowin' and reapin,' you get back what you give out. There's no better way to learn to stop doing something wrong than to have to take a dose of your own bitter medicine.

"Jesus wasn't saying that we shouldn't judge, or decide, between right and wrong, or healthy and harmful—stuff like that. He was referring to hypocritical judging. Like I said, that's the kind of judgin' we do when we forget about our own sin and just look at other people's instead. Doing that is dangerous—it's like throwing out a big ol' heavy boomerang that goes way out and then, without warning, it turns back and ends up conking you hard, right on your own head," he said, smacking his forehead with his fist.

I watched Rick shift in his seat. *Finally, we're getting somewhere now.* I sat perfectly still but inwardly started to cheer Brandon on, like he was aiming his basketball from the free throw line in the last seconds of the game.

"That's the cure. That's the boomerang—whatever you hypocritically throw out there concerning others will absolutely come back on you in one way or another. If you're mean to someone at some point, someone will be mean to you. If you refuse to forgive, someone will withhold forgiveness from you. The situations may be miles or years apart, but you will get back on yourself all the judgments you send out. You end up bindin' yourself to the same sentence you pronounce on others."

Brandon added that the Pharisees' boomerang came back to conk them in the form of Jesus. They would receive the same scrutiny from Jesus that they had been doling out to everyone else. Instead of repenting and letting Jesus love them and change them, though, they got mad and started plotting to "take him out."

"If we don't act like the Pharisees, though, and instead take our whoopin' from our judgments like a smart kid would, we end up humbled—" he paused to inhale deeply, "and humility is a sweet, nice thing—"

He abruptly stopped talking and thrust his head up with his eyes closed. "—mm, I just caught a whiff of ginger."

He shook his head and looked down at an elderly woman sitting in the third pew. "Dora, is that your gingerbread doughnuts callin' at me from the coffee room?"

"Yesiree, Pastor—made a fresh batch first thing this morning," Dora replied.

Brandon's expression changed instantly from serious to childlike. "Got the butter and cream cheese frosting on 'em?"

"Yep."

"Oooowee, doooeeey! Guess it's quittin' time, folks!"

He promptly closed his Bible and announced that he would continue his study of the Pharisees in his next sermon and wanted each parishioner to think during the week about ways that they might be acting like a Pharisee themselves.

I snuck a peek at Rick. He seemed momentarily lost in thought.

My heart lifted. Maybe Rick was feeling conviction as the Holy Spirit washed over his troubled and fault-finding soul. How silly of me to lose faith, even briefly, in God's ability to change hearts and heal relationships. Brandon's voice faded as my mind wandered. I was warmed by a vision of me magnanimously forgiving Rick as he humbly confessed his sin of judgment against me. I pictured his adoring eyes, looking up at me in gratitude for the selfless mercy I would extend toward him.

I couldn't help it. I reached over and squeezed Rick's hand. He squeezed back and smiled at me. Just before Brandon started to deliver the benediction, a young woman near the back stood and said that something needed to be clarified concerning one of the announcements.

"I'm sorry, Pastor," she said, "but I think you forgot to mention where we're going to meet for this month's ladies Bible study luncheon."

The pastor laughed. "Go ahead, tell us, Patti—we wouldn't want you hard-workin' gals to miss out on your fellowship time."

"Ladies," the young woman raised her voice, "we'll be meeting at noon on Thursday at Bison Jack's Saloon. See y'all then!"

12

Once I recovered from the shocking news that the ladies met in a dumpy tavern for their Bible study, I started formulating The Plan. My new purpose energized me, even in the middle of mushrooming pregnancy misery. I now second-guessed all the second-guessing I had been doing about whether or not we should have come to Montana in the first place. The people of Buffalo Jump Community Church needed help, and I was now convinced that God had brought me in from the outside to provide the fresh perspective they required to get on track. I certainly knew how to combat unhealthy eating—it was just a matter of education—and educate I could. As a teacher, I automatically started thinking of what information I was to convey and the most creative way in which to convey it. My level ride was promising to turn upward again.

The potluck, which I had scorned at first, now seemed like the optimal occasion for a hands-on introductory lesson. As often happens when God is moving in someone's heart, I opened Rick's Bible to a random scripture on the way home and took it as a divine mandate for my nutrition mission. It was in the last chapter of Genesis where Joseph spoke to his brothers about their betrayal of him,

"You intended to harm me, but God intended it for good,
to accomplish what is now being done, the saving of many lives."

To me, that verse said that I could take that harmful potluck cholesterolfest and turn it into an opportunity in which many lives could be changed, or even indirectly, saved.

My vision enlarged, my borders stretched, and I began to compare myself to a relief worker in a developing nation, working to teach the underinformed. Except, on this mission field, I didn't have to worry about malaria or squalid outdoor facilities. In my new calling, Gracie's place now seemed luxurious. It was a base of important operations and a comfortable one at that. *Thank you for a shower and clean toilet, Lord. I promise to serve You well here.*

I got right to work. Even though both Rick and Win showed no signs of repentance from their respective sins against me, I knew that I would have to let it all go and love them anyway. It wouldn't be easy—Rick was still acting too happy to be feeling any conviction for his accusations against me, and Win had still not said a word about being responsible for destroying my mother's car. I just couldn't get over how a person could do something so injurious to others and not take responsibility for it. But I knew that God was calling me to a higher standard now, and so I did my best to be civil to both perpetrators.

The Plan first involved concocting a super healthy, yet super tasty side dish to contribute to the picnic. When people begged for the recipe, I could provide it on handouts that included nutrition information about that dish and a brief write-up on how to prepare other wholesome and appealing meals. I could sneak in a few facts and statistics about health risks associated with high fat diets. Maybe I could even add fun graphics or a word find puzzle that would appeal to children. It was all entirely doable.

As I turned on Hank's computer in the dining room, I forced myself to exercise patience with the absurdly slow dial-up internet connection. The chattering and chirping of the dialing signal made the computer sound like a birdcage. I drummed my fingers on the computer desk, wanting the busy birds to stop flitting around and get out of the way of the crucial stream of information that I needed to tap into. Every cell in my body ached to have Hal back.

I had to admit that Hal wouldn't have worked well in this prairie desert deceivingly named Montana anyway. Some checking around revealed that the closest wireless signal was thirty miles away in Range City. The high-speed cable option was ruled out by the fact that only the Grassview residents who had cable TV could get that piped into their homes. Hank and Gracie's place, being two miles outside the city limits was out of cable reach. A company that provided DSL service informed me that they had not bothered to adapt the local phone lines to their option because of such a high cost for such a small population. Cell phone service was too spotty to allow cell card internet, and a satellite dish was too outrageously priced to even consider as a short-term solution for my summer internet needs. Moreover, even if a dish was cheaper, Rick said he wouldn't want to mess with Gracie and Hank's marital bliss. I would have to make my peace with dial-up. Like a stinky outhouse in a campground, it was better than nothing.

Finally after six tries and four and a half minutes, the birds quieted and the dial-up connected. Before I started my recipe search, I went to Facebook. I had been out of contact with my social circle for exactly four interminable days.

Predictably my home page was plastered with dozens of posts. I would have normally delved right in, reading each person's message and responding to them all. Having such an important ministry task awaiting me on this day, though, combined with the painful wait between clicks, caused me to check only the updates of my closest friends.

I did put a few extra minutes into my own update, though. My friends often complimented me on my good writing skills, so I had a reputation to uphold. I wrote:

"It's clear that we were, indeed, swimming against the enemy's tide in our trip to Grassview. Satan pulled out every weapon in his arsenal, including the decimation of our vehicle to keep us from getting here safely. But we forged ahead and almost immediately a ministry opportunity presented itself. Pray for me as I start teaching the hungry locals about godly nutrition practices; the people here seem to eat as though there's no tomorrow. (Which there might not be for some, considering the amount of fat they consume.) The locals are friendly but obviously backwards, and not just in their food choices. BTW: I'll be posting more Fashion Fails soon. :)"

I added both Gracie's landline and Rick's cell phone numbers to the end of my status in case someone wanted to call me and clicked "post" to submit my report. It felt satisfying to be back in the game.

I typed in the address of my favorite recipe website. It was good that I wasn't searching for emergency information. A life could be lost in the amount of time it took for the home page to show up. I found myself staring with baited breath at the little green rectangles that crawled ever so slowly through their box on the bottom tool bar. It was worse than waiting for an off-key performer to stop singing.

It took a full half hour for me to complete my search, but it was worth the time. I found a recipe for a special asparagus/bulgur/crab salad that would be just the ticket. This dish utilized fresh crab meat for protein, something that the landlocked Montanans probably didn't get much of and something that I could easily procure, even in the hinterlands of Grassview. All it would take is an email to Josh. I knew he could easily overnight a pound or two of ice-packed Maryland Blue crab meat to Gracie's house.

The best part of using seafood in this dish, though, was that when people tried the recipe for themselves, they could substitute locally-caught river fish for the crab meat. That fit in perfectly with my "Eat Green, Eat Lean, Eat Local" theme.

The bulgur wouldn't be a problem, either, because I brought a bag of it with me. Before we left home, I put a box together of some nonperishable food items, thinking that access to whole foods could be limited in Montana. I now smiled at my foresight.

I could really see the hand of God working, though, when it came to the last main ingredient—asparagus. When I lamented out loud that the little grocery store in Grassview might not have quality fresh asparagus on hand, Win piped up with the exact and beautiful answer to my concern.

"Asparagus? Why this part of Montana is loaded with it this time of year," she said while peering over my shoulder at the recipe I had printed off.

"What do you mean, loaded with it?" I asked.

"Oh, it grows wild everywhere around here," Win exclaimed, "in the valley bottoms and in all the ditches along the county roads. In fact, this is the perfect time of year to find it!"

That cinched it for me. An abundant supply of a fresh, local, organic ingredient that Win was most happy to hunt out and harvest for me—it couldn't have worked out better. She skipped off right away, wearing a camouflage patterned hat and carrying a plastic bucket.

Before disconnecting the molasses internet pipeline, I typed out an email to my hairstylist, Josie. I was curious to hear if she knew anything about the Pump-Up hair poofer that Win talked about. It sounded silly…and yet my hair was not doing well in the windy climate. It needed a boost.

I spent the next hour carefully crafting my nutrition information sheets, then, as an afterthought, dialed back up the Web to check my email before I got off the computer altogether. There was plenty time to use the bathroom while the birds chirped.

This connection happened in less than four minutes. That encouraged me. Seeing that Josie had already replied encouraged me further. Drumming my fingers yet again, I daydreamed about getting my shiny, beefy hairstyle back while the little green bars did their lazy walk. I frowned, though, when I clicked on the subject line that she had simply entitled, "NO!" Her reply appeared in less than a minute. It said:

Haley—

Nice to hear from you. Funny—your name came up just yesterday in the shop. Your cousin, Polly, came in upon your sister's referral. Polly needed her hair done for an awards ceremony she had to go to. Wow—to think that Polly has already made her first million at such a young age! And to receive the Humanitarian Engineer of the

Year award on top of that…such an amazing story about how her software engineering project boosted an entire African nation's economy. Unbelievable—and how modest of you not to brag about your cousin!

Now, to answer your question—Do not, I repeat DO NOT use the 'Pump-Up' crown poofer. It is a dangerous product. I just got back from a hair emergency call in a small town where I helped detangle a Pump-Up disaster. Not enough time to go into detail, but basically a windstorm at a May Day parade twisted a lady's long hair around and around her Pump-Up so high that people thought she was one of the Shriner's auxiliary wives. Little kids started running up to her, begging for candy, and some old men tried to push her onto a miniature bike. They kept yelling for her to ride it into the street and do "the figure eight." Not only was she humiliated, but we had to cut a lot of her hair off to get the poofer out. It was one of the more awful hair tragedies that I've seen in my career. Please take heed—DO NOT order the Pump-up!

Peace out, Josie

I finished reading and sat back in my chair, feeling like I had just dodged a bullet. I was glad I had consulted an expert first. I vowed right there and then to never, ever again take any of Win's products or suggestions seriously. I would never be so desperate as to resort to that woman's foolishness. It was just too risky.

And what about Polly? No one in the family had said anything to me about her for years. The last I heard she was in a tech college somewhere and had won some sort of calculus quiz bowl competition. Mom had read it to me from a relative's Christmas letter. I remember laughing with Danielle over the fact that Polly's first place prize was a typical geek thing—a Star Trek movie collection set. *Hmm, a millionaire now?* Disquieted, I got up to put the teakettle on. I needed my herbal energy tea.

I had a lot of important work to do.

━━◆◆◆━━

I could feel Rick's phone vibrating in my jacket pocket as I walked over to the salad table but couldn't answer it at the moment. Both my hands were occupied with carrying the large crystal serving bowl that contained the creative ministry tool disguised as a healthful side dish. It was probably just Josh calling again anyway. He had tried earlier, but I couldn't take the time away from my task to call him back. I figured he was simply checking to make sure that the crab had arrived, so I made a mental note to return his calls later.

I was thankful that even though Grassview was beyond the reach of overnight express service, two-day delivery was still available. Josh had assured me that the crab was packed in dry ice and would weather the second day just fine. I had made up my mind to trust him on this, even if my rebellious younger brother had not always proven to be trustworthy.

As a part of my Christian witness, the asparagus/bulgur/crab salad was everything I had hoped it would be. I had worked on both its taste and presentation to craft a result that was worthy of its calling. Although it was my inspired brainchild, I knew that it was also the product of teamwork. Josh's crab was pungent and robust, while Win's contribution of wild asparagus stalks were delicate, tender, and tasty beyond imagination. Rick's support came in the form of printer-fixing expertise so the flyers could be printed, and Gracie, without even knowing it, had done her share by simply having such a brilliant glass bowl in her collection. I capped it all off with an artistic garnish. I tied the tiniest asparagus stalks into bundles that resembled wheat sheaves and placed them in a row pattern on top of the salad. A final spritz of lime chili dressing lent a wonderful bouquet intended to pique the eater's senses.

The handouts, on the other hand, were not as satisfactory as I would have liked. I couldn't get all the information that I wanted, and I wasn't happy with how the pictures looked when they printed off. I had worked as hard on them as I had on the salad, absorbed in the same intensity that I stepped into when I was developing a new test or curriculum for my class. I took these things seriously. Too seriously, Rick always said. But he didn't understand the responsibility I felt toward the jobs that I was assigned to. Second-rate results were not an option for me. Short on time, though, I ended up having to accept the flyers the way they were and pray that the message would come through.

Pushing aside a salami/bacon/iceberg lettuce slaw and a marshmallow/whipped cream/coconut ambrosia, I made room for my offering. It definitely outshone its table mates, proving that the healthiest choice need not be the homeliest.

Several ladies joined me at the table and commented on my "pretty" salad. I could only hope that they would try it and ask for the recipe. My recipe sheets were tucked neatly in a folder on the dash of the car, waiting to be utilized for the glory of God's kingdom. The other food choices were every bit as unwholesome as I anticipated. There was no end to the sticky gelatin salads and nary a morsel of fruit could be seen in, or even on, the creamy, fudgey, and buttery dessert concoctions that filled one sagging card table to its edges—a table that could finance many cardiologists' and dentists' vacations.

"Oh, look, Pofu's hot and ready to fry," one of the ladies said, pointing to a long, wooden trailer on which two, fifty-five gallon metal barrels were affixed.

My assumption that Pofu was a carnival-stand type, outdoor catering kind of fryer was bad enough, but the reality of this homemade atrocity was appalling. A series of hoses and valves connected the barrels to a giant propane tank, and two long-armed stands were stationed over each of the drums. Fryer baskets hung from the stands by chains that were attached to pulleys. Steam rose from the open tops of the charred, oil-stained drums, sending a sleazy smell on a furtive slide around the church parking lot. I wrinkled my nose, convinced that the apparatus would be put to better use in a nineteenth century oil refinery.

"What's on the menu for today, Ken?" someone shouted.

Ken, sensibly outfitted with a welding mask, long gloves, and industrial apron, shouted back, "Breaded cube steak cutlets and chicken-fried meatballs in this one," he pointed to the barrel on his left, "and batter coated mushrooms, cheese sticks, and onion rings in this one." He pointed to the barrel on his right.

"Yay, onion rings!" a young boy, standing beside me exclaimed.

My heart sunk for the poor child. *Was anyone looking out for his health? These entrees could make him quite ill. Don't these people know?* My next thought made me smile. *Of course they don't know—that's why I'm here, right Lord? To shine my light in this darkness.*

At least one person had the sense to take traffic cones and cordon off a wide space around the trailer. A splattered sign was put in front of the cones that read, "DANGER—HOT OIL, KEEP BACK." It was obvious that the food was dangerous on all counts.

Beside me stood a middle-aged lady who had introduced herself as Judy. She spoke glowingly of the Carter's benevolence. "Ken and Charla are some of the most generous people in our community. They could make a lot of money off Pofu, but they always donate their services instead to our local rodeos and school events."

I was not impressed. "People must eat a lot of fried food around here."

"Well, somewhat. Mostly just at Grassview's special gatherings, though." She looked beyond me and smiled wistfully. "I must say, we have had some interesting times with Pofu over the years. Ken has fried everything imaginable. One year, at the electric co-op barbecue, some guys skinned a entire pig and dredged it with corn meal, and lowered the whole thing—"

"Oh, excuse me," I hated to be rude, but I had to cut her off. It was either that or throw up on her shoes. For some reason, I was starting to feel queasy.

I went over to the side dish table where I saw two women standing over my salad. They had each taken a small scoop, and one put some on her child's plate. *Probably the only healthy thing that child will eat all day.* I was torn between quickly grabbing the info sheets out of the ca or staying to eavesdrop on their comments.

I stayed, pretending to watch the frying action while they talked. "Hmm, what is this?" asked the one I recognized as Patti.

"I'm not sure—I think the new gal brought it. Looks gourmet, maybe," a red-haired lady answered.

"Gourmet? Does it have some exotic ingredients?"

"Well, let's see—what's this fish stuff?" She chewed a bite. "Hmm, fishy."

I was surprised. *Fish stuff? Don't they know crab when they taste it? I paid an arm and a leg for that 'fish stuff'!*

"Yeah, fishy. It tastes a little strong, maybe." Patti poked at her portion with her fork. "What're the grains? They're not rice."

"I'm pretty sure it's bulgur. My health nut sister puts it in everything."

"What's bulgur? Is it exotic?"

"No, just wheat as far as I know."

"Wheat? Oh."

Both women looked out at the field behind the church, where the green rows of new wheat reached to the farthest horizon. In unison, they looked back at their plates..

"Hmm. Lots of asparagus too."

"Yep. This reminds me I should go out and get some before it's gone."

"Oh, it won't be gone for awhile. Bumper crop this year. Jake said he saw a huge bunch growing by the sewage treatment plant."

"Hmm. The new gal must not have had time to go grocery shopping." Patti might as well have kicked my coaster car herself. I was going down, yet again.

"Tastes okay, though."

"Yeah, and she dressed it up cute, too." Patti, glancing away from my salad, looked at a dish that had just arrived. She brightened and smiled. "Ooh, look—Bonnie brought her cheese and butter bread pudding! Better get some before it's gone."

"Oh, yeah, her Cheese Royale. Hurry, it's to die for!"

I was devastated. So much work. So much time. So much purpose. All down the drain in a matter of seconds. I lingered at the food line like a dejected puppy waiting for even the tiniest scrap to fall. All I needed was one, just one person to show interest in my salad and ask me about it. Surprisingly, it was the children who took the most. They seemed to like the looks of the little wheat sheaves. They played with them, though, instead of eating them, and didn't bother to ask for the recipe.

Rick finally came through the line, absentmindedly dishing his plate up while talking a mile a minute with the rancher beside him. I sadly watched as even my own husband passed over my special dish. I would not be enlightening the masses at this picnic, after all. Balancing a plate piled high with dripping meatballs, Rick followed his new friend over to a row of folding chairs and sat down. I sank into the chair next to him.

"Hi, Haley. Aren't you going to eat?" he sounded genuinely concerned. My fragile emotions were giving me mixed messages. Part of me wanted to just melt into his warm and protective arms, and part of me wanted to push his face down into his plate and squish it around in his meatballs.

"No, I'm not feeling well."

"Oh, dear, well, we don't have to stay long. After I finish eating, we can go whenever you want."

He turned to his friend and continued his conversation. "So, you're saying that Ken Carter made that fryer himself?"

"Oh, yeah. Ken and his sons can make anything. They reuse all kinds of scrap metal and junk and build whatever they need without ever havin' to buy new stuff."

Rick was in awe. "Wow, so they're really into recycling."

"Guess you could call it that. I just call it smart. And cheap," he laughed.

"So Ken did all the welding himself?"

"Yeah, he didn't make the winches, though. They're old engine hoists from his son's truck rebuilding shop. Work good as fry basket lifters."

"What about all the vegetable oil? That can't be cheap."

"You mentioned that recycling stuff—there's an old hippie guy in town who's always talkin' about the environment. Uses the word, 'green' a lot. Anyway, he got one of Ken's sons to help him convert an old, cheap econobox car into a cookin' oil burner."

"Wow! I read about that somewhere—you mean it burns vegetable oil instead of gas, right?" Rick was on the edge of his seat.

"Yep. He shares the cost of the oil with Ken. When the oil starts gettin' old, Ken drains it out and gives it to Spider—the hippie guy—and everybody's happy. He filters it through the legs of old jeans. Still works out to be lots cheaper than gas."

Rick looked starstruck, like he was talking to John Deere himself. "Amazing! But he probably can't take the car on long trips, right? I mean, would he have to go to burger joints to, um, gas up?"

The guy laughed. "Nope. He just carries some big cans of cookin' oil on a little trailer that he tows behind him when he has to drive too far from home. Works pretty slick...ha, 'scuse the pun."

"Ha, good one." Rick was enjoying this conversation way too much. "Wow, a cheap car that's good for the environment." He turned to me. "Haley, we need to look into this."

My glare was all the answer I would give. Inside my brain, though, I had plenty of feedback to offer. *Sure, I'll look into anything that a man named Spider has built. Seeing as how I'll apparently never be the answer to anyone's culinary dreams, I might as well tour the country in a rusting little McGreasy Mobile. Win can come along, too. It can be a traveling fondue fantasy for her and her snacks. She can fry crackers at every stop.*

"I need to go home now, Rick."

"Sure, Sweetie. I'll finish these last bites and go find Win. Meet you at the car."

I was really feeling sick to my stomach and really glad that my snappy little hybrid was locked safely up in our garage at home. Maybe I should have locked up some of me back there too. It was starting to feel like the real Haley could get lost somewhere out there in the land of Bad Hair, Bad Food, and Bar-based Bible Studies.

As I walked away, a huge wind gust whipped up a swirling dust devil right in the lot. The dirt covered my hair and stung my eyes. It dawned on me that Rick had left the car windows open. He had announced earlier that because we were now living in crime-free Montana, we could take a summer off from locking our vehicles. I rushed toward the station wagon as fast as my leaden body would allow, but was too late.

All my recipe sheets had flown directly out the passenger window and were soaring wildly like white birds that had been freed from a cage. Not a one had been asked for; and all my valuable information fluttered away, diving and swirling into the arms of the endless field. My project was now destined instead to rot and eventually nourish the soil of the very wheat whose nutrients it, in turn, extolled.

13

The rejection I suffered from the spurning of my salad would prove small when compared to the stab of horror that Josh's phone messages inflicted when I finally listened to them.

The first message simply said, "Sis, I have something important to tell you regarding the crab. Please call me back right away."

He had yelled his second message into the phone. "Hales—why haven't you called back? I accidentally sent you expired crabmeat. Do not eat the crab. I repeat, DO NOT EAT THE CRAB!"

Due to the time difference between Maryland and Montana, I got him out of bed when I did finally call him back. He snapped awake instantly when I said that it was too late—I had used the crabmeat in a salad that was served at a public function.

He proceeded to freak out, yelling a stream of incoherent sentences, punctuated several times with the words, "lawsuit" and "put us under." When I could finally get him to slow down and talk nicely, he said that he hadn't realized until Wednesday morning that he had made a huge mistake. When his coworker, Shelley, cleaned out the deli case, she set a tub of older crabmeat right beside the one that Josh had waiting on the counter to prepare for sending. In his rush, he grabbed the expired meat. It wasn't until the next day that he found the tub in the cooler with his markings on it, indicating that it was to be sent to Montana. It didn't take much investigating to find out what had happened.

When he got to that part, Josh resumed his ranting and incoherency. He chastised me for not returning his calls and bellowed that "there better not be any lawsuit-happy people in my new corner of the universe." I tried to keep my voice even and asked him how toxic the expired crab might be. He said that the crab wasn't necessarily rotten but that it was older than would be considered safe by the market's standards. When I asked him if it could make people sick, he answered with a vague, "maybe, maybe not." I gently reminded him that even if I didn't call back soon enough, he was responsible for sickening innocent people, not me. He was the one who sent out bad crab in the first place. How was I to know that it wasn't good?

The next morning, I tried to stay in bed after Rick's alarm rang, but my thoughts refused to let me sleep. Thankfully, I hadn't gotten sick. I had lain awake for the better part of the night feeling mildly nauseated, but it could have been much worse. I wasn't sure if my absence of illness was because I had only eaten a small portion of the salad, or if the crab really was okay. Rick was perfectly fine, but that was because he was more interested in filling his plate with lard balls than with anything good for him. Guiltily, he admitted that he hadn't even tasted any of my salad.

I knew better than to go by Win. I figured she had developed a gut of steel from a lifetime of eating leftovers from her warm purse. That fact that she ate a big helping of the salad and remained as healthy as a horse didn't mean a thing. She could probably drink water out of the sewers of Mexico City one day and go on an all-day toiletless hot air balloon ride the next without a shred of worry.

I did worry, though, about the other picnickers, principally the children. Had any of them had fallen ill? I was absolutely anguished that I, of all people, was responsible for jeopardizing the health of young children. How could I let that happen?

I joined Rick in the kitchen and asked his opinion about what I should do. His answer was a cheerfully pragmatic, "just 'fess up." That seemed way too uncomplicated to me. Josh's heated references to lawsuits hung in my mind like the shadow of a stalker in a dark alley. I didn't know these people yet, and I had no way of knowing how they might react to the news that the stranger who had pulled into their little town had secretly poisoned their food supply.

A terrible scene instantly flashed through my mind. I saw myself standing on a platform in the middle of the town, like Hester Prynne in *The Scarlet Letter.* A crowd of accusing and tongue-clicking villagers were gazing upon me and pointing at the huge letter "B" for Botulism that was emblazoned upon the chest of my billowy maternity muumuu. *I'm a pariah, a veritable Typhoid Mary. A menace to the town of Grassview.*

But, then, what if nobody did get sick? If the crab was actually just fine, my unnecessary confession could stir up a "mass psychogenic illness" reaction. I learned that term after an incident in the teacher's lounge at the high school. That was the day that Miss Haney screamed that toxic gases were leaking into our break room. As everyone starting smelling the terrible smells, they reported dizziness, headaches, immediate nausea. I felt it too. All of the teachers in the room fell ill within ten minutes of each other. Panic ensued, and an emergency response team was called in, but the toxic gases merely turned out to be some Korean food that the Family and Consumer Sciences teacher was warming in the microwave. It was ethnic food day, and all the microwaves in Mrs. Percy's classroom were full, so she was warming the fermented cabbage kimchi in the teacher's lounge. It was amazing how quickly our symptoms disappeared when we found out that we were wrong about the source. I remember being alarmed at how suggestible I and everybody else was. I was sure that the good people of Buffalo Jump Community Church could be no less gullible than a group of east coast professional educators.

Sitting with Rick at the breakfast table, I bemoaned, "Rick, help me! How do I deal with this without causing a huge panic?"

Rick cocked his head to one side and looked up at the calendar in Gracie's kitchen. "Well, it's Thursday, right? Just go to the ladies' luncheon and talk to them about it there. They seem like a reasonable bunch."

"What? The luncheon at the bar?"

"Yeah, why not? It would be simpler to talk to a small informal group than to try to call a bunch of people. Most of the kids' moms would probably be there."

He had a point. Earlier I vowed that I wouldn't attend that Bible study lunch-thing out of pure principle. A Bible study in a bar? The concept was irreverent, disrespectful. Might as well get up on stage at a techno rave party, preach the gospel, pop some ecstasy, sing the old hymn, "I'll Fly Away," and throw myself into the welcoming arms of a mosh pit.

And yet....even missionaries in Third World countries had no choice but to go to unsuitable places sometimes. I couldn't let one little mistake thwart my entire mission. I needed to find out what had happened and pray that God would give me the wisdom and creativity I needed to make it right. Surely, all was not lost.

⬥•◦•⬥

My roller coaster had bottomed out again. It was to be a tortured day of inner conflict and upheaval for me. The smoky, rancid beer odor greeted me with a cloying hug as I stood in front of Bison Jack's entrance. I cringed, knowing full well that it would stick to me until my next shower. In some ways, it was worse than walking into Scary Larry's—I might as well have been skulking off to have an adulterous affair for all the guilt and shame that I felt about having lunch in a seedy tavern. *What if my Sunday school students back at home saw me now? What would their parents say if they found out that their children's mentor and example was hanging out in a grimy sinkhole of moral vitiation? Forget that—what would my own mother say?*

Another voice, my dad's, intruded on my already troubled thoughts. His warning to me when I was going off to college reverberated in my head. "If you're ever unsure about whether or not you should go to a certain place, just ask yourself how you would feel if Jesus returned at that exact moment and met you there. Think about this—how would you feel if Jesus came back to earth and caught you in a bar?"

Rusty cowbells clanked when Win opened the door and held it for me. As I hesitated with my heart pounding, a giant wind gust swept down the sidewalk and banged the tavern's overhead sign against its own bracket. Instinctually, I dove inside, momentarily engulfed in sheer terror at the prospect of having my skull fractured by a flying giant neon beer mug. I silently prayed a highly unorthodox prayer that asked Jesus to delay His second coming, in case it had been planned for that day. I decided to get the lunch over with as quickly as possible.

"Hello, gals. So glad you decided to come." Naomi Stanton's chenille voice smoothed a path for us through the dusky room. She was wearing her church jeans. The puzzling idea hit me that she belonged in her clothes. For her, they weren't a mistake, or a Fashion Fail; they were just an honest reflection of who she was. Which I still didn't like.

Inside, a heavy cloud of fresh cigarette smoke joined the stale odors. This couldn't be good for the baby. As my eyes adjusted to the dimness, however, it became evident that the bar wasn't quite as bad as I had envisioned. There were clean wooden tables and green countertop booths. The only patrons were two older farmers sitting at the bar, smoking and drinking coffee. They both doffed their hats and said hello as Naomi led us past them toward the back. I recognized one of the smokers as an usher at church on Sunday.

Another smoker was off to one side, sitting alone with her ashtray in a booth. She was a young, heavily made-up woman, with fiercely bleached, strawish hair that brushed the shoulders of a tight, low-cut T-shirt. Naomi smiled at her as we walked by.

The back room was a bit brighter. Several larger windows lined the outside wall, with one open just wide enough to let in fresh air. There were two long tables with checkered plastic tablecloths and vases of plastic flowers. A collection of rusting horseshoes was nailed to one wall and a huge black velvet painting of a sheepdog was affixed to the opposite. There was also one of the revolting hooved animal leg lamps standing on a shelf bracket in between two windows. I couldn't help but think about the last church ladies' luncheon I had attended—my baby shower. I felt a stab of homesickness as I recalled the silky elegance and opulent flair my peers at Artos & Ichthus wove into all our gatherings. In contrast, Buffalo Jump ladies met in surroundings woven with all the opulence of burlap.

My body tensed when Naomi introduced us to the other seven ladies already seated. They didn't represent any one particular age range. In fact, it appeared that there was one woman from each adult decade, with Naomi being the eldest. They all recognized me from church and from the picnic. I waited in fear for the conversation to turn to the serious matter of food poisoning, but they nonchalantly continued to make pleasant small talk. They peppered me with friendly questions about where I was from, how my pregnancy was going, where Rick was working, and so on.

Finally, the dreaded topic was broached. Patti started with, "Didn't the picnic turn out great yesterday?"

I caught my breath.

Thirty-something Jeannie answered, "Yeah, a lot of people showed up. But—" she clutched her stomach. I did the same. "—we had way too many desserts. I pigged out, big time."

"Me, too," youngish Brooke spoke up, "and the kids. I couldn't keep them out of the cookies. They got sick—had me up several times in the night."

"Are you sure it was the cookies that made them sick? Scott's Uncle Herb is visiting from Idaho and he's a diabetic. He didn't touch the desserts, but he said he was up all night with intestinal troubles."

My heart started pounding and the mystery spot on my right hand started itching. Rubbing it with my clammy left hand under the table only made it worse. It had recently begun itching more than hurting, but it still wouldn't go away.

Sporting a shrieking red curly perm cap, middle-aged Marlene chimed in. "Really? I was kind of sick to my stomach too, and my little granddaughter was in and out of the bathroom all night. Said she felt fine this morning, though. I thought it might have something to do with Elsie's salami slaw. We both ate some."

My itchy hand trembled as I pulled it up from my lap and took a sip from my water glass. I decided to stay quiet and see where the talk would lead.

"Hmm," Brooke commented, "my kids love Elsie's meat salads. That might have been it."

"Yep, especially since she left early this morning for her trip to Cheyenne. She always cleans out her fridge before she goes—knowin' Elsie, that meat might have been pretty dated," Naomi said.

"Well, even if it was, it's not such a bad thing. Uncle Herb said he actually felt pretty good this morning. Said that whatever it was, it worked better than the expensive GastroKleen he usually buys."

The ladies laughed. Win, sitting beside me guffawed and hit the table. I offered a weak, phony smile.

So nobody suspects my salad. I didn't eat any of the salami stuff, but I was sick so I'm sure it was the crab. And I saw the kids all eating it. What should I do? Speak up... like crows flocking to road kill, rationalizations started to gather in the reasoning part of my brain...*or not?*

I mentally reviewed my options. Take the blame or let Elsie take it? *It doesn't sound like the big deal I worried it would be.* A large, sparkly silver lining was revealing itself in the middle of my dark clouds. *Maybe God took what Satan intended for evil and made it work for good, anyway. I mean, it was probably good for the kids' bodies to get rid of all the frying fat, right? And Uncle Herb feels better than ever. In fact, in a strange, but opportune way, these women could end up being thankful for the episode. So if I allow them to think it was Elsie, I'm humbly letting her get the credit.*

Patti spoke again "Gals, do you think we should talk to Elsie about this when she gets back next month?"

"You know," Naomi answered, "I don't think so. Let's let this one go and just keep an eye on what she brings to our potlucks. I don't want her to feel bad."

The ladies all agreed. So did I.

The discussion took a different turn when someone asked us about our trip from Pennsylvania. I was glad to let Win answer that one. She even surprised me by telling the story of the van incident and succinctly stating that it was her fault. Just like that, she took the blame. Luckily, everyone was too riveted by Win's dramatic narration to notice the astonished, yet pained expression on my face as she talked. My satisfaction that she had finally seen the light was tinged with an odd guilty feeling. I found myself hunching down slightly in my chair.

A few minutes later, the bleached blonde who had been smoking in a booth at the front of the bar suddenly appeared in the doorway.

"Oh, good, you're back," Brooke smiled warmly as she addressed the young woman. "Gals, this is Kendra—she's new in town. Kendra, come sit beside me."

Saturated with heavy tobacco odors, Kendra sat down in the empty chair between Brooke and me. She seemed nervous and her hands shook. Pointing to each of us in turn, Brooke quickly rattled off all our names and kindly reassured Kendra that we wouldn't hold her to remembering them all right away.

I was grateful for the conversation diversion that Kendra provided, despite the headache that her smell gave me.

"Where are you from, Kendra?" Marlene asked.

"Great Falls. My boyfriend and I got here three days ago." Kendra's voice was quiet and trembly.

"They moved in next to us at the trailer court," Brooke explained, "and Kendra doesn't know anyone yet. Thought it would be nice for her to join us for lunch and meet some of her new neighbors."

Poor Kendra was nervous and obviously out of her element. I questioned whether it was wise of Brooke to invite her to a Bible study. Kendra didn't seem to be the type of person who would ever go to church. Of course, I had to remind myself that we were in a bar, so someone like Kendra would feel more at home there than in church.

Joanne joined in. "Nice to have you here, Kendra. What brought you and your boyfriend to Grassview?"

Kendra looked down and fidgeted with her hands while she spoke. "A job. Curt—my boyfriend—is taking over the Salt Lick Saloon for a few months for his mom."

"Oh, so your boyfriend is Sue Birky's boy! That makes sense!" Marlene boomed. It would seem that she was born without voice volume control capabilities. "I just heard the other day that Sue was going to Fargo for the summer to take care of her sister, Mona. Mona just got diagnosed with cancer, you know. Oh, put that one on the prayer list, Jeannie." Marlene's voice speed control seemed set a little high, as well.

"Yeah, Sue's nice," Kendra replied. She continued to fidget and avoided looking anyone in the eye.

I really felt bad for Kendra. It must have been quite intimidating for her to be surrounded by a group of church ladies. It brought me back to the time at Artos & Ichthus when Dolores brought a down-and-outer type woman to one of our functions. Dolores had the foresight, however, to warn us all ahead of time that a struggling addict was coming so we could adjust our whole study to minister to her. We agreed that God must have put her in our collective path for a reason, most likely to be convicted by the Truth.

Lorna had coached us beforehand, reminding us that setting the indigent woman at ease was the important first step to softening her heart toward the Gospel message. However, Lorna had admonished us to resist the temptation to lower our own standards in the name of making the woman feel comfortable. I remembered being only a few minutes into the study when we watched shrewd Lorna seize the opportunity to put her own admonishment into practice. She had nicely, but firmly announced that "we don't use that kind of language here" when the scruffy woman used a profanity.

The woman seemed a bit taken aback but didn't say another cuss word the entire time. Of course, she did seem to shut down after that, but Lorna said later that usually that was a good sign—it meant that the person was listening instead of talking, thus allowing more Truth to settle into her heart. The woman never came back, but Lorna said even that was a good sign—our study was probably only meant to function as a seed planting session that day.

Sitting across the table from me, Marlene changed the subject again. She commented on how pretty my navy blue kurta top was and talked about how much maternity clothes had changed since her day. I secretly wished that once again the wind hadn't flattened my hair. A tiny part of me wanted to be the "city gal" who would impress these style-deprived rural woman with my fashion sense. Maybe I could even help them update their own looks—some had real potential—or at least give them pointers on how to fix their hair and get rid of those infernal ponytails and scalp-hugging perm caps.

With the touchy subject of food poisoning out of the way, I let my mind wander. As I snuck peeks at Kendra's abused hair and pondered the other ladies' style ignorance, something poked at the discouraged part of my heart. It was, unbelievably enough, another ministry idea. *Maybe these ladies don't worry about nutrition because they have low self-esteem.* I sat up a little straighter. *Wow, I haven't thought about that concept before. Is it possible that people don't feed their bodies properly when they don't feel good about the way they look?*

That's it—a hair ministry! Is this why You've brought me out here, Lord? I started thinking about the possibility of having Josie send out some hairstyle books that I could bring to the next luncheon. *Hmm, those books are expensive, though, and postage isn't cheap....maybe I could get our church's missions board to donate them. I could send out a letter that outlined the plight of the cloistered ranch wife, the never-ending bad hair day of the rural Montana woman. My car climbed.* I was feeling almost tipsy from the flow of ideas that were pouring into my brain.

The waitress, Dolly, showed up and Patti ordered rib platters for everyone. I normally would have equated eating pork ribs with ingesting drain cleaner, but this time I didn't bat an eye. I knew that missionaries sometimes ended up eating grasshoppers and sheep eyeballs when they went to foreign lands. Even if I was used to eating fresh salads and spelt wraps at our women's Bible studies at home, I realized I would have to be more adaptable if I was going to make it in my mission field here.

My idea expanded as the ladies chatted. It was all coming together. *I'll name my ministry "Manes of Mercy," and we'll shower these women with God's love through helping them boost their self-respect. I could take their pictures, but instead of Fashion Fails, they could be the "before" pictures for a Mercy Makeover Facebook album—huh?*

"....a beer."

Kendra's drink order crashed in on my daydream and halted my coaster ascent.

"I'll take whatever you have on tap today."

Dolly scribbled on her pad and turned to me with her pencil poised.

"Ma'am?"

"Um, uh, water's fine," I stammered.

This was a curious situation. I looked over at Naomi. As the leader of the Bible study, I was anxious to see how she would handle this turn of events. I knew Kendra would feel embarrassed when she realized that Christian women don't drink beer at Bible studies. It would be a necessary type of discomfort, though, as God was clearly introducing her to a higher standard.

Naomi looked up with an odd, unreadable expression on her face. "Hmm—you know, Dolly, I'll take a beer too."

14

I was completely blown away.

What is wrong with Naomi? This is a Bible study, for Pete's sake, and she's the leader!

This would never happen at Artos & Ichthus. Our leadership team, though young, knew the ways of the world. They were not prudes, in any sense—they respected personal freedom and choices that were sometimes divergent with theirs—but they also valued clear-thinking and sober-mindedness.

How can we ever hope to bring Kendra to Jesus if no one shows her a better way? What if she's an alcoholic? Naomi wasn't just being inappropriate herself, she was being reckless. Lorna would never be that careless with people's lives. She would have reported the incident to Mitch who would pull Naomi out of leadership immediately.

"You know what?" Marlene said. "I'm thinking a margarita with my lunch would be lovely. Dolly, do you have any limes, today?"

"Sure do. Blended or on the rocks?"

"Oh, let's blend it—in honor of spring!" Marlene hollered like it was 1999.

I was repulsed but no longer surprised. A group will only go as high as the leader will take it, as Dad would say. Apparently Naomi, as self-appointed Captain of the Lemmings, was bent on leading the whole Bible study pack, along with their respective Christian testimonies, over the cliff and into the fatal depths of the pagan sea.

Thankfully, the rest of the ladies ordered coffee and soft drinks. Dolly left and Naomi spoke up. "Okay, let's get started while we wait for our food. Because we wrapped up our beatitudes study last month, I thought we could just use this meeting to talk about which topic we want to tackle next."

I exhaled loudly. In one big puff of air my pungent ministry notions left my insides like an acrid cloud of smoke, leaving my sails to fall limp against my missions' mast. I was halted, dead in the water yet again. This group had problems that went way beyond anything my experience and faith could solve.

Indignation now filled the place in my spirit from which my ministry dreams exited. My suspicions about treacherous Naomi were confirmed.

How had she wormed her way into the trusting hearts of the good people of Buffalo Jump Community Church? How had she duped them into allowing her to not only hold a leadership position but to drink beer with a non-Christian at a Bible study? Naomi was dangerous, pure and simple.

Jeannie spoke up. "I like the idea of sticking to a series rather than studying a new concept every month."

"Me too," Marlene nodded her blazing head.

"What about just going on through the book of Matthew?" Brooke asked.

"Well, I think I'm on the right track with what I have in mind," Naomi commented, opening her Bible right alongside the huge mug of beer that Dolly had set in front of her.

Once again, I was without a Bible. In fact, it hadn't even occurred to me to bring one. Hal still hadn't come back; and besides that, I was going to a saloon, for pity's sake. Kendra didn't have a Bible either, though, so maybe I was doing my part to make her feel comfortable. Too comfortable.

Win pulled out a shiny, blue cylindrical bundle from her purse. Some tartar sauce packets fell out with it. "Glad I always have my 'Everlasting Word' with me."

She unsnapped a strap from around the cylinder and unrolled it. It flopped open, revealing itself to be a book with thin cloth-like pages.

"Wow."

"Well, I'll be!"

"Cool."

The women watched, fascinated.

"Is that a Bible?" Naomi asked.

"Yep," Win replied with an air of triumph, "and it really is everlasting. It's made by the EternaGear Company and has a lifetime warranty." She held it up with all the theatrics of a shopping channel hostess. "The pages are coated with a patented, unique polymer vinyl compound that holds up to just about anything. It's waterproof and fire resistant. Let me demonstrate."

I sat back in my chair and just let Win do her thing. I was irritated but there seemed to be no point in trying to stop her. The old lady could dance on the table for all I cared. Beer drinking and margarita swilling had swiftly erased all traces of respectability from this meeting, and there was no propriety here for anyone, even a concerned missionary, to protect.

Win turned the pages to the book of Genesis and, with a flourish, poured a generous amount of water over the account of Noah's flood. Everyone gasped. I rolled my eyes. She wiped it with a fistful of napkins and riffled the pages.

"Voila! Good as new," she announced. "Now watch this."

Everyone sat spellbound while Win pulled a lighter out of one of her purse compartments. The arrival of steaming rib racks and fries caused her to put the lighter back, though, and mercifully shut the sideshow down.

"Clear the table, please. These are hot," Dolly said as she set the food down in front of us. She brought three whole rolls of paper towels and placed them at intervals on the table.

I bristled as Naomi said grace and then took a gulp of her beer. She resumed her discussion while we all ate. To be polite, I nicely cut a piece of meat from the bone with my knife and fork and ate a tiny bit. It was, admittedly, juicy and tasty. In fact, it was fabulous. The other ladies pulled off long strips of paper towels and started eating their ribs with their fingers.

I guiltily cut off a tiny bit more, then threw caution to the winds and picked my ribs right off my plate. The smoky barbecue sauce was delectable. It tasted amazing. With a gusto borne from hopelessness and despair, I dove into my plate of ribs like someone who had never even heard of tofu. Charmaine was almost two thousand miles away, anyway. She would never have to know that I hadn't worked out in over a week, was wearing flip-flops in public restrooms and was chowing down on greasy pork ribs like a relapsing addict. *What happens in Grassview stays in Grassview.*

Naomi resumed talking as if she was a legitimate Bible teacher. Which she wasn't. "So, I was thinkin' that a study on how love beats sin is a good one to follow the beatitudes. Maybe comparing some of Jesus' teaching on love in Matthew with Paul's teaching in Galatians. It would go along with what Pastor Brandon's been preachin' on, you know, the Pharisees' pride and sins. Those guys thought that obeying the rules and keeping up appearances made them God's special people. Jesus, though, came along and taught that it was love, and love only, that fulfilled the whole Jewish law and made them God's children."

She put her rib bone down and wiped her hands on a paper towel. "Let me show you what I'm talkin' about. Why don't we get our Bibles out right now." She pushed her beer mug back with her Bible. "Let's see—I think we should start in the book of Matthew. Here it is—Matthew twenty-two, thirty-six."

Some shuffling ensued as the ladies passed around the paper towel rolls. They wiped the pig grease from their fingers and shoved their plates around to make room for their Bibles.

I was reduced to looking on at Win's Everlasting Word. The waterproof coating on the page reflected just enough light to keep me from seeing the words clearly. Win bobbed her head and fiddled with her glasses. I squinted my eyes but it didn't help. I gave up and just listened.

Naomi cleared her throat. "This is talking about a time when one of the Pharisees who was a big-wig law expert tried to trap Jesus with a question. It goes like this—"

She took a gulp of her beer and started reading. "—'Teacher, which is the most important commandment in the law of Moses?' Jesus replied, 'You must love the Lord your God with all your heart, all your soul, and all your mind. This is the first and greatest commandment. A second is equally important: Love your neighbor as yourself. The entire law and all the demands of the prophets are based on these two commandments.'"

Naomi looked up. "Girls, this is it. All there is to bein' a Christian is right here. Love God, love others, and you can throw out all the rules."

I felt the blood drain from my face. *Is she promoting some sort of liberal "everything goes; let's just love each other" doctrine?* My evangelical, fundamental sensibilities were offended, causing my pig rib to slide onto my plate from my greasy fingers. Naomi sounded like a holdover from the 1969 Woodstock festival, proving that even a slight amount of alcohol could impair someone enough to fall into error.

"What do you mean, Naomi?" Jeannie asked. She looked innocent and vulnerable. It saddened me to think that Naomi could be misleading someone who was genuinely hungry to learn the truth of scripture. I had a sudden desire to whisk Jeannie back to Philly with me and have her sit in on one of our church's expository Bible studies. Those were taught by qualified leaders.

"Well, hon, I mean that when you look at all the things that are listed as sins in the Bible, you see that every last one is just a hurtful, unloving act. Sometimes it seems that churches have kind of misused the whole of idea of sin."

Naomi paused to take another sip of her beer. "Sins are things we do that hurt ourselves or others. When God brought in the ten commandments and the law, I think He was giving His people a list of the things that they needed to avoid, and the things they needed to do in order to stay safe."

"Kinda like a parent's rules for their kids, right?" Brooke asked.

"Yep, you could say that."

"What?" The shriek popped out of my mouth involuntarily, as if someone had just poked me with a pin. I certainly didn't want to debate with a self-appointed, unschooled theologian, but I couldn't just let her false teaching go unchallenged in front of the gullible ladies. I swallowed hard and lowered my voice. "What about serial killers or rapists or Hitler for that matter? Was he just being unsafe?" I purposely aimed my cynicism straight at Naomi.

She didn't even blink. "Well, from what I read in the Bible, it seems that all sins stem from the same source—the original sin that Adam messed with in the garden. When he let sin get into his system, it's like it got into his DNA or somethin'. It's been passed down to every human born since, like a bad trait in a sire bull. So whether someone does a huge, nasty, evil thing or a small, hidden, bad thing, it's all coming from the same pool of stinkwater. When the sweetest little pastor's wife says a little lie, she's dipping a finger into the same pool that Hitler swam around in while he murdered millions."

"Good grief, Naomi, that's illogical—you can't make a comparison like that!" My mind jumped to a time, ten years earlier, when my dad came home from a church board meeting and related how he had to put the kibosh on a film series that the pastor had proposed for a youth group study. The subject of the series was mercy, and the films had something to do with criminals who had been given a second chance. Dad said the preview made it look like the criminals weren't really that bad after all. He went on to say the film could promote a dangerous message on grace and love that young people could misinterpret.

Naomi gazed directly into my eyes. "Haley, nobody's denyin' that the consequences of some sins are much huger than others, but the fact is that sin is sin. We can't get too caught up in degrees of sin, or we start down the same path that the legalists in Jesus' time did. All the things that God said were sin are things that He knew would eventually mess up our lives in one way or another. Stealing, lying, drunkenness, sexual sin—those things always end up in some sort of pain and God loves us enough to warn us to stay away from them. Like a good Dad would."

Naomi paused and took another sip of her beer. *Yeah, and my good dad warned me about people like you, Naomi.*

"I'm afraid that a lot of Christians—myself included—have twisted sin into being something that we use to measure each other against. Instead of lookin' at people who sin as fellow strugglers, they look at them as bad, worse, and evil. They set up a standard that makes some people look better or more holy according to the degree of good or bad things they do. Christians that aren't addicted to anything or don't do anything that's considered 'bad' are looked up to. People who mess up are judged."

"We can get pretty prideful about ourselves if we aren't doing things that look bad on the outside, right?" Marlene asked.

"Yep, and like Brandon says—pride is a doozy of a sin in and of itself!"

Naomi laughed. "Pride is sin because it makes us think more highly of ourselves than we do of others. That's not loving. Pride also keeps us separated from those we're supposed to love. When we think we're better than someone, we stay above them, like the Pharisees did with the rest of God's people. It's amazing how crafty the ol' devil is—he can use our 'Christian' behavior to separate us from the only thing that Jesus said we ever have to do to please Him—love others. While we're loving others, they're loving us. We get help from them to fight our own stuff. God made it so that we need each other. It's kinda like team ropin'—it takes two riders to pull the steer down."

Jeannie leaned forward. "Yeah, but that means you have to be totally honest and open with people about what's really going on in your heart."

"Or in your home," Patti said quietly, looking down at her plate.

Having no idea how to reply, I sat in awkward silence. I didn't agree with Naomi but wasn't sure how to word a rebuttal. I wished Pastor Mitch was there. He would have gently, but firmly, set Naomi straight.

"And another funny thing, ladies, is that when you boil it all back down to Adam in the garden, you see that all sin goes back to serving self, which is just plain ol' garden-variety idolatry. Satan tempted Adam and Eve to question God, which meant that they pulled God off His throne and put themselves first. When you think about it, all sin comes from putting our own selfish needs before God and others. Our need for attention from other people or our wanting to be distracted, entertained, and pleased can all become sin because it puts us first. Makes us sort of entitled, like royalty. Loving God means we know He's the king—not our selfishness."

"Yes!" Win exclaimed through a mouthful of rib meat. "That's why the first commandment is the first one!" A piece of pork dangled from her chin. "I've never seen it that way before. Hmm, makes me wonder what other new things are out there waiting for an eighty-year-old woman to learn..." She trailed off as her mind roamed off again to its strange and happy place.

"Naomi, sin is not that simple," I broke in. "We can't just love it away. There's stuff that we have to do—our witness will be compromised if we don't make sure we live right. How can we spread the Gospel if we just look like the rest of the world? We're supposed to avoid even the appearance of evil!"

I looked directly down at her beer, then back into her eagle eyes. Naomi's toxic love doctrine and Win's lack of manners were equally irritating. I just wanted to finish the discussion and get out of the saloon.

Naomi stared right back at me. "Well, I don't see where appearances have much to do with love. I mean, in times of trouble, who are you most likely to turn to for help—the one who looks the best or the one who loves you the most? Besides that, our love is our witness, not our self-righteous perfect behavior. When someone's witness is tainted, it's usually because they did something unloving toward others or even toward themselves. That's why Jesus said that loving God and loving others would fulfill the entire law. If you really love someone, you won't steal from them, cheat on them, gossip about them, or even try to look better than them."

She stopped to flip through her Bible pages. "You know, I've got a cross reference here to Galatians five, thirteen. Yes, here it is—'For you have been called to live in freedom, my brothers and sisters. But don't use your freedom to satisfy your sinful nature. Instead, use your freedom to serve one another in love. For the whole law can be summed up in this one command: Love your neighbor as yourself.'"

"Does anyone know where I could find a used chainsaw for sale?" Win broke in while intently arranging her fries in an organized lattice pattern on her plate.

"Huh?" Several of us interjected the same syllable at the same moment. Win threw her nonsense into the middle of our conversation like a heavy bookend, shoring up the other end of Naomi's tangled doctrine. I felt squashed in between the two old ladies' irrationalities.

"Ice carving! It's one thing that's still left for me to learn! I saw an ad the other day for an online course in food artistry and ice carving." Win smiled with satisfaction at her fry art.

"I say go for it, Winifred!" Marlene perked up. "None of us is too old to learn something new. And Naomi, I like your study idea. I think I could get a lot out of it."

The other ladies all agreed with Marlene, so the matter was settled—at least it was with them. For me, everything was unsettled. My coaster car had gone up and down so many times in such a short period that I felt spent, sickened, and tired. I almost felt like I didn't even know who I was anymore. My gaze traveled from the sheepdog painting to the hooved animal leg lamp, to the way Marlene's ketchup-red perm clashed with her green boozy drink, to the disgusting empty rib bones on my own plate. It was all so surreal, so stupid, that it defied even a Facebook report. It was just as well that I didn't have Hal. He didn't fit in here, either.

The conversation turned to babies as they started asking me more about my pregnancy. As jarred and frustrated as I felt, I did the right thing and put my friendly face back on and reactivated my cheery voice. I had already done enough damage to my witness that day by simply being in that place—I didn't want to make things worse by letting my anger show. Self control was a fruit of the Spirit, after all.

"That's great that you know you're having a girl, Haley. Have you settled on a name?" Brooke asked.

"Well, not quite—Rick and I have had a hard time agreeing on that. We both want something unusual but not too weird, and we are both partial to nature-type names."

"Nature—like plants or trees?"

"Well, sort of. I like Dawn or maybe Rose. I'm leaning toward something one-syllable. Rick wants Fern, but I'm holding out for something a little less old-fashioned. We're praying about it. I didn't realize that choosing a name would be so hard for us."

"My brother and I were both named after my Dad's best cow dogs," Bonnie, in her forties, piped in.

I politely chuckled at her cute little joke. No one else did.

"Dad always said that Bonnie was the best Australian shepherd he ever owned. She could work cattle like nobody's business. I like it that I'm named after her."

"My cousin, Glenn, is named after his mother's best barrel racing horse," Patti stated.

Patti's words sent a trickle of fear through my veins, shoving aside even my ministry worries. It was a thought that was almost as scary as Naomi's dangerous teaching.

We have to get the baby's named pinned down before Rick comes home from his ranch job with a special cow's name for our daughter. I would NEVER saddle my child with the disgrace of being named after barnyard livestock!

15

"Ouch!" I yelled as I peeled the thrashing shirt sleeve away from my watering eyes. The wind whipped it into my face, almost wiping my contacts right off my corneas. Win had insisted that we hang the laundry out. The breezes were wonderfully warm, she said, and it would be such a pity to waste all the electricity that the dryer consumed for something that the "breath of our prairie sister" could do faster, and for free. It was true that the towels on one end of the clothesline were almost dry before we reached the other end, but I was frustrated with battling the clothes to make them stay attached to the line.

There was one frustrating battle I had managed to win, however, and that was my fight with elastic-waisted pants. The victory was bittersweet, though, considering that it involved me making the most humbling concession I had ever been forced to stoop to in my life so far.

Unbelievably enough...I was wearing the lederhosen.

Like a mega batch of yeast dough in a hot kitchen, my little girl was growing at an alarming rate. The pork ribs seemed to be an even more potent baby growth stimulator than the Ohio burrito. She was crowding out her space, making my abdomen expand exponentially to accommodate her. My belly became so huge, round, and smooth that it gave my waistbands absolutely nothing to adhere to. Every waistband of every pair of maternity pants, stretchy capris, shorts, warm-ups, and sweats did the same thing—slide down. I'd pull them back up and zoop, back down they would go. Over and over, again and again. If I went into a store, I'd have to hang on to the waistband of whatever I was wearing the whole time I shopped. It was terrible. I was in constant fear of my pants falling down to my knees. Nobody had told me this would happen.

In desperation I resorted to wrapping duct tape around the tops of my pants. It was sticky and itchy, though, and I went through so many rolls that Rick started complaining about the expense. I had to replace the long strips of tape every time I went to the bathroom, which, considering the lack of room left for my bladder, was almost continual at times.

I was in the middle of a self-pity fest when I chanced upon the lederhosen in a box of baby things. I hadn't intended to bring them along but figured that Rick must have mistakenly stuck them in the box when he packed some of the shower gifts for me. In a frenzy of despondency, I waddled to the bedroom and tried them on. The result was a strange and special moment of sheer, unadulterated relief.

The lederhosen felt wonderful. I put them on over a stretchy T-shirt and let my huge belly pop right out onto the elastic panel shelf. The suspender straps held the shorts snugly in place as I walked in and out of each room. Lyla Wittenbow was a gem. A true American hero. Of course, I knew I looked ridiculous, so wearing them in public was not an option, but they quickly became my standard uniform for around-the-house wear.

I had changed into the lederhosen the minute we arrived home from our lunch at Bison Jack's. I was especially thankful to be wearing them at the clothesline. I could reach up and over my head without any fear of my shorts falling to my ankles. I was not so thankful, however, for Win's companionship. I had already had too much time with her. She was driving me crazy.

"I'm glad you're wearing the lederhosen, dear," Win said, grasping a clothespin with her arthritic, claw-like fingers. "You look so uncomfortable in your trousers. You know, I would be happy to sew you some maternity dresses if that would help. When I was a teenager, I made some for our neighbor, Mrs. Gradle. She was pregnant with twins and she grew so huge in her eighth month that she could hardly walk. Her husband took to hauling her around in a wheelbarrow whenever they left the house…"

I sighed. I just didn't have the energy to fight my way into her rushing conversation stream and insert an emphatic "no thank you" to her dress offer. I had already ruled out dresses for two important reasons. First, I had discovered in my second trimester that dresses made me look like a walking beanbag chair. Being on the short side, I just didn't have enough leg length to balance the width of a voluminous hemline.

Second, my no-dress decision was affirmed when, at a South Dakota convenience store, I had watched a wind gust pull an older woman's skirt right up her back, revealing her pantyhosed derriere to everyone in the parking lot. It was a strange and terrible spectacle to behold—she was grasping a giant slurpee bucket in one hand, a towering ice cream cone in the other, with her teeth gripping her car keys. I blushed, knowing she had no choice but to march to her car, shamefully exposed the whole way. If I were her, I would either never wear a dress again or forever duct tape the inside of my hem to my pantyhose, which would be just as tricky and expensive as wearing pants, which looked much better than a dress in the first place.

Win's ridiculously rambling sentences flowed on. "…Being just after the war, dress material was hard to afford, but I found some banquet-sized

Christmas tablecloths that were sitting unused in mother's attic. There was enough material for two dresses. Mrs. Gradle was thrilled—she had outgrown everything she owned by that time. Even though it was August, she was so desperate that she didn't mind that one dress was in a red and green poinsettia print, and the other was covered with Santa faces—oh, oh!"

A gust pulled a pair of Rick's boxers from her bird-like grasp. "These naughty little undies just want to dance free with the wind, don't they?" Win giggled and picked up a garden rake to retrieve the underwear from the top of a leering totem pole. I sighed again and wrestled another shirt onto the line.

"It's a three clothespin day, that's for sure!" Win started adding an extra clothespin to the top of all the underwear waistbands. As usual, she was completely oblivious to my disgruntlement.

Having nothing to say to her, I let her chatter on while my thoughts went elsewhere. I felt drained from my Bible study experience at the saloon. In fact, my entire first week in Grassview had drained me. It was now Thursday afternoon, and Rick still showed no indication that he was going to repent of his judgments against me. Instead, he seemed happier than ever. My initial exultation over Pastor Brandon's sermon on Sunday had faded into yet another missed opportunity for marital healing.

Rick had returned home from his first day at the Diamond Butte ranch in high spirits. He gushed about the enormity of the ranch—40,000 acres—and the fact that he instantly saw some basic operational improvements that could be made. He said he had worried at first that his lack of ranch experience could hinder his job performance, but when he approached the foreman with some ideas concerning their antiquated financial tracking methods, the guy was receptive. He said that Boss Bill expressed relief at the owner's decision to hire Rick's outfit to help them make changes.

On Tuesday, Rick had arrived home even more excited about his venture. He was given an ATV to drive through the wheat fields with Bill in order to get a feel for the crop production. Rick was especially excited to toss aside his dress clothes and wear jeans to work. He said it was like someone had let him out of a dark basement and that he had finally found the perfect work environment.

Perfect environment? I was incredulous. Particularly so as I stood at the clothesline on Thursday, duking it out with a flapping nightgown. Contrary to Rick, I felt like I had been locked up.

My cellmate, Win, gaily prattled on. She was definitely a candidate for ADHD meds. "You know, this sky and this weather bring back so many precious memories. I think I was introduced to the two personalities of Montana in the summer of '49 when I came out from Wisconsin to work as a cook in a logging camp. It was in the mountains of the far Northwest corner of the state—a scenic Eden of sorts. I was only nineteen, and my family thought I was crazy to step out on such an adventure. But I wouldn't be deterred. The allure of the wild west beckoned me like the aroma of bacon grease to a grizzly bear."

Lord, help me. I grabbed a fistful of socks, determined to get the clothesline ordeal over with. I already had more than enough of Win's outrageous stories. "Living in the beauty of the mountains was unlike anything I had experienced in the Midwest. I seized every opportunity to explore the forests and ridgelines. When I was fired from my cooking job, I started driving a logging truck and had even more time to admire the scenery."

I glanced dubiously at Win's little body, knowing that she had always been petite. It didn't seem likely that a small young girl could drive an old timey logging truck on scary mountain roads. While I was mentally mulling over the right way to confront her lying habit, an unexpectedly sad thought hit me. Could Win possibly be in the early stages of dementia? I knew I needed to talk to Rick about this. For the moment, though, I decided to humor her.

"Why were you fired?"

"I think it was simply because my ideas about cooking clashed with the dominant woman cook. I can't quite remember all the details, but I can still see that large lady's red face when she fumed about something unusual that I added to her stew."

This part of the story I could believe. I finished the socks and leaned against the leering totem pole.

"Anyway, I spent much time observing the peaky vistas and the gorgeous flora and fauna and, oh—the incredible smells! Those matchless smells that one can only smell in such a setting—pungent pine, cedar and wild rose bushes. And tastes too."

"Tastes?"

"Oh, Haley, have you ever sampled a real Montana huckleberry?"

"Um, no."

"You haven't truly lived until you do. In the high country those deep purple beauties get as big as a nine-year-old's thumb and taste like, oh, it's hard to describe a huckleberry's flavor. Hmm. Melodious—that's it."

"Melodious? That's a sound."

"Absolutely! If tastes were sounds then huckleberries would taste like a musky, mountain melody. Orchestral, really—the way the slopes have millions of the sparkling fruit singing out their sweet aroma."

Win's puzzling description was somehow forming pictures in my mind. I thought wistfully about the brochures that were left on the table back home.

"Anyway, it was all dazzling to the senses. I got there in early summer and stayed until late September. That's when I heard that a sugar beet factory in Billings was hiring drivers to haul beets in from the fields."

Win paused, holding a shirt in her hand, and looked up. I wondered if her neck would ever get stiff from so much sky gazing.

"Ah, yes, the prairie scenery presented herself to me in that hot, dusty September. It didn't take long for me to be as fascinated with her unique persona as I had been with Miss Mountain's. It still amazes me how different the east side of Montana is from the west side."

I sighed. I would have loved to make such a comparison with my own eyes.

"My long days driving a beet truck along the highway taught me to interpret the immense sky painting like an art critic. At first, I thought that in contrast to Miss Mountains, Miss Prairie was dull and devoid of scenery. One day, when a late summer storm moved in, my eyes were opened to the fact that Miss Prairie's sky was her beauty. You know, they don't call Montana, 'Big Sky Country' for nothing. In fact, I began to appreciate the sky vista so much that later on, during a return trip to the west side, I felt like the mountains were actually blocking the view."

I had no choice but to wait this one out. Her eyes were glazed over, envisioning things, real or not, from her distant past.

"I saw Miss Prairie's wild side during a storm that day. It was terrifying and exhilarating at the same time. She put on black, flailing robes and whipped the hills, the cliffs, and the gullies with furious rain. She tossed lightning bolts between the clouds and some fell to the ground. I was hooked. I sat in the cab of that ol' dump truck and just watched. It was better than any movie I had ever seen."

"Weren't you afraid?"

"Oh yes, it was wonderful! After the beet harvest ended, I stayed in Billings for the winter. That's when I met Naomi—her dad hired me to run his contract mail route. Once again, I found myself driving on back roads in the middle of eastern Montana. I did that for almost a full year, so I became well acquainted with Miss Prairie's temperament through all the seasons."

My feet were killing me from wearing the flimsy, unsupportive flip-flops. I looked around for a place to sit. The back of a faded donkey statue looked as good a place as any.

Win continued, "I learned to appreciate Miss Prairie's raw-boned beauty.

She is like a plain, strong woman. She doesn't get all gussied up in the lacy leaves and flower decorations like Miss Mountains, but she has her own un-tamed intrigue. She can appear dull and brown for a long time until, unex-pectedly, her temper flares into a raging storm. Whereas Miss Mountains will politely change from one season to the next, Miss Prairie kicks and screams the whole way."

The wind agitated the clothes into another frenzy. The towels snapped, sounding like balloons popping. I hung onto my hair and shifted my position on the donkey. Absentmindedly I also started pondering the sky while Win's nonsensical word pictures began to slyly coalesce with what my eyes were observing in the realm above. It was kind of nice to take my mind off my marriage and ministry problems.

Win added more clothespins to a tablecloth as she talked. "If you're here when it snows or rains, you'll see what I mean. Miss Prairie never allows pre-cipitation to fall gently, ladylike—her rain and snow always bluster sideways. Umbrellas don't do a bit of good on the plains. They make the Prairie mad and she tends to destroy them."

A bawling wind chime startled both me and Herman and I shook myself, as if I had almost fallen asleep while driving. I had to regather my wits—I couldn't let myself be pulled into Win's poetic madness. She quieted and gazed out at a distant spot near the horizon. I looked but only saw dingy hills.

"Oh!" Win exclaimed. "Let's go for a walk. I think I see some green!"

"What?"

"Miss Prairie is slipping into her fancy spring dress, and she won't wear it for long. We need to walk—nay, dance with her on the hills before the sun and the wind get jealous and steal the green satin away. It is her only femi-nine garment, and she can be quite self-conscious in it. Miss Prairie dislikes pretentiousness."

Pretentiousness. I had to hand it to Win. She used another great vocabu-lary word. If she could only have channeled her storytelling into more legiti-mate avenues when she was younger, she might have made it as a writer for the tabloids.

I struggled to stand up. The donkey's back had a sway that had me hemmed in on both sides of my swollen belly. Win rushed over and offered to help. Her hand, though small, offered a grip that was surprisingly warm and strong. She pulled me right up.

"Aunt Win, sorry. I don't think I could take a walk right now." I knew Charmaine would protest. I was supposed to be taking at least one Keepin' Cool Cardio Stroll a day, but that was in my previous life. That was the life over which I had some control. The life in which I didn't expend all my energy swimming against a tidal wave of felonious food and foreign religious practices.

"I'm going to go in and take a nap instead." I needed a break from all her strange talk, anyway. "Please feel free to go without me."

"I just might do that. Miss Prairie and I need to get reacquainted," she announced, leaping onto the back deck. "Must get a different hat first, though."

I felt large, old, and sluggish as I watched her skip through the back door. She clearly possessed the metabolism of a hummingbird, while mine was slowing like it was preparing for winter hibernation. I shuffled into the house, intent on taking a very long nap.

16

Win hit a high note that made my skin tingle and the hair on my arms stand up. Nevertheless, I kept my hands steady on the wheel. After nearly colliding with an espresso stand in Range City, I discovered that the tanker's steering system was hair-trigger sensitive. I couldn't let the straightness of the highway lull me into inattention, even for a moment. For that reason, I suppose it was helpful that Win's singing was so strident.

It was just after lunch and we were heading back to Gracie's after spending a morning in the relative sophistication of Range City. My early morning doctor appointment was uneventful, and I was thankful for the time to shop in a real grocery store afterward. Even lunch in a fast food chain in a town with a population of 5,000 was a treat. The only glitch in the morning occurred when we returned to the car in the clinic parking lot. The electronic door lock and seat adjusting system of the early 70s were now tired and unreliable. We made sure to leave the doors unlocked after Win had ended up crawling through the rear hatch to pull up the unresponsive front locks.

My prenatal appointment set my mind at ease. The balding obstetrician, dressed as he was in jeans and a striped shirt, seemed sufficiently qualified. He assured me that backaches, heartburn, and extreme bladder urgency were all perfectly normal for this stage of the game. The baby's heartbeat was strong and Dr. Swartzky pronounced my pregnancy to be as healthy as a heifer's.

The doctor couldn't give me a clear diagnosis for my hand injury, though. He was surprised that it had hung on so long without healing. He said he suspected it was some sort of bug bite reaction, possibly a spider bite. He commented that the way the two spots were placed actually made it look like the puncture wounds of a snake bite.

"It can't be a snake bite," I stated with a sniff, "I know exactly when it happened. I was indoors in our church basement."

Dr. Swartzky laughed. "Ha—have you ever had the building checked for snakes?"

"Excuse me?"

"Heh, just joshin'. You would have known right away if it had been a snake—might not even be sittin' here right now if that was the case."

I couldn't believe he could be so flippant about something as grave as my own demise.

He concluded the appointment by reassuring me that it was probably nothing more serious than a mild allergic reaction to a bug bite and gave me a sample tube of a topical ointment. He said that because I was only three weeks away from my due date, he would need to see me again in another week. I wasn't sure if I wanted to go back so soon but knew I didn't have any other choice. It was either see him or the livestock veterinarian in Grassview.

I would have liked to spend more time checking out other stores in Range City, but I needed the entire afternoon at home to get ready for dinner guests. Rick had invited the Diamond Butte ranch owner and his wife to visit with us for the evening. The owners were actually from Houston and only visited the Montana operation a few times a year. Rick wanted to have a personal talk with Mel Connor and, of course, had the hidden intention of soliciting business with his other ranches.

At first, I was not excited about the prospect of entertaining guests, especially the refined type, at Gracie's house. I was truly embarrassed to host a dinner party in the knickknack festival booth on the carnival property. But then I started to think that maybe I was supposed to connect with Mel Connor's wife, Tina. Maybe I could offer her something the local women couldn't, like a shared understanding of the outside world—the cosmopolitan perspective, perhaps. Being from Houston, she might feel as out of place in Grassview as I did.

That idea invigorated me. I decided to work with what I had. I started by insisting that Rick do something about the ridiculous yard. He responded with a begrudging, halfhearted attempt at herding some of the most offensive statues into a corner by the back fence. He spent precious time drawing up a chart of where all the objects stood before he moved them so he'd know where to put them back and stuck the special map up on the fridge. It consisted of weird shapes and arrows drawn inside a large square with captions like, "fire engine and miner's cart here," and "wooden goat here," and "lighthouse inside circle flowerbed." An asterisked footnote said, "Put glass bottles back in miner's cart. Sunglasses go back on goat." It appeared that he was much more worried about offending Gracie than he was about protecting my concerns.

Inside the house, I worried that it might be dangerous for visitors to enter unawares into our temporary shop of horrors. I had considered boxing up the trinkets, but realized that it would take more time and more boxes than we could scare up in a week, let alone a day. The only solution I could come up with was to apologize profusely for the clutter and bowl the guests over with the most impressive gourmet meal that I could possibly create. I also vowed to look as chic as my pregnancy would allow. Of course, that would involve my hair being perfect.

Win had been singing and reciting her original works for me the whole way home. It was tiring but not unbearable. Some of her songs were genuinely clever. As an English teacher, I was surprised by her extensive knowledge of poetry and famous poets. I laughed when she told me that I could be a poet. I informed her that I loved technical writing and teaching literature, but poetry was not my forte and never would be. Not content to leave it at that, Win had gone on to assert that stories and poems were "birthed," and that when people were born, their stories were born. She rambled on about how we are all walking stories that are lived out, instead of read, and all of us carry a lesson. Her talk dizzied me the way discussing the size of the universe did.

"I'm pretty sure that's Naomi's place," Win pointed out the car window toward a hybrid trailer clump, not far off the highway.

It was a squat and squarish abode, a May-December marriage between a washed up beauty queen of a single wide trailer, and a round-domed, turquoise and silver codger of a trailer from an even more distant antiquity. Listless, rusty cars lolled on the lawn near the mobile home, like ill-conceived, sickly children from the hapless union.

"That's her house?" I was repulsed, but not surprised.

"Yes. It's the same one she's lived in for thirty years. Her husband, Bill, put the addition on when their third child was born."

"Addition? How do the trailers stay attached?"

"I'm not sure, but whatever holds them together has been effective. It's outlasted Bill—he was killed in an accident ten years ago." Win paused and then said thoughtfully, "I'd love to stop and say hi to Naomi. Do we have time?"

I would never go inside that hovel heap. It looked like the kind of place where the odors of stale fried food and mildew thrived. "Sorry, Aunt Win, I'm afraid we don't have time."

"Okay," Win said wistfully as she gazed at the ramshackle property.

The tiniest twinge of compassion poked my heart when we passed the ailing acreage. It was apparent that Naomi was in desperate need of more suitable shelter.

"Aunt Win, do you know if anyone from Buffalo Jump Church has done anything to help Naomi out?"

I thought about how Artos & Ichthus had ministries set up to care for the poor and downtrodden. We certainly wouldn't have left one of our own to live in abject poverty.

"Help her in what way?"

"Oh, you know—maybe do some work on her, uh, house or bring her food or something."

"I don't know, dear, but I don't think she needs it. She seems comfortable enough. Besides, I think she puts most of her resources into her livestock and other things."

Hmph, like a drinking habit, perhaps? Dismissing my moment of compassion as hormone-induced, I decided Naomi could take care of herself. I had more pressing matters to deal with that day. I looked at my watch and pushed on the gas. Time was wasting.

Win, noticing my urgency asked, "What time will our guests be arriving?"

"Rick told them to follow him home when he gets off at five, and I've got tons to do before then."

"Don't get all knotted up about this, Haley. I'm here to help, remember? Just give me some tasks and let me work my magic."

Win bobbed her head and bounced a bit in her seat. I thought about Bruce and recalled how he did have a knack for entertaining visitors. I hoped Win would behave herself enough to be considered charming to our guests. I knew asking her to stay quiet and uninvolved would be asking too much.

In spite of all Win's foibles, I did appreciate her offer of help, though. She had spent the day before dusting every inch of the living room. She did a thorough job, singing and talking to herself and the figurines the whole time. By the time the setting sun shone through the living room window, the glass monkeys on the Wizard of Oz chess set sparkled breathtakingly.

Overall, Win's behavior was disturbing enough for me to finally broach the subject of her possible dementia with Rick. We had ended the previous evening in a whispered argument in which he defended his great aunt's mental faculties. He insisted that her stories were true—possibly maximized, but true—and that she simply had an unusually colorful past.

I had felt defeated and wanted to cry. "Well, even if she isn't losing her mind, she's making me lose mine. Rick, I don't want to consider home schooling our daughter anymore."

Rick looked perplexed. "What does that have to do with Win?"

"Rick, what if our little girl turns out to have a weird personality and is *chatty?*"

"So?"

The tears broke forth. "Oh, Rick! I can't stand the idea of being home with that for twelve years!"

At that point he conceded that it probably wouldn't be a bad idea for me to have a break from her. We talked about how we could get her to Wyoming to visit other relatives there. That idea had done much to calm me.

Remembering that conversation from the night before helped me stay calm all day.

"Since you've offered, Win, why don't you clean the bathroom while I start the food prep," I said as we pulled into the driveway. "Oh, and I want to deep condition my hair—maybe I'll do that first."

"Insecurity clogs the channel."

"What?"

"One's river of love can't flow when one lets the silty deposits of insecurities choke up one's streambed."

Oh, great. I really don't have time for this. I pushed hard to get the monumental driver door to swing open and attempted to exit the car quickly, desperate for the bathroom. I couldn't do it, though. I got stuck. The car was too close to the ground, and my huge stomach was jammed too close to the steering wheel. I struggled and grunted with one foot outside but couldn't muster enough leverage to slide myself out.

Win was completely oblivious to my distress and kept talking. "Our worries over being accepted can pile up inside our hearts and block our honesty—who we really are without all the bells and whistles. Insecurities make our rivers dishonest and shallow."

"Oof—help me, Aunt Winnie."

"Well, dear," she was still in the car, staring out her window, "you need the humility dredge."

"Win! Not that—look at me, I'm stuck!"

"Oh dear. Here let me help." She got out her side and came around to me. She pulled and I pushed, but I didn't pop free until I remembered to push the switch back that controlled the seat position. I felt stupid and large. My stress was sapping me of my common sense.

"Ooh, I mustn't forget my fries," Win sprinted back around to the other side of the car to retrieve her mysterious purchases. Before we left the fast food restaurant, she had ordered two huge to-go bags of spiral-shaped french fries to take home. She also bought two large bottles of yellow and blue food color in the grocery store but had avoided giving a reason for either purchase. I could only hope that she was planning a project for another day.

I lumbered into the house. Win was smart enough to keep quiet while she put the groceries away. I skimmed over the recipes I had printed off Hank's computer and started pulling out the ingredients for pesto chicken lasagna, a main dish that could be assembled ahead and baked later. The original recipe was actually for shrimp lasagna, but I had decided to swear off seafood for awhile and substituted it with chicken instead.

I felt lucky to have had the chance to go to the bigger grocery store that morning in Range City. The Grassview store would certainly not have fresh basil or, even better, the unexpected sun-dried tomato artisan bread loaves that were sitting on the upscale store shelf, waiting there just for me, like a sweepstakes prize check in the mailbox. I took time to offer thanks for those. A fresh green salad and a showy chocolate meringue with whipped cream and strawberries would round out the dinner nicely. I had decided against serving an appetizer when Rick said that we'd have to have an early dinner. The Connors planned to keep the visit short due to the fact that they were leaving for Denver the next morning. Appetizer or not, I was determined to make a meal fit for visiting dignitaries. I would pull this one off.

I worked in the kitchen until late afternoon and went to the bedroom to take care of my appearance. I turned my music up and sang to the baby while I showered and primped. For the first time in weeks, my hair had finally turned out the way it was supposed to. Just the right amount of height and just the right amount of straight. The conditioner made it gleam. I actually felt like a respectable woman again. Mel's wife was bound to see that I was not a country hick.

At four-twenty, I went back to the kitchen to take out the meringue and put in the lasagna. I felt good. I was even humming one of Win's crazy songs—a country waltz ballad concoction about watching the Montana Sky instead of TV. It was corny but catchy.

I should have known, though, that things were going too well. If I had only spent even ten fewer minutes on my hair, I might have stopped Win before the whole disaster got set in motion and maybe things could have turned out differently. Crying over spilled milk—or cream, in this case—can't change a thing. Once it's spilled, there's no going back.

17

"Win! What...are...you...doing?" I screeched, immobilized with shock as I stared into the kitchen.

Mysterious blue and yellow splotches spilled from mixing bowls on the counter. The beaters were dripping into an azure puddle which ran down the front of a cupboard door. A large cookie sheet sat in the middle of the kitchen table with a bizarre pattern of dark blue, yellow and green spirals laid out on it. A closer look revealed that the spirals were the fast food fries that had been dipped in some sort of paint. I was appalled. Horrified. Mad.

"Haley, it's okay dear. I'll clean this up in a jiffy." Win beamed and held up the cookie sheet like a presentation. "It's a food rendition of Van Gogh's Starry Night, a masterpiece appetizer and it's completely edible."

I exhaled long and spoke quietly. "Aunt Win," my voice was phony, scary sweet, "We will not be serving an appetizer tonight. And just what did you use for the, um, paint?"

"Whipping cream."

"Whipping cream? The cream I bought today?" I had resorted to shrieking again.

"Yes. It was one ingredient I didn't think you needed for tonight."

"I didn't need? It's for the meringue! The meringue will be naked without it—naked, I tell you, naked!"

Win cringed and looked tearful. I had never seen her like that before. "Haley, I'm sorry."

I growled and started throwing utensils into the sink. Win leapt up and started wiping the counters, muttering apologetically. I knew I had to get a hold of myself. This was an emergency, and I had to stay calm and think clearly. I would have to save my furor for later.

"Aunt Win, you keep cleaning up and I'll run to the Grassview store. It should only take a few minutes."

"Haley, I used your whipping cream, so it's only fair for me to go. I can drive the car."

"No. You haven't driven in years. This is not the time for a refresher course."

"But I've driven all sorts of big trucks and machinery. It would be no problem."

"No, I'm going." *You've probably never driven most of what your dying memory is telling you that you have, woman. You need help.*

"But, Haley, dear—the lederhosen. You're still wearing them."

She had a point there. I was leaving the lederhosen on until the last possible minute. Win might be weird but she wasn't stupid. She was well aware that I wore them for comfort not for looks. She also knew that unlike Missie the Truck Driver, I would rather eat worms than wear the lederhosen in public. My choice of stylish evening clothes—brown maternity pants and the cream-colored kurta blouse—were hanging in the bathroom, waiting to be donned and taped to me at exactly four fifty-five.

"Okay, let's do this—I'll drive and you come with me to go into the store and buy the whipping cream. We can still be back in time for me to change clothes and you to clean this mess."

"Sounds like a plan to me!" Win rushed to get her purse from her bedroom.

I slipped on my flashy flip-flops and stalked out the back door. "Eeeek!" A spray of dust granules slapped my face. *Oh, no. The wind. My hair. My perfect hair.*

I retreated back into the house just as the apish weather station started howling a song I hadn't heard it play before.

"Oh dear," Win said as she stepped back into the kitchen, "I think that song is called, 'Bad Moon Rising.' We might be in for a bit of a storm."

My skin prickled while I stood, thrust unwillingly into a tragic dilemma. The wind and the dust would most certainly ruin my impressive hairstyle the moment I went out. The two choices facing me were each unthinkable—the dessert or my hair? Which one to sacrifice?

Like a barbershop quartet from the insane asylum, four dissonant voices assaulted me at once. Herman hooted, the back porch wind chimes intoned, and the weather station howled while the kitchen clock joined in, heckling me with its four-thirty ding-dong. I broke out in a sweat, glancing over at my undressed, brown meringue. It looked like a kid's mud pie.

One other option crept like a faint scent into my pained consciousness. If I hadn't been so pressed for time, I might have thought it through long enough to wisely reject it. I might have recalled a certain vow I had made with myself only days before. I was rushed, though, and just like a person who starts downing a big piece of cake before they remember that they had sworn off sugar only the day before, I said an inner "yes" to that risky option.

I gulped, gathered my courage, and slowly turned to meet Win's gaze.

She looked at me sympathetically and nodded knowingly. Without a word, she hurried back into her bedroom to help me in the only way she could.

"The main thing to remember is to keep the helmet strapped on just a wee bit tighter than feels comfortable. Whatever you do, don't give in to the temptation to loosen the chin strap. You're risking hair and spline entanglement if you let the Preservadoo fall forward or move backward on your head once it's set in place."

I felt ridiculous, yet oddly empowered. I had a plan, and I didn't have to sacrifice my hair or the dessert. I was in control again.

The clear plastic bubble contained dozens of blunt, toothpick-like projections that rested around my skull. Unlike a regular hat, the Preservadoo enabled my hair to be sheltered from the elements, but not squished flat.

Win pulled gently on the chin strap. "Do you feel pressure?"

"Yes, it's starting to hurt." I was determined to be stalwart.

"Good. We'll leave it there."

I glanced at the evil clock. "We have to go, now!" I marched with confidence into the face of the wind.

"Just DON'T loosen the strap!" Win yelled as she followed me onto the back deck.

The helmet dramatically increased the circumference of my head, so I had to lower myself with extreme caution into the cruise ship. I knew speed was of the utmost importance if we were to get this all done in the next fifteen minutes. I tromped on the gas pedal and the beast responded with a roar.

Win chattered as if everything was just fine, and she hadn't come close to being murdered only minutes before. "The infomercial was really inspirational. Apparently, the lady who invented the Preservadoo got the idea for it from contributing cakes to a cake walk. She ran out of things to transport the cakes in so she started wrapping the rest in plastic wrap. She found that when she inserted toothpicks around the layers she could keep the plastic wrap from touching the frosting. When she envisioned her head as a cake, the idea took off. If we had time, I'd show you the DVD."

I only half listened as I sped down the highway. I remembered that Rick said he'd call me if our guests' time schedule changed for any reason. He knew to call Win's phone if our internet usage tied up the landline.

"Aunt Win, do you have your phone with you?" I really hoped that Rick would call and say that the Connors were running late.

"It should still be in your purse."

"Oh, that's right." I had kept her silly buggish phone with me while we were in Range City earlier. Win had abandoned her wrist strap harness after she poked her eye badly during a chat with her sister, Penny.

I felt around with my right hand on the seat beside me. *Uh-oh.* My purse wasn't there. In all the hubbub, I had forgotten my purse.

I glanced over at Win. Thankfully, she had hers. We didn't have a phone with us, but at least we could still buy the whipping cream. Win always seemed to have cash on hand.

"How's the Preservadoo feeling, dear?"

"Okay." It hurt, but I figured that was par for the course when wearing such an appliance. The pain did seem to be centered on my right temple, however. Without thinking, I sat up higher and tried to see the side of my head in the rearview mirror.

"HALEY—watch out!" Win's screech startled my bladder.

Oh, no! I looked up just in time to see that I was half off the road, heading straight for the ditch at sixty-five miles per hour. *Stupid touchy steering!* I panicked, over corrected, and found myself lurching into the ditch on the other side of the road. It was all happening too fast to even think. I swayed and swerved several times, snaking my way from side to side down the thankfully empty highway before I rolled to a stop. Waves of dust lapped at the sides of the beast as it sank into dry dock in the ditch on the right side. A center of gravity as low as that of an aircraft carrier was the only thing that had kept the vehicle from rolling over.

"Oh, my!" Win clutched her chest and gasped for air. For the first time since I had known her, she didn't have anything else to say.

"Uh—*phoof*—are you okay—*phoo*—Aunt Winnie?" I too could hardly catch my breath.

"Yes, I'll be fine." She inhaled and exhaled deeply and then actually smiled. "I think the angels were protecting us. Are you okay, dear?"

My heart pounded and my whole body shook. "I think so." A pang of guilty alarm accompanied the realization that I could have given Win a heart attack.

A blaze of pain on my scalp reminded that I was wearing the contraption. Operating on nothing but sensory instinct, I reached up...and loosened the strap.

"Haley, NO!" Win's smile immediately twisted into a look of horror.

It was too late. The Preservadoo immediately slid back an inch on my head, raking my scalp with all the tenderness of a mauling grizzly bear. I tried to yank it off my head, but it slid to one side, painfully twisting sections of my hair in the process. I pulled down the visor to see how it was situated and saw a sight even worse than the mangled strands that were sticking out the sides of the hat—flashing blue and red lights pulling up behind me.

Panicking, I grasped the death bubble with both hands and pulled hard. It was useless. What had started out as the perfect solution to my earlier conundrum was now grabbing onto my hair with savage tentacles, tangling, mangling, abusing the power of my costly hairspray and using it against me. I wrestled and tugged on it in vain.

Aunt Win looked back and her smile returned. "Oh, good, maybe the nice officer can help us."

Tap, tap. "Ma'am, turn off your engine and open the window."

I turned sheepishly to look into the wide face of a female officer. She was shielding her eyes and tapping on the window. "Open up, Ma'am."

I pressed down on the window button, but, like one's child being naughty at the worst possible time, it wouldn't respond. "It won't open!" I yelled loudly through the glass. I turned off the engine and started to open the door.

"STOP! Put your hands back on the steering wheel where I can see them—both of them."

Yikes. I had to let the Preservadoo cruelly slide to one side and choke me with the chin strap in order to comply. I needed to get that stupid thing off my head but didn't dare disobey her stern command. The roundish, stocky woman was wielding the authority of her tan deputy sheriff's uniform to the fullest. I continued to tremble from disbelief and fright.

"Passenger—both hands on the dash, NOW!"

"Oh, my," Win said with a measure of glee as she scooted to the front of the gigantic seat and placed her wrinkled palms on the dashboard.

The lady officer, one hand grasping the gun in her belt holster, slowly opened my door with the other. "Ma'am, you were driving erratically. You could have killed yourself and your passenger, or even another motorist. I was behind you and have it all on camera. What do you have to say for yourself?"

"Um, uh, I was going to the store in Grassview and, um—"

She didn't let me finish. "I need to see your license, insurance, and registration. You may take your hands off the wheel. Slowly, please."

I tried to lean over to reach the glove back in front of Win, but my huge belly was crammed against the steering wheel.

The officer's voice was tinged with impatience. "Passenger—do it for her. You may slowly take your hands down and open the glove box."

Win complied with exaggerated slow motion movements and unlatched the glove box. I was relieved to see the car's information on top. Win pulled the documents out and handed them over. The officer took them from me and spoke as she looked over the paperwork.

"Ma'am, what is that on your head?"

I gulped. "It's called a Preserv..." I trailed off, not really sure how to explain it. For once, Win stayed silent.

"Is that a medical device? Do you have a condition?"

"Um, no."

She frowned. "License, please."

"Uh, it's not with me—I forgot my purse."

Her eyes narrowed ominously. "Ma'am, I'm going to ask you to exit the car slowly, keeping your hands where I can see them."

"What?"

"You heard me, Ma'am. Do exactly as I say and no one will get hurt."

I slowly placed my left foot onto the ground. Cautiously, so as not to upset the malicious helmet further, I lowered my head and attempted to pull my cumbersome body out of the car. Inconveniently enough, I got stuck again. Only this time, the seat switch would not go back.

"Ooof," I grunted.

"Is there a problem, Ma'am?"

"I'm stuck. The seat won't go back—this happens sometimes."

She bent down toward me and tried the switch for herself. Nothing. "Hmmm, must be a short circuit somewhere. I take it that you're pregnant, and not just large?"

My fear was giving way to intense irritation. "Yes."

"So you were not just endangering yourself and your elderly passenger, but the life of an innocent child." She clucked her tongue. "You should be ashamed, Ma'am."

"Listen, I can explain—"

"I bet you can. I don't have time for your excuses. I'm going to have to call for backup."

"What?"

"Ma'am, this is a crime scene. You were driving erratically, are now wrecked by the side of the road—"

"I'm not wrecked!"

"—you have no license or ID, and you're wearing an unknown apparatus. As soon as we can get you out of there, I'm going to conduct a field sobriety test."

"This is ludicrous!" Anger took over, spurring me to heroic strength. I grabbed onto the roof of the car, planted my left foot on the ground, and pulled myself up and out in one mighty heave. The Preservadoo hit the top of the door opening as I got out but stayed fixed to the side of my head like a baby baboon clinging to its mother. Grunting, I pivoted to get my right foot out, promptly lost my balance, and lurched forward toward the officer.

"Hold it right there!" The deputy stepped back and actually pulled her gun.

I grabbed the car's door frame to regain my footing. Ditch mud oozed between my bare toes, sullying the plastic jewels on the flip-flops.

"Put your hands up!"

What? I was outraged. I threw my hands up while I stood in front of the door and started yelling, "What is your problem? I'm an innocent citizen—I accidentally left my purse at home and I made a driving mistake—I'm not a criminal!"

A newer sedan with a load of gawking passengers slowed to a crawl as it passed us. I was, confessedly, a bizarre and sorry spectacle standing by the side of the highway with my hands up like a felon. A big-bellied, red-faced female felon, with a jaunty plastic bubble strapped to one side of my head, wearing lederhosen shorts that revealed my skinny legs and muddy, flip-flopped feet. Even worse, my blinding white legs prickled with the stubby hair that I had been unable to shave off for weeks because I could no longer reach them over my stomach.

Two of the gawkers leaned out their car windows, held up cell phones, and snapped pictures of me.

I was a bonafide Fashion Fail.

A Fashion Freak. A Fashion Fool. A Fashion Farce.

And I would have given just about anything at that moment to be wearing filthy jeans, a raggedy plaid shirt, and a dingy, winterish hat with dangling ear flaps. That would have been a huge step up on the ladder of respectability.

Of course, it was only fitting that two more vehicles, approaching from the north slowed to pass us. The first was none other than our own flatbed pickup, driven by my dear astonished husband.

The second was a polished, snazzy black sports car with Texas plates.

18

Rick, feigning concern and attempting to pass off his laughing outburst as choking, rushed to my aid after he pulled his truck over. Thinking fast on his feet and knowing my need to have the scene cleared of spectators, he directed our guests, Mel and Tina Connor, to take Win with them and go on ahead to Gracie's place. He set about the task of convincing the deputy that I wasn't a drugged-up criminal or escapee from a mental hospital or abductor of innocent old ladies. He even sweet-talked her out of fining me for not carrying my driver's license. Finally, he managed to help me rip the Preservadoo off my head. Needless to say, I meekly reversed the ship's course and followed Rick home without the whipping cream.

I mentally leafed through my entire stockpile of synonyms for the word "embarrassment" as I drove. Words that I had rarely thought about in my previous life in Philly were now beginning to lose their effect from recent overuse. *Humiliation...disgrace...degradation...mortification...indignity...* Hadn't I just used these all a week earlier after the van explosion and the Trav-a-lav disaster?

How can you do this to me, God? My shame started souring into anger as I prayed while I drove. *Why, God? How could You let this happen? What have I ever done to deserve this? My reputation, my witness, my purpose—is this fun for You, God?*

The souring gelled, curdling into a sticky, mad goo of emotion. My coaster car got stuck in it. *Do you have me where you want me now, God? In a place where I can't use the teaching talent You gave me, and all my efforts to help others or to be a witness for Your glory are smashed by Your iron fist of ruin and shame?*

The boat sailed down the highway with a crazy woman at the helm. *Well, fine then, God. If that's how You want it, You can have it. Go ahead, just keep on creating people like me to be your playthings. I'll tell You this—if I were a science teacher, I wouldn't skip the evolution chapter in the biology book!*

The Connors were about fifteen minutes ahead of us. I wasn't sure if Win would take them into the house or wait outside for us to show up. I really hoped that she would keep them outside, maybe take them on a tour of the yard or something. Anything to keep them out of the house until we had a chance to change and clean up. This was doubly important as the back door was the only entrance into the house. Gracie kept the front door permanently locked because she used it as interior wall space for a shelving unit to be propped against. That meant that the guests would have to be led through Win's bright blue and yellow hazmat site on their way to the living room. That prospect bothered me, but then how much more damage could the dirty kitchen do to my already mutilated reputation?

Sure enough, I could see that no one was outside when I parked the car. Win had led them in and Rick had just joined them. *Great.* I rushed through the back door and slid furtively into the bathroom to change, glad that at the very least my nice outfit was still hanging untouched. My hair, though, was a complete loss. All I could do was quickly secure my limp, exhausted tangles into a stringy ponytail and secure it with a rubber band. Before I left the bathroom, I took a moment to pray that I could still salvage an unsoiled pearl of dignity from the swine manure heap of my circumstances.

I inhaled and forged ahead into the living room with a forced smile. Gorgeous Tina flashed me a sneery, quizzical look, then stood with her husband to shake my hand. My heart lurched.

Both of them held small paper plates of brilliant blue curls. As if my earlier degradation was not enough, Win had gone ahead and served her appetizer. Things could hardly get worse.

Mel Connor was smartly dressed and congenial. I winced when he smiled, though. His teeth were blue. Rick, with blue dribbles at the corners of his mouth, was managing to artfully explain away my whole highway debacle. His gift of gab definitely came in handy at a time like this.

Tina, delicately holding her plate away from her like it was a dirty diaper, was more beautiful, polished, and refined than I could ever have imagined. Everything about her looked expensive. Politely subdued emanations of enticing eau de parfum quietly hovered around her, whispering haikus of water lilies and cherry blossoms. Her cream-colored pantsuit was tailored, but not too formal, and her shimmering, summer wheat-toned haircut could have come straight from one of Josie's books. Like exquisite silk, her tresses flowed gracefully above her shoulders as she moved. From her understated, gleaming diamond earrings to her impeccable Italian leather shoes, she was truly elegant, a perfect specimen of good taste and fashion. I was in awe.

She reminded me of one of Gracie's nicest display pieces. She was like the captivating, six-inch-high glass swan that sat on the living room window sill. Its iridescent finish glistened, reflecting different colors depending on the angle of the light source. I, on the other hand, was the acrylic Oompa-Loompa bowl from the Willy Wonka snack set, complete with a bellyful of fossilized candy corn.

When Mel and Rick's discussion turned to ranch matters, I tried to strike up a conversation with Tina. She was somewhat guarded and less friendly than her husband, so it wasn't an easy task. I floundered about, unmoored as it were, trying to grab onto even a small piece of common ground.

For a moment it struck me as strange that I was not on a level playing field with the first urbanite I had encountered in over a week. The thought of how she had gazed upon me in all my glory beside the road reminded me that I didn't even deserve to be in the same stadium with Tina, let alone on the field with her. It actually seemed quite fitting—and very much a vital part of God's cruel plan for me—to be playing hostess in a home containing more junky baubles than a two-bit tourist trap, serving bright blue french fries on paper plates, and wearing a ratty, dreadlocky ponytail. I felt awkward, childish, apologetic, pathetic.

After a few feeble attempts at small talk, I resorted to flattery. "Your shoes are really attractive. They look incredibly comfortable—I'd love to find a pair just like them. Did you get them in Houston?"

Tina smiled patronizingly and set her plate of untouched Van Gogh sky pieces down on an end table. "Oh, good heavens, no. I bought these directly from a manufacturer's outlet in Italy. I was with a tour group in Naples."

"Oh..." my voice quieted as I realized that I must have absentmindedly slipped the muddy flip-flops back on after I changed into my pants. I discreetly tucked my feet under my chair without looking down.

Tina seemed to open up once we hit on the subject of style. "I took that European trip last fall. I went with my art club members and we squeezed in a couple of visits to fashion design houses in addition to our scheduled museum tours." Her voice became slightly animated. "I found some incredible deals on suits and shoes. You should get a group together and go sometime." She looked down at my feet.

I squirmed, offended that she automatically assumed that I had never visited a European design house. Of course I hadn't but it still stung.

I spoke through a stiff smile, "With a new baby on the way, I don't think it's likely that we'll be traveling overseas anytime in the near future."

"Well, when you can go, I'd highly recommend it." Tina paused and looked me up and down in an uncomfortable instant. "Attractive clothing is well worth the sacrifice."

For some reason I felt obliged to offer a needless apology. "My pregnancy is, um, at the stage where I'm running out of nice clothes that fit comfortably. I don't want to buy new things at this point, though, so I'm not wearing, um, outfits like my usual ones."

Why did I just say that? Earlier, I was actually feeling quite proud of my beaded kurta blouse and matching necklace. I thought that I was hip for a pregnant lady until this ravishing swan-woman landed on the edge of my mucky duck pond.

"You know, if you and Rick are still here in early August, I'll have to invite you to a spa day that I'm planning. It's a thank-you to the ranch women who always work so hard during harvest. I'm thinking of having my hairstylist from Dallas fly in for the weekend."

"Oh, uh, sure. If we're still here, that is."

She stretched her elegant neck out slightly, cocked her head to one side, and blatantly scrutinized my ragged ponytail. My need to apologize was being eclipsed by my desire to throw blue french fries at her creamy plumage.

"I definitely think you should come. Nigel, my stylist, could do amazing things with the women's hair—" she paused and arched her eyebrows, "—and with yours too. I'll Facebook the date when it's solidified."

A wave of indignation washed over me, temporarily paralyzing my vocal cords. Inside my head, though, wrathful words screamed at the presumptive woman. *How dare you! You have no right to compare me to those ranch women—I know just as much, no, probably more than you about current hairstyles! I'm just having a bad hair moment—you have no right to form an opinion of me when you haven't even gotten to know me yet. Believe me—I am NOT one of them.*

"Let me check my calendar right now." She reached into the luxurious designer handbag that sat at her feet and pulled out a smart phone. It looked like the most advanced one on the market. Probably the kind that could read Shakespeare out loud to her in Italian. It probably monitored the stock market and automatically bought gold futures for her. It probably pressed her suits, conditioned her hair, and spread her caviar on crackers for her.

My scathing thoughts were interrupted by a ridiculous ice cream truck song coming from my dingy purse on the dining room table.

"Oh, there's where you put your purse, Haley!" Win jumped up and pulled her silly green bug phone from my handbag. "Hello? Oh hi, Beverly, how are you?"

Tina looked on with an amused smile.

"Um, that's not my phone," I said quietly.

I stopped there, knowing that there was no point in going on about how I too owned a smart phone but that it was in the repair shop. I would just sound like a wannabe. Tina Connor would simply never know that, if it had been up to me, if things had been in my control, if God wasn't so bent on torturing me, I would have been serving wasabi scallop wontons and sushi bundles tied with seaweed strips on chic, square luncheon plates. I would have beefy hair that would swing lustily, outshining hers by a thousand lumens; and I could tell the story of how my international connections had gotten me my hand-beaded designer kurta top straight from India.

But alas, too much damage had been done, and Tina and I were both aware that I had no business attempting to go up her ladder. The rungs she climbed up on were gleaming and slick and I couldn't get a foothold on them in my tractionless flip-flops. I could hurt myself trying.

Even though Win went into the kitchen, her squawking voice rang through the living room. "Really?...Is it an herbal supplement?...So, has Bootsie stopped piddling on the area rug altogether?...Really?...Well, that could be just the ticket for Haley's bladder control problem..."

I intended to jump out of my chair and run to the kitchen to shush Win, but my body could not obey my intentions. Instead, I grunted and worked my way to a standing position.

"Excuse me while I check on our dinner," I said, breathing hard from my exertion.

"Certainly," Tina replied with her head down as she clicked away on her phone. Bored with our circus, she was most likely texting her personal trainer.

As I waddled into the kitchen, I rubbed my tender scalp. My head hurt, but not just from the Preservadoo. It felt like something had conked me right in the middle of the forehead.

19

A backache and false labor contractions sent me out of bed early. Rick stirred when I hauled myself up but immediately went back to sleep. My physical symptoms and tortured thoughts combined to kill any hopes I might have for sleeping in late. It was Rick's fault—once again, he had incited an argument right before bedtime.

This time, it was about two things. The first was the fact that he found Friday's Preservadoo episode highly amusing. He had said that it was hilarious, and I should just see it as an entertaining story to tell our friends. I told him that I felt awful about it and certainly did not want to recount it to anyone, ever. When he said I should just loosen up, I accused him of being callous toward my suffering. I couldn't get him to see how badly I needed comfort, not dismissal.

Our second point of contention had to do with the horror I still felt about Thursday's Bible study/beerfest/frat party. I needed Rick to understand the impact that incident had on me and that it made me not want to go back to Buffalo Jump Church. I told him that I did not want to go to a church where a Bible study leader would lower her standards to match those of someone who was in desperate need of being taught to raise hers. It was incongruent—as impossible as trying to combine unlike terms.

In frustration, I had stated, "Beer-drinking and Bible teaching can't go together, just like x's and y's can't be added together in an equation."

"Wow, you're channeling your dad," Rick had replied.

"I am not—why can't you just listen to me?"

Our marriage had fallen even deeper into the ditch. I didn't see how we could pull it out by ourselves.

———•◦•◦•———

A rhythmic whistling snore, coming from Win's bedroom, was loud enough to hear in the kitchen. I tip-toed around, not wanting to generate a puff of air or any humidity with my breath that would set off a sensor in the yapping weather station. I gingerly put a cup of tea water in the microwave and turned on Hank's computer. I needed my friends now more than ever.

The chirping birds inside the computer tower settled down much faster than usual. I logged on to Facebook and the home page came up in fifty seconds. Lorna's post appeared first. It read:

Another fruitful study at the church last night. Nilima brought several Hindu friends who were bowled over by the beauty and simplicity of our sanctuary. They said they will come for our Sunday morning service. Imagine that! It's a perfect example of how important it is for us to remain tasteful and pleasing to the secular world. God is obviously blessing our efforts.

Really, now. So glad God is blessing you. How nice that He's your friend.
I decided to check my personal messages instead. There was one from Charmaine.

Thanks for letting me know about your phone issues. I'll just use Facebook instead of texting until you get your cell back. To answer your question about sudden growth, there's not much you can do at this late stage. Just be glad that you've stayed in shape and eaten well up to this point. I'm sure you're still as sleek and beautiful as ever. As long as you're still doing your Sitting Still Stretches and your Keepin' Cool Cardio Strolls and eating all your usual kick-butt healthy foods, you'll be fine. Can't wait to hear about your easy delivery!

Kick-butt healthy foods. Like burritos and pork ribs? Sleek and beautiful. Like a giant mushroom, perhaps, or one of those competition pumpkins that has to be loaded on a truck with a forklift?
I clicked on the next message. It was from Stacie.

Hope you're recovering from your car explosion. I'm not doing so great. Went on another nightmare blind date last night. :(Why I keep putting myself through these things I'll never know. He's some accountant for a car dealership but talked like he owned the whole business. Was dressed in an expensive suit and acted snotty with our server. It made me mad. At one point, I noticed that Special Date's hairdo shifted. Yep, he was wearing a rug, all right. It drove me crazy to watch his part slowly sink toward one ear while he bragged about himself. Was too wrapped up in impressing me to feel it, I guess. Made me wonder what else about him was fake. So, HAVE YOU FOUND A COWBOY FOR ME YET? lol. Actually, at this point

I'd take just about any guy who was real and honest and down to earth. That would be a refreshing change. Call me sometime. Miss you. :)

I laughed. Good ol' Stacie made me smile again. I always thought that as a Christian, I would be the one to help her; but by just being herself, she always ended up making me feel better.

I went back to my home page and scanned the rest of the messages. I wouldn't admit it to Rick, but a lot of the postings did suddenly seem sort of petty and boasty. I decided not to bother updating my own pitiful status. There was no way to honestly relate it in a way that wouldn't contradict everything I had previously written about God's holy growth within my soul, my nutrition mission, swimming against the enemy's tide, and all the rest of my blah, blah, blah. I had raised my own faith bar so high that even I couldn't reach it anymore.

If I was really brave and honest I would post something like: "I am now huge and enjoy wearing maternity lederhosen in public. I've stopped shaving my legs, eat pork ribs with my fingers, and live in a house that has a four-foot-wide wooden catfish nailed to the wall in the bathroom. I drive a massive all-metal gas guzzling station wagon and sometimes go into ditches. I was unruly this week and a policewoman pulled a gun on me. I also went to a saloon for lunch this week. I am mad at my husband and I am mad at God. God doesn't like me anymore."

Lorna wouldn't approve, she'd say I wasn't being a good witness, but Stacie would hug me.

I disconnected the internet, suddenly dissatisfied with the whole game and gazed out the window. Something about the way the sun was hitting the unfolding leaf buds on a bush outside caught my attention. There was a curious brightness, almost a glow, varnishing the bushes and the old cottonwood tree behind the house. It begged further inspection, so I slipped on my flip-flops and went out the back door with my steaming tea mug in hand.

The breezes were the faintest I had experienced so far in Montana. They played lightly around my face, flitting and teasing, but not overpowering. I sat down on a plastic lawn chair by the back fence and drank my tea, ignoring Herman's persistent hoots the way a mother might ignore a tantrumming child's demands.

The sunshine had given everything its early morning bath, and all that I could see—the house, the landscape, even the lawn ornaments—appeared fresh and ready to face the new day. It was peaceful. More peaceful than staring at a computer screen could ever be.

Sadly, the serenity outside of me couldn't touch the anarchy that had erupted inside of me. I started talking out loud to God, complaining to Him, challenging Him, telling Him that He was unfair. Didn't all the things I had done for Him make any difference at all? I had worked hard to look and talk and behave like a Christian all my life—even through a difficult childhood with a control freak for a father—and ruination of my life was my reward? Even as I let my honest resentment pour out, however, I knew God wasn't hearing me. Maybe He wasn't who I thought He was, after all.

A sweet meadowlark, sitting on the clothesline, listened to every word I said, though. When I finally stopped talking, the bird started singing his distinctive and repetitive lark song. His cheery lyrics sounded sympathetic. I wondered if he had ever done anything stupid in front of the other birds. Probably not. He was too naturally pretty to ever need a hairdo protector, and he certainly didn't care if anyone caught a glimpse of him toileting. He was free from expectation and convention. I wished I could be free. Not free from the toileting part, of course, but free from what?

I thought of Bruce the budgie, who had lived a long and happy life, thanks to Josh's vigilant protection of his freedom. Josh let Bruce fly around outside his cage whenever Dad wasn't home. Josh was so patient and diligent in his training with Bruce that the bird could even be trusted to fly around in the backyard for short periods of time without straying far. Bruce always came back—he knew where the love was.

After Bruce died, it seemed that Josh transferred his protection of Bruce's freedom to the protection of his own. Leaving home immediately after graduation, Josh flew as far as he could from Dad's rules and Dad's church. But up to this point, he hadn't gone back. He said he had a relationship with God, but it couldn't be boxed in by a church. And he liked it that way.

He went so far into rebellion that he said he forgave Dad for his rigidity. He once announced, "One of the best things that ever happened to me was that Dad ran me out of the traditional church. It drove me to freedom."

I appreciated that Josh wanted to distance himself from a regular church setting but knew that he needed to stay in fellowship with other believers. I had taken him with me to Artos & Ichthus, certain he would love it, but two different visits there only seemed to amuse him instead of capturing him. He said it wasn't much different from any other evangelical church, just in a cooler package. He said he felt like his relationship with God would still be judged by how often he attended services or how much he read his Bible, and that the church measured its own effectiveness by how snazzy their music was and how good they looked.

Stacie reacted similarly went I invited her to a Sunday morning service. I couldn't figure out why. Because she had grown up in a dry, old-school church, I thought she would love our hip and modern worship. I was sure she would find a whole new Jesus there. She didn't, though, and I often wondered what was wrong with her.

I looked around Gracie's yard and frowned. My thoughts were getting me nowhere. My coaster car was stuck on a nauseating circular track, spinning me around and around, making me sicker and more tired with every lap. I wanted off.

Out of nowhere, a deviously fanciful notion struck me. It was an urge.

An urge to get back at God. An urge to rebel.

An overwhelming desire to throw off all my burdens pulsed through me. I struggled to my feet, not sure what I would do next but open to just about anything. I didn't want to be myself anymore. I suddenly wanted to be rough, a heathen, a renegade. I felt like my pulled-back hair, ratty bathrobe, and dirty flip-flops were the uniform of a proud soldier, a soldier deliberately fighting for the wrong side.

The baby fluttered around inside me as I stepped onto the muddy grass, my eyes set toward a low hill just a few hundred yards from the backyard fence. The hill was outside the property line.

It was outside the boundaries.

Gracie and Hank's property bordered an enormous tract of public land that was leased to ranchers for livestock grazing purposes. Hank had explained that eastern Montana was dotted with such government-owned ranges. Up until that morning, I had been too afraid of snakes to entertain the slightest bit of interest in exploring the area. Rick insisted there was nothing to worry about, but I had turned down his repeated invitations for even a leisurely walk with him out there.

Now, though, I inexplicably longed to go there. I was determined to haul my mushroom mass up to a higher, forbidden place. A place where I could see my miserable life from a different perspective.

I reached the opening in the back fence that led to the vast prairie beyond. I hesitated, though.

Rattlesnakes.

My heart started to beat harder while I scanned the hillside, not sure what a snake on the ground would look like or how camouflaged a deadly rattler on a greening hillside might be.

Fear battled desire inside me. I was disgusted at myself for being afraid. Fear had imprisoned me in different ways my whole life and I wanted desperately to laugh in its face this time. *But rattlesnakes kill people, right?*

"Hoo-hoo, hoo-hoo," Herman hooted from his spot by the back door. A mosquito must have exhaled near him. The bright morning sun had recharged his solar cells and he was extra animated, straining at any and every hint of sound and motion in the vicinity. Garden pests were probably shaking in their boots for acres around, repelled by the terrifying sound of the fake hooting.

That's it!

I've read that even sane people can have insane moments. Maybe even several in a lifetime. Stacie told me once that her own mother had a breakdown during a period of high stress. She acted fine but kept lining food up neatly in the top dishwasher rack. Bread slices one day, sausages the next. Stacie said that the scary part was that her usually intelligent, aware mom kept insisting that it was normal practice to put food in the dishwasher. A temporary stint on anti-depressants combined with a nice vacation brought Stacie's mom back to sanity eventually.

And so, in the middle of my elevated stress and despair, the idea of using Herman as a snake shield seemed perfectly fine, even brilliant. I calmly walked over to the back steps, picked the hooting statue up and marched right through the fence opening.

I held Herman upside-down as I hiked, reasoning that a snake could better perceive the hooting vibrations if I kept the owl's head speaker close to the ground. Overcome by the rhythmic motion of my plodding feet, Herman's head spun wildly while he hooted and hooted. It was wonderful. I was confident that snakes would run from him like vampires fleeing from a cross made of garlic cloves.

I was feeling better. Not just better—elated. My coaster car abruptly exited its roundabout and started climbing an upward track at the same slow pace my feet kept on the hill.

I would have loved to run up the hill, arms outstretched like Julie Andrews in *The Sound of Music*. Only, instead of singing, "The Hills Are Alive," I'd belt out "Born to Be Wild." And it wouldn't be the tepid school band version that I putzed out on my clarinet in the woodwind section of middle school. It would be the full rockin' Steppenwolf version. And I wouldn't lightly run up the hill with a perfect little nun hairdo. I would hellishly crest the hill in a spray of mud on my mean Harley Hawg. I'd be wearing a stretchy tank top under the leather lederhosen to show off my muscular arms and my shiny, beefy hair would bounce and flow gloriously from under my fantastical helmet with attached wings—one that I would have traded my digital food scale for in Larry's shop. I would rev my deafening, mufflerless motor and lean forward as I executed a bold jump over a mound of dirt.

My imagination soared out of control as I lugged hooting Herman up the hill. I drifted farther into a mad reverie, blissfully unaware that I was losing my mind.

I smiled, envisioning the shocked expressions on the faces of my family and friends who would already be assembled on the hilltop to greet me. Expecting their usual Nice Haley Girl to sweetly embrace them, they would be totally unprepared to be peppered by rocks and uprooted sagebrush as Naughty Harley Girl popped an outrageously dangerous wheelie right in front of them.

Danielle would be there. Mom would be there. Lorna would be there.

Dad would be there.

And I wouldn't care.

It wouldn't make one bit of difference what they thought because I didn't care anymore. I was no longer a Christian. I would just be a bad person who enjoyed being that way. No more important mission assignments. No more life purpose. No more perfect church services. No more wifely guilt. No more Facebook status updates to write in pious Christianese. No more hair products. No more expectation. No more demand. *No more...no more...no more...*

The baby kicked harder this time. Dementedly exhilarated, I wondered if there was a casino in Range City. That would solve our name issue. I'd ride there to birth our daughter next to a slot machine and name her Golden Nugget. I'd keep wearing my lederhosen postpartum and take to the road in my Harley with Nuggie strapped in her car seat behind me. I'd keep the visor of my helmet up to show off all the ear and face piercings that Larry kindly riveted into me back in Ohio and head all the way to Houston just to rev my deafening motor in front of Tina Connor's house at six am. I'd wait until she flitted out of her house in her ultra-plush, white designer bathrobe to plead with me to stop the noise and spray her with mud as I spun off into the sunrise. She would raise her fist at me and threaten to call the police, but I would laugh with delight. No cop could catch me and Nuggie, ever...

Breathing hard, I reached the top of the hill. It was just high enough to allow for a wider perspective of the area than I could get from Gracie's yard. The range of view was probably forty or fifty miles in all directions. About a half a mile away, I could see the Basin River winding its way North toward

Grassview, and farther off in the distance, I could make out the line of higher hills that the map named Garrison Ridge. Except for the cluster of buildings that comprised tiny Grassview, the landscape was almost completely void of anything but prairie, hills, and sky. That suddenly seemed okay, though. Unlike the city, there were no boundaries, no straight, concrete lines to box me in. For the briefest moment, I was free.

"Haley, what are you doing?"

"Aaah!" The baby and I both jumped. I almost dropped Herman. Rick had appeared from nowhere and stood beside me, openmouthed.

"What the—" Rick's shocked expression was overdone. He acted like he had never seen a pregnant woman minding her own business at the top of a deserted hill, clutching an upside-down hooting garden statue before.

"Rick, don't scare me like that! How'd you get here?"

"Uh, same way you did—up the hill. What's going on with you? And what's with that?" He pointed at Herman. "I know you don't like the owl, Haley, but it's Gracie's. You can't just take someone's stuff and throw it over a cliff because you don't like it."

"I'm not—" I stopped short.

Even though his wild curls were springing up in all directions and he was wearing pajama sweats and a faded John Wayne T-shirt, Rick reeked of stability. He stood beside me, unfashionable, unsophisticated, yet muscular and achingly good-looking. Somewhere, somehow, the tables had turned and he was the grounded one. I knew I had temporarily departed earth to fly dangerously up among the clouds of silliness. Rick had come just in time, tugging on my kite strings, pulling me back to earth, reeling me in, saving me from the deadly power lines of emotional unhingement.

I looked down at Herman, then back at Rick. I flushed with raw shame. It made my hand itch. I dropped Herman to the ground. Agreeing with Rick's assumption that I had hiked up the hill merely to toss Herman over a cliff was the out I needed. No one ever need know that in a moment sheer madness I had used a fake owl as a snake shield. It was not Facebook material. My regrettable daydream wasn't ever going to see the light of day, either—not even on a therapist's couch. I needed to put my scandalous thoughts back in their cage and throw a blanket over them.

"Um, you're right. I'm being impulsive. I, uh, couldn't stand the hooting anymore and, well, just grabbed him and, ahem, came up here. "

"Well, you shouldn't steal people's stuff, and you sure shouldn't be walking around out here by yourself."

I stiffened at Rick's scolding. Defensive anger rose up in me, replacing my shame. "Stealing? You're calling me a thief?"

I yelled loud enough to activate one of our dysfunctional, but handy, communication patterns. It was the one where, if I responded in a mean enough and loud enough tone, Rick would back down. It was in his nature to always do that.

"Okay, okay—calm down. I know you're not a thief. I guess you're just not thinking this through." He spoke softer and moved closer to me. At my feet, Herman hooted. The ground muffled the sound. Unable to spin in a supine position, his head repeatedly whirred and clicked against a rock. He looked sad. A snake somewhere nearby was probably laughing.

Rick stood quietly beside me for a minute before asking, "How long have you been out here?"

I rubbed my hand. "A while."

"Are you cold?" Rick's voice became genuinely tender.

"No." I kept my tone flat.

He touched my shoulder. "We should go back to the house."

The last thing I wanted to do was return to my depressing reality, but having no supportive shoes and no motorcycle nearby, I knew he was right.

Rick bent down and picked Herman up. "Are you still planning on going to church? It's getting late and you need time to get ready."

I hadn't completely returned to earth. A little piece of Naughty Harley Girl still lingered inside of me. If she could have, she would have sneered, *"Yeah, right, church. Like I'd be caught dead in a church. I wouldn't go to church even if they gave out free tattoo certificates there. I'm goin' to Vegas, Mister, and you ain't goin' along."*

But Nice Haley Girl, returning from her sanity sabbatical, overpowered Harley Girl. With a lifetime of duty and obligation exercises behind her, Nice Girl was much stronger.

I sighed. "Yes, I'm ready and I'm going to church."

I was mad that Rick even had to ask. He should have known after all these years with me that church attendance was a non-negotiable. My dad had worked out a ratio for that one too. It proved that the number of crimes committed on Sunday mornings in certain areas was directly proportional to the number of church attendees in said communities. As kids, when we protested having to go to church, even when we were on vacation, Dad would remind us that we could end up costing the taxpayers a lot of money some day when we became yet another inmate in an already overcrowded system. And we better not expect him to visit us in jail if that happened—it was much better to just go to church and avoid the temptation to start robbing ATM machines, setting school buildings on fire, or writing bad checks at convenience stores.

"Um, your hair…" Rick glanced questioningly at my ponytail.

"My hair's fine. I just need to get dressed." I lifted my chin slightly.

Rick's eyes widened. "Oookay."

Herman bellowed like a noisy toddler as Rick toted him back to the house. I followed, slogging down the hill on puffy feet. My spirits descended along with the rest of me. I felt like I was drowning from an overdose.

An imagination overdose. A momentary dream of scandalous freedom that was already calling to me, enticing me to come back for more.

20

Overloaded with leaden guilt, my coaster car had derailed. It was nearly impossible to drag it over the rocks and dirt into the church with me.

Our trip to church had been completely silent. Even Win, decked out in purple gingham and eyelet lace, was smart enough to allow plenty of room in the car for my thick, dark mood. I brooded as we drove, feeling deep remorse over my brush with spiritual homicide. My daydream of being bad and running away was shameful. I couldn't believe that I had even for a moment entertained the thought that I no longer wanted to be a Christian. It just wasn't right, especially for an expectant mother.

It made me even madder at Rick. Part of my indiscretion was clearly his fault. His mishandling of our marriage had driven me to the kind of despair that can make a respectable woman go crazy. Harley crazy.

I took a deep breath as I stood on the sanctuary threshold, determined to get right with God and get back on track. I would regain my dignity and reestablish my ministry purpose.

"Hi, Haley!" Brooke waved at me from the other side of the sanctuary.

Oof. Someone grabbed my shoulders from behind. "Hi, Haley—baby still on the inside?" It was cardinal-haired Marlene.

"Haley!" Jeannie ran up, attempting to hug me around the baby. Her kind gesture was as awkward as Rick's muddled Heimlich maneuver.

I wasn't expecting such a warm reception. The church women treated me as if they had known me all my life. Like I was one of them—like I belonged. I flushed, wishing they wouldn't be so nice to me. They didn't know that only an hour earlier I had privately backslidden on a lonely hilltop. They didn't know that I was failing in my God-given mission to enlighten them, and even worse, they still didn't know that I was the one who had poisoned their children. I felt like a crooked life insurance salesman accepting gifts from elderly people that I was covertly swindling.

On top of everything, I was dressed like a failure. At least in that respect, I was being honest, though. My lack of reverence on the inside was now officially mirrored on my outside. I was now down to the only outfit beside the lederhosen that I could squeeze my fully mushroomed body into. In my old life, I would never have dreamed that I would show up in church in old stretch pants, a T-shirt, and flip-flops with sullied fake jewels. The pants were not supposed to be Capri length, but my circumference had pulled them up above my ankles, making them look like ugly highwaters. Several inches of my hairy, unshaven legs stuck out below the pants' hem, suggesting that I had pulled my trousers on over the bottom half of an ape costume. And, the icing on the cake was the fact that my shirt was stretched so tight around my middle that the bands of necessary duct tape showed through, making my midsection look lumpy as well as shockingly round.

When Jeannie backed away from me, I caught sight of Naomi ambling through the church doors. Kendra was with her. I turned around quickly, pretending that I didn't see them. The very presence of Naomi made my skin crawl. As a woman with low standards, she had no business mentoring an ignorant young woman. I might have been temporarily backslidden, but unlike Naomi, I wasn't going to stay in my pitiful state. I had every intention of repenting and winning back God's favor. In fact, at that exact moment, it felt like I was already being handed an opportunity to redeem myself.

I watched Naomi take Kendra over to meet Brandon and a galvanizing flash of determination shot through me. Yet another new mission plunked down, right there in front of me. *Wow, thank You, God. Thank You for giving me another chance.*

I sensed a new call. A heavenly calling. In the name of protecting the whole church from her dangerous influence, I was assigned to take Naomi down.

Fueled by a desperate need to reclaim my spiritual credibility, my mind went back into planning mode. I would start by informing Brandon about the degeneration of Thursday's Bible study. He needed to see that Naomi could endanger Buffalo Jump church's reputation in the community. He needed to know that Naomi didn't seem to care one bit about reputation, whether it was the church's or her own. Maybe he didn't know about Naomi's squalid living conditions—conditions which would deprive her of the accountability a good reputation provides.

The time had come for Brandon to mature as a pastor and step up to the hard job of administering church discipline to one of his own. My dad would be quite proud of me for taking this on.

The crying man started the worship service off with a peppy song. Win sat in the pew beside me since it was Naomi's turn to man the nursery. Margarita Marlene had pulled Kendra with a hug into the seat beside her. They were right in front of us. Again, Kendra's offensive tobacco odor assaulted me. I almost felt like I was back at Bison Jack's. I wanted to move, but Rick was happily settled in beside me and most likely would balk at sitting somewhere else.

As I struggled to sing the fuzzy words projected on the tablecloth, I noticed an odd odor wafting in and around Kendra's smell. It was the scent of something that I couldn't quite place. Sort of plasticky, or soapy, with a hint of magic marker, maybe. It kept floating in and out of my consciousness as I tried to pay attention to the organ honky-tonk. Just before the singing ended, it finally dawned on me that I had smelled that same smell in the car. *Win.*

She was on my left, and I leaned over and sniffed her. It was definitely Win. She smelled like a banana dipped in turpentine. I sneezed.

Without taking her eyes off the pastor up front, she whispered, "Lotion legs."

Now what? I looked down at her legs and realized that they were shiny. She was wearing some sort of odoriferous, shimmering hosiery. I didn't want to ask, didn't want to know, didn't even want to go there. I was through worrying about her antics. She could cover her legs in cake batter for all I cared. I sneezed again.

Win leaned over to say something, but I put my finger to my lips and shushed her. She turned and dug out a small plastic sack from her purse. I tried to ignore it, but she pushed it in front of my face. It read:

LOTIONLEGS
THE FANTASTIC ALL-DAY MOISTURIZING PANTYHOSE
SOFTEN YOUR LEGS WITHOUT THE HASSLE
OF APPLYING LOTION
A TRUE MORNING TIME-SAVER!

I pushed the silly bag away and bowed my head as Brandon started praying. Not wanting my mascara to smear, I kept my eyes open. One line on the bulletin in my lap called out to me. It was the title of the sermon: "What Will Jesus Catch You Doing When He Returns?" I gasped. I couldn't believe it. Was Brandon going to preach on Dad's philosophy? My thoughts raced. I had already given up on Rick—but...*Naomi! Is this sermon intended for Naomi? Had someone already beaten me to the punch and reported her beer drinking to him? Is Brandon creatively confronting both Marlene and Naomi by simply laying it all out in a Sunday sermon?*

I could hardly wait for the prayer to end. "Aunt Win," I whispered. "Quick, go take the nursery for Naomi—she needs, um, might want to hear the sermon today."

Win looked like she was about to protest, then cocked her head and whispered back, "You know, I think I'll do that. Brooke's toddler twins are really cute."

She and Glory! do-si-doed up and out of the pew, skirts rustling like Scarlet O'Hara. A stray gum wrapper and a piece of tissue hitched a ride on her sticky pantyhose.

Brandon had already started talking. "...and last week we also discussed the Pharisees' showiness—what was the word I used, folks?"

"Ostentation!" Several people yelled it at once. I felt like I was at a pep rally.

"Good job, folks! Glad you remembered. And we talked about their pride and hypocrisy as well. Today, I thought we'd take a look at another word you hear used more often in church than anywhere else."

He paused to smile, then shouted, "Potluck!"

I didn't laugh, but everyone else did, including Naomi, who had just emerged from the nursery and slipped into the pew in front of me. She squeezed Kendra's shoulders as she sat down beside her. My skin bristled.

"Ha, ha just kidding. The real word I'm studying right now is 'legalism.'" He paused to look at a piece of paper he pulled out of his Bible. "The dictionary definition of legalism is 'strict adherence to a literal interpretation of a law, rule, or religious or moral code.'"

He looked up and cleared his throat. "For the Pharisees, legalism was a way of life. They believed their connection to God and their salvation hinged on following the rules of the law absolutely perfectly. It must have gotten pretty old to have to live the way they did. And they held every other Jewish person to their standard, making life really hard for the regular people to feel they could ever be close to God. It should have been Good News to all the Jewish leaders to have Jesus come along and tell them they wouldn't have to do that anymore. But as we all know, that wasn't the case.

"Those Pharisees had invested so much, had so many centuries of tradition backing their cause that they just couldn't walk away from it. Following Jesus and accepting His preachin' would have stripped them of everything they did that gave them power and glory. It's like the wind of the Holy Spirit blew right out of Jesus and kept mussin' up their hair and blowin' dirt on their robes every time they came too close to Him."

The baby moved, feeling like she was purposely trying to find my bladder so she could rest her head against it. I hoped Brandon would get to the point of his sermon quickly.

He looked around the crowd, then smiled at a younger cowboy near the back. "Kinda like that tornado on your property last year, huh, Jason? Stripped the roof off your barn and blew loads of your pretty topsoil all the way into North Dakota, didn't it?"

"Yep, sure did." The cowboy's voice was smooth and low.

"That's what the Holy Spirit does when He follows Jesus into our lives. Blows all the stuff off our outsides, exposes what's inside. The Pharisees got mad every time they were around Jesus because He kept talkin' about their insides. Wouldn't let them get away with covering up and pretending. Deep down, I think they knew that if they admitted that Jesus was the Son of God, then He would be right, they would be exposed, and everything they ever believed in would be turned upside down. They wouldn't be teachers anymore, and they'd have to lower themselves to be students. That thought probably put their undies in a bunch. You know, we can be like that too when we start thinkin' we always have to teach everybody—when we forget that sometimes we need to shut up and learn and stop thinking that everywhere we go we have something to contribute. That's not very humble, is it? Believe me, I'm talkin' to myself here. As a preacher, sometimes I forget that I'm a student too. And sometimes God uses the most surprising situations and people to teach me things.

"When it came to legalism—their strict obeying of the rules of the Old Law—they weren't necessarily wrong. Good Jews were expected to carry out certain duties and to avoid certain things. And the Pharisees had been doing their job of protecting God's law for scads of years, just like God had commanded through Moses. But, somewhere along the line, they had lost sight of God's original intent—the spirit of the law. They had gotten so caught up in obeying every single bit of every single rule, or the 'letter of the Law,' as Paul called it, that they no longer fulfilled the spirit of the Law. Jesus was forcing them to look at the spirit of the Law, which was love."

"Amen, Brother Brandon." Naomi's white head nodded as she spoke brazenly into the crowd's hush. I bristled again. For me, her comeuppance couldn't come soon enough. But Brandon kept on going as if he had gotten his sermons mixed up, and the title in the bulletin wasn't going to be the point of this one.

"The Pharisees' legalism made them blind. They lost sight of God's love. They were trained to only see people as obedient or disobedient. Clean or unclean. In a way, they had become like racists. They judged the content of people's character by what they saw on the outside. That's what legalism does to us today too. When we decide whether or not someone is a Christian by how they look on the outside, we're almost being as nasty as an ol' Ku Klux Klan member."

Brandon leaned forward and squinted his eyes. "I'm not jokin' here, folks. When taken to the extreme, legalism produces the same type of hate that racism does. It's nothin' to mess with. The biggest danger of becoming legalistic is that we end up propping ourselves up with externals and never, ever deal with our hearts." He paused.

"Hmm. This is where I was going to have us turn to second Corinthians three, but something just hit me. I was talking to Naomi about this the other day, and she came up with a great word picture about this very thing—" he paused and cocked his head to one side, "—in fact, you know what?"

He looked over in our direction. "Naomi, I see you're not coverin' the nursery today. Why don't you come up and tell us all the same thing you said to me about legalism. Don't mean to put you on the spot—but you can say it better than I did. Would you mind?"

Even though I could only see the back of Naomi's head, I was sure she was smiling. "Heh—well, I guess I don't mind. Sure, why not?" I saw her pat Kendra's knee before she stood and slowly strode to the pulpit.

I was horrified. *For heaven's sake, what does Brandon think he's doing? He's supposed to correct her, not let her preach!*

My heart pounded as I watched Brandon step back and give his place at the pulpit over to Naomi. This wasn't right. As usual, Rick looked attentive and cheerful. *Why am I the only one to see through this woman, Lord?*

I decided my mission was confirmed by this turn of events. Brandon definitely needed my insight into Naomi. How could he be so oblivious to the danger she posed? I would waste no time after the service was over—I would ask Brandon to speak to me privately and make sure that he understood that Naomi was not fit for leadership. In the meantime, I would have to sit and endure whatever twisted love doctrine she was going to try and fool the people with this time.

She addressed Brandon first. "You're referrin' to when I talked about Gramma's corset, right?"

"Yeah, that one. Tell everybody what you told me," Brandon replied.

Gramma's corset?

"Well, when Brandon and I talked a little bit the other day about his preachin' on the subject of legalism, I told him it made me think of my Gramma Frances. She used to tell my sisters and me stories of how she had to wear an undergarment called a 'corset' when she was younger. All the ladies wore them back then. They were a girdle-type thing that they cinched up tight around their middles and it made them look really small-waisted. Having a teensy hourglass figure was all the rage, apparently."

What does this have to do with anything? Is she getting senile like Win, or has she fried too many brain cells from too much beer?

"Gramma showed us one of her old corsets once. It had rows of vertical ribbing called 'boning' sewed all around it. The stiff strips made a rigid frame that wrapped around a lady's stomach, and when its crisscross laces were pulled tight, it sucked her whole gut in. Everything, flesh on the outside, organs on the inside, got pushed either up or down in order to make it look like the woman was way skinnier than she really was. It was almost a kind of cheating—the ladies could look like they were toned up without ever exercising or eating right."

This is disgusting. Pastor Mitch would have kicked Naomi out by now.

"Gramma said it was awful uncomfortable, that at times it really hurt bad to wear one of those corsets, and that women often had problems later on in life because they injured themselves from wearing 'em too long. Displaced organs and something she called 'puddin' middle happened. The women's torsos would get all mushy and squishy from never having to use their own abdominal muscles to have a smaller waist. The longer a woman wore one, the weaker her internal muscle strength got.

"When Brandon and I were talking about how legalism works, I thought of all those poor ladies and their puddin' middles. When Christians rely on external structure to set them apart as 'holy' they can actually be keepin' themselves from ever getting strong in their faith. Strong faith springs from our hearts and gets its shape and form from having to exercise love, over and over.

It takes time and patience and a good dose of the Holy Spirit to know how to love from the inside out. It doesn't worry about appearances or what people think; it just loves others more than self. Legalism—good behavior and good deeds—can make a Christian look all pretty and perfect on the outside but allows messed up motives to squish around on the inside. These motives are like learning the Bible just to show off how much you know or helpin' someone just to make yourself look sacrificial and be someone's hero. We're supposed to do that stuff out of a heart that truly loves God and wants to help others. If you do good works just because it's what a pretty Christian is supposed to do, then you're just wearing a damaging corset. Instead, we need to be building up our love abs."

"Preach it, sister!" Marlene hollered.

"Amen!" several others yelled.

To my absolute horror, Brandon dropped to the floor beside the pulpit and started doing sit-ups. Naomi laughed and started counting.

"One, two, three…" the rest of the congregation joined in.

The pep rally had deteriorated into a Richard Simmons infomercial. Brandon was ridiculously Movin,' Groovin,' and Losin' it on the church platform. The baby was movin' and groovin' inside me and I was about to lose my breakfast.

Rick, with a grin as big as Margarita Marlene's, counted along with the rest of the studio audience. It was so corny that it was humiliating to be there. I sat helplessly wringing my hands in my lap, desperately wishing for the church service travesty to play itself out quickly.

In front of me, Kendra's unswerving, yellow hair stiffly defied the movement of her shoulders as she also clapped and counted. *What kind of message is this group sending to this ignorant young woman? That church is a place to be foolish? That Christians can throw away the rules and just have fun?*

After fifty ridiculous sit-ups, Brandon finally stood up, pink-cheeked but not breathing hard. He raised his hands in the air like he had just scored a touchdown. The crowd cheered. *He's just showing off. What a ridiculous excuse for a pastor.* My anger was not about to dissipate anytime soon.

"Good job, pastor boy!" Old Naomi high-fived him, then patted his stomach. "Nice abs. Are your insides just as strong?"

"By the grace of God and through the power of the Holy Spirit, I hope so!" Brandon's voice boomed. He tugged on his belt, straightened his bolo tie and stepped back up to the pulpit. "Ha, ha—that was fun. You can sit down now, Naomi. Thanks for your good words."

Naomi returned to her place beside Kendra, and Brandon resumed as though nothing ridiculous had just happened.

"So folks, do you get what Naomi was trying to say? We can't rely on outside props to make us a Christian. We need to get strong from the inside before we try to fix our outside conduct. In fact, we can end up damaging our relationship with Jesus if we just do stuff to appear righteous. Our hearts can get hard and brittle when we neglect to exercise them through loving others. Jesus put it in a real interesting way in Matthew twenty-three, verse twenty-seven. Turn there and read along with me, please."

I stared straight ahead. I no longer trusted his doctrine or him, for that matter. I couldn't confide in him about Naomi—he was just like her. Buffalo Jump Community Church was a sham.

"Woe to you, teachers of the law and Pharisees, you hypocrites! You are like whitewashed tombs, which look beautiful on the outside but on the inside are full of dead men's bones and everything unclean. In the same way, on the outside you appear to people as righteous but on the inside you are full of hypocrisy and wickedness."

Brandon looked up. "Here Jesus was talking about the Jewish practice of making burial spots—their graves—visible so people wouldn't accidentally step on them and become unceremonially clean. He was sayin' that the Pharisees were brushing good deeds like white paint over the top of their sin, making them like 'white-washed tombs, beautiful on the outside, but full of dead men's bones' on the inside. I think he meant that the Pharisees' arrogant good deeds actually became the evidence of their internal sin. Their duty-filling behaviors were actually the outside warning flags that they were full of dead, rotten sin on the inside!" He stopped to pat his stomach before continuing, "'and just what were those inside sins?' you ask."

I haven't asked. I don't care. I don't care about the Pharisees. I care about Kendra and everyone else that Naomi is leading astray. What about that, Pastor-boy? Huh?

"Well, first, those arrogant leaders were full of stinky pride—Jesus had talked about that earlier in chapter twenty-three—the kind of pride that craved people's attention, honor, and adoration. The kind of self-centered pride that made them worry more about themselves than about others. Pride is sin, people, there's no way around it."

A few "amens" echoed again in response to Brandon's words. Naomi, of course, was among them.

"Next, they made such a big deal out of the teensiest technicalities in the law that they neglected the much bigger and important matters—justice, compassion, and faithfulness. Folks, you can be the cleanest-living person on earth and still be sinning big time, everyday." He was getting worked up. "What about greed, deceit, gluttony, gossip, and unforgiveness? These inside sins are even more dangerous than outside sins because they are tolerated in many of our modern churches. They're the socially acceptable sins that can stay nicely hidden inside our weak hearts. As long as we wear our pretty, good behavior corsets to church on Sunday and make sure to show up every time the doors are open, we figure we're all fine.

"And another thing—later on in the New Testament, Paul said that the New Covenant that Jesus taught about would involve having the law 'written on our hearts and put in our minds.' So it makes sense to me that if we don't stop lookin' at everybody else's actions more than we look inside our own hearts, we won't be ready to receive the new law in the new way that Jesus was bringin' in," he turned to smile directly at Naomi, "the law of love."

Poor Kendra looked over at Naomi and smiled. Naomi smiled back. It was awful.

Brandon walked around to the front of the pulpit. "So what was the remedy for all this legalism?"

His worthless rhetorical questions were getting old. I wouldn't have ever guessed that a man could be a cowboy, a pastor, and a drama queen all at once.

"The remedy, the cure, folks, for legalism is the same for us as it was for the Pharisees—repentance. Repentance—to turn away from the wrong and turn toward the right…"

I grabbed my right hand with my left. On top of the itching, the original pain starting flaring up again. I rubbed it while my mind raced. Repentance? *Isn't that supposed to be preached to unsaved people? To people who don't believe in God? If these people really are Christians, a repentance message shouldn't be necessary.* I glanced over at Rick. *Unless, of course, someone is mistreating one's wife.*

"…Repentance doesn't have to be some formal big deal. It just involves prayin' and tellin' God that you know that your thoughts and attitudes are bad ones; and even though you think you're some special Christian, you see now that you're no better than an investment embezzler or a meth cooker. That's all you have to do, folks. Admit you're a dumb sheep like everyone else on this planet. Jesus likes it when we're honest like that. He loves us so much and will forgive you and help you to start dealin' with your bad heart from that point on. That's the humility I was talking about last week. You'll not only be forgiven, you'll be a whole lot more compassionate toward others too. And you'll sure be easier to live with."

A few chuckles, including a loud one from Rick, rippled through the group. I wasn't one bit amused. I was furious.

"Repentance is the key to stepping into God's kingdom—the heart place we can live in right now where He rules and reigns over our lives. It was the one thing, though, that the Pharisees were completely unwilling to do. Their pride not only kept them from admitting guilt, they guilted others into being just like them. Worse than that, in verse thirteen, Jesus tells them that they 'shut the kingdom of heaven in men's faces.' They themselves refused to enter and kept others from entering too. Repentance is the Door to the Kingdom, folks! Are you refusing to repent of your sin? Are you avoiding this by judging someone else's instead? We all know that addictions and abuse can ruin homes and lives, but loved ones, think about this—how many marriages and homes are ruined by selfishness, critical attitudes, disrespect, greed, pride, self-centeredness, vanity, and unforgiveness? Aren't those things just as dirty and toxic and expensive as alcoholism or a gambling addiction?"

The baby kicked, and it felt like her foot got lodged under my bottom rib. It hurt. I shifted around on the pew but it didn't help. I really needed to just get up and get to the bathroom, but like someone rubber-necking at an auto wreck on the highway, I didn't want to miss any of the sermon carnage. I felt constrained to stay in spite of my disgust.

"Folks, let me put it this way—a good test of whether or not you're harboring socially acceptable, whitewashed sin is to ask yourself this: How would I feel if Jesus returned and caught me in the middle of ...whatever. You fill in the blanks."

There it was—my father's warning. But it now seemed meaningless in the face of Brandon's convoluted reasoning. Too familiar disappointment constricted my throat as tears sprung to my eyes.

Brandon slowly walked closer to the congregation, suddenly appearing older, even taller. He narrowed his eyes and said, "Ask this: would I want Jesus to come back and find me on the phone...gossipin'? Would I want Jesus to come back and find me sittin' in a slimy pool of pride, puttin' someone else down, or refusin' to forgive them? Would I want Jesus to come back and find me bein' snotty and mean to someone in my own family? Would I want Jesus to come back and find me...in church...goin' back for FOURTHS in the church potluck line?"

A few gasps, then a reverent hush fell over the entire congregation. Brandon paused to let the dust settle.

"And so, folks, let me tell you—the Pharisees were guilty, you're all guilty, and I'm the guiltiest of all. We're all a bunch of sin-spawning trout, swimming our way upstream in this muddy river of life. And no amount of good behavior or good appearances or perfect church attendance can touch our sin. In fact, you know what, folks? Sometimes the ones who brag about bein' in church 'every time the doors are open' and think everyone else should do the same are the weakest Christians of all. They're wearing attendance corsets! Sometimes, even pastors need to stay home on a Sunday morning once in awhile and show the Gospel to their neighbors by helping 'em get their hay in, or helpin' em fix their broke-down equipment. You know, make the drive to Range City for parts, or something like that."

"Amen, brother," several voices chimed together.

"Hey, now wait a minute—don't get too agreeable about pastors stayin' home." Brandon laughed. "Makes me nervous. Anyway, maybe we need to stop worryin' about what we shouldn't do, and just start thinkin' about what we can do—acts of love and care for others. And especially when those acts are outside our comfort zone. The ones that might seem weird, outside the box, or even uncomfortable could be the things that we're called to do. That's true love. And remember—true love automatically fulfills the requirements of the law."

He paused again and resumed his place behind the pulpit before continuing, "let me ask you again—what will Jesus find you doing, or even thinking about, when He—"

My bladder couldn't wait another moment. I grabbed a roll of duct tape from my purse and rushed out.

I lingered a little while in the bathroom, trying to rein in my crushing disappointment and confusion. Buffalo Jump Church had nothing to offer me and I had nothing to offer it.

I longed to go back to Artos & Ichthus. At least there I could count on orderliness and proper procedure. My friends there respected clean living. For some reason, Brandon didn't put any emphasis on conduct. His teaching on heart issues was entirely too intangible, subjective, and corny for me to agree with.

It made me admire Artos & Ichthus's emergent philosophies all the more. I thought about my home church's ministry to the poor. For all Brandon's talk about acts of love, he didn't seem to care that Naomi lived like a pauper. My church friends, on the other hand, would make Naomi's situation their business and promptly do something about it. They would find a way to improve her living conditions and hold her to a higher standard.

Defeated, I smoothed my ponytail and reentered the sanctuary. The service was already over and people were milling about. I felt like I did in the room with Tina Connor. Unsettled. Unmoored.

Naomi was talking to Brandon. She smiled like she loved the sermon. Without warning, she looked right over at me, causing me to shiver. *Yikes.* She smiled and waved at me. I knew it. I could see it.

She was gloating.

She had stayed below the radar, dodged the bullet again. The pastor's sermon had contained nothing convicting for her, and so she loved every minute of it. Receiving no response from me, save a fixed frown, Naomi simply turned to hug someone else. My heart pounded with anger. How could she be so content with herself?

"Haley!" Win emerged from the nursery. She was struggling under the weight of two toddlers perched on each of her hips. "I won't be ready to go for a little while. I told Brooke that I'd continue to watch the twins while she helped clean the coffee pots. We had so much fun!" She kissed each of the cherub's smeary cheeks. Her hair was frazzled, her glasses were askew, and a long piece of ripped crinoline fluttered from Glory's! hemline. Worst of all, her legs were hairy with cracker crumbs, paper scraps, and other pieces of miscellaneous detritus. The pantyhose's adhesion qualities must have rivaled that of pine pitch.

It was disturbing. Even more disturbing, though, was the sight of Kendra, sobbing, as she walked to the front and sank to her knees at the altar. An out-of-the-box urge to go up and put my arm around her rose inside of me. It only lingered for an instant, though, as I watched Naomi leave her group of adoring fans and rush to Kendra's side. Brandon joined her and I saw them bow their heads.

Poor Kendra.

She might be undergoing a conversion experience, but it's under the guidance of unqualified oafs. What a terrible start for someone so obviously in need.

Rick guffawed loudly from the doorway. He was telling jokes like everything was just peachy in his life, like he wasn't failing miserably in his marriage, like he was fine with the way things were. He and Naomi both seemed to have a gift for denial, for living above the stuff that caused the rest of us realists to suffer and stew. It wasn't right and it wasn't fair.

They had no right to be so happy, so…free.

21

"Haley, dear, I'm really not sure we should be out on the road today." Win gazed out the passenger window of the car.

The struggle to keep my emotions reined in was now officially over. My feelings died when my expectations died. My coaster car remained completely derailed, wheels buried in a heap of miry negativity. In a way, it was good to be stuck because then I couldn't go any farther down, and I now entertained zero hope of climbing upward. I felt like my life had come to a halt, and I was destined to be forever pregnant—forever fat, achy, incontinent, and purposeless.

I really wasn't even missing Hal anymore. What good was advanced communication technology when all one had to communicate was darkness, despair, and unchecked fluid retention?

I replied to Win through tightened lips. "I told you, Aunt Winnie, it's just fine. It's May, for heaven's sake, not the middle of winter. It's one of the warmest mornings we've had since we got here."

Win kept looking out her window. "I have to admit that Miss Prairie is delightfully dressed this morning. Although she can change her outfit at the drop of a hat, if she's gets the whim to do so. Sudden storms are her specialty."

"Well, even if it does storm, I'm perfectly able to drive on a rainy highway." I was actually more concerned about my worsening back pain and nausea than about the weather conditions, but I was afraid if I mentioned it, she would insist on returning home.

"I just don't know," Win spoke in an unusually quiet tone. "I don't like the looks of that band of clouds way off on the horizon," she said, pointing toward the west.

A push on the accelerator was my answer. I wasn't about to go back, and I wasn't interested in more climate talk. For one thing, just before we left, the weather melodies yapper, finally on its last legs, had gotten bizarrely stuck on the song, "Let It Snow, Let It Snow, Let It Snow!" It almost drove me loony before we could get out of the house.

And the storm warning I heard on the radio earlier didn't alarm me because it was just another hokey report from Grassview's little local station. The station was so low budget that their main announcer was Spider the hippie guy. He conducted most of his broadcasts from his cell phone while he sat in his greasy little car on a high hill to ensure good reception.

I might have respected the weather report more if Hal had delivered it, but then respect would have constrained me to obey it. And I didn't want to. I knew I was fine on the road. Even if a storm did crop up, it would probably be in the afternoon. I had plenty of time to get Win to the bus station in Range City and get myself back home before lunchtime.

Rick had already tried to talk me out of taking Win to Range City that day. He, too, felt uneasy about me making the drive by myself. He said that if I would just wait until his day off on Wednesday, we could all go together. He had even suggested that we use the opportunity to have lunch at a fancier restaurant after we dropped Win off. He wanted to celebrate his career success.

In a conference call on Sunday night, Jerry had sprung the good news that Rick was now designated their company's Agricultural Business Manager. It was a new position that Rick had skillfully carved out for himself by being so knowledgeable about farming and crop production.

Rick was so excited about the promotion that his victory leap in the living room almost knocked over a shelving unit. Fortunately, the only objects that fell to the floor were Gracie's sequin-studded, Styrofoam fruits. When Rick reached to retrieve the apple from where it rolled under the couch, he also found a little resin bear figurine. Win took it, blew off the dust, and set it beside a vase of plastic sunflowers. She said that the bear had come out of its dark hibernation now and needed to be placed into summer. Rick had smiled at Win and announced that we, too, were being freed from the dark—that we could put our financial concerns to rest and that I could stay home fulltime without worry.

My relief at this news was tinged with an inexplicable grumpy feeling, though. I didn't want to lend any more credibility to Rick's farming obsession than absolutely necessary. I wasn't ready to concede that all his research and endless talk about grass and plants and fertilizers ultimately benefited me. Moreover, even though I appreciated the financial advantage the promotion offered, it didn't seem fair that Rick should be rewarded for something that was more like play than work for him. So I had stubbornly refused his celebratory lunch offer. On top of that, I needed to get away from Win immediately. Even two more days with her was too much. She was driving me crazy with her constant happiness.

The plan was for Win to take the bus from Range City south to Buffalo, Wyoming, and then west over the mountains to the small town where Rick's cousins would pick her up. They had opened up some sort of guest lodge in the high country there and were gracious enough to host their elderly great-aunt for a couple of weeks. They even asked her if she might be able to assist their cook in the lodge kitchen. Win jumped at that request. "Of course!" she had replied. I knew that the unsuspecting cousins had no idea of what they were getting themselves into.

I had managed, however, to recognize a feeble ray of silver lining inside my black mood. At the last minute, Win had grabbed Herman to take with her as a problem solving experiment for the cousins. They had mentioned in a phone conversation that they were having a serious issue with swallows building nests in the eaves of their log lodge. The birds were a terrible nuisance. Win thought that mounting Herman on a high pole beside the building might solve their problem, and so, because Gracie was gone anyway and wouldn't miss him, Win toted the owl along. She also sweetly reassured me that Herman's absence would only be temporary. If he succeeded at swallow repelling, she said she would order another owl off the internet for the cousins. I told her that her reassurance wasn't necessary. I wouldn't miss Herman. At all.

After driving along in silence for a little while, Win spoke up. "You know, these colors make me think of my mother's china closet."

I sighed, reminding myself that I wouldn't have to put up with Win's stupid comments for much longer.

"What colors?" I asked.

"The prairie colors."

"The prairie is brown."

"Not entirely. Look at the part of the sky that's still not clouded over," she said, pointing toward the east. "I've watched it change from powder blue to cornflower blue as the sun grows higher. It's now the color of Mother's wedgewood blue butter plate. And the new grass on the hillsides is her depression glass pedestal cake plate, while the brown grass is her crockery bread bowl."

I would never have admitted it to anyone in a million years, but I did sort of understand her comparisons. My mind started wandering as I drove. I started thinking about my own Grandma Lily's house and a time when life wasn't so complicated.

As a little girl, I loved spending time in Grandma's old country home with the low ceilings, pink bathroom fixtures, and a kitchen that always smelled bready. She kept a drawer full of candy bars and a glass-doored cupboard full of assorted fancy tea cups. Grandma wasn't protective of her stuff.

The tea cup collection contained many rare and antique pieces, but she would let me empty the cupboard and sort and resort the cups according to color and size. Each piece had a story, either about the person or place where it came from, and Grandma patiently retold the stories every time I asked her to. I treasured my time with her, so her early death from cancer when I was a teenager was devastating.

It struck me that I would have been thrilled to visit Gracie's place when I was a little girl. I could see myself skipping happily among the fascinating lawn ornaments, completely oblivious to my messy hair or muddy shoes. Inside the house, I would have spent hours, or even days, admiring, arranging, and rearranging her trinkets. I would have asked a hundred questions about each one and asked if I could reorganize them. I have a feeling that Gracie would have kindly said yes.

A small plaque that Gracie hung in the baby's room came to mind. It bore a Bible verse that read, "...whoever humbles himself like this child is the greatest in the kingdom of heaven." I pondered that for a moment before another of Win's odd remarks broke my reverie.

"Hmm, that weather front in the west makes me think of the Soviet army before Gorbachev came along. It's marching in, not skipping in." She stared out the passenger window, her face so close she fogged the glass.

She wiped the window with her sleeve and continued her sky scrutiny. "The whitish band of clouds is now in front of some meaner looking blackish ones..." she trailed off, then commented, "I think we're in for quite a tempest. I bet the church will have to cancel the branding party that was planned at Naomi's tomorrow."

"Branding party?" I wrinkled my nose. Just hearing Naomi's name pushed my coaster car further into the dirt.

"Yes, didn't you see it in the church bulletin yesterday? A whole group from the congregation is planning to help Naomi and her son, Jeff, round up and work on their cattle herd tomorrow."

I was surprised. I must not have read the entire bulletin. "That sounds like a big job. Are they going out to her place?"

"Of course, where else would her cows be?" Win's voice carried an unusually agitated edge.

"So the church people will finally see how Naomi lives?"

"Haley, Naomi's gone to that church for a decade! They know perfectly well how she lives. From what I hear, people like going to her place—she hosts get-togethers all the time."

It was hard for me to imagine what kind of fun could be had in Naomi's grungy setting. It seemed almost as wrong as partying in a starving African family's thatched hut while ignoring their desperate plight. "I thought she was poor."

"I told you that she seems quite comfortable."

"Well, yeah, but someone can get comfortable in their poverty and just sort of resign themselves to it."

"I don't think it's that way for Naomi. Between what they own and what they lease, she and Jeff work several thousand acres. What you can see from the highway is only a small part of their land. Naomi's not wealthy, but she and Bill managed to make a decent living on that piece."

"Mmph."

Win unbuckled her seatbelt and leaned forward, her cheek almost resting on the dashboard as she peered up and through the top of the windshield. "Those clouds are not typical for May." She lingered for a moment at the dashboard and scooted back into her seat. "I really think they might cancel the branding tomorrow. That would be disappointing."

"Mmph."

"It's a day devoted to taking care of the spring calf crop," Win replied to a question that I hadn't asked. I didn't care to know about a branding party. Was she hearing voices in her head now too?

She chattered on. "It's a social event and work party rolled into one. The women usually cook up a huge feast, and everyone pitches in with all the necessary branding and vaccinating of the calves. They usually tag ears and castrate the little guys, as well."

"Oh." Apparently Buffalo Jump church did take care of their own, but not in the way that I would have expected. I still couldn't picture a decent picnic taking place on Naomi's desolate property. I also couldn't picture any of my Artos & Ichthus friends making a party out of mutilating someone's baby cows.

Win fell quiet while she turned her attention back to the world outside the car. Her silence allowed me a moment to ruminate over the foreignness of Buffalo Jump's church ministry. I thought of the kindness of my friends back home and how hard they worked to bless me. Would they do the same for Naomi? That was an interesting thought. I knew Dolores wouldn't be of any help at all. In fact, she'd probably get out her bullhorn and stage a protest.

I flinched from a painful twinge in my lower back, but it was eclipsed by the advent of new questions in my mind. I knew there was a proper place for Dolores and her convictions, but obviously, it wasn't in Grassview. *So how do we know what real ministry is and isn't?*

"Love. That's it," Win stated matter-of-factly.

I sat up, straightening my hurting back. She did it again—she answered the question I hadn't asked. I wondered if there was a qualified gerontologist in Wyoming that could help with senility. Or maybe a neurologist.

"Haley, that's it. I have my answer. I just got the distinct feeling that God is reminding me that I have to stop fretting over this storm."

"What are you talking about, Aunt Win?" I realized that she was answering her own inner thoughts not mine.

"God just reminded me that He loves us and that He'll take care of us. Even an unusual spring storm can't change that. I need to stop worrying about you driving in this."

"Aunt Win, I didn't know you were that worried about me." The faintest bit of softness crept into my heart. "I'm sure this is just a big thunderstorm and those are usually over fast. I can always wait it out in Range City if I have to."

"I'm glad to know you'll do that if you need to. It doesn't hurt to be cautious, dear." She stretched over to pat my shoulder but could barely reach me. Her fingers brushed against my elbow instead. "Of course, in that case you might need to prepare for a long wait. Every storm has a predestined duration; once it starts, only God can stop it."

She leaned her head against the window and continued staring at the clouds. "I do know that sometimes Miss Prairie's thunder tantrums are the worst when a frigid front meets up with a warm front." She lowered her voice. "It has been quite warm lately, and I'd be willing to bet more than cookies that snow is in the approaching air."

I snickered. "Snow? It's almost the end of May! Winter can't just come crashing in on spring; that would be wrong."

She waited a moment before answering. "Hmm. Nobody seems to think it's wrong when spring crashes in on winter, when an unexpected chinook, or thaw, happens in January—they almost accept it as their due somehow."

"Lawns are green; flowers and leaves are out—it just wouldn't be right for snow to come now."

"Like I've said before, Haley, Miss Prairie is highly unpredictable."

◆•◆◆•◆

The first storm wave didn't hit until the bus motored out of the feed store parking lot. We had passed by the depot twice, until a local informed us that Stanley's Feed and Seed doubled as the bus station. How silly of me to miss the writing on the store window that said, "Zapz-It Wild Oat Herbicide— Explorer Bus Lines Tickets Sold Here."

It took two friendly farmers to help the driver load Win's leaden suitcases into the cargo hold. Watching them made me feel rotten about teasing Rick when he had struggled to load the baggage into the car that morning. It surprised me to think that my husband was as strong as two farmers put together. Why hadn't I noticed that before? I guessed that our metropolitan life didn't ordinarily offer Rick the physical challenges, or maybe the opportunities, to demonstrate his strength to me.

Sadly, Montana living was only making me look stupid. The dreary prairie with all its hokey people and houses and church services was blowing away everything that I had ever taken pride in—my proficiency as an educator, my respectable living quarters, my smartphone, my perfect hairdo. Good heavens, even decent shoes were denied me. *I want to go back home, Lord.*

In the middle of Win hugging me, talking to my tummy, and telling the baby that she couldn't wait to read her first chapter, a fierce wind gust pushed an empty plastic garbage bin into the side of the bus. I was actually glad that my hair was securely pulled back in a high ponytail.

"Promise me you'll wait for the storm to pass if it looks unsafe on the road, okay, Haley honey?"

I assured her I would. She boarded the bus with Herman under one arm and her purse under the other. Herman had stayed eerily quiet when Win talked with the driver about storing her statue in the overhead baggage bin inside the bus. The minute the driver turned his back, though, Herman had spun his head to look at me and hoot good-bye. I shivered, wondering if we should have had him exorcised back in Ohio after all.

I waved as the bus pulled onto the street and a prickly feeling crept up my throat. My hormones were playing tricks on me, making me think I was sad to see her leave.

I hurried to the car, took to the helm, and steered the craft onto the street. Dirt clouds, propelled by giant gusts, ran across the road and scattered litter and leaves in all directions. Even though the upscale grocery store beckoned to me as I passed it, I drove ahead, turning onto the main highway.

I was beginning to feel terrible. My back still hurt and I was getting a headache. I thought about driving to Dr. Swartzky's office since I was in Range City anyway but figured he would say it was normal to be tired, nauseated, and achy at this point in the game. Putting away Win's concerns over me driving in the storm, I kept heading south. I just wanted to get back to

Gracie's as quickly as possible and spend the rest of the day on the couch with my feet up.

Win's green bug phone warbled from its spot on the seat beside me. She had insisted I keep it since she'd be out of service in the mountains anyway. I could see Rick's number displayed on the front and decided to ignore it. I would be home in less than a half hour and would call him back then. I knew he was just checking on me. He was probably going to chew me out for being on the road or, worse yet, deliver more appeasing sweet talk, something I had experienced too much of lately. I was holding out for true repentance from him. I simply couldn't let him get away with his insensitivity anymore. He owed it to me and the baby.

When I was about fifteen miles outside of Range City, the clouds turned ominous. They blackened menacingly and lowered almost to the ground. A smudgy grayness coated the fields and hills, tarnishing the morning colors. I imagined Win saying that Miss Prairie, in a fit of artistic madness, was smearing strokes of charcoal over the pretty landscape that she had just painted the day before. Win probably would have gone on to call the subsequent lightning bolts static electricity created by the rubbing action of Miss Prairie's cloud robes against the hill carpet. *Uh-oh, wait a minute*—I deliberately focused my thoughts back onto the road—*I definitely need this break from Win. I'm thinking her language. Next thing I know, I'll be writing corny poetry.*

The darkness and the wind speed increased, forcing me to turn on my headlights. Even the low-centered tonnage of the monster car was barely a match for the driving wind gusts that bore down from the west. I had to fight with the sensitive steering to keep the car on the road. What had always appeared to be an empty landscape now didn't seem very empty as the wind churned up bushes and plants and threw them across the road.

Just ahead, I watched a terrified family of fairy-tale sized tumbleweeds running for their lives from the chasing gales. They swooped onto the road right in front of me and momentarily blocked my vision as they rolled over my hood and windshield. One unlucky tumbleweed got caught in the very middle of the front grill and hung on, looking like an oversized, Texas Longhorn hood ornament.

As the first raindrops hit the windshield, stirrings of alarm trickled through my limbs, making me grip the steering wheel tighter. I bit my bottom lip and reminded myself that I had driven in many a Philadelphia rainstorm. And that was always on a busy multi-lane freeway. This empty highway was a cakewalk compared to that.

Or was it?

Suddenly, seemingly from out of nowhere, a wall of rain slammed the driver side of the car, making it almost impossible to see the road. Rivers of water washed over the windshield, making a mockery out of the frenzied wipers. I leaned forward, barely able to see the lines of the highway.

This was no Philadelphia rainstorm. This onslaught couldn't even be called a rainstorm. I briefly recalled something Win had said about prairie storms—something about how prairie rain never falls gently down, but always blusters sideways. I had thought that comment was just another exaggeration, another meandering of her muddled mind, but the force of the blustering rain against my window now validated her words.

Lightning flashed across the western sky, and a cold, frightening thought struck me.

What else is Win right about, Lord?

22

I had no option but to plow ahead. The highway had virtually no shoulders, and the ditches were filling with mud and water. I knew that if I tried to pull off to the side, I could get stuck. I struggled to stay in my lane, not sure if it was helpful or scary that there was hardly any traffic.

The giant windshield wipers, set on high speed, worked as hard and fast as any I had ever seen but still only offered intermittent nanoseconds of visibility. My ripples of alarm became breakers of fear, and I started praying in time to the wipers, chanting, "Please God, help, help, help, help me see…"

For the briefest moment, I thought the rain had let up, but it was only holding back to let the next line of assault forces through. Hail. Huge, golf ball hail. The noise of it pounding the outside of Gracie's station wagon was so loud, I couldn't even hear my own cries. I was terrified that the windshield would shatter as I watched the stones bounce like rubber balls off the hood, denting it before my eyes. Ironically, the tumbleweed hood ornament held fast, bravely facing her doom like Rose at the prow of the *Titanic*.

I was close to panic, not knowing if it was safer to keep driving or to stop. Keeping a death grip on the steering wheel with one hand, I grabbed the bug phone with the other. *I have to call Rick—he'll know what to do.*

As soon as I saw the blank screen, I knew my exact location on the highway. I had previously named this ten-mile stretch "No Man's Land" because it was completely devoid of cell phone coverage. It would be a while before I would have reception again. If only I had talked to Rick when I had the chance. I would have given almost anything to hear his optimistic voice at that moment.

My fear and helplessness brought forth memories of my dad. Another one of his favorite reproofs flashed through my mind. This time he pounded me with scripture. "The way of a fool seems right to him, but a wise man listens to advice."

For the first time ever, I wanted to shout, to scream back at him. *I know, I know, Dad—I'm a guilty fool. I should have listened to the warnings. Just like I should have listened when you warned me not to waste money on a college education. You were right all along—I might never use my teaching degree again. I'm a sinner and a fool—are you happy? You win!*

A surge of longing and love for Rick instantly poured into my heart. I didn't want to hear my dad's voice anymore. I needed to hear my husband's.

I cried out, "Lord, I'm sorry for being so critical of Rick and for taking him so for granted. Please forgive me!" The hail ball blitz promptly intensified.

Finally, I saw headlights approaching me through the hail. Even though I wasn't sure what it would accomplish, I flashed my lights at the oncoming vehicle. It turned out to be a semi-truck barreling unafraid through the elements that were so threatening to me and my smaller ship. It simply flashed its lights back, apparently thinking I was communicating "howdy" and raced on by. Its wake engulfed me completely for a terrifying two seconds.

My worry that the hail might shatter the windshield began to subside when the hailstones started squishing against the glass, allowing the windshield wipers to push them off. It only took an instant, however, for me to realize that the squishiness of the hail signaled something worse, much worse.

Snow?

Snow! Again, Win was right...*please forgive me, Lord, for disrespecting her!*

A second gush of love and respect, this time for Aunt Win, flooded my heart as a blinding, frenzied cloud of winter enveloped the car—barging in on my spring, daring me to guess where the edge of the road was. I accelerated, thinking only that I needed to get home fast. The moment I did, though, I knew it was a mistake. The slushy snow was already piling up on the road, making it slick. The car swerved, but this time I knew to avoid over-correcting and stayed on the road. In frustration, I slowed back down.

It dawned on me that I might find refuge in a picnic area that was only a couple miles ahead. I had noted that spot on my first drive to Range City, commenting to Win that it was the only place on the entire thirty-mile stretch that had any trees. It was located just off the road where the highway bridge crossed the Basin River and might provide a bit of shelter to park under. Surely this would be over soon.

I leaned forward as far as my stomach would allow and strained to see ahead. The whiteness was terrifying. In a matter of minutes, the blowing, swirling, raging snow had already formed drifts across the road, indicating that the temperature had plummeted at a phenomenal rate. I would never doubt anyone's stories concerning prairie blizzards again. I might even consider keeping the weather yapper around for a little longer.

The appearance of a guard rail to my right signaled the start of the Basin River bridge. I knew the turn-in to the picnic area would be at the end of the bridge. I drove carefully, grateful for something to guide me. Right before I was to turn off, though, something bumped underneath the car. Then another, and another. I was running over objects of some sort. I slowed to a crawl and saw that tree branches, already covered in snow, littered the highway.

I guessed that the combination of wind and heavy snow was drastically pruning the group of venerable cottonwoods lining the river shore at the picnic area. Some of the branches were huge, and I had to dodge them like an obstacle course. I couldn't see them until I was practically on top of them. I barely made it around one branch that was more like an entire cottonwood cut in half. Smaller branches, propelled by the blizzard gusts, continued to hit the car and bounce off the windows. I drove ahead in fear, knowing that the picnic area would be more of a death trap than a shelter.

I had no option but to keep driving and praying. At least the car was warm, and it was getting me closer to home with every mile. I still hadn't met any other cars, and what could someone else do for me, anyway? Even though it wasn't a four-wheel-drive, Gracie's enormous vehicle was somehow getting me through. I tried to calm myself with logic. *As long as I can stay on the road, I'll be okay.*

It was at about that exact moment that the illogical, the unthinkable oc-curred. I was seized with such a violent back spasm that I almost threw up. It couldn't be.

It just…couldn't…be…*dear Lord, NOT NOW!*

23

Surely this was a nightmare. Surely I wasn't in labor. Not yet, not two weeks early. Not while I was driving by myself in the worst blizzard I had ever seen, miles away from any medical help.

This can't be a contraction if it's in my lower back, right, God? As if it was answering my question, another spasm followed on the heels of the last. I gasped, then moaned. I remembered reading something about "back labor" in one of my pregnancy books, and I moaned again.

I tried to think. My doctor was in Range City, but I was closer to Grassview. Grassview didn't have a hospital, but the memory of Bonnie mentioning how the local livestock veterinarian had delivered several Grassview babies kept me driving north. It seemed too risky to turn back.

The contraction gripped me and I instinctively sped up. I was desperate to get to help. The car swerved, however, constraining me to slow down again. *This just can't be happening!*

The snowstorm was unbelievable. It was worsening at the same rate as my contractions. I absolutely could not see more than a few feet in front of the car. There were no tracks to follow, and no oncoming vehicles to help me get my bearings. I had the heat on and the blower fan going full blast, but the window kept fogging up on the inside.

Suddenly, the blower fan went silent. I pounded on the dash to no avail. The electrical system had glitched again. Fog immediately formed on the windshield and my efforts at wiping only smeared it around. I tried to lower my side window. Of course, it wouldn't budge.

In sheer terror, I started bawling like the baby I was about to birth.

"Oh, God, help me!" I blubbered. An even bigger contraction ensued and I felt a sudden, wet warmth envelope my legs and the seat of the car.

My water broke.

I drove straight into white oblivion. "Please God, please—send me someone, anyone—to help!" I cried uncontrollably. "Baby, don't come yet, please don't come yet—ow!" Nothing could have prepared me for the severity of the contractions.

A shape appeared on the opposite side of the road. I tapped on the brakes to slow down. Wiping my side window vigorously created just enough visibility to reveal that the shape was a mailbox. A mailbox would only be at the end of someone's driveway. *Thank You, Lord.*

Moaning, I inched the car along the right edge of the road, praying that the driveway was on my side of the highway and not the other. Not only was I in no condition to get out and walk to find it, I was wearing the stupid flip-flops.

Almost immediately, a wide spot opened up. It was definitely the entrance to a driveway. I cranked the steering wheel to the right and pressed on the gas. The window fogged again. I wiped it just in time to see that I had turned too soon. The right front wheel missed the turnoff and sank down into a deep trench instead. The car was stuck. *A tractor would be nice right about now.*

I sat, almost suffocating in fear, knowing that my fate and the fate of my child rested solely in the hands of the One who created us both. I was as helpless as my own baby.

I had no choice but to pour out my defenseless and broken heart. "Oh, God, I need a miracle! I need you so bad—*ouch*—please come to me now. God, I'm so sorry, so sorry that I've been—*ow*—so stupid about everything. Just send help, now, please!"

A gripping, compelling sense of urgency rose up in me as I prayed. It was horrible and wonderful all at once. It overshadowed everything that I felt about myself, physically or emotionally, at that moment. It was my assignment, my mission, my purpose. Right then and there I knew God had appointed me to protect my child's life, with my own if necessary, and I was completely willing to do it. It was the most important thing that would ever be asked of me. Everything else that I had ever worried about paled in comparison to the saving of my daughter's life.

The next contraction hit with a vengeance. It felt like my entire back was ripping in two. I screamed out, "Oh God—don't take me yet! Please save us both!"

I threw my head against my hands on the steering wheel and sobbed. "I know, God, I know You're the Creator of her life and mine. I'm so sorry that I thought what I did about the evolution chapter and all that—forgive me, please! Just please let us both live, PLEASE!"

And right at that very moment, I heard a low buzzing sound motoring toward me from the driveway to my right. I looked up through the fogged windshield and saw a dark form driving around the front of the car. Indescribable relief flooded through me as a person walked up to my door and opened it.

No less amazing than the parting of the Red Sea, my deliverance had arrived.

The answer to my prayers—my miracle—was sent in the form of Naomi Stanton on an ATV.

I didn't recognize her at first. She had on an odd pair of goggles that covered half her face. Even through the howling wind, though, the moment I heard her voice, I knew exactly who my rescuer was. Strong, capable Naomi was somehow able to get me positioned in front of her on the four-wheeler's seat and carefully drive us down the lane to her little home. Because I was shivering wildly, she wrapped one arm protectively around me and steered with the other. My toes were frozen numb but I didn't care. Getting my daughter to safety was the only thing that mattered. Win could probably order me some kind of toe replacement things from one of her sources if mine froze off, anyway.

Naomi helped me up the steps and into the front door of her shanty's addition. I was in no shape to take in much, but I did register a vague awareness of how clean and sweet-smelling the home was. It wasn't crowded like Gracie's. Right inside the door stood a carved credenza, topped only with an elegant pottery vase and an antique birdcage. A small woodstove beside an overstuffed couch radiated blessed warmth. As she helped me onto the couch, another contraction hit hard.

"Naomi, I think I'm in labor," I gasped.

"I picked up on that, dear. How far apart are your contractions?"

"I'm, ohhhh, not sure, ooooww—"

"Here, put your feet up," she spoke calmly. "That's good, now, take a deep breath and let it out slowly…good. Did you take childbirth classes?"

"Yes, mmph."

"Okay, try to remember your breathing technique. Work on that while I see about either gettin' you to town, or gettin' help out here."

I inhaled and exhaled slowly. The pain eased slightly. "Rick, I need Rick. He'd remember the breathing stuff," I said as tears started flowing again. "Naomi—I need Rick!"

"I know, darlin'. I'll do my best, but the radio just said that the highway is closed. Visibility is down to zero and the roads are driftin' in as we speak. It looks like we're in for the worst May blizzard anyone has seen around these parts in fifty years. That's why I was out on the four-wheeler—I thought I was just goin' to survey the condition of the highway, but it must have been God tellin' me to go. Amazin' how He works that way."

"Oh, Naomi, I'm so scared," I started breathing too fast.

"It's okay, Haley. This isn't new to me—I'm a nurse. Now try to breathe slowly."

"You're a nurse?"

"Yes, dear, I'm an RN. Been retired for over twenty years now, but I've helped birth a lot of babies in my time."

"I had no idea."

"Well, we haven't really gotten to know each other yet, have we?" She walked across the room and picked up a cordless phone. "Phones are still working fine."

A faint spark of hope lit. "Oh good, I need to try Rick's phone. Depending on where he's at, he might have reception."

Naomi handed me the phone. "Okay, but hurry—we need to figure things out. This baby isn't going to wait much longer. If nothing else, Jeff happened to be over when the storm hit. He went out to check on the cattle, but he should be back any minute. His pickup is a four-wheel-drive, so he might be able to get you to town."

I dialed Rick's number, grateful for a break between contractions. Praying silently, I waited through three rings. *Please, Lord!*

"Hello?" The connection was scratchy.

"Rick—"

"Haley, where are you? I just made it home and saw you weren't back yet so I headed down the highway to look for you. I'm about eight miles south—where are you?"

"Rick, my car got stuck, but it was right at Naomi Stanton's place, and I'm here, now—"

"You got stuck? Are you okay?"

"Well, yes and no—I'm in labor—"

"What? You say you're what? I'm...my way...now!" The reception started breaking up. "...where....actly is...omi's place?"

A white gust whooshed Jeff through the door while I was on the phone. He talked quietly to Naomi.

I was worried that Rick could lose service any moment. "Here, Rick, can you still hear me? Let me give the phone to Naomi—she can give you directions."

Jeff, a lanky, bearded man, looked at me with his mother's eyes and stretched out his hand. "Ma'am, I'll talk to your husband."

He took the phone and explained that the road was drifting in fast, and no amount of four-wheel-drive was going to make it through for anybody. When he finally figured out that Rick was only a couple miles away, though, Jeff conceded that Rick might as well keep going. If he didn't show up in fifteen minutes, Jeff said he was going to go looking for him. Between the phrases, "Are you still there?" and "Can you hear me?" Jeff finally lost the call.

The pain came back, but I closed my eyes and took a deep breath. "In through your mouth, out through your nose," Naomi coached in a soothing voice.

"Ooww!" The contractions were getting harder. I did my best to breathe steadily.

Naomi put one hand on my belly while she studied her watch. Just having her warm hand on me soothed me a little. She didn't look the least bit gloating or manipulative. She looked powerful. And merciful.

The pain abated. Naomi stood and said, "About a minute long. It's been about, what, three minutes since the last one?"

"I'm not sure."

"Well, I'll keep timin' them, dear. Try to relax in between pains." She positioned a pillow behind my head. "I'm gonna go get you some dry clothes to change into."

"So there's no way we'll make it to the nurse's office?"

"No, Haley, I think it would be too risky at this point to try. I'm confident that we can do this together with God's help. He's right here with us."

I teared up again. "I know."

She disappeared for few minutes into the back of the trailer and returned with a large blue bathrobe. She gently helped me change my clothes, just like a nurse in the hospital would. I sank back into the couch to wait for another contraction.

But another one didn't come. We waited three minutes, four, five…eight. Nothing.

Naomi stayed cheerful. "I've seen this many times, hon. It's not unusual for labor to start out fast and then slow down for awhile. We just got to be patient."

I felt a glimmer of hope. Maybe I could make it to town after all.

Jeff emerged from another room and announced he was going back out. "If your husband doesn't show up in ten minutes, Miss Haley, I'm going to head down the highway in the four-wheeler." He started putting his boots back on.

"Here, Jeff, wear these. They really do work quite well." Naomi picked up the goggles she had been wearing.

"Mom, I told you before—this contraption doesn't work for me. That dang wiper attachment hypnotizes me, makes me woozy," Jeff donned his cowboy hat on top of a close-fitting knit cap.

"I think you'd really find them helpful today," Naomi replied. "There's still plenty of juice in the battery, and you only have to turn on the windshield wipers when you need them. They'll keep your range of view clear."

Jeff growled. "Fine, but I'm just going to keep them in the carrier. I'll put 'em on if I need 'em." He went out the door with the goggles' wires and straps trailing behind him.

"What are those?" I asked.

"They're called the Clear 'n' Cool Pro 2000. Winifred ordered them for me off the TV. They came with a passel of detachable accessories—a windshield-wiper unit, a cooling fan unit, and flip-up magnifiers for map readin.' They're the handiest ATV goggles I've ever owned. Can't figure out why Jeff won't give them a chance."

Just then, a whistle came from the birdcage by the door, startling me. I hadn't noticed the bird in there.

"Sadie, be quiet," Naomi said.

I looked over and saw a pretty songbird sitting dutifully inside the cage. The door to the cage was wide open, but the bird stayed inside.

My curiosity momentarily trumped my crisis. "Is that a meadowlark?"

"Sure is. My granddaughter, Lacey, picked the injured thing up in the field. Poor birdie was just a little chick, dyin' in the grass at the time. She's healin' up but doesn't realize she can come out of her cage. She doesn't understand that the door is open." Bruce the Budgie would never have done that. It struck me that he and Win both knew freedom when they saw it.

Naomi kept talking quietly. "Lacey's off on a mission trip overseas right now. Wanted me to look after the bird for her."

"Oof—where did she go?" I asked while awkwardly repositioning myself on the couch.

"Africa. Been there several times myself. I'm gettin' too old to go on those trips anymore, though. Would rather just give the money to the young'uns that want to go. Can't take anymore of those blasted plane rides. Bunch you up like steers in a storm on those flights. Any pain, yet?"

"No, no pain, but I don't feel good." I put my hand on my stomach. "Should we be worried? I mean, with my water breaking and all?"

"No, I'm not worried. Like I said, I've seen this before. In the hospital, we'd sometimes put a woman on an IV drip to restart her contractions, but we usually tried to wait it out. Sometimes we'd get the gal to walk around to try and speed things up, but with your water gushin' and all, I think the baby might be better off if you don't move around too much."

"So if the contractions don't start back up and it stops snowing, do you think we could make it into town?"

Naomi bit her lip. "Hmm, probably not. Unless your contractions don't start up again, it stops snowin', and the highway gets cleared. Seems like a lot to ask for. I have a feelin' your young'un will show up before all that happens."

My heart lurched. It was all so scary. "Naomi, don't take this wrong, but I'm terrified to have the baby here!"

Naomi smiled. "No offense taken. It might not be ideal, but it's warm and dry in here. A whole lot better'n you birthin' all by yourself in a ditched car."

She had a point.

"You know," she said as she stood up, "I have something I think you'd be interested in. Might take your mind off things a little. Sometimes just relaxin' helps get labor goin' again."

She disappeared again into the back room and returned this time with a faded, black photo album.

"These pictures go way, way back. They're from the first summer Win and I met." She chuckled. "You'll get a kick out of them."

She sat down on the couch beside me and opened the album. White-bordered black and white photos with scalloped edges rested in tiny corner brackets glued on the brittle pages. The ancient pictures showed a tall, lanky Naomi towering above an impish little Winifred. I was amazed to see that even a span of sixty years hadn't erased all the traces of resemblance to how they looked now.

"There's Win, wavin' from her beet truck. She was one of the best truck drivers around. Careful, but quick. Drivin' a log truck in the mountains probably prepared her for haulin' beets."

"So Win did drive big trucks?"

"Oh, yes. And just about anything else that could be driven. Tractors, heavy equipment—even the big harvester for our neighbor that summer. She wasn't afraid of anything."

"Oh." I didn't know what to say. I almost felt dizzy with regret and conviction. I had been misjudging Aunt Win and assuming things about her all along. She hadn't deserved any of it.

"And here's Win riding on the back of a big sheep—"

Naomi was cut short by Jeff bursting through the doorway. "The four-wheeler's dead as a doornail. Won't start."

"But I just used it to pick up Haley!"

"I know but now something's busted. It's been longer'n fifteen minutes."

"Naomi!" A huge contraction suddenly hit. I didn't think I could stand it. "I need Rick!"

Naomi looked at her watch. "Okay, dear." She looked up. "Jeff, saddle up Blue Sky. She's not afraid of snow."

"Yep," was all Jeff said and disappeared through the door into freezing white obscurity.

I broke out in a sweat and started panting hard. I couldn't even try to breathe right. I started moaning instead. Naomi tried to time the contraction, but it wouldn't let up.

"Owww!" I yelled. It felt like my back was splitting in two.

The contraction abated momentarily but then slammed me again. Naomi looked away from her watch and announced, "Honey, I think we should get ready. I do believe it's time."

She guided me to her bedroom where earlier she had arranged clean towels on top of a plastic shower curtain on her bed. I was in too much distress to question her about anything except the retrieval of Rick. She continued to talk in a tranquil voice as she helped me position myself against pillows at the head of the bed.

"Sky is the bravest, steadiest horse I've ever owned. If Rick is stuck, then Sky will get Jeff right to him. A horse is more reliable than a four-wheeler any day."

"Naomi, I'm really scared."

"I know, hon. Let's pray." Naomi prayed, asking God for safety, health, wisdom, and courage, and began to give instructions in a more commanding voice.

Right in the middle of the ordeal, I uttered through a grimace, "Naomi, I'm sorry."

"Sorry? For what?"

"Ooooouch—Naomi, I—" In spite of my travail, I was compelled to repent. "I thought mean thoughts about you, and I've been proud and—"

"Oh, Haley, don't worry about that! You're forgiven a million times over—now just focus on yourself and do what I tell you. Here, squeeze my hand." She reached for my right hand.

"NO! I can't—that hand hurts. I have an injury—two spots—"

Naomi pulled my hand up to her face. "I don't see anything. You need to grip something in order to push hard."

I went ahead and grabbed her hand, realizing that it suddenly felt fine. It didn't hurt at all. My entire torso was saturated in pain, but my hand felt like it was healed. The injury had disappeared. Completely. No marks, no pain, no itching. Like the weird bite had never even been there.

"Haley, it's time to push. Ready?"

A surge of gratitude and love for Naomi spilled like a third wave, massaging life back into my weak and dry heart. "Oww! Yes, I'm ready—ohhhhh!"

And with that, Naomi gently guided me through the agonizingly amazing process of bringing new life into the world.

24

I was smiling and crying and holding the most exquisite treasure I had ever laid eyes on. Our precious, wiggling daughter had a wash of dark hair and beautiful round eyes. Ten fingers, ten toes—flawless in every way. Naomi had a basin of water and towels waiting to clean off my sweet little girl, but I couldn't let her go—even for a moment. I found myself instinctively cradling her to my breast and cooing at her.

The door burst open and Rick rushed in. He was wearing the Clear 'n' Cool Pro 2000 goggles. Not bothering to switch the miniature windshield wipers off, he pushed the glasses up onto his forehead and came straight to me. He dropped to his knees to gaze in awe at our daughter's pinched and gorgeous little face.

"She's so beautiful!" he whispered, tears streaming down his face. The wiper attachment arms kept dutifully swiping the glasses perched above his brow.

"Her name is Sky," I announced.

"Sky...that's perfect, Haley. Just perfect. Thank you." Rick kissed us both. "I'm so sorry I wasn't here, Haley—I tried, I really did."

Naomi spoke up. "You only missed it by a few minutes, Rick. At least you're here now."

I turned to snuggle my face against Rick's, but barely missed stabbing my eye out on the goggle's wiper projectiles. I bent down and lowered my head to his chest instead. "I'm so glad I have you now. Everything's going to be all right."

I meant it. As I listened to my husband's heart beat to the tempo of the whirring and clicking Clear 'n' Cool Pro 2000 goggles, I knew we'd be okay.

"Oh, Haley, I was so scared for you," Rick choked. "I was so afraid of losing you and the baby—" he paused to wipe his face, "—and all I could think about is how I didn't want to live without you!" He kissed my cheek again. "Haley, you're an amazing woman."

Even though after pains still gripped me, a warmth unlike anything I had ever known blanketed me. I felt loved, really loved. And I had done nothing to deserve it. I couldn't even take credit for surrendering to God. He had given me no choice. I was just a little kid, as helpless as my own new baby, but apparently that was all I needed to be.

Just like everybody else.

Suddenly, Sadie sang a beautiful meadowlark call from the other side of the room. I looked over and saw her perched cautiously on the threshold of the little wire doorway. She was close to stepping out.

Nestling my nose against tiny Sky's downy head, I let my poetically quirky thoughts run wild and free.

Ah, sweet humility has dredged my soul,
making way for true love to flow,
And sweeps me through the door of Repentance.
At the welcoming gate, brothers and sisters await
To applaud the release of my sentence—

What was that? My poem's flow stopped for a moment. I looked up. I could have sworn I saw something dash out the bedroom door. Something close to the floor, black, slithery…*A snake? No way. I'm just seeing things. My blood sugar is probably really low right now.*

I rested my cheek back against Sky's velvetness and let the rest of my emerging poem dance with abandon through my consciousness.

Tolerant, diverse, trendy, aware—
My family I now see everywhere;
They're hippies and pig-fryers, businessmen, bauble-buyers,
Mullet-bearers, ponytail-wearers,
Proper ladies in suits, improper old ladies in boots,
Trailer-dwellers, fireworks-sellers
Beer-drinkers, deep-thinkers,
Moms and dads and kids, drivers of trucks and snappy hybrids...

I think the boomerang must have knocked some self out of me.

Woe to Me
by Haley Ewing

Woe to me, I'm beginning to see
That way down deep inside of me
Lives an ignorant, arrogant Pharisee.

Oh, my, a sweet Christian I strive to be;
With good works and deeds done sacrificially.
But, truth be known, these things really just serve me.

For my heart, so needy, desperate for attention,
Makes me do things just for recognition—
Not like Jesus, who avoided a reputation.

How I wash and polish my sparkly outside,
Ignoring my sinful motives inside
And judge everybody else in my pride.

Why, I would never utter profanity,
And would never attend an R-rated movie,
But, I join in gossip, so wicked and filthy.

Oh, I'm so practiced in my noble generosity
That directs me to tithe to a respectable ministry,
While, at home, I withhold forgiveness from my family.

And, at church fellowship, I mention my neighbor's junk.
"How awful that last night that smoker was drunk,"
I sermonize while I gluttonize on fruit pies at potluck.

I list all the commandments our culture violates—
Oh, the world out there, how it steals, kills and fornicates!
Yet, though love fills the law, I seethe with hidden hate.

Woe to me, for I am selfish, filled with greed,
Always wanting and grasping for more than I need,
And like that old emperor, my nakedness I don't see.

Dear Lord, how I must come down from that place
Of pride and presumption, and just fall on my face,
Finally seeing what I am—a sinner saved by grace.

Woe to me, I'm an ignorant, arrogant Pharisee.
Woe to me, Lord, please send your forgiveness to me!

The Stormy Big Sky
by Winifred Louise Harkins

(Set to a country waltz tune)
1. The smell of dust, of blowing dust
And the sound of a shingle, loosened by a gust
Sends us fleeing our basement den,
Leaving behind our TV again.
Like frenzied deer, we sprint out the door,
Eager to watch this thunderstorm.
For our entertainment is right outdoors,
Up on the Montana sky.

Chorus:
You can have your videos and DVDs;
Watch your sports or your MTV.
Lower your morals with network prime time;
Buy a big dish, rope a satellite.
But I'll watch the best that money can't buy
Just let me see the stormy Big Sky—
I love to watch my Montana sky.

2. The horizons surround a heavenly stage
Where black clouds are gathering, filled with rage.
Lightning debuts, the wind starts to howl
We watch the high drama roll in from the south.
Action, adventure we anticipate;
Like nothing that Hollywood could duplicate.
No greater production has ever been made
Than found on the Montana sky.

(Chorus)

3. Sometimes the sunset makes the lightning glow red
As it dances between the clouds overhead.
Thunder echoes in stereo sound
And the silver screen sky is the biggest around.
The weatherman tells us to go get inside,
"You never know where that lightning might strike."
But I'll take my chances on the patio
Just to watch the Lord's own reality show.
For only God could direct this show,
Produced on the Montana sky.
(Chorus)
Ending: Come with me now, watch the Montana Sky.

About the Author

Willow Feller, a recovering Pharisee, lives in the woods of North Idaho with her husband, Mike, and as of recently, none of the six rambunctious kids that they managed to raise and sequentially kick out of the nest. The nest-emptying has opened up writing time for Willow, resulting in the publication of this, her first novel. Together, Willow and Mike enjoy all the usual hyphenated Idaho activities: trail-ambling, huckleberry-picking, firewood-cutting, supposed deer resistant flower-planting, and seed catalog false advertising-lamenting.

More of Willow's stories can be read at www.willowfeller.com.

Laugh out loud at one wacky, improbable, uproarious disaster after another!

"I didn't even know who I was anymore. My gaze wandered from the hooved animal leg lamp, to the way Marlene's ketchup-red perm clashed with her green drink, to the disgusting rib bones on my own plate. It was all so stupidly surreal, so shameful—it defied the most outrageous Facebook post."

Facing a cataclysmic identity crisis, pregnant Haley is battling for her very life—her life as an eco-chic, vegan Christian, that is. She hadn't counted on being thrust into a war zone when she agreed to leave her East Coast life and go with her husband, Rick, to the Montana outback for the summer. And she certainly hadn't counted on attending a ladies Bible study in a smoky, rancid saloon. Rather than run from it, though, Haley decides it is her God-given mission to subdue and educate the redneck forces that discount her superior vocabulary and sophisticated hairdo. With no help from Rick or his freaky Aunt Win, Haley dives headfirst into her mission only to find herself sucked irretrievably into a maelstrom of humiliating mishaps.

With tensions mushrooming as fast as her belly, will Haley see that she is actually living out the reality of the scripture, "Do not judge, or you too will be judged"? And just how many car explosions and massive wardrobe malfunctions will it take for her to realize that it is her own judgments of others that are boomeranging back on her?

"...It's hilarious! You should definitely all indulge in in some witty Christian fiction." —Cora Roberts, author, *No Other Rock*

"This book is hilarious, fast-paced, and well-written. I laughed out loud so often that my husband wanted me to read it to him. We're both waiting for the sequel!" —Valerie Thompson, M.Ed.

E**v**ergreen
PRESS

Biblical Solutions for Breakthrough Living ™

FICTION / Christian / Humor